THE SISTERS MAO

THE
SISTERS
MAO

GAVIN McCREA

SCRIBE
Melbourne • London

Scribe Publications
2 John St, Clerkenwell, London, WC1N 2ES, United Kingdom
18–20 Edward St, Brunswick, Victoria 3056, Australia
3754 Pleasant Ave, Suite 100, Minneapolis, Minnesota 55409, USA

Published by Scribe 2021

This book is a work of fiction. Any references to historical events, real
people, or real places are used fictitiously. Other names, characters, places
and events are products of the author's imagination, and any resemblance
to actual events, places or persons, living or dead, is entirely coincidental.

Endpaper posters used with permission of The Poster Workshop
www.posterworkshop.co.uk

Typeset in Minion Pro by the publishers

Printed and bound in the UK by CPI Group (UK) Ltd, Croydon CR0 4YY

Scribe is committed to the sustainable use of natural resources and the use
of paper products made responsibly from those resources.

978 1 912854 39 4 (UK hardback)
978 1 913348 02 1 (UK paperback)
978 1 950354 79 5 (US hardback)
978 1 925713 57 2 (Australian paperback)
978 1 925548 24 2 (ebook)

Catalogue records for this book are available from the
National Library of Australia and the British Library.

scribepublications.co.uk
scribepublications.com
scribepublications.com.au

To Iñaki

And in memory of
Margaret McCrea

When talk of revolution has gone the rounds three times,
You may commit yourself,
And people will believe you.

—I CHING

CONTENTS

THE OPENING

My dear Mao,

This morning they came while it was still night to give me my meal. I was especially hungry, having found no sleep to escape the needs of my body, so it was with some eagerness that I took the bowl from them and went to eat under the window where sometimes there is sufficient light to pick out the grubs which, for their amusement rather than my nourishment, they push into my food. And there, on that square of floor where the night illuminated the night, I noticed something that I would like to relate to you, something that has roused me from my dumbness and brought me finally to address you. I noticed, my love, that I was watching my own fingers touching the chopsticks, the rice, the grubs, and that I was not watching the objects themselves. My gaze was fixed not on that which was hungered after but instead on that which was doing the hungering. And I understood — then — that I was changed. I had become aware of myself. Through sleeplessness and privation I had gained the capacity to look from above and afar at my own being, and my being had accordingly become the being of another, as single and as separate, and I realised that I would be capable, at last, of criticising my shortcomings and mistakes, and of rectifying them before you, as before a judge.

You know I have always found it hard to calm my mind down. I have lived an undisciplined life. I have had difficulty persevering. I have been too fond of wandering my own way. I have jumped from one track to another, serving Qin in the morning and Chu in the evening. But in that moment — in that long and quiet moment — I became clear. I saw black turn to white, and white turn to black, and I was, perhaps for the first time, a subject to myself. Old defences, which have long formed a wall around me, fell, and I was left with a naked figure in my sights.

It was a shock to hold audience with myself in this way; such a

3

shock that when I heard a scream come from one of the other cells I thought it might have come from my own mouth. The sensation was that of being both infinitely light and infinitely substantial. The bowl, which had suddenly begun to feel like a boulder in my hands, passed through my fingers as a feather passes through air. I watched as I watched the food, my precious food, spill onto the floor, and I was surprised to see that I reacted with neither anger nor despair. I did not kick. I did not curse. I did not crawl around scooping the mess up, as yesterday I might desperately have done. For I found that I was no longer in want of it. I found, indeed, that I had no desires at all. In each organ I was satisfied and full.

The bowl, being cheap bamboo, bounced and then rolled around on its lip before settling upside down on the ground. The noise of this drew the attention of the sentry in the passage outside. The hatch on the door slid across, and I sensed her eye peering in through the grille — and I do not lie to you, honoured husband, I swear I am being truthful when I tell you that, right then, it was me who was occupying the sentry's position. I, too, was on the outside looking in. I was seeing what she was seeing. Her eye was my own, scrutinising my actions, penetrating to my thoughts.

And, oh Great Saviour, what bliss I felt then! After the shock, what joy! A joy which sits within me still and seems invulnerable to disruption. For I have reached the point which every revolutionary, every Chinese, every Communist in the world hopes to reach in life: the point from which it is possible to begin the total criticism of oneself.

A lifetime of rehearsing, and suddenly the performance begins.

Your little actress,

Jiang Qing

I

IRIS

1968

<u>i.</u>

Iris had never been to this flat before. Nor would she have been here now had she not, over the course of four days and nights, exhausted all the venues on her usual circuit. She had left home on Wednesday with the intention of dropping into the Speakeasy for one drink only. That drink turned into a heavy night at Happening 66, followed by a forty-eight-hour crawl of the bedsits and squats of Earl's Court. At some stage on Saturday, at the bar in Middle Earth, she lost sight of her last reliable acquaintance. With a lack of alternatives, she decided to metamorphose a group of professional types into friends. After selling them some trips, she attached herself to them as a kind of counsellor and guide (there were things they did not know that they were supposed to know) and together they went on to an impromptu Sunday blowout on a bit of wasteland in Notting Hill. Then, when that was raided, she accompanied them here, to this place on Portobello Road. (A further act of generosity on her part. She would have been better off calling it a day and getting some proper sleep, but her expertise was something she could neither refuse nor keep to herself.)

The digs, which she treated to a full inspection on arrival, came from a different epoch of taste. The conventional flowered wallpaper and the dark carpets were evidence of this and had purposely not been removed. Instead they had been casually overlaid with some cheap tokens of modernity: indoor plants, striped Kazakh rugs, framed cinema posters, ornaments with Buddhist motifs. In the sitting room a gas heater had been fitted into the fireplace cavity, and air-sofas placed in an L in front. The adjoining dining room had been emptied of table and chairs in favour of cushions and beanbags, which were arranged on the floor to form a circular dancing space. Under a spotlight, where once a dresser had had pride of place, sat an extensive Bang & Olufsen hifi. A train of LPs skirted the walls. From mounted speakers Pink Floyd now blared.

—You cats are into some plastic shit, she said.

At which the group — designers and advertisers and marketeers — all laughed because they had decided, as a unit, to be amused by her. In the face of her unconcealed disdain, they behaved warmly towards her. Welcomed her into their fold. Established effortlessly that she was not expected to be like them: these days everyone partied with everyone.

—Fine, she said, for she understood their game and was too far in to fight it. Now which one of you nasty little bureaucrats is going to light me a cancerette?

All the same, she was uncertain about how much she could achieve with them. They were older than what she was used to. And sharper. More preoccupied by style. Spoiled by constant talk of success. With a habit of presenting themselves with a full and immediate declaration of personality — *In my line of work you have to be X, I'm such a fan of Y, If there's something I can't bloody stand, it's Z* — which aroused in her a distinct feeling of mistrust. A person could spend a lifetime fighting to get such people to accept truths that the underground freaks accepted at once.

As she danced amongst them now, she deliberately avoided their eyes. Coming from them, the eyes, were fine threads of light which threatened to entangle her and return her to the world from which the LSD had delivered her. By lowering her gaze and focussing instead on the bodies — on the luminous patterns which the arms traced in the air, or the sparks that exploded where the hips touched — she was able to keep herself here, firmly in the experience.

A fact lost on crowds like this: tripping, the good kind, required concentration. Discipline. Without it, one's journey was likely to remain superficial, devoid of lessons, susceptible to the negative emotions that so quickly turned it into a breakdown. Iris had been taking LSD on a regular basis for two years, and in that time had had a host of terrifying trips from which she thought she might never recover. In every case her mistake had been the same: she had approached what was deadly serious as something light. The trick, which a person only learned after a lot of practice, was to give all one's attention to the hallucinations, and to behave towards them, not as if they were real, but as real. Not as one's own imaginary property but as actually existing out there. Getting to such a place was not easy. The mind was an insecure god; it transformed anything that lay outside its comprehension into something to be feared. But for Iris, giving up — submitting once and for all to the limits of mind — was not an option. She was going to persevere. Row harder against the water. Push further. What she craved, simply, was to see things, all things, as they were. And in seeing them, to be united with them, no distinctions; she and they as one.

Craving such union now, she reached up to grab the objects that were swimming just beyond her vision. Then, looking at her hands, she laughed at how odd it was to feel that she was not the same as them. Her hands were objects just like the colours and the shapes they were trying to catch, belonging to no one. The more often she tripped, the less odd this feeling became, so it was crucial, in this moment, to remember how revolutionary it actually was. Nothing less than an end to one-sidedness. A switching to the third person. A self-overturning.

Fathoming this once more, she released a wild cry, and all the electricity in the room passed through her. Her body arched backwards and was convulsed in a ripple. And then another. And another. Every part of her participated in this undulatory, rhythmical wave, which only by coincidence matched the beat of the music. The flowing of her limbs, which had been enclosed within itself, not moving beyond its own borders, now oozed onto other surfaces in space. And the reverse: the current of the room spread onto her limbs. The result was a churning pool of primitive colours, the pressure of which she felt all around her.

The ocean parted as a man (possibly the owner of the flat, possibly not) came to dance directly in front of her. He mimicked her movements, as if by doing so he might absorb some of her ferocity. Iris, deeming him to be in need of reassurance, gave him a smile. In response, he seized her arm. She did not want to be seized in this way, yet she allowed it, for the velvet of his jacket, when it brushed her skin, gave her a nice sensation. Below a glowing halo of blond hair, his eyes pulsated. In his irises, Iris could make out tiny crystals, each made up of a perfect geometrical arrangement, from which shafts of light flashed. She saw the magnificence of every little grain.

He brought his mouth close to her ear. She felt the tickle of his beard as far away as her toes.

—Some of us here are into groups.

He had to shout to be heard over Syd Barrett's guitar riff in 'Interstellar Overdrive'.

—You might or mightn't be into that, it's up to you. You can stay where you are or come with us. We're going to the bedroom. Over there. You can join in at any time, or you can go home, the decision is completely yours. Like completely. Whatever you decide is a-okay, okay?

She thought she was being asked to leave, and, having no desire to do so, felt her spirit dip. Colour drained from her view.

—Haha. Right on, the man said.

His mouth, when it opened, engulfed the entire lower half of his face. When it closed, it disappeared entirely.

—I can always tell when a bird is up for it. From a mile off I could tell.

She was puzzled. It felt like she was hesitating, holding back, yet her body was definitely moving forward, yes, definitely following him towards the corridor. Her hand in his, his step leading hers, she felt on the outside of her own wishes. A perplexing sensation. One which deserved some reflecting upon. But there was no time. The bedroom was already here and she was in it. A dim, vaporous cave. Incense and candles burning to cover the smell. The air too heavy to breathe with comfort. Lots of little noises — whisperings, rustlings, the wet sounds of mouth and tongue — yet in sum, eerily quiet; the sound of the music outside like distant bells.

It took a moment for her to adjust. It was just wilderness at first, but then she began noticing things, as though parts were being added to the scene. An oriental wall hanging. A large bed, four people on that. A chair, another two people in that. In a second chair, a solitary figure. By the window, a couple in a standing embrace. Two, three, how many? loitering around, watching or waiting.

To her surprise — she had expected him to try to seduce her — the blond man released her hand and moved away across the room, stripping off his jacket and shirt as he went. She, suddenly alone in the doorway, did not know what to do except make herself invisible, somehow, amongst these bodies. Spotting an empty bit of back wall, she dropped onto all fours — *whoosh!* — and crawled over the rug towards it. Once at her destination, she turned around like a dog in grass — the shag as dense as forest undergrowth — and then sat with her legs crossed, a hand placed unconsciously on her kaftan in order to keep it from rising up and showing her knickers.

From here, the perspective was that of a child looking up at a massive adult world. The lines of the room did not meet in right angles but were warped so that the back wall receded sharply, tunnel-like, to a point of light far off. The effect was to shrink the bodies on the far side of the bed, and to make giants out of those on the near side. With detached curiosity, she studied the giants, then the dwarfs. Here, there, up, down, backwards and sideways: all of them convinced that their fucking was making the world a better place.

Imagining themselves to be liberated when in fact they were wearing the same armour and playing the same games.

From experience she knew not to express such judgements on the scene. When she had done so in the past, she had been told that she was afraid of sexuality. That she was a puritan. A prude. An accusation which stung, but one which she could not wholly deny. It was true, she did fear sex, at least some aspects of it, and was tentative as a result, and often lonely. Most men she found boring and invasive. The few she let in, when subsequently they tried to take ownership of her, she rejected them outright. Capable of neither free love nor traditional relationships: it was an impossible way to be, and she knew it. Her aversion to contact was itself a form of attachment. She prided herself on being able to take care of herself, yet more often than not this translated into a painful withholding. A disengagement. A retreat into this position here. The squatter in the corner.

The room leaned and swayed as she searched it for an entry point. (*What she was dealing with was a form of repression which — yes, now — she had to conquer.*) Amongst the different configurations of bodies, she did not see anything capable of leading up to passion. But she had to move in. It was not possible to love at a distance.

The figure alone in the chair.

That?

Squinting, she saw what it was. A balding head. An athletic figure grown flabby at the waist. Dark hair covering his shoulders and chest and curling high off his legs. With his feet planted wide on the floor and his knees splayed out, he was a man, one that was taking sugar cubes from a side table and putting them under his foreskin, and inviting people, both men and women, to come and suck them out.

Taking up her position between his legs, she giggled like a woman who had stopped trying to be interesting and now wanted only to please.

—Don't laugh, the man said. I'm offering you the gift of divine sight.

She hated him then. Nevertheless she took his penis in. Used her lips to peel the top back. The sugar cube fell out onto her tongue, and for a moment she froze. As a rule she only did drugs from her own batches because they had been tested by people she trusted. There were stories going around of acid cut with strychnine.

She pushed the sugar cube into her cheek to let it dissolve.

Fuck the stories.

The man's grip on her skull began to feel crushing, so she jerked herself free, and, heaving in air, let her body fall backwards onto the floor. Feeling red flashes of self-righteous rage, she bent her knees and spread her legs: a naughty girl showing her knickers to the world.

An instant then, and she felt a pair of hands trying to pull the knickers down. Blindly — her eyes still closed — she slapped at the hands to stop them, for she had her money, all of the takings, in a pouch tied around her waist and tucked into her underwear, and she did not want it stolen. Instead she prised her knickers to one side as an invitation to whomever it was to proceed that way. Another instant, and she felt a tongue on the rim of her vagina. Then felt it enter, slowly, slowly, then faster, thrusting. And, simultaneously, a finger on her clitoris, rubbing and pinching.

To begin with, there was nothing. But after a time, by applying herself to the sensations, she brought on something, which slowly built into something more. She arched her back, the crown of her head rocking on the floor, and opened her eyes. The world around her was phasing into ever intenser beauty, ever deeper significance. Which was all right until it got too much to bear. No longer a garden, attractive and thrilling, now it was a massive wave rolling over, and crashing, and crashing, and she could hardly breathe.

Then nothing. The unremarkable sight of feet and legs. A patch of old wallpaper.

She turned to look down the length of her own body. Pushed away the woman who was crouched there. Easy. But then the action of rolling onto her side and getting her limbs underneath her consumed most of her energy, leaving her in a state of physical fatigue. She felt overtaken by heaviness and fell back onto the carpet face down. Thoughts came which she was incapable of organising. Her body grew progressively more dense, more tightly packed, until she found herself at last reduced to stone. She could not move.

This is too much.

Up, she said to herself. For she had to rise, to surface.

Up. Up. Up.

Excruciating moments passed in which she wanted to scream but could not. Motionless, she had an attack of frustration, a tantrum. She wanted to beat her head against the floor and flail her arms about—

All of a sudden — minutes, hours later — she felt as if she had stood up.

—I've got up, she said, genuinely surprised.

She made it to the bathroom. Once there, she immediately fell back down, and every time she thought she could stand up, would collapse again, and crash into the washbasin. The safest place, she decided, was on the floor.

For what seemed like a vast amount of time she gazed without knowing, or even without wishing to know.

Vomiting was like all of the tension passing out of her body.

Back in the sitting room, she danced alone. Everyone else was lying about, extinguished by the sugar cubes. The man who had previously been in charge of choosing the music had receded into a corner to rub his back up and down against the wall, and offer an exhaustive commentary on the sensations this yielded, with the result that the same side of a Cream album was being played over and over. When it reached its end, Iris went to the hifi, lifted the stylus and dropped it back to a point near the start.

At some point came the phenomenon of dawn. Sitting on the couch, bodies scattered around her like so many cushions, she watched the morning light illuminate the thin blue curtain. Feeling once more the aloofness, the separateness, the desire to stay quiet, she stared fixedly at the shadows falling on the folds: stripes of deep blue alternating with stripes of an incandescence like blue fire. In a blink, the colours rose to a higher power and then fell back down. Between one colour and the next, Iris could make out innumerable fine shades of difference.

If one always saw like this, she thought, one would never want to do anything else but see. There would be no reason to do anything else. The causes for which, at ordinary times, one was prepared to act and suffer, would become uninteresting. Apartheid? Civil rights? The war? Theatre? Art? She would not be bothered about any of that, for the good reason that what she saw directly before her would be enough.

Time was lengthened out. The night had had twenty-four hours, but now here came the day. Curtains drawn back. And light, hateful light, let in.

People were moaning and shielding their eyes. Those with jobs had left or had called in their excuses and gone for an afternoon breakfast, the owner of the flat among them. What remained were the scum. The dross. Those who lived without money or ambition, and who saw with different eyes. The brightness had begun to be again: *would they be able to see in it?*

She came to understand that she was lying across a beanbag, her head on a man's lap. The man was caressing her forehead, as a nurse might a patient, or a mother her sleeping child. Blinking up at him, she waited to hear what she would say.

—Am I—? is what eventually came. Am I—?

—You're a fine thing, the man said.

—No, I mean—

She shook her epileptic bracelet in front of his eyes:

—Did you see? Was I—?

—I know what you mean. You told me. I been over here watching. You're all good.

She had no memory of telling this man about her epilepsy or anything else. As far as she was concerned, she had never set eyes on him before. She put her hand under her kaftan. Felt for her purse. Then rubbed her knickers. Sniffed her fingers. There was no smell of piss, which probably meant she had not had a seizure. She usually pissed herself if the seizure was big enough, and the ones that came after a few nights of partying were always big. She had no scientific evidence or anything, but she had a theory that LSD kept the fits at bay, put them off until she had come down and gone to bed to recover. The problem then was, they struck with a vengeance.

She sat up:

—The time?

—Plenty of it, sweets.

The man was — the fact dawned — a Negro. But not a hip Negro. He did not have a West Indian accent, and if he belonged to the Rastafarians he was not showing it. No dreadlocks. No beard. No beads. Just a loose and uneven afro, isolated bits of stubble, a grubby white t-shirt, and a crumpled pair of trousers with a high waist and a pleat, like those worn by middle-aged men or by boys who thought they were older than themselves.

Oh God. One of those.

Once again in control of her voluntary system, she got up with only a minimum of hesitation.

—Where you off to? the Negro said.

—Blowing, she said.

—For?

—For the good of my health.

She went into the bedroom. Paused briefly to survey the mess, then waded through it to the wardrobe, in which she found a pair of jeans. She pulled them on. Too big. But they stayed up when she tucked her kaftan into them and used her headscarf as a belt. Thus protected against the day, she left.

The Negro's voice came after her down the stairs:

—Iris, hold it—

—Sorry, mate, she called back. Gotta split, yeah?

Out on the street, she remembered that she was in Notting Hill. Significance had obviously returned to its everyday level, for Notting Hill was once again the pits.

—I was only asking where you're off to.

She jumped. The Negro was beside her.

—Jesus. Home, man. Where d'you think?

—Home?

—*Da-ding*. Double your money.

She started to walk. A wind blew in her face. Cold for May. The last of the market stalls were packing up. Bits of fruit and veg littered the ground. Mentally she mapped out the route to King's Cross. She always felt like a god after going through a trip, for she had seen what ordinary mortals could not, so although it was a fair distance, she decided to go on foot. She was hungry and foolishly had left the flat without drinking anything, but then again she was divine — her spirit, she had once been told, had the power of nine cows and two tigers — so, if she met with no aggro, she would make it.

—You got anything to eat at home? the Negro said.

—You read my mind, she said.

—Nice one.

He said this in the tone of someone who presumed he was coming with her. And in point of fact he was coming with her. She stopped. He stopped.

—Wait a sec, she said. Did w—?

—Chill, miss thing. Nothing happened.

Feeling a cold panic rise up her legs, she stared into the black spaces of her memory.

—On your honour?

The Negro lay his palm over his heart:

—Don't be fretting. I made sure you was protected.

She believed him because she so gravely had to. The sensation, then, was not so much relief as a temporary freezing of the inevitable self-disgust.

—Yeah? she said. Well, thanks for that.

The Negro laughed:

—In return, you said we'd go for grub. Your treat.

—Chancer.

—Only telling you what you said.

—Wasn't there anything to eat up there? Did you check the cupboards?

—Cobwebs.

—Where you living? D'you have a room?

—If you can call it that. Down Ladbroke Grove.

—That's just around the corner. Don't you have a can of something you can open?

—All out till my dole on Thursday.

—I'm sorry about that, mate. I am. I'd like to help you out, but I live in King's Cross. You won't want to go all that way just for a bit of toast.

—King's Cross?

He thought for a second.

—Don't have any better offers.

—Aw, mate, don't be—

—What?

—The coloured caffs, what about them? That one on Westbourne Park Road, the Rio?

He laughed:

—You know the Rio?

—Yeah, I know the Rio. I've been out with some spades. No one there who'd shout you some foo-foo?

He laughed again, shaking his head:

—No one shouting me nothing at the Rio.

—Oh, well, that's got to change, my friend. That's your community there. Not cool not to be plugged in.

She took off again.

He caught up right away.

Flick and fuck: a sticker.

They walked in silence for a while. With her head turned slightly towards the road, she tried to remain oblivious to him, but a slap-slapping sound eventually drew her attention to his feet. He was wearing flip-flops. His toes were filthy. His nails long and black.

—Where're you from? she said.

—Been in London for years, too long probably.

—And before that?

—Grew up in Portsmouth.

—No, I mean originally.

—Oh, originally? Portsmouth.

She nodded down at his feet:

—Is this what they're wearing these days in Portsmouth?

He curled his toes upwards so that he walked like a penguin for a few steps.

—Friend of mine gave me these.

—Aren't you cold?

—What's it to you?

She did not quite know what it was to her — but it was something. She herself did not like to change her clothes. She rarely washed and did not brush her teeth. After a childhood spent under supervision because of her epilepsy, scrubbed regularly with carbon soap to remove the stink of piss, instilled with impeccable manners in preparation for those times when she would have to apologise to the world for disturbing it, she was now going on the offensive, displaying a fabulous neglect of personal hygiene. *Let the world smell me. Let them be disturbed.* Perhaps she was experiencing this Negro's displays of grossness, so similar to her own, as a sort of test. Was he the genuine article? Most people on the scene were just fashionable fakes with their own self-interest at heart. Only a few, a very few had abandoned it all to live the real underground life. Which camp did this Negro belong to? She would give herself till Paddington to find out.

As they walked, passers-by greeted them with a variety of disapproving looks. Crossing a road, a little girl pointed at the Negro and said to her mother:

—Look, Mummy, a blackie.

A minute later, a well-dressed man reeled off a string of swear words in a mumbling undertone. Another man, no more than ten paces on, said:

—Ain't natural.

And then louder from behind:

—Stay away from our women!

Iris was accustomed to gaining a certain kind of attention in public, on account of her clothes and her hennaed hair that went down to her waist, but there was a quality to these reproaches that was new, directed not at the way one chose to live but at the way one was born, which struck her as especially stupid. Wanting to show defiance, she dropped her hand and allowed it to brush against the Negro's, so that if he wished he would be able to take it, but he did not.

—You don't remember my name, do you? he said instead.

He showed no signs of having heard the insults, but being here, beside her, he must have, and they must have cut.

—It's Keith.

—I knew that.

—No, you never asked.

They walked in silence for another minute. Then she said:

—I'm not ignorant, you know.

—Oh no?

—No. In school they don't tell you anything about it, but my parents were communists, serious ones, so they taught me.

—Communists?

—S'right. Full-on Russia lovers. Right up to the end. The last to leave the Party, out of all of their friends. And even then they only left because they were forced to, because it got to the point where they couldn't ignore the evidence any more.

—The evidence?

—The gulags, mate.

Keith looked at her vacantly.

She shook her head and sighed. It hurt her, somewhere, that the scene cats did not have a clue about what was happening in the world.

—Don't worry about it. All I'm saying is, my folks were commies. Into oppression with a big O. Which meant they spent a lot of time educating us about, you know, *you*. And I'm not just talking about *To Kill a* fucking *Mockingbird*. I'm talking about history lessons and lectures and photographic exhibitions, the whole jingbang.

—That right? Your folks sound cool.

—Communism isn't cool mate. It fucks you up. Kills the spirit. Allows no space for people like you and me.

—Like me?

—I'm not talking about Negros now, I'm talking about people who want to cop out and to do their own thing. Individuals. Freaks.

—Right.

—That said, what my parents have become since isn't any better. My mother's gone full circle and openly votes Tory. My father calls himself a Christian. Did you hear what I said? A *Christian*. They're more fucked up now than they ever were, if that makes you feel better.

—Feel better about what?

Nonplussed, she examined Keith's face. The truth was that for her, as for her parents, Negroes were more a concept than a reality. A highly approved concept but a concept nonetheless. The difference with this Negro was, he was actually here and not making any sign of disappearing.

—I'm in no way a racialist but you spades can be—

—What?

She was going to say prickly but she went for:

—Pushy. You don't take no, do you?

—That's funny, he said. Pushy is what we think you are. Politely getting your way all the time.

—Nah, we're just afraid. If you were white, I'd have told you to fuck off ages ago.

—Are you going to tell me to fuck off now? Cause I will if you want.

She filled her cheeks with air and looked up and down the road.

In friendships she had the truth or nothing, and Keith was showing himself to be equal to that, at least. But he was asking too much to expect her not to feel that he was asking too much.

—All right, she said, exhaling loudly. Fuck it.

—Fuck what?

—Come on. Back to mine. I'm not saying no because inside I'm feeling a yes — well, actually a maybe *verging* on a yes. But any funny business, any, you know, tomfuckery, and I'll scream and say you did this.

She pulled up her sleeve and showed him old bruises from past seizures.

—Jesus, he said.

—Ahuhn, she said, yanking her sleeve back down. And you should know something else. Where I live, it's a group. There's a few of us.

—You squatting?

—Yeah, man.

It took a few seconds for this lie to make itself felt in her system.

—Scratch that, she said then. I don't know why I—. We're not really squatting. The building belongs to my mother. We're an urban commune, sort of. An art and performance collective.

—Porno and that, he laughed. Swingers. I get it.

—You wish. There won't be any of that caper. We're performers all right. But we do street theatre. Happenings. That sort of shit.

—Right on.

—And, look, I apologise in advance for my sister, Eva. She's a politico and, I mean, the antithesis of laid back.

—No stress. I've handled my share of politicos. What's her trip?

—She's a commie.

—Like your parents?

—Don't say that to her, she'll take your head off you. Her whole deal is, she's trying to show them where they went wrong. The problem isn't communism itself, *it's communism as practised in Russia*. That's what she says. *Russia fucked it up, and now it's too late to fix it there.* So if the workers' paradise is going to materialise, it has to be somewhere else. She's putting her money on China.

—China the place?

—Of course the fucking place. You know Mao?

—Mo? Don't think I do. Where's he jive?

Iris laughed:

—Whatever, man. All you need to know is, my sister's a Maoist, which means she's a fucking pain. The commune isn't supposed to have a leader, everything is meant to be like this joint effort, but let's face the facts, she's the leader. She'll probably make you chip in and do something for your dinner. Some fixing up or something. That's the way it works.

—Dig it.

—I can't promise you haute cuisine either, in case that's what you're used to. But we'll find something. But afterwards you have to split. No hanging around.

—Roger that. No hanging around.

They got a bus up the Euston Road as far as King's Cross station. She paid for the tickets because Keith had nothing in his pockets. Although the money was not much, just a few of the new pence, she did not like spending it, for technically it was not hers. She had already spent her share of the takings (on what, she did not want to recall) and was now dipping into Simon's: Simon, her uncle, her father's brother, who also happened to be her supplier, and who was not going to be happy. She had outstanding debts to him, and his patience with her was running out, his threats escalating. She was not looking forward to facing him.

From the bus stop, they doubled back on Euston Road and took a right onto Midland Road. The high walls of the station on the right side and the goods depot on the left offered respite from the wind, though this was short-lived: they became exposed to the weather once again as they went past the railway lines. Between the gaps in the corrugated iron fence, the windows of the moving trains flashed; signal lights twinkled red and green. The gasworks, which loomed over the tracks, came in and out of their vision; its stink invaded their noses. The bridge at the foot of St Pancras Road was covered with advance publicity of a film. Underneath, men slept. Women, recognising Iris as belonging to the commune, waved at her. Iris made a concerted effort to smile and wave back. Every profession had its dignity.

After the coal depot and before the flat blocks, they turned onto Chenies Place and then onto Purchese Street. At the school, they took a right onto the Somers Town terraces, where Iris instinctively noted the familiar distinctions between the streets: washing on every clothesline, then none at all; whitened steps and frosted glass, then railings and iron bars; emptiness, then bodies and noise. Iris navigated them through. Outside the solitary fish and chip shop, men fell quiet as they passed. On the steps of the houses, women stopped their work and gave narrow stares. Children, roaming unsupervised, jeered by making monkey impressions. Iris told the children that if they did not shut up, she would never again invite them into the commune to make things.

—Aw what, Miss Iris? said one. You ain't serious.

—I am too, she said. Now bloody behave.

Keith walked through the packs of children without acknowledging them. Hands in his pockets, face lifted, gaze raised above the chimney stacks: tough was the surface that could withstand such constant grinding.

The commune, up ahead, was spread over two buildings. The first was a large red-brick warehouse on the corner of a crossroads. Graffiti and boarded doors covered the bottom third of the façade; the middle third was a windowless belt of plain red bricks; on the upper third the brickwork was arranged to spell out TYTELL MEDS EST 1904. The second building, an adjoining three-storey Victorian residence, had once been a temperance house for the local workers. Access to the commune was through the temperance house door.

Painted bright red, with a distinctive — but long broken — Chinese lantern hanging over it, the door was meant to be kept open during the day, as a welcoming in, but for some reason it had been boarded and chained.

Approaching from the perpendicular terrace, Iris saw the change.

—What the fuck? she said, feeling too worn out to adapt to new circumstances.

She went to the door and pulled at the lock. Took a few steps back and scoured, senselessly, the windowless walls for any signs of life.

—*Where. House*, said Keith, reading the large letters written in white paint across a board next to the door. Oh, *Wherehouse*. I get it. Is this it?

—Yeah, but—

—And *Tytell Meds*? said Keith, pointing up at the factory wall. What's that about?

She looked up and down the street. A silence had settled on everything, which made her fear the world ahead.

—It was once a pill factory.

—Nice.

—Nah, nothing like that. Just painkillers, tonics, that sort of stuff. Big operation, though. Exported all over the world. Germany, mostly. Sod's luck. When the war started, it became a coal store. And was left empty after that.

—Your family was in the painkiller business?

—Painkillers? My family? No. My parents bought this building in the fifties, when it was already derelict, and converted it into a—

Suddenly furious, she took a running kick at the boarding on the door.

—theatre! Fuck!

—Hey, take it easy.

With one hand Keith took her wrist, and with the other he warmed the space between her shoulder blades, as if burping a baby.

She shook him off:

—It's locked. It's never locked. Something's going on.

—Okay, calm down. We'll figure it out.

He blinked at her the questions he was unwilling to speak.

—Before you ask, she said, I left without the key. Don't normally need it, do I?

—I didn't say anything, he said.

She went round the side of the temperance house steps and, crouching down, reached in through the bars and knocked on the basement window.

—Neel? Neel? You there?

—What do you want? came a voice.

—Neel, it's Iris. I forgot my key. Let us in the window, can you?

Neel was one of two Indian medical students whom the group rented the unwanted lower rooms to. Neel, in the front basement, and Sid, in the back, were not part of the commune, but their contributions covered some of the building's expenses, and it was handy to have them there for emergencies. Neel always had rice and lentils if the kitchen ever ran out, and Sid could usually be paid to steal prescription medicine from the hospital; some of Iris's worst comedowns had been cushioned by morphine from the University College.

The latch on the window clicked, and she pushed it open.

—You're a star, Neel! she called after the figure that was already scuttling back into the dark of the flat. Do you know where everyone is?

—Not my problem!

The two central bars of the grille covering the window were for show only; they were in fact broken and could be easily twisted out. The sound of the bars hitting the ground where Iris threw them reverberated around the nearby terrace. She slid through the gap, landing heavily on the kitchenette counter inside, causing spoons left in unwashed cups to jingle. She jumped down, ran through the flat — two weeks late with the rent, Neel and Sid were skulking in their rooms — and out of the door, then up the basement stairs to the hall. She opened the front door and helped Keith to duck under the chains.

—Jesus, he said, squinting at the by-now ragged posters of Che and Fidel and Ho Chi Minh and — larger and a little less ragged than the others — Mao.

—Hmm, what? I can't hear you.

Iris was checking under the stairs and out the back for signs of life.

—I said, Jesus. This place.

—Oh yeah, she said, returning. It's boss, isn't it? Was a temperance house originally, but that closed down after the war, and the building was left vacant. My parents, when they were planning their theatre, wanted all of the actors to live together, as a sort of community, so they bought here as well and turned it into the lodging house. A community of *alcoholics*, I guess, was the idea.

Keith gazed at her blankly.

—That was a joke, spade. Wait here.

In the kitchen out back, mould was growing in half-filled cups of tea; what little remained in the vegetable rack had shrivelled and sprouted. Up the main stairs, the common room was empty; the sleeping bags and foam beds that were usually piled into the corner, gone. Up again, on the second floor, the doors of all the bedrooms, except her own, were closed and locked. Nobody answered her knocking. She checked the landing lights: still working.

She came back down to the hall. Gave Keith a half-full packet of kidney beans.

—This is all there is.

Her hands freed, she clutched her hips and thought for a moment.

—This situation is seriously off.

The Wherehouse commune was never deserted like this. People wandered in and out at all times. Not just the eight core members, but their friends also, and friends of those friends. Only the previous week, a handful of Dutch travellers, distant acquaintances of Eva's boyfriend, had come unannounced and slept for four nights on the common-room floor. This open-door policy was not without its difficulties. The people Wherehouse attracted, members and visitors alike, were the sort who did not feel easy in society. Creative and bright and funny as they often were, they also had their idiosyncrasies. Having abandoned the centre for the fringe, they had become sensitive to rules and sceptical of programmes and were tricky to manage as a consequence. Soon after Eva became a Maoist — senseless to try to put exact dates on these things, but Iris estimated that the cycle of Eva's conversion had probably been completed by the winter of sixty-six — a manifesto was adopted aimed at bringing into the commune only people with a minimum grade of political knowledge. But this had proved impossible to implement, and in reality no matter how screwy people were, as long as they agreed to hate capitalism and imperialism and most of all America, they were acceptable. And it worked the other way too: as individual as everybody insisted on feeling, there was safety in the pack; comfort in knowing that someone sympathetic would always be around. If the price of this was an occasional dip into Mao's *Sayings*, most were willing to pay it. Keeping the peace really just meant getting the balance right.

—When was the last time you were home? said Keith.

She shrugged. Counted back.

—Four, five days? If the place is left empty like this, it'll be filled with squatters inside a week.

—No one left a message? Did you check the fridge?

—Fridge?

She smiled at his goodness.

—You know, Keith, I'm glad you came.

He cleared his throat, embarrassed.

She thought he might kiss her then, but he did not, which was a relief. It was not what she wanted for them either.

—Let's try next door.

He held up the packet of beans:

—Shouldn't we put these on first?

—What? Oh!

Laughing, she knocked it out of his hands onto the floor.

—You settle too easily. We'll find better than that yet.

She led him down the hall to the old scullery, a wall of which had been partially removed to give access to the theatre without having to go outside. It had been Eva's idea, to knock through, one of her many which turned out to be unpopular, for it allowed the cats which lived in the theatre (last count, eleven) to stray into the lodging house. Neel and Sid in particular objected to this feline infestation, on hygiene grounds, and threatened to call the council unless it was contained. A solution was found whereby a board was fixed onto a rail, which could be slid across to block the entrance. Painted onto this board were cutesy illustrations of cats defecating, and the words:

KEEP ~~SHIT~~ SHUT.

As soon as Iris rolled the board back, the smell assaulted them: a torrent of piss and shit and ammonia.

—Whoaff! said Keith, slapping his hand to his face.

—Ach, Christ.

Going through into the foyer, she untied the bandana from her wrist and put it over her mouth. Dollops of shit dotted the floor. From various positions around the room — under the furniture, on the ledges — cats meowed.

—I thought cats were supposed to be clean, said Keith.

—Normally they go outside, she said. The door is meant to be left open during the day, and at night we leave a window in the back ajar. No, this, my friend, is a protest.

Iris offered Keith her bandana. He refused it with shake of his head. She shrugged and tied it back on her wrist. The smell was not so disturbing when you just took it.

—From what I can see, they've been left alone more or less since I've been out. How would you like it? To be stranded here without food and company for that length?

Keith sucked his teeth as if to say that being stranded was something an intelligent being these days learned to get used to.

She blew through her lips and peered round:

—And as usual it's left to me to clean up.

—You gonna clean all of this?

Iris gave him a patronising look:

—You ever lived in a commune? Nah, didn't think so. Anyone who's lived this life knows it's always like this. There's always one or two who do the dirty work.

—Doesn't sound fair to me.

—It's not.

Although Iris had a mother, she had always had a feeling of missing a mother. This feeling did not have so much to do with missing her own specific mother (she hoped never to see *her* again), but with missing what she believed a mother should be. A warmth or a certain kind of touch. An order and cleanliness in a room. Iris, wanting that others should never feel the same lack, acted — unofficially, for in the commune there were no fixed roles — as a sort of housemother. Cleaning. Cooking. Shopping. Housekeeping. Teaching. When it came to the collective's artistic work, she preferred the sewing and the painting and the gluing and the planning to the presenting and the performing. Steered away from acting by her parents — *an epileptic on the boards would be a danger to everyone* — and fearful of the limelight as a result, she preferred to make her mark behind the scenes.

—The only thing I mind, I mean what really bothers me is that they've gone somewhere, you know? That they've left without telling me.

—You don't know where they might've gone?

—That's the thing. I haven't the foggiest.

The thought that she had been left alone was awful. Anger leaked away, leaving sadness as she took the key from the hook and unlocked the chains on the foyer door. Keith helped her to remove the boards and railings. Clearly he had noticed she was having feelings and wanted to take them away, because when he next spoke, he did so brightly.

—So this was your parents' theatre, huh? he said.

She swallowed. Ran her forearm across her nose.

—Back when I was ten we all came to live here. My family and all the actors.

—Your parents moved you into a pill factory?

She laughed:

—Yeah. I mean, we slept next door in the lodging house. But we spent most of our time here in the theatre.

—Fuck. That's—

—Round the bend? Believe it. In fairness, we were only here a few months in the end. The theatre didn't stay open for long.

—What happened?

—Don't know.

—You don't remember?

—I do. It's just—

—A long story?

She inhaled loudly, deeply, as if seeking in this single breath the force to carry her whole life.

—A long story, yeah.

With the boards and railings cleared, and the door flung open, light and air poured in. Several of the cats dashed out.

Keith removed the dirt from his hands by clapping them.

—So when did you and your sister decide to move back in?

—Three years ago.

—Your parents gave you the place?

—My parents aren't together any more. It's my mother's.

—She gave it to you?

—Not exactly.

—You just took it over? She doesn't know you're here?

—No, she knows we're here, but we're not supposed to be. Every so often she threatens to kick us out and put the building on the market.

Keith was peering around the foyer, taking it in. Concrete floor, bare brick walls, metal beams: he was struggling to see how this could have been anything but what it was built to be.

—So your idea was always to start this group? This happenings club?

—Eva wanted to try it. It was her idea initially.

That was not strictly true. Iris had been involved at every step.

—What about you?

—I came round.

She climbed over the counter of the old box office and retrieved a carton of dried cat food from the cupboard. She handed the box to Keith.

—This what we're having? he said.

—Shut up and put some into the bowls. And some water too, please. There's a tap in the toilet, which is in the auditorium, through those doors there.

He did not look happy.

—I told you you'd have to work. I'm not asking you to pick up the shit. I'll do that.

—Okay.

—Good. I'll be a back in a minute. Stay down here.

—Where you going?

—I just need to check on a thing. A minute and I'll be back, and then we'll get some grub.

He pouted.

She slapped him on the shoulder, as a man might do to say *Cheer up, son*, and left the foyer by the low passageway leading to what had once been the bar: a large, high-ceilinged room with a mezzanine that wrapped round three sides. She went up the mezzanine stairs. Knocked on the old office door, which was now her uncle's bedroom.

—Who is it?

—It's me. Open up.

Yin yang. Black white. Circle line circle. For Iris, being the founder of a commune, and now its caretaker, meant being recognised as MOTHER; the nourisher of something of her own, which in her mind was the same as being good. But it was also true that, by going out to sell and bringing home the earnings, she was being FATHER too. The provider. The bread earner. A role as important as its opposite, which she performed just as well, but which the group refused to acknowledge.

Among the Wherehouse members there existed an assumption — unspoken yet no less real for this — that all the expenses which their own meagre contributions failed to meet were covered by Thurlow family money, in the form of trusts to Iris and Eva. Iris's drug dealing, far from being the main show, was thought to be a side act. Less to do with generating an income than with keeping the less creative members (Iris) occupied, and maintaining the group's reputation — for lawlessness, for danger — within the avant-garde arts scene. Despite the inaccuracy of this view (the Thurlows were indeed rich, but Iris and Eva themselves had been cut off from their trusts by reason of their lifestyles) the sisters did not contradict it, because they found that it made for the better running of things. The members were happy to believe themselves part of a system which took from those who had better and gave to those who had worse. There were fewer quarrels. Relations were more fluid. Envy and competition were dampened. With money relegated to a secondary concern, everyone felt free to pursue the greater task of making art — and more and better art was made.

—Iris? Halle-fucking-lujah. Are you alone?

—Open the door, Simon.

—Are. You. Al—

—It's just me. Let me in.

She heard him pushing back his chair. Knocking things over.

—Simon, for ff—

The door swung open. His eyebrows were worried, his face bitter. He checked up and down the mezzanine corridor.

—Get in here, he said, pulling her by the sleeve.

—Oi, watch the threads.

He slammed the door behind her. Locked it.

The room was filled with smoke and reeked of the man who rarely left it. The bricked-up windows meant the only light came from a lamp on the desk. Directly under the beam, on a piece of silver kitchen foil, was a mound of crystal acid.

The soles of Simon's old boots squeaked as he walked back to his chair behind the desk. As ever, he was wearing a dressing gown with the stains of previous meals scattered across the flaring lapels. Visible underneath the gown, for he left it untied, were a vest, trousers and braces from a suit made for a few shillings in the fifties, which he kept in use by darning the holes himself with a needle and thread. He sat down and immediately resumed his work: dissolving the crystals in distilled water and dropping the mixture onto sheets of blotting paper to make single trips. Without looking up, he made a gesture to indicate that Iris could sit where she liked, though there were few options, only a stool or the floor. She chose to stand.

—Simon? she said. What's going on? Where is every—

—Shh, he said. Hear that?

—What?

He jabbed his ill-fitting artificial arm in the direction of the wireless radio on the shelf:

—That.

It was tuned to the war. The volume turned right up.

—They're going to lose, you know. Beaten—

He shook his head, laughed a bit manically.

—by a bunch of peasants.

—Simon, listen to me, I need to know where—

He lurched out of his chair and smashed his prosthesis down on the radio to turn it off.

—*Simon* listen? How about *Iris* listen for a change.

He pointed the index finger of his good hand, a real shivering finger, between her eyes.

—You've been gone for a week. No word. Not a tinkle.

The one finger turned into five, hovering over the mound on the table.

—Look at all of this. I've needed your help. I told you to get back as soon as possible. You knew this consignment was due.

—Sorry, said Iris.

—Where you been?

—Out.

—For a week?

—For as long as I fucking well want.

—Oh, I see.

The monk-like baldness of Simon's crown made it look as though his worries had worn through. There were scabs where he had tried to scratch these worries away. He stopped scratching now and rested his elbows on the table. Spread his arms out in a V.

—Did you hear that, ladies and gents? he said, addressing an imaginary audience sitting behind her. The little missy thinks she's free to do what she likes, for as long as she likes. What do you make of that, hmm?

A pause while he brought his hands together, skin wrapping over wood, and rested his chin on top.

—Yes, yes, uh-huh, I quite agree, he said, nodding. I also think it's time she came back into the world and got real. She has a job to do, and until it's done, she's not free to do what she wants, is she? She's not free at all. She's the opposite of free.

Iris joined the game by turning her head to the invisible public by the back wall.

—That's right, she said, she's a slave. Iris here, a slave to this man, and on top of that, to this whole fucking group. A double bloody slave.

Her eyes flicked across to meet his:

—And for future reference, Simon, throwing ammonia on the floor isn't a help to anyone. Picking up the shit would have taken less time and effort.

Simon did not consume the drugs that he sold, but he did drink, in binges, and when drunk, liked to disparage the Wherehouse collective, its performances, its mission. Most of the communards were frightened of him. They understood that he was necessary somehow, that he had an undeclared function, but his roughness and his belligerence were menacing to them, his right-wing rants were something they had joined the commune to get away from, and so they kept their distance. Even Eva, who was related to him, who understood that his touch of madness did not make him dangerous, even she shrank from being alone in a room with him. Iris, though, was not afraid. In her life there had been no one kinder to her than Simon, and despite everything she loved him.

He picked a half-smoked cigarette from the ashtray and relit it. He had bitten his fingernails so low that he did not have any left — except, that is, for the nail on the little finger, which he kept long for scratching.

—What I gave you to sell wasn't much. It could have been shifted in a day.

—What can I say, Simon? Business was slow. There's a lot of stuff going round. People's palates are tired. They want new experiences. Tastes are changing.

—Bollocks. There's always buyers.

He sucked in a mouthful of smoke. Funnelled it out his nose. Scratched some more.

—When you want to be fast, you can be fast.

—I didn't think there was a special rush. We're hardly stuck.

—We're always stuck, Thurlow. The fucking phone rental being the latest thing. They cut that off yesterday.

—The dirty fuck-offs.

—It was that or the lights. I had to make a choice.

She shook her head for a moment, disgusted:

—At least we have the lights. They're the main thing.

Simon mumbled something inaudible. As if his words had become caught, he hacked up a glob of phlegm. Released it into a balled-up handkerchief which he produced from his dressing gown pocket. Licking his broken lips, he poured himself some vodka from a bottle on the floor.

—Huh? he said as an offering.

—Nah, she said.

Simon slugged the vodka down:

—Did you flog everything at least?

—More or less.

Jamming her hands into her new jeans, she untied the pouch and tossed it onto the table. The gust of air this created caused some acid crystals to scatter.

—Ahrk!

Simon brushed them back onto the silver foil.

—Mind what you're fucking doing.

He crushed his cigarette into the ashtray, opened the pouch, emptied the money out and began to count it.

She took a seat on the stool and watched him.

He finished counting and gurgled unhappily.

—Before you go off on one, she said, about being short or whatever, I was obliged to give out some complimentaries. It was a quiet weekend. There weren't many heads about. I had to get in with a new crowd. And you know how that is. Trust has to be won. People like to sample the product.

—*A new crowd*, he muttered, taking her off unkindly. *Trust had to be won.*

—Oh fuck off, Simon, she said.

—*Oh fuck off, Simon*, he said, and twisted round to unlock the cupboard behind him.

Arranged on the cupboard shelves were lines of tins, each one marked with a number that corresponded to a particular expense: electricity, gas, phone, repairs, plumbing, cleaning, food. He distributed the takings, in an apparently random fashion, though more probably according to a carefully calculated ratio, among three or four of the tins. This done, he scribbled a figure onto a slip of paper and put it into the last tin, the one containing Iris's IOUs.

—You'll get your money back, she said.

—Damn right I will, he said.

Before, there had been a trust. When Iris reached eighteen, her grandparents on her mother's side — the rich ones, the Thurlows — began to give her a monthly allowance, which she had to go in person to collect. At these meetings in her grandparents' Tudor doll house in Cheam, she was called into the study, where her grandfather would, while slowing making out a cheque, issue a series of softly spoken yet unsubtle warnings. While he did not expect her to want to enter the family's hotel business — *hotels are rough places for women* — he would not tolerate her becoming an actress or a communist like her mother, and he did expect her to marry correctly, as her mother had failed so handsomely to do. This meant having a mind with which to make the correct marriage choice, which meant having an education, which meant not ever dropping out. Naturally her grandparents had hoped for Oxbridge, and were disappointed when this did not transpire, though they eventually came round to the merits of an education in the city. Geography at the London King's was the lie that they had been told. As a matter of fact, Iris was registered at Hornsey College of Art, where she lasted a year and half before leaving to volunteer full time at the Poster Workshop on Camden Road. When the truth of this eventually reached her grandparents — through which channel? it could only have been her mother — they cut her off without ceremony. Now her entire income came from the National Assistance she drew in two different boroughs, and from selling Simon's acid. It was enough. She could eat. She could buy music and clothes. She could go out whenever she wanted. She remained the single greatest contributor to the commune coffers. Yet this experience of losing her family allowance, of no longer being someone to whom things simply came and instead having to scrounge and to graft without security or guarantees, taught her to despise money as a medium. After reading an article in a newsletter on the idea of a moneyless society, she now wondered whether anarchism might be the appropriate attitude to have. For, according to the anarchist, in the new era money would be of no use.

—I'm not being funny, said Iris now, but if you actually made a product people wanted to buy, a stronger product, business would pick up, and I'd be able to repay you quicker.

—The product's not the problem.

He was pointing at her again, despite knowing how much she hated that; how easily it could set her off.

—It's you. Far as I'm concerned, you're on your last chance. Any more of this messing and I'll get someone else.

She scoffed:

—Who?

—I don't know. Your sister.

—Leave it out.

—Or her bloke. What's his name?

She laughed:

—Glorious idea.

—Or someone from outside. I wouldn't rule that out.

—Give it a rest. It's a shit job you have me doing, and I do it well.

—*Well* is a stretch.

He tapped the table with his single fingernail.

—Just don't get complacent, Iris. You're blood and I care about you, but I won't be an idiot for you.

Simon did not go out, and, except drinking, he did not do anything that cost. In everything, money was his motivation. Far from living in Wherehouse out of a love of art, or a desire for an alternative style of life, or an allegiance to family, he was here because there was no rent to pay and it gave him access to a cheap and willing labour force (again, Iris). Everything he earned off her back — a seventy/thirty split in his favour — that did not go on vodka went into one of those tins. Which tin? She was not sure. What she was sure of was that one day he would disappear with it, his savings box, and she would never see him again. She hated having this presentiment, but this was not the same as hating him.

—Paris, he said now, out of nothing.

—What?

—You wanted to know where everyone is. They're in Paris.

—You're joking.

—That's where they are.

—All of them?

—In a van. Guess who had to stump up for the rental.

—When?

—Thursday. Or was it Friday? Before the weekend. They looked for you. Not very hard, mind, but they did a sweep round.

—Just like that?

—Just like that.

—Why Paris?

—If they were to go anywhere, it'd be there, wouldn't it?

The anxiety was already there, a toxicant in her veins. Information. She needed information. Only that would protect her against the nothingness which was vast about her.

—What're you on about? What's happening in Paris?

—Where've you been stuck? Under a rock?

—Can't you just tell me, please, what's going on? So I can get your face out of mine and—

A knock on the door. Instinctively Simon wrapped his arms around the drugs, and folded his body over them, as a shield. Iris jumped to her feet and put herself in front of the desk, a second wall.

—Is that you, Keith? she said.

—I heard voices, Keith said.

—Go downstairs. Wait for me there.

—Everything all right, thing?

—Yeah. Just wait downstairs.

—I can't find a tap that works.

—Okay, I'll be down in a minute.

Footsteps.

Silence.

—Who the fuck is that? Simon rasped.

—A mate.

—What fucking mate? You said you were alone.

—He's just a friend.

—Did you have him selling with you?

—No. He's outside of this.

—He better be. Check to see he's gone.

—Chill out. He's cool.

—Check.

She unlocked the door and looked out. Keith was on his way down the stairs. He turned to look up at her.

—Everything all right, Keith? she said.

—I picked up the shit.

—You're a pet. I owe you.

—I put it in a plastic bag I found. Left it out the back by the other bins.

He showed her the cat's bowl that he was holding.

—I couldn't find the tap, though.

—The tap is where I told you it was. You were checking up on me.

—I heard voices.

—I'm here with my uncle. Everything's fine. Go back to the auditorium and I'll see you there in a sec.

Back in the room, Simon had come round to the front of the desk, and was leaning against it uncomfortably, his left leg planted on the ground, his right leg bent and resting on the edge, his foot dangling.

—Fuck's sake, Iris, he said.

—Don't worry about him.

—*Don't worry about him.*

Something switched in her then.

—Right, that's it.

She stormed over to him, reached around, and between a finger and thumb grasped a corner of the silver foil:

—If you don't tell me right now what's going on, what the deal is with Paris, I'll—

—Calm the fuck down.

He grabbed her arm. Glad to see that he knew her — the nervous impulse to pursue a goal at any price that overtook her in moments of frustration — she released the foil and sat back down on the stool.

There had been a telegram.

—That was what started it. The what-you-call-it, the *exodus*.

—A telegram from who?

She already knew the answer. From Max. Max whom the sisters also called *uncle*, even though he was not in fact a relative, merely their parents' best friend from Cambridge.

—Max is in Paris?

—There's some kind of rebellion going on.

—God, the faggot never misses a thing.

—It's all over the newspapers.

—First I've heard of it.

Max's telegram had been sent to their father's second wife, Doris. Doris was a *body artist*, and Max was her collaborator. COME IMMEDIATELY, the telegram had said. YOUR MOMENT HAS ARRIVED.

—Great. Another one of Doris's moments. Did she go?

—Does the Pope shit?

—And Papa?

—Not your father's game any more, is it?

—So Doris went without him?

—Ahuhn, and now I'd say he's terrified she's not coming back.

—She's forever not coming back. Then she always does.

—One of these times, she won't. Mark me.

As soon as Doris had left for Paris, Iris's father made a rare visit to Wherehouse in order to urge the group to follow her there. The youth revolution was happening, he told them. The spirit of Mao had arrived in Europe. This was *their* moment.

—For fuck's sake. He doesn't give a fuck about Mao. The slime-bag just wants them to find Doris and make sure she comes home.

—He didn't say as much, said Simon, but that's my guess too.

Iris pulled her cheeks down with the palm of her hands:

—And the group just did what he said?

No delay; as if complying with orders, they had left. And now who knew when they would return and for how long Iris would have to suffer the offence of solitude.

—I blame your sister, said Simon. Your father manipulates her. She thinks she can't say no to him.

There was a moment of silence between them now, as Simon watched what Iris would do. She felt his gaze on her; she could hear him wondering.

—A revolution? she said then.

—Is what they're calling it.

—I should go too.

—Now stop right there. They're calling it this big thing, but you know that's just the media talking. It'll come to naught. Won't change a thing.

—I should be there. To see.

—It'll be over before it starts, just watch. Afterwards the poor will still be shafted, and the war will go on, and the big bang will eventually wipe us out, thank Christ.

—They wouldn't run off like that for nothing.

—Them? They're just chasing a thrill.

—They won't do well without me. There are things they need me for.

—Don't take it personally, Iris. No one is saying you're not important. You've got your own talents. You should just stay and make the revolution from here.

With an unconscious glance, he referred to the drugs on the table.

—Not from over there. In somebody else's head. Your father. Your sister. Doris. Forget about them for once, and their bloody pointless crusades, and focus on what we have to do here. Keeping things afloat at home.

She pointed at the pile of acid and shook her head:

—Shifting that will have to wait till I get back.

He slapped his thigh, then used the slapping hand to appeal to her:

—Don't be a bloody pain, Iris! This stuff can't just sit here. What if there's a raid, hmm? and I'm arrested? What'd you do then? How'd you feel about that? No, it needs to be sold, a-sap. And you're not going anywhere till it is.

—I heard acid is a killer to get in France. I'll sell it there.

Simon clutched his head as if to keep it fixed on:

—Oh man, you rub me wrong, you do.

—Lend me some money for the ticket, will you?

—No money. You're staying here.

—Fine. I'll find the money elsewhere.

Defiance stayed with her only as far as the door. As soon as she was on the other side, she felt a weakening, and she knew Simon was right. Exhausted, penniless, a fear of boats: she was not going to Paris. Glowering, she went back into the office.

—All right, she said.

—All right what?

—Just give me enough to make a call.

—Talking to your father won't win you anything.

—Ten pence, Simon, please.

—The phone here is out.

—I'll go to a box.

Grumbling but obviously pleased, he stuck his hand into a jar of ready cash that he kept in a drawer. Held out two shillings.

—Use this. You'll be hard pressed to find a phone that'll take the new money.

She put the coins into her pouch and tied it once more around her waist.

—Don't be long, Simon said. You look like the living dead. Come back, soon as you can, and get some sleep. You can help me with the rest of this tomorrow.

—All right.

—And leave your bedroom door unlocked. In case—

In case she had a fit. In case he had to get inside to help her. What would a day in her life look like that did not come with precautions?

On the way downstairs, she thought about Paris, and the pictures most people had of the life there. Of loafing in cafés, and crossing the Seine, and living on chocolate and bread. Well now, in place of those things, there was revolution, whatever that looked like. With the politicos in charge, there would be marches, and speeches against the war, and Mao's *Sayings*. No one would be talking about love, and there would be no drugs, no music, which meant none of it could be real. Not like what was happening in San Francisco, where the people, the seekers from everywhere, were plugging out and getting in touch with themselves and doing only what they really wanted to do, following their inner paths, which was the truly selfless way, the greatest gift that humans could give to the world right now, and, in the long run, the only means of bringing about peace. *Get some fucking LSD into the White House water supply* — this is what she liked to tell Eva — *blast some Steppenwolf through the Oval Office windows, and see how long the war lasts then!*

On entering the auditorium, full of this, she was struck by the sight of what she had forgotten. Wherehouse had converted the auditorium — a windowless room, cavernous, unevenly lit by a rig of lights above a bare stage near the back wall — into a workshop space. The stalls had been cleared away and two lines of workbenches set out. On top of these benches, still there, exactly as the group had left them, were boxes containing bamboo strips and paper and tubs of paste, and all around, in piles on the floor, were unfinished Chinese lanterns. The completed ones were laid out on the stage floor, in groups according to their design: water lily, lotus flower, fan, aeroplane. Around thirty in all. Together making a beautiful but sad impression. This was what struck Iris as she came in: everywhere lanterns, so many in number, yet giving no light.

Keith was kneeling on the stage, examining a small rabbit lantern by holding it above his head and craning his neck to look up through its bottom.

—What's all this? he said.

—This?

She looked about uncertainly.

—Don't quite know yet. The bones of a performance piece.

—You made all of these? said Keith, jumping down from the stage and coming to join her on the workshop floor.

—Some of them, she said. It's a group effort.

She weaved her way around the benches. Picked up from the floor what had fallen. Closed jars of glue that had been left open. Put hardened brushes into the pots of dirty water. There were twenty-one steps to making a lantern. As she inspected the unfinished pieces, she tried to determine which step they were at, and whether it was worth continuing with them or discarding them and starting over.

—So you put candles in them? said Keith, who was following her closely. And they light up? Is that it? I'd like to see them lit up.

—Yeah, it's nice.

—What are you going to use them for?

—Don't know yet. A happening. I told you, Eva's obsessed with China at the mo. It was her idea.

This was not strictly true, either. The lanterns idea had been as much hers as Eva's, though neither sister could properly take credit for it, since all of this stuff — Russia versus China and hip-hip-hurrah for the wretched of the earth — had come down to them from their parents.

—I like them, said Keith now. They're beautiful. Innocent.

—Innocent?

She looked around again, taking in the work.

—Yeah, innocent, I guess you're right. Like deserted children.

She directed Keith's attention to the line of ochre-coloured boiler suits hanging from hooks on the back wall.

—And it looks like they're going to stay deserted for a while longer. Everyone's gone to *Paris*.

He looked at her blankly. Paris signified nothing to him.

—What's happening there?

—Revolution, apparently. Interested?

—What about food?

—After that.

—Revolution? I don't know.

—Be something to do.

—Paris?

—Yeah.

Keith drew his eyebrows together, worried:

—Don't have a passport.

—Me neither.

Shooing a cat off a workbench, she leaned her now aching body onto newly freed space. Looked about as if seeking something in the surrounding air.

—Listen, I've to make a quick call. You want to stay here, or come with?

—So you weren't serious about Paris?

—I guess I wasn't.

—Are we going to eat here?

She thought for a second:

—You'd better come with.

They went — plodding, in silence — to a phone kiosk on Euston Road.

Her father answered immediately.

—Papa?

—Eva?

—It's Iris.

—Sorry, darling, how are you? I thought you were—. Are you in Paris as well?

—Have you been sitting beside the phone?

—What? No.

—You sure?

—

—Papa?

—What?

—Can you call me back? I don't have any money.

—So you're here, in London? All right.

She replaced the receiver and only then realised that she had forgotten to give her father the kiosk's number. He would call the theatre, presuming she was ringing from there. Deliberately, delicately, as if holding a porcelain cup, she lifted the receiver again, then banged it furiously against the top of the coin box. Through the glass, Keith made a gesture expressive of *You crazy bint, what the fuck?*

She kicked open the kiosk door:

—Come on. We're going to my father's.

At this, his face expressed real distress.

—Relax, she said. It's not far. We'll eat there.

—Your old man's okay with that?

—Sure.

She could see he was not convinced.

—He's not that bad. You just have to ignore absolutely everything he says.

JIANG QING

1974

ii.

Ash-coloured clouds drifted from west to east. Little by little the light changed. The trees in the garden trembled. On the paths, fallen leaves, swept up by the breeze, rustled impatiently. Autumn: the pensive season, the reminiscing season, and in the chrysanthemum enclosure, Jiang Qing stood bent over her tripod, immersed. Framed in the viewfinder was a single specimen of brilliant white, its outer petals reaching out hopefully, its inner petals curling inwards to clasp its yellow heart; if the wind were to catch it and turn it ever so slightly in her direction, it would make a perfect picture. For a long minute she watched and did not move. The ends of her skirt whipped at her shins. Her fringe, those strands which had struggled free of the hairband, tickled her forehead. The skin on her bare arms rose into pimples. But — being human after all and bound by the same restrictions — her focus eventually weakened. Memories seeped in. Thoughts and visions. And now, as some painful event gripped her, she shivered.

Without pressing the shutter button, she took her eye away. Straightened up. Stepped back from the camera. Conscious of a strain in her lower back, she brought a hand to rest there.

In accordance with her precise instructions, her attendants had set up three of her cameras, spaced three metres apart, in the line of an arc, pointing towards the same flower, which she had chosen the day before and marked with a ribbon. To the right was her medium format Rolleiflex. To the left, her Shanghai 4 twin-lens. In the centre, where she stood, her Kiev 88. Her cameras were her most precious possessions. Her jewels. Locked in special cases and stored in a dedicated cupboard. Cleaned and inspected for marks and scuffs after every use. Which was not meant to suggest that she was a photographer of talent; rather it was the meticulousness of a hobbyist who took her work seriously and did not feel beyond the perfectionist streak which would have the best possible or nothing.

She moved over to the Rolleiflex. Checked the shutter speed before popping open the viewfinder and placing her eye to it. Her photography tutor had taught her to keep her back straight and look down into the finder from a distance, but this was a good example of why one must beware of teachers and the prejudices hidden in their lessons, for when one examined that pose critically, one could see it was reactionary, attractive only to people who were afraid of looking like a peasant and who generally delighted in themselves. The fact was, in order to see one's subject in all its details, and to get the best results thereby, it was necessary to bend over like a good proletarian and get close.

Finding her chrysanthemum to be both off-centre and blurred, she adjusted the Rolleiflex's angle and focus. In the newly sharpened image, the day looked gloomier than it actually was, the colours appeared darkened, so that the flower was now a flourish in the shadows, its mood even more ambivalent than before: where it was open it seemed expectant and where it was closed defensive, as if it were readying itself for a rainstorm that would both nourish and lash it.

She glanced up at the clouds: they threatened rain but were unlikely to give it. If *Chrysanthemum in a Rainstorm* was a scene she wanted to capture, she would have to help it into existence by artificial means. Moving quickly in case the light changed once more, she dipped her fingertips into the bowl of water that she kept on her worktable and sprinkled it over the flower. She then slid a bamboo partition into the flowerbed, arranging it in such a way that it would prevent any gusts from blowing the moisture from the petals.

Hastening back to the camera, she whipped off her glasses, rubbed the lenses vigorously, then replaced them, pushing them roughly up the bridge of her nose. Unhappy with the image the Rolleiflex was giving her, and wondering if perhaps the problem was her eyesight, she shrouded her head with a square of velvet and peered through one eye and then the other. After turning the focus in either direction several times, unable to find clarity at the centre without losing it around the edges, she decided the fault was not with her but with the Rolleiflex, and so abandoned it for the Shanghai.

Her tutor had a theory that looking and seeing were two distinct manners of perceiving. Looking referred to the ordinary way in which one was accustomed to perceive the world, with the naked eye, tainted by thoughts. Seeing, on the other hand, could only happen with the aid of the camera lens, and entailed a complex process of communing, through the machine, with the essence of things. She had always struggled to make out what exactly this meant, but now, thanks to the Shanghai, she thought she understood. For the chrysanthemum was white, she saw, and contained everything that was itself; in the drops of water that clung to the flower's surface were the colours of the world. To see such, and to seize it, was to quench one's thirst for company, for relations, for love.

—Forgive me, Commander.

She felt her attendant's presence over her shoulder but refused to be interrupted by it. One of the water drops, too heavy for its perch at the top of a petal, was on the cusp of dribbling down. If it did so, it would leave behind a track like pearls. She would not budge until—

Click. There it was. *Click-click.* She had got it. *Click.* A final one for safety.

—What is it? she said only then.

—We have finally received a response from Comrade Song Yaojin.

—Did he call?

—He sent a letter.

—A letter?

Jiang Qing uncurled herself. Came to stand tall over the deed completed. She glanced in the attendant's direction. He was holding a white envelope, its lip torn open.

—Remind me, what do you go by, soldier?

—My humble name is Xinhua.

—Soldier Xinhua—

It was hard to keep track.

—I asked you to get Comrade Song on the phone. I wanted to speak to him personally.

—And I tried, Commander. I've been calling all week, but never managed to catch him at home. I left several messages with his mother. She said he would call back. But it seems he has preferred to respond with a letter.

Jiang Qing went to her worktable and wiped her clammy hands with a towel:

—You've had a look, I see.

The boy was nervous; the new ones tended to be.

—With respect, Commander, I've been instructed to open and stamp all official corres—

—Yes, yes. And?

—It says no.

—No?

The attendant, having memorised in advance the main points, did not need to refer to what was written:

—Comrade Song says that, regretfully, on account of his advancing years and the toll that almost three decades of dancing at an elite level has taken on his body, compounded by his recent period of re-education in the countryside, he asks that his retirement be respected and that he be relieved of the obligation to participate in the upcoming perform—

—Ah, you dog!

The attendant jumped.

—What did you do wrong? When you called, in these messages you left, did you approach the subject properly? Using the right language? The correct tone?

—I followed your instructions.

—Stressing the importance of the occasion?

—Yes, Commander.

—Saying, expressly, who was coming? I mean, mentioning our guest, by name?

—Mrs Marcos, Commander?

—Mrs Marcos, precisely.

The attendant bowed his head.

—I did, Commander. I mentioned Mrs Marcos by name as you ordered, as many times as I could without sounding profane. And I took pains to emphasise the size of the occasion, calling it *a gala performance*, which is the term you told me to use. I was explicit about all of that, and Comrade Song's mother assured me that she had made full note of my words. I spoke to her several times, and each time she was eager to stress that her son would be certain to oblige, there was nothing he would not do for the Party, given the eternal debt he owed it, after all it had done for him. Still, unfortunately, his response, as laid out in this letter, i—

—Enough.

She threw down the towel.

—I've heard quite enough.

She went back to the chrysanthemum. Pinched the stem just below the bract and shook off the water. *That no-good motherfucker. He's not going to get out of this. An eternal debt to the Party? Pah! Everything he owes, he owes to me and me alone.* From the pocket of her apron she took a pair of secateurs. Snipped the stem. Handed the flower to the attendant.

—Put this in a vase in my study.

She lay a finger across the stem, a third of the way up:

—Water to here.

The attendant made a mark with his fingernail.

—Find a good place for it. On the rose-shaped table, perhaps. Or—

—On your desk?

—No, not there. Then call for my cars.

—To come directly?

—No delay. I'll visit Comrade Song myself, speak to him man to man, which in these times, it seems, is the only way to make oneself heard. It's what I should have done in the first place.

—I'll have to get authorisation for the cars, Commander.

—Then do so.

—The reason for your journey? For the form?

—Important Propaganda Committee business. Related to the imminent gala performance in honour of the First Lady of the Philippines. No need to be more specific than that. I'll use my seal to sign off on it.

Jiang Qing walked the line of the cameras, closing the viewfinders one by one.

—Tell me, Soldier, she said on her way back, is Comrade Song's dossier too heavy to carry?

—I shouldn't say so. A single binder. Full but portable.

—In that case, put it on my desk where I can see it. I'll take it with me to read on the way.

—Right away.

—And, Soldier, get the Volgas.

—Commander?

—The Volgas. Rather than the Fords. The Russians are no longer our friends, but, provenance aside, they're good cars and plainer. This is a personal visit and a delicate situation. I don't want to make a splash. Once you've done all that, find my daughter please. I'm going to need her help.

—Will your daughter be accompanying you, Commander?

—She will, so she'll have to get changed for the Outside. Inform her of this, and if she doesn't like it, well, she has no choice. Is that clear?

The attendant saluted.

Jiang Qing waved him off:

—Oh and have someone take these cameras in. As soon as possible. I don't want them left out here to be shat on.

Excited, she hurried back. These days she rarely got out of the Compound, and it was only when the opportunity for an excursion arose that she remembered how claustrophobic it was in here, amongst all of this splendour, and how much she enjoyed to ride in the car through the city, and to see the masses, and to be with them. She took a different route to her Separate Residence: over the bridge as she had come, but then around the bamboo thicket rather than through it, and along the edge of the lake, avoiding the central courtyards — a greater distance to walk, but unlikely to be populated by people she did not want to see. And indeed her only encounter before reaching the sentinel at the entrance of her Residence was with a gardener, on his knees scraping moss from the base of an imperial tablet. Jiang Qing had wanted these tablets dug out, or at least their evil inscriptions polished away, but her husband had intervened to keep them. *Leave them be*, he had said. *No one is going to see them.*

The gardener bowed his head as she passed.

—I'm no one, Comrade, she said to him. Labour is the master.

Back in her bedroom, she wiped her arms to the elbows and her neck to the armpits with hot towels handed to her by a female attendant. She changed out of her jumper and skirt into a navy Lenin suit. To replace her white plastic sandals, she picked an old pair of low-heeled leather shoes. She brushed her hair, but only lightly for fear of slackening her perm, then tied it into a bun and covered it with a flat cap.

Hot chicken broth had been prepared for her as a pick-me-up and placed on a side table in the study. She sipped at this but did not have the patience to finish it.

—Go and see what's keeping my daughter, she told a third attendant.

The chrysanthemum had been put in a thin porcelain flute and placed on the rose-shaped table. Shaking her head, no, she moved it to the desk. There, without sitting down, she opened Song Yaojin's dossier and flicked through it until the attendant returned.

—Your daughter has asked me to tell you that she won't be leaving the Compound this afternoon.

Jiang Qing resumed her flicking:

—Won't she now.

—She said she was busy. That her hands are full with the baby.

Jiang Qing shut the dossier. Lifted it. Held it in both palms as if to weigh it. Then put it under her arm. Turned to face the window. Outside, beyond the roof tiles of the neighbouring building, and framed by the ornamental gate, autumn's first colours were emerging from the green. Purple. Red. Orange. Yellow—

—All right, I'll deal with it. You can go.

Fires in dreamland.

Across the courtyard, in the guest rooms, she found her daughter, Li Na, sitting spread-legged on the bed, playing Patience with dominos. She was in her pyjamas and must have recently painted her toenails, for there were folded tissues slotted into the spaces between her toes, and the smell of lacquer in the air. On the bedside table, a tape recorder was playing a Linguaphone lesson. Li Na's daughter, Jiang Qing's granddaughter, was on a blanket on the floor, surrounded by wooden bricks with which she was too young to do much except suck.

—Get changed, Jiang Qing said.

The tape-recorder bleeped, and Li Na said something in English.

—Did you hear me? Jiang Qing said.

Another bleep, and Li Na again spoke, louder this time.

Jiang Qing searched the machine for the stop button, but the script was in Russian so it was easier just to unplug it.

—Ma? Li Na said then without turning from her game. What are you doing, Ma?

—You shouldn't be listening to such tapes.

—They're from the research library. I have Babba's consent.

—The Chairman's consent.

—I have the Chairman's consent.

—You have no such thing.

Jiang Qing walked round the bed to face her daughter:

—Now up and into your clothes. I need your help.

—Put the tape back on.

—Up, I said.

—I don't get it, I thought you wanted me to be able to speak to Mrs Marcos. Impress her with my fluency.

—The Chairman's *Sayings* are idiomatic and available in English. Everyone else uses those to learn. Are you special or something, that you need another way?

Li Na leaned back onto her hands, bent her knees and planted her feet on the mattress; her nails gleamed but showed no colour; that the varnish was clear did not make the offence any less egregious. Drawing her chin into the pouch that hung down from under her ears, and pursing her lips into a shape expressing defiance, Li Na fixed on Jiang Qing through the pillars of her shins. Her pyjama top, purchased at a different juncture in her life, was now a couple of sizes too small and strained against the bulge of her breasts and belly. From the gaps between the buttons where the two edges of silk did not meet, stretch-marked patches of flesh peeked; though she tried not to, Jiang Qing could not help studying them.

—Ma?

Feelings of pity contracted Jiang Qing's heart. If her daughter was in this state, it was not wholly her daughter's fault. Li Na belonged to the least fortunate generation. Li Na and her peers had not seen with their own eyes the difference between before and after. They had not witnessed the difficult process of transformation; the hard and bitter struggles. They thought China's current greatness had just fallen out of the sky, and therefore they could not understand anything.

—What are you looking at, Ma?

In their ignorance, they spent their time knocking back good food and drink, and did not have a care in the world.

Li Na kicked the dominoes off the mattress and onto the floor:

—Ma!

Jiang Qing flinched:

—Do you think you're better than your mother, is that why you won't do as she says?

—Oh goddess of mercy, hear me.

—I asked you to come to Beijing to help me. You were glad to be asked. You said you needed a break from the countryside. Anything I might give you to do, you said, couldn't possibly be as tedious as farm work. Weren't those your words?

—Not exactly.

—Yet now that you're here, when I ask for your help, you refuse.

—I want to help, Ma—

—Oh you do.

—but if you want me to do something, you're going to have to give me more notice. I can't just drop everything in a flash. You just shout and expect me to be ready.

—An army would be dressed and in formation by now. The truth is you're unwilling to lift a finger. I hope you're not like this with your husband.

—My husband is fine and has plenty of help.

—What would he say if he saw you here with me, hmm? being so stubborn and lazy? a bad example of a daughter?

Laughing, Li Na swiped a sheet of paper from the side table.

—Lazy and stubborn? Let's have a look, shall we, at the evidence? The famous itinerary?

She unfolded the sheet and held up its printed side.

—See those ticks? I've agreed to everything you've assigned to me. You've heard no argument from me about any task you've given me for the coming week. But what's this here? A blank space. Nothing in the box for today. A beautiful bit of white, which I understood to mean time off. I thought you were being kind and giving me a day to recuperate after my long journey.

—That was the intention, daughter of mine, but heaven forbid you might be a bit flexible, or put yourself out. You'll have plenty of time to recuperate once Mrs Marcos is come and gone.

Li Na scrunched the sheet and threw it off the side of the bed:

—Well, thank you, mother, for your generosity.

Jiang Qing put Song Yaojin's dossier down on the bed. Bent over and picked up the itinerary. Smoothed it onto the surface of the table. Took a long breath. Her daughter was pushing her into a corner from which she would then be unable to liberate herself without being vicious.

—You know how important this event is to me. You know what it represents. And how much needs to be done to make it perfect.

—It's all I've been hearing from you for weeks. Late-night phone calls to the farm. Urgent telegrams.

—Shouldn't I call? Counting on my daughter's advice and support, is that wrong of me?

Li Na sighed:

—No, Ma.

Family feelings were not always correct. Sometimes they were a cloak for selfishness and counterrevolutionary urgings. How often over the years had Jiang Qing witnessed otherwise sane and rational people affording protection to perpetrators of heinous anti-Party offences for no other reason than their being a relative of some kind? What utility did these attachments have in revolution, where actions, not blood, proved one's worth? The good revolutionary had to be prepared to draw a line of demarcation between herself and any member of her family found guilty by the people of harming the cause. To this end, she had to learn to cut back on family feelings, and when necessary to get rid of them altogether. No one ever said this was easy. One had to work hard to keep one's system clear.

—Look, daughter, said Jiang Qing with some sadness, I don't mean to bother you. Or to be on top of you. But I don't think you realise what it's like either.

—What what's like?

—The Compound. Living here. There are people around all the time, yes, but even so, it can get—. Well, it can be—

—Lonely?

—I wouldn't use that word.

—What word would you use?

—I don't know. Not that one.

—Whatever, Ma. You don't have to tell me. I remember what it was like.

—Ach, it was different when you were here. We used to have those picnics in the pavilion, do you remember? and your father would recite his poems.

Li Na shrugged.

—It's another world since you left and your father got bad. I spend my days in the company of strangers. The attendants are changed so often, I'm forever having to get used to new faces. I have my friends in the Party, plenty enough. But they have jobs and are busy, and anyway too much socialising can put a strain on more important purposes. I'm not complaining, revolutionary daughter, I don't as a rule. It's just that from time to time it feels like—

Exile. A kind of exile. And the woman in exile is weak.

—What, Ma? What does it feel like?

Jiang Qing sensed suddenly that they had veered into dangerous territory.

—Nothing, she said for the benefit of the bugs which might or might not be hidden in the room. I don't know what I'm saying.

Jiang Qing began to pick up the dominoes that her daughter had kicked off the bed.

—Ma, said Li Na, for fuck's sake. Stop picking things up.

Jiang Qing held out a handful of the tiles to her daughter:

—I just wish you would show me some understanding. This is a busy time, the busiest, and I'm depending on you, my only daughter, my only child, to remember her obligations to her mother.

Li Na took the dominoes from her mother and dropped them into her lap.

—It's just not a good moment, Ma. Travelling with the baby has me worn out, and the dinner last night went on late. Can't you get someone else, just for today? So that I can relax for a little more?

—You've had all morning to relax. Do you know how many in this world aren't in possession of such leisure?

—So I'm to be denied it too, is that it? We're all to be equally denied?

—Your problem is you've been denied too little. You grew up on comfort and have been spoiled by it. You're too little used to giving anything of yourself.

Jiang Qing knew that in the long run Li Na was unsuited to life outside the city and would eventually be beaten by the roughness of it. What Li Na ought to have done was follow Jiang Qing's advice and attach herself to a high Party cadre, an older man who would have helped her to advance — an intelligent woman knew how to do this without becoming subservient. But no, it was contrary to Jiang Qing's guidance that Li Na ran, and a farmer that she took, a man who treated her well but was not much to look at and would never truly satisfy her. To Jiang Qing, the ugly child they had produced was a testimony to their incompatibility.

—I can't be blamed for how I was raised, said Li Na now.

—This again? Jiang Qing said matter-of-factly, with no ire in her voice.

—You're right. Forget I said anything.

—You're accusing me of being a bad parent, is that it? Are you going to give me the stick, now, about my not being around enough? Of neglecting you and, crime of all crimes, sending you away for a good education?

—No. I don't want to talk about any of that.

—Well good. Spare your breath. Because I already see in your eyes that's what you're thinking.

Unbelievably, her daughter did not think her upbringing had been easy. On occasion, during a quarrel, or with her mouth loosened by drink, Li Na would complain that Jiang Qing and the Chairman — but especially her — had not shown her enough warmth. *I never heard any loving words in the home*, she would say. *I was hugged only rarely. Kissed even less. And slapped even less than that,* Jiang Qing would reply, *for your father forbade it.* But this was not good enough for Li Na. She wanted what she could never have: a mother and a father who were just a mother and a father.

—All right, Ma, Li Na said, say I go with you. What about the baby? What would I do with her?

Shaking her head, *Don't even try that one with me,* Jiang Qing pressed the buzzer to call the attendant.

The attendant opened the door and stood, too casually Jiang Qing thought, with a hand resting on the knob. Jiang Qing gestured to the child.

—She needs to go to the creche. Sign her in for two hours. Actually, make it three, to be on the safe side.

The attendant picked the child up underneath the arms, and left the room holding it at arm's length.

Watching this, Li Na tilted her head to one side and scratched her scalp fiercely with a single finger.

Jiang Qing picked up Song Yaojin's dossier and wrapped both arms around it:

—I'll wait for you in the car.

The chauffeur started the engine as soon as Jiang Qing got in.

—You can leave it off, she said to him. We're waiting for my daughter.

He obeyed, and they sat in silence for a few minutes.

—Is it the same with your children? Jiang Qing said then.

—I haven't been blessed with children, he said.

—Oh well, she said in a commiserating tone, it's not everyone's fate.

Li Na got into the car wearing prescription shades and a fake fur collar on her jacket. Attached to a strap slung around her body was a small leather bag.

—Where are we going anyway? she said, heaving herself onto the seat opposite.

Jiang Qing did not answer. She and her daughter were like iron and steel. Unless they tried to compromise with each other, they would just continue to crash heads, and both would feel the pain. The car moved off, and Jiang Qing drew back a corner of the lace window blind, so as not to have to look at her.

They left the Compound by the West Gate, where the Party complaints office was located. From the office doors, long queues of people snaked out the gate and down the road along the Compound wall. Many of those waiting were peasants, who would have travelled a long way to be seen and have their grievances heard. In all likelihood, this was their first trip to the capital, and in all likelihood their last. When the chauffeur sounded the horn in an effort to herd some of them out of the car's path, Li Na sank down in her seat and put a hand over her face, as if anyone could possibly see her in here.

—What are you embarrassed about? Jiang Qing said, unable to hold herself in any longer. Look at you. How you're dressed. Like a rich woman in an American movie. Yet you want us to think you have shame?

—Leave me alone, Ma.

—Do you think these peasants here can afford to have a second suit for the city?

—I don't think these peasants give a shit about what I'm wearing.

Jiang Qing was not without self-regard. She liked the freshness of a skirt in the summer, and in the winter when everyone wore thick clothes, she had hers cut to fit tightly, so as to show off her figure. But these were private vanities. Having given so much, she was entitled to some selfishness, as long as it stayed hidden. Outside, there could be no place for bad practices and bad attitudes. Nothing should be done that would show contempt for the toiling masses or damage the Party's reputation among them. The effort to modernise China required a strict code of conduct; deviations had to be exposed and shamed.

—What do you have there? said Jiang Qing, gesturing at her daughter's bag.

—My things.

—What things? What could you possibly need?

—Just my things.

—Have you got your Treasure Book in there?

—Hmm?

—Your Treasure Book. Your father's *Sayings*.

—Yes, Ma.

—Show me.

—It's in there, don't worry.

—Don't lie to me, daughter.

—Leave me be, Ma. I'm a grown woman.

The fact of this knocked Jiang Qing back: thirty-four years old, Li
Na was now, and still testing the limits of what she was allowed to do;
still learning how to be Chinese. If she was like this, Jiang Qing had to
face that she herself had a part to play in making it so, for she was her
mother, her daughter's first teacher.

—Very well. You're right. We should just sit and enjoy the ride in
peace.

She settled back and opened Song Yaojin's dossier, ran a finger
along the script as if meditating on it — but now, from nowhere, she
threw it to one side, pounced into the seat beside Li Na, grabbed the
bag, opened it, stuck her hand in, rummaged about.

Her daughter yanked on the strap and screamed:

—Get off me, you witch! Let go!

—As I thought, Jiang Qing said. No book.

—You've lost grip of yourself, Ma, you know that?

—You're a little liar.

—I thought it was in there. And if it's not, what's the big problem?
I don't need to bring it everywhere I go.

Breathless, Jiang Qing returned to her seat. Re-pinned her bun.
Tucked any errant hairs back into her cap.

—In the West, she said in between breaths, the youths carry it in
their breast pockets. They're proud to be seen with it.

—Yeah? said Li Na. Well, I carry it here.

She tapped her temple.

—And here.

She placed a hand on her chest.

—Which is the important thing, isn't it? To have it on the inside. Do the Westerners have it there, do you think?

Their first stop was a shoe shop in Dashilar. Jiang Qing's bodyguards, who had been riding in separate cars, one in front and one behind, cleared the alleyway of cyclists and pedestrians before taking up positions on either side of the shop's entrance. Only once this had been done, and a new quiet had settled on the immediate area, did the chauffeur open the car door.

Li Na moved to get out first, but Jiang Qing stopped her:

—Take those glasses off.

—They're just glasses, Ma.

—No one knows who you are.

—Of course they do. Look at these fucking cars.

Jiang Qing shook her head and sighed.

Biting her lip, Li Na conceded:

—All right.

She folded the glasses into a case and put the case into her bag. Her naked eyes were dark and tired. One of them was bordered with red styes. She blinked and squinted:

—Have they been warned we're coming?

—No. This is a private errand.

—There's a shop in the Compound, Ma.

—They wouldn't have what I want. I'm after a gift. Of a quite specific nature. I want you to help me choose it.

Inside, the shopkeeper was standing behind the counter; the wife by the storeroom door. Both were stiff and obviously afraid.

—Good afternoon to you, said Jiang Qing, and a thousand years to the Chairman.

—And a thousand years more, the man said, addressing Jiang Qing's feet.

Two shelves lined the walls on either side. Jiang Qing went up the shop floor on the right side, inspecting the stock, which was entirely made up of standard liberation shoes in black, navy and grey. She paused at the back wall to glance through the small window that gave into the workshop. Neither the man, a pace to her right, nor the woman, a pace to her left, moved or said a word. Jiang Qing did not have the magic word that would put them at ease, so she came away. At the end of the shelf on the other side, she picked up a grey shoe and turned it over in her hands. On the sole had been painted:

LET'S STIR THE COUNTRY

She bent and folded the shoe to see how durable it was.

—I must be mistaken, she said as she did this. Have I come to the right place?

The man, a grey-haired comrade of seventy or more, replied in a strong Beijing accent, which, even after all these years, Jiang Qing had to strain her ear to understand:

—Tell me, revolutionary sister, what exactly were you looking for?

She put the shoe back on the shelf:

—What's the name of your shop?

—The alley is called Dazhalan Jie. We're just the Dazhalan Jie shoe shop.

—Are there others?

—No, sister. This is the only one.

—In that case, I must've been given inaccurate information. I was told you make ballet slippers.

The man sucked air in through the gaps in his teeth, then froze a moment, open-mouthed, his tongue turning over, as he formulated a response.

—Your information is correct, sister. We are in fact the suppliers of slippers to the Central Ballet. But we do not make such things for use by the ordinary comrade. I cannot sell them to just anyone, you understand?

—I understand, revolutionary father. There's no need to fear. I have the permission.

He knew who she was, of course he did. He was pretending not to know because he could see that Jiang Qing was pretending not to be herself, and he understood that this was a test.

—Do you dance, sister? Are you looking for slippers for yourself?

At this insincerity Jiang Qing laughed sincerely.

—You are kind, father. Unfortunately I've advanced beyond the age for anything more strenuous than a brisk walk and a few stretches.

—But you danced at one time?

—You know, I might have. Had I been given the chance. My feet—. Well, I don't need to tell you how it was back then.

The man nodded pensively:

—The old society was indeed a cruel one.

Jiang Qing matched his movements:

—How far we've come, hmm?

—How far.

—And we don't dwell. We keep our eyes fixed on the glory of the now.

—Fixed, fixed.

For thirty years after her marriage to the Chairman, she had been kept in obscurity by the Party; for thirty years, cloistered and disguised by other names, forbidden to assume any public role in government affairs; for thirty whole years chained up in the shadows waiting for her moment, her opportunity to shine. It had not been a healthy time. In truth it had made her sick, and she would never go back to it. She was happier now, being known. It felt better to be recognised. Far from being an aberrant state, it was for her the natural one. She had always expected to get here, so when she did, it simply felt like a coming into herself; she accepted it without amazement or alarm. But, as with every natural thing, fame was divided into two sides, a light and a dark. The dark side, which few talked about, was the alienation. The better she was known, the harder it became for her to know others. People did not act naturally around her. She who had once loved commune life and had enjoyed being in the thick of a crowd was now unable to prevent her very presence from creating a barrier between herself and others; everyone constantly, pitilessly made her remember who she was. No one bothered about the woman of flesh and blood who stood before them, with her humour, her sensitivity, her tenderness — and her weaknesses, too, of which she had as many as anyone else, only she no longer had a right to forgiveness for them. Everyone presumed to know her, and judged her as known, which meant she was not permitted to get to know anyone as herself, a situation which made her long for the plain and the ordinary in human exchange: the simple request, the throwaway comment, the smirk, the wink.

—So this must be the dancer here then, the man said, turning to direct a quivering smile at Li Na, who had taken up a non-participatory position beside the door.

—Ah!—

Jiang Qing did not need to look round in order to call to mind her daughter's wide hips and her gourd-shaped tits.

—Quite the ticket you are. In fact I'm looking for a gift for one of our revolutionary brothers.

—A man's slipper?

—For a friend of mine who also happens to be one of China's finest dancers.

The man showed no sign of surprise at this news.

—Is he in the Central Ballet?

—Recently retired. Though too early, in my opinion.

The man waved a hand at his wife and said:

—Get the ledger!

Then:

—If you give me the dancer's name, I can check his shoe size. I keep a list of sizes for all the Central Ballet dancers.

The wife, falling out of the respectful posture she had held until now, hurried to the counter.

—No need, revolutionary mother, Jiang Qing said to her. I know the man's size. He takes a forty-two.

The wife, who had produced the ledger from a drawer, looked to her husband, unsure of what to do. The man extended an open palm in his wife's direction.

—Sister, he said to Jiang Qing, are you sure you don't want to double check? Sometimes a dancer will go for a tighter shoe because they eventually stretch.

—That won't be necessary, she said. I know he's a forty-two.

A fluttering of his fingers told his wife to put the ledger away.

—You're the boss.

Jiang Qing's husband had found a way. His conversational style, his relaxed and easy-going manner, his method of encouraging people to speak without restraint, and probing their mind without revealing his: he was, in the presence of people, both a god and a human, and this was what made him great. Jiang Qing wished that what he did would rub off on her.

The man shuffled over to a cabinet, opened it with a key and pulled out a long drawer.

—This is the men's range, if you'd care to have a look?

Jiang Qing joined the man at the cabinet. He reeked of wine and smoke and sweat, against which she closed her nose. In the drawer there were displayed two models of slipper: one unadorned, the other with a small bow sown onto the front. Each came in four colours: white, grey, navy and black. The man picked out the navy and black samples of both models and put them to one side.

—These are the colours we have in stock in size forty-two. If you want white or grey, you'll have to wait a day while we make them.

—I see. And of the navy and black, is one of superior quality?

—They are both of superior quality, sister.

—Hmm.

Jiang Qing tapped a tooth.

—I'm not sure. Daughter of mine, come and help me choose.

Her daughter reluctantly approached.

—What do you think? said Jiang Qing. Which do you prefer?

—Ahm, said Li Na, I don't know. I can't see so well without my—. Aren't they more or less the same?

Jiang Qing clucked her tongue.

—How about that one? said Li Na.

She pointed, predictably enough, at the black slipper with the bow.

—That one? said Jiang Qing.

Sighing, she turned to the man:

—We'll take the plain navy one now. And we'll order a white one with the bow to be made.

—Very well. Would you like me to post the white one to you?

—No need. I'll have someone come and pick it up. Tomorrow?

—We'll have it waiting.

The man opened a second cabinet, which was filled with the different sizes of navy slipper and extracted a forty-two. He was about to close the cabinet door again, when Jiang Qing noticed a stack of boxes which had been pushed to the back so that it was half-hidden by the slippers. From the top box, whose lid had not been properly replaced, a bright green ribbon had escaped, and was dangling down, wafting with the current created by the opening and closing of the cabinet door.

—What are they? said Jiang Qing.

—They? said the man, who had shut the door and was already fiddling with the lock and key.

—Those boxes.

—Boxes?

—In the cabinet. Western-style shoe boxes.

—Oh those? They're nothing. A mistaken order. They need to be sent back.

—I was under the impression that you made all of your own shoes.

—We do, most often. But from time to time we get requests, from the theatre troupes and the like, for which we don't have the materials. So we have to order from outside.

—Did you say theatre troupes?

—Did I? I meant—. I don't know what I meant. My mind is no longer quite with me.

—It's the years catching up.

—That'd be it.

—We've seen so much.

—Enough for five generations, sister.

—And many more, father. But, tell me, from where do you order these special shoes?

—Oh I can't remember. I have it written somewhere.

—You've forgotten that also?

—I can check—

—I'd rather just see them directly.

—See what?

—The shoes. I bet I can tell where they're from, just by looking at them.

—You want to see the shoes?

—That's right, I want to see the shoes.

The man re-opened the cabinet with gestures whose slowness and deliberateness made his anxiety all the more palpable. Reaching into the gloom behind the slippers, he removed the box and opened its lid. Presented the contents to Jiang Qing as a boy might the neighbour's chicken he has accidentally killed. Lying on their side, wrapped in thin paper, was a pair of green leather sandals made according to a fashion from Hong Kong, it was likely, with embroidered leaves running across the front, and cut away so that the big toe would be open to the weather.

At first Jiang Qing said nothing, and the room waited. Li Na had gone hot and was touching her face with the back of her hand. The shopkeeper and his wife stood bowed and absolutely still. Until Jiang Qing — cheerfully, unfazed — waved the shoe away.

—Fancy, she said. I, for one, wouldn't get my feet into them.

In silence, unwilling to show even relief, the man knelt to put the box back in the cabinet. Jiang Qing brought the navy slippers to the counter herself. The wife wrapped them in newspaper and, without raising her eyes, pushed them across towards Jiang Qing. Then the wife stepped back, towards the wall, seemingly uninterested in taking payment. Jiang Qing had to count out the coupons once, twice, and then again because the woman was refusing to oversee it.

—Do you want to get paid or not? said Jiang Qing.

The woman did not open her mouth. Kept her gaze on the floor.

—Yes, said the man, coming to stand beside his wife. Thank you.

—That's half, said Jiang Qing, who did not need to hear the price of something to know how much she would pay. I'll send the rest with the messenger tomorrow.

—So we should expect someone?

—In the morning.

He picked up a pen and, with more than a hint of bravado, dipped it into the pot:

—What's the name, for the docket?

—Put down Lan Ping, said Jiang Qing, giving her old Shanghai stage name. That's it. *Lan. Ping.*

Song Yaojin lived in a courtyard house in Dongcheng. On the way there, Li Na was quiet for a time, brooding, but then said:

—Was that it? Was that all you wanted me for?

Jiang Qing laughed:

—Gracious sakes alive, child, loosen up. I'm having a nice time. Practically nothing comes to my ear in Beijing. It's good to be out and to see.

Jiang Qing pinched herself between the eyes, for her laughter had risen up her nose and made her feel light in the head.

—If you feel you're lacking something to do—

She handed Li Na the wrapped slippers.

—you can give these to Comrade Song.

—What? No.

—You see? You're impossible.

—I don't even know him.

—You used to play as children.

—I remember seeing him dance when you took me to the Academy. But we weren't friends. We never played.

—Your memory is defective.

—You're making stuff up.

—Just give him the shoes, daughter. He'll remember you, even if you don't remember him.

Until relatively recently Song Yaojin and his parents had lived in the best house in the courtyard: a three-roomed building behind a wooden fence-gate on the north side, facing south. Three years ago, however, soon after Song Yaojin was sent away for rehabilitation, that house was given to a Party official, and Song Yaojin's parents were moved into a small out-of-business factory situated in the southwest corner. This dwelling had just a single room, a storeroom and a toilet. The kitchen was a gas cooker partitioned off with a board. Song Yaojin's father died soon after the move, so when Song Yaojin was allowed to return to the city, there was space for him here, in the room with his widow-mother, and half a bed to sleep on.

The widow now served them tea, the water for which they watched her take from the toilet cistern.

—Oh, just boiled water for me, revolutionary widow, said Jiang Qing. Tea after noon only gives me a headache.

It was Jiang Qing's first visit since the move, and she was pleasantly surprised. It could have been worse. There was little furnishing — a table for writing, a table for eating, a chest of drawers, a bookcase, a tattered armchair — but in such a confined space any more than this would have created clutter. In the old house, there had been a cupboard on top of which were displayed the gifts that Jiang Qing had sent, like jars of fruit and scented candles, but that was gone now. The only decoration was a portrait of the Chairman, and it was enough. From the bed, however, there came an odour of rotting straw.

—You should have a modern bed, said Jiang Qing. I'll see what I can do.

The widow smiled briefly and went back to looking at her lap.

—And the Party man, your neighbour in the old house, he doesn't mind that we phone?

The widow shook her head.

—He doesn't make a fuss about you walking in to use it?

Again the widow shook her head.

—My son won't be long, she said then, for they were waiting for Song Yaojin to return from a walk.

When he came, he behaved as if their presence confirmed what he had expected to find and was not enough to be considered strange. He walked through the room with a light step, like someone who was in better shape than anyone else, and for whom things were easier. He sat down on the bed, which creaked beneath him, and replaced his outdoor shoes with something for the inside. Coming to the table, he emptied the contents of his pockets onto the tray in front of them: a notebook and pencil, a handkerchief, a couple of coins, a coupon. Jiang Qing thought he looked drunk.

—Commander Jiang, he said.

—Comrade Song, she said.

The widow gave her son her chair and went out to the washing line with a basin of wet clothes. Song Yaojin tossed the tea from the widow's cup and served himself from a bottle of wine. He held the bottle up as an offering to the visitors. They declined by shaking their heads in unison.

—And you, Li Na? he said, slurping. What are you doing here? Are you back in Beijing for good?

Li Na looked surprised that Song Yaojin would know anything about her life.

Jiang Qing pulled a face: *I told you so.*

—I'm just back for a visit, said Li Na, ignoring her mother. I've come to help Ma with this thing.

—Ah yes, said Song Yaojin, this thing.

—She's not sure how long she'll stay, said Jiang Qing. In the countryside, I mean. Our doors are always open for her, if she ever wanted to come back to the city, and I think one day she might.

—Whatever, Ma, murmured Li Na.

—You never know, daughter of mine.

Saying this, Jiang Qing gave Song Yaojin a knowing look. Song

Yaojin, who had double-folded eyelids which made his eyes appear larger, more vulnerable, received this look and returned one in his own style. But then, as if to protect himself against further exchanges of this type, he planted his elbows on the table and raised up his cup with both hands, so as to obstruct the full view of his face. In this pose, his eyes were visible only when he drank; the rest of the time, while he waited to drink, they were hidden.

—And what about you, Comrade Song? Jiang Qing asked him. How are you?

—How am I? he said, pondering the question as though it were deep.

He sloshed some wine around his mouth. Swallowed. Bared his teeth.

—Let me see.

Thanks to the nutritious diet that he had received, first as a young trainee at the Academy, then as a professional dancer at the Central Ballet, Song Yaojin had always been fair-skinned and well developed. The training had made him muscular but seamless; no rough edges. Now, though, after his time amongst the peasants, he was darker, like red earth, and, whereas his stomach had softened and bloated out, his limbs had thinned and hardened. His once unlined face had cracked in places. His button nose had lost its shine. And still; still he was beautiful.

—Let me ask you, Commander Jiang, do you remember—?

Song Yaojin faltered.

—Comrade? said Jiang Qing.

—I'm sorry. It's perhaps egotistical of me to bring it up.

—Go ahead. We are all red here. And close.

Song Yaojin sipped from his cup, and their eyes met: several tones of black vibrating.

—Do you remember—

His eyes disappeared once more.

—when I danced for the first time the role of the ARMY CAPTAIN in *The Red Detachment of Women*?

Jiang Qing nodded and smiled:

—I'll never forget it.

—Did you happen to be there, Li Na? Song Yaojin asked.

—I don't think so, said Li Na.

—It was in the auditorium of the Great Hall of the People. You've been there, I take it? Well, picture, if you can, the whole of the Beijing Party in the Great Hall, filling every seat, thousands and thousands of people.

—Wow, said Li Na.

—Yeah, wow, said Song Yaojin. I'd never performed in front of so many, but as a trainee I had often dared to wonder what it must feel like to receive the applause of such a large crowd.

—It must be quite a feeling, said Li Na.

—You'd think so, wouldn't you? said Song Yaojin.

—Well, isn't it? said Jiang Qing, suddenly piqued.

Without feeling that she was doing so, she clenched her jaw. She did not like how this conversation was taking shape. She was not in control of it, did not know its orientation, and wondered, jadedly, if she was being asked to read between the lines to find it out.

—During the performance, Song Yaojin said, I remember I danced like a madman and felt many things. But at the end, during the applause—

He put the cup down, revealing eyes that had given up their defence.

—during the applause, I felt nothing. No, not nothing. I felt something, but it was an empty something. Like I'd poured all my emotions into a bucket and then poured them back over myself, so that all I was left with was the feeling of cold on my skin and a desperate need for a blanket to cover myself with.

Jiang Qing tapped her fingernails on the table, once to express her irritation; a second time, her social advantage.

—Comrade Song, you are being unfair to your experience, surely. You must have felt—

—No.

Caught mid-swig, Song Yaojin had to swallow quickly in order to get the word out.

—That was all I felt. Nothing more than what I've described. I do remember having a thought, though. A very specific thought. When we'd had our bows, and I came off stage, something occurred to me, a question, and do you know what it was?

Li Na shook her head.

Feeling restricted, Jiang Qing eased the collar of her suit.

—I remember it like it was yesterday, Song Yaojin said. I stepped out of the lights and into the wings, and the thing I asked myself, before anything else, was: *What's it going to be like when I can't do this any more?* Not: *When can I do that again?* But: *When is this going to end? What am I going to do with myself when I have to stop doing this?*

Without asking, as an insistence, he threw out the contents of the visitors' cups and filled them with wine.

—And, do you know, just like that, a voice in my head answered immediately—

He clicked his fingers.

—almost as soon as I'd asked the question.

—And what did it say? said Li Na.

Jiang Qing shot her a glare.

—It said, said Song Yaojin, *If I can't dance, it'd be better to be dead.*

Song Yaojin had never been a difficult person to control. That he seemed to be beyond her influence now frightened Jiang Qing, and she burst out:

—But of course! Yours is a vocation. A life's work. All dancers who are truly dancers feel this way. They're incapable of imagining a life in which they aren't dancing. And I'm here to tell you, Comrade, that you don't have to imagine any such thing. You don't have to stop.

Song Yaojin lifted the bottle to the ineffectual evening light coming through the window. He swirled the remaining liquid around before tipping it into his cup.

—But don't you see, Commander? I want to stop.

Gripping the bottle by its neck and pointing it straight down, he shook out the last drops. When no more came, he put the bottle onto its side on the table and spun it around. Stopped it by slapping a hand on it.

—It's over and I'm glad that it is.

—No, said Jiang Qing, for she could now see the dark place he had receded to, you can't say that. I won't hear it from you.

—I'm sorry, Commander. But it's the truth. You are China's great patron. Supervisor of all the arts. Therefore you know that ballet is a very specific design of movement and physicality. One can master it for a certain amount of time, to a certain degree, but then at a certain point, usually at an age much younger than mine, it becomes too hard. You, Commander Jiang, have watched me work for twenty-five years, and in that time I demonstrated my mastery through concrete achievements, each of which brought me honour and pride, but with every year that passed the costs increased and the results diminished, this can't have passed your notice. Now I've reached the stage where I know that if I continue, not only will I be doing a disservice to my art, my body will end by devouring itself.

Jiang Qing knocked a knuckle on the wood:

—Stop. Don't go on. You're sounding like a pessimistic old man.

—But look at me, Commander. You see that's what I am.

—I can see what I've always seen. A man too powerful for the room. For any room! You've always had a terrifying strength. So much so that the troupe used to be afraid of you, don't you remember that? Maybe you're a little out of shape these days, yes. But not to the extent that justifies retirement.

—You don't understand, Commander. Inside, in here—

Song Yaojin beat on his chest.

—I don't have anything left. I'm finished.

—On the contrary, I understand perfectly. You're simply using a false idea of age to hold yourself back. You're refusing to respond to your powers, which are real and visible for all to see. For an artist of your experience, the wise thing is not to give up but to use what you have well.

Jiang Qing jabbed her daughter in the ribs as a signal to give Song Yaojin his gift.

—I've never been one to waste time on the impossible, Comrade. If I thought you weren't equal to my demands, I wouldn't have come here. And I wouldn't have brought you this.

Song Yaojin appeared humbled by the offering but not surprised. He accepted it gracefully, with two hands and head bowed, as someone accustomed to receiving. He opened the wrapping on his lap. Stared down at the slippers, unmoved.

—What I'm proposing is a new beginning for you, Jiang Qing said, examining him for a weakening, a change. I'm giving you a chance to resume your career. Prolong it. See it through to its natural end, if indeed it has an end, for you are the virile kind, born to be the man who proves that he deserves his talent.

Song Yaojin looked up from his lap. He did not have to shed any tears for Jiang Qing to know that he was crying. Pain, unlike pleasure, wore no mask. Behind joy and laughter there could lurk another temperament, one that was coarse and callous, but behind sorrow there could only be sorrow. Song Yaojin got up and put the slippers on the end of the bed. There he stayed, with his back turned, and for that moment his shadow was more in the room than he was.

—I thank you, Commander, he said, turning his head first, then his body, I thank you for this kind gift, and for your offer. Truly, I feel blessed to have been noticed by you and to have had your protection all these years.

With a single unsteady step, he shortened the distance between them. Jiang Qing would have preferred him to sit down directly, for she did not want to see a lifetime of hard training so casually undermined.

—You gave me my weapon, which was my art. You moulded and remoulded me so that I could be, not only a dancer, but a revolutionary, a soldier in the Chairman's great crusade. Thanks to you, I've had a place in the Party and a purpose in the revolution. It has been a charmed life, no doubt about it, and I can never repay you for having allowed me to live it.

From a shelf whose contents were concealed by a little curtain, he took a second bottle. Uncorked it. Then sat, heavily, like a worker exhausted.

—But, Commander, as I wrote in my letter, and what I'm trying to tell you now is, I've changed. Completely. I don't believe—. No, believe is the wrong word. I don't live for dance any more. I no longer want to do it. I can't. The thought of not dancing doesn't terrify me as it once did. Stopping doesn't signify death any more. If you ask me today what I want to do, it's to go on living as I do now, with my good mother, in peace, forgetting that I've ever lived differently. For twenty-five years I gave to the revolution, and I can continue to give to it, as is my duty, but only by not taking away from it. The best I can do is look after what you see here, in this house, and know that that is—

The door creaked open.

—enough, Song Yaojin trailed off.

The widow returned from the courtyard to a place changed. The curtain on the shelf open. A pair of slippers on the bed. Wine in two cups untouched. She saw all of this, though she barely lifted her eyes as she deposited the basin in the space beside the toilet and went to sit with her woolwork in the armchair. Watching her, Jiang Qing was reminded of how much responsibility a child felt when he carried his entire family's dreams on his shoulders; what a heavy burden he carried once he realised that he had to succeed. Song Yaojin had joined the Academy at ten years old. Already then he was behaving like a miniature adult, having been made to understand at an even earlier age that his role in life was to fulfil his family's expectations; that he would be loved not for himself but only for what he produced. If he was anything like Jiang Qing — and she was sure that he was — he would have lost touch with his own feelings at around four or five. After that, he existed in himself and for himself only insofar as he existed in and for others; that is, he existed only by being recognised and acknowledged.

—Revolutionary widow, Jiang Qing said now, addressing the other side of the room, can you hear me? Yes? Do you love your son? Do you truly love him?

The widow narrowed her eyes as if to say, *What kind of question is that?*

—Then on no account, Jiang Qing went on, must you let your son isolate himself here. If he does, what will happen to him when you pass away, do you reckon? Will he marry? Do you believe there is still a chance of that? Will someone have him at this stage?

The widow shifted her eyes to her son, then back to Jiang Qing.

—I look at your son, old widow, and I see a man still with the strength of nine cows. He should be on the stage. That's where he belongs. In front of the people. Where he can be of use to them. Not stuck in here. A stone in a box.

The widow cleared her throat loudly.

—Well? said Jiang Qing. What do you say? Have you lost your tongue, woman?

Song Yaojin intervened by thrusting his right hand into the expanse between the two.

—Did you see this? he said, uncurling his index finger, the top of which was missing.

The widow, who in order to listen had laid her needles down on top of the skein of coloured wool, resumed her work.

Jiang Qing looked at Song Yaojin's deformity and nodded:

—When you came in, I saw it, yes. It's a pity.

—And this.

He turned over his hand to show the marks of labour on the palm.

—Uh-huh, said Jiang Qing. What of it?

—And my feet, he said. My feet, if you saw them, would shock you, they are so bad.

—A bit of chapping will hardly keep you from dancing.

—Plus—

He pointed a thumb over his shoulder.

—two herniated discs. From pushing carts. In all my years of dancing, I was blessed, I had no serious injuries. But now to cross from one side of this room to another is agony. The pain I feel just walking—

—You're in pain now?

—When I move I am.

—It doesn't seem that way. Your movements look fluid to me.

Song Yaojin sighed.

—Look, I'm grateful for your offer, Commander, but I simply cannot take on such a demanding role. It would be the end of me.

Jiang Qing would never have dared to have an affair. She had had opportunities, and had come close, but at the critical moment had always stepped back, for to have pushed on would have provided the Chairman with cause to get rid of her. As a substitute, she allowed herself to be amused by men, to admire them, to help them. The men she chose, they understood that her attentions were chaste and posed no risk to their moral standards or political reputations; they understood that, quite the reverse, to be under Jiang Qing's care was to occupy a position of almost unrivalled privilege, a position moreover that was relatively easy to maintain; all that was asked of them was to show some humbleness from time to time, and a little gratitude. Not rocket science. Unfortunately, for some of the men, even this was too much to manage. Their being male did not render them immune to the green-eyed illness, jealousy, or to feelings of supremacy. In such states of stress, they fought with one another for her regard; on occasion they lashed out and caused real harm. Song Yaojin, because he was both famous and young, and both young and handsome, was the object of some of the more savage attacks. The worst of these: a rumour, put out three years ago, when Song Yaojin was at the height of his celebrity, which said that he had been engaging in perverted sexual activities in Temple of Heaven Park. Jiang Qing had a policy of ignoring malicious talk amongst the men in her protection, but she could not let such a serious allegation go uninvestigated. When her team confronted Song Yaojin, he defended himself as vehemently as she would have expected, but in doing so regrettably used a method that aggravated the situation: in the course of his denials, he claimed to have had open relationships with a number of women, many of whom were married, and all of whom he named. It was a scandal.

One which Jiang Qing could not contain. It was out of her hands. He had had to go.

—Comrade Song, Jiang Qing said now, you've done your years of labour, yet I can see that in your heart you're still a little master. You need someone to fawn on you and tell you you're the best. All right, so you can't dance the main part. So what? You don't have to be the ARMY CAPTAIN. You could dance another, less taxing role. The LANDLORD, for instance. THE TYRANT And if that didn't work, there's nothing to say we couldn't write a new scene, or a new character for you. I'm open to all kinds of solutions. My one worry is that, despite your expressions of gratitude, you've lost the ability to show respect to me, as a woman, and as your leader. I'm not convinced that you haven't forgotten that it was me who made it possible for you to follow your calling. That I paved the way for you to do what you must do.

—Please believe me, Commander, I haven't forgotten.

—Then you won't have forgotten either, Comrade, that I'm not in the business of rehabilitation. As a rule, I don't give people second chances. Yet here I am, out of the goodness of my heart, giving you a second chance. And what a second chance it is, wouldn't you agree, old widow, hmm? performing for the First Lady of the Philippines? It would be glorious. Nothing less than the final act of your son's reintegration. By stepping onto that stage, he'd be clean again, a revolutionary once more, don't you want that for him?

When perverts were discovered in the ranks, the convention was to send them to a pig farm to scrub their filthy minds. On their return, most cleaned toilets for the rest of their lives. But Jiang Qing — the generous, the innocent — had given Song Yaojin a choice: either he could go to the pig farm, and hazard never returning to the stage again; or he could send his mother and father away in his place, to a camp in the Great Northern Wilderness, and he could continue to dance without interruption. Jiang Qing presented this to Song Yaojin as a choice, but of course she was aware that it was no such thing. Boys like Song Yaojin, the good ones, the chosen ones, could never accept that class struggle ought also to be waged in the home. Opposing the family meant separating family feelings from revolutionary ones, and such a task, simple to most communists, was beyond them.

—Do you think it's a small hurt for a mother, to see her son in decline?

The widow was speaking now, in the form of questions, but in a tone that made them unanswerable, the final word.

—Every life ought to contain a turn and return, I'll give you that, but can we call it glorious to put a broken man on the stage, for the world to leer at?

She shook her head and tutted.

—No, no. From such a thing, nothing furthers.

Dark had fallen, and with it an uneasy muteness, by the time they got back to the Compound. In Jiang Qing's Separate Apartment the lamps had been lit and the radiators turned on. Coming into the study — alone because her daughter had immediately scuttled off to her room — Jiang Qing cast about for a target. With the back of her hand, at full swing, she knocked the chrysanthemum off the desk. Which felt good in the doing, but once done was a let-down. The vase had not shattered. Only some water had chugged out onto the rug, and a few petals had scattered about. Unsatisfying. There was more in her that would have to come out. But as she watched her attendant clean up the spill, and as she imagined the violence that could in that instant so straightforwardly be inflicted upon her, she thought: no. That was what the attendant, what *everyone* expected of her. They had become so used to her rage that it had become for them just more of the same air. Some of them had even grown to enjoy it, it seemed: the act of turning their cheek, an excuse to feel superior. And if there was something that Jiang Qing knew about herself, it was that she was superior to anyone who felt that way.

From the phone on the desk, she made two calls. The first was to the leader of her most trusted band of Red Guards, to whom she provided the address of the shoe shop in Dashilar and descriptions of its owner and his wife. Her order, which she said ought to be carried out without delay, was that these two be arrested, and a public tribunal staged at which they would be struggled against and purified.

—How hard should we go? the Red Guard asked.

—Hard, she said.

Her second call was to Chao Ying, her director at the Central Ballet.

—Call everybody, she said to him. All of the dancers and the entire crew. I want everyone in the Great Hall for rehearsals tomorrow.

—

—Hello? Director Chao? Did you hear me?

A pause and then:

—With respect, Commander, didn't we agree that there was no need for rehearsals? The troupe has been dancing *The Red Detachment of Woman* for years. It's the model. They know it back to front. Wouldn't more rehearsals be a waste of time? All we'd be doing is gilding the lily.

—This is not a discussion, Director Chao. I'm informing you of a decision I've made.

—But Commander, I must ask you to reconsider. Most of the dancers are, as you know, just back from touring and need some rest. There is a danger that more practice now would lead to confusion, or, more grave, boredom and lethargy. In my professional view, it would be counterproductive.

—The gala performance is Saturday week. That gives us nine days.

—Nine whole days! But, but why?

It was times when things were constantly changing, that the people liked to know about. When it came to periods of calm, they were bored and looked away. It was not that they liked chaos; rather, that a reign of peace could last long was unendurable to them.

—I've come to the conclusion, she said, that the model is old and needs changing.

EVA

1968

<u>iii.</u>

The hitch thing was out. They paid their own fares now like every-body else. With an advance from the Wherehouse budget they rented a white van and bought a ticket for the ferry — to Ostend, it turned out, because the ports in France were closed. During the crossing, on the upper deck, surrounded by some British but by many more French returning, they performed a short piece from their repertoire.

Entitled *Agent Orange*, it was what they termed ghost theatre, a performance which involved the public as participants in the action without their knowing it. To begin they sat separately on the benches, or mingled in the crowd, minding their own business and pretending not to know each other. Then gradually, one by one, they became aware of liquid raining on their heads, then of the smell of chemicals in the air, then of symptoms of an illness. They began to clutch their stomachs and groan, to gasp for breath, to shudder, to splutter, to blubber incoherent phrases, to double over, to wretch, to stagger about, until, as if overcome by panic, they dropped to the ground and writhed at the other passengers' feet. During rehearsals for the piece, they had practised responses to every imaginable intervention from the public. They were ready to incorporate any kind of interruption, including acts of violence, though in previous performances these had occurred only rarely. Ideally spectators would mimic the group by joining them on the ground and thrashing about and screaming, in so doing lending substance to the work's principal idea, which was that no one was immune to the horrors of Vietnam. But in this instance on the ferry, the spectators took them for clowns; instead of joining in they backed away, and from a safe distance by the railings laughed or clapped or shouted insults. Which for the group did not signify failure exactly. But neither could they claim a great success.

From Ostend they drove to Brussels and stayed overnight at the Free University, where there was an occupation in progress. Half of the group slept in the van, the other half on the floor of dormitory rooms which the students had opened up to visitors. In the morning they performed a second piece in the quad. Some members had been fearful that the carnival atmosphere on the campus made performing impossible. They felt that, with so many bodies milling about, drinking and singing and chanting and cheering, any attempt to mount a scene or to communicate a message that was not a slogan would fail. But Eva disagreed.

—What on earth are we afraid of? she said, for she was a founder of the group and one of its more outspoken members. A bit of disorder? We need to trust each other, and the people here, the situation. Trust is revolutionary change.

After some discussion they decided on *Sayings* because it was a piece in which they did not play characters but were themselves, real people going through a real experience. *An exercise in authenticity* is what they called it, which in the circumstances seemed suitable. Wearing their everyday clothes, they split up and spread themselves around the quad. Individually and according to their own impulses, they approached people — students, professors, members of the public, it did not matter — and told them a single fact about their own experience of living under the controlling powers of state and money.

—I can't live without a salary, they said.

Or:

—I'm not allowed to take my clothes off in public.

Or:

—I'm barred from travelling without a passport.

Or:

—I can't do anything for the Third World.

Or whatever came up when they abandoned the need to explain and dispensed with the category of right or wrong and instead just spoke the truth about their incarceration in the system.

Eva, because she had good French, and because she was a woman in a predominantly male crowd, found that she had an advantage. She could get a man's attention merely by stepping into his path and was able to hold that attention using an unforced look of concern until, with a single phrase well spoken, she convinced him not only of her presence but of her existence. In this way, she initiated a number of worthwhile encounters. The most rewarding of these was with an older man whom she approached outside the library, and whose shoulders she felt bold enough to grasp, and to whom she said:

—I don't know how to stop the war.

The man, possibly a lecturer, responded by twitching his moustache as if in deep thought and, after a significant pause, saying:

—I know that I should know, mademoiselle, but I don't either. I'm sorry.

Looking into his eyes, young into old, she felt the flash that came when one communed deeply with another person; hearing his words, it was confirmed for her that there were no longer strangers when one spoke simply and truthfully. Communication had power so long as one did what one was not expected to.

Not everyone in the group had such promising experiences. At one point, Eva saw her boyfriend, Álvaro, accost a young student by shouting into his face in English:

—Don't you get it, Comrade, don't you get it?

Eva watched as the student violently jostled Álvaro and told him to fuck off, and then as Álvaro stormed away back to the van.

When the group regathered there later, a number of the members were, like Álvaro, in a state of dejection. One after the other, they judged themselves unqualified to perform in such overheated conditions. The occupation, they said, was greater than any individual and beyond the control of any group; anything they did was bound to be swallowed up by it.

Listening to them, Eva understood that they were unhappy because they wanted recognition instantly.

—Have patience, she said to them. Our journey has only begun. We're feeling our way in. Integration won't come just like that. We're going to have to work hard for it. We'll find a way to make a contribution, you'll see. In Paris there'll be plenty of opportunities.

That night, after a majority vote in favour of continuing their journey, they travelled to Paris as a caravan: cars and motorbikes and vans and coaches, all crammed with students and their rucksacks and their rolled-up sleeping bags, everyone so young, so far from grown up that Eva marvelled at the occasion and the seriousness with which it was being enjoyed. Radios blared, horns blasted, drivers swigged from bottles of wine, passengers thrust their limbs out of windows, and several times they almost got killed on the road, driving through the mist in their vision. Nearing the Paris ring road, the Wherehouse group separated from the procession and left the van in a quiet street in Bagnolet, for they had heard that vehicles were being destroyed in the city itself. From there they walked through the Twentieth, into the Eleventh, past the Bastille, across the Pont de Sully, arriving at the Latin Quarter as the birds were beginning to sing and the sky to lighten.

On boulevard Saint-Germain it looked like the morning after a giant storm. Rows of windows had been smashed. Shops boarded up. Trees felled. Cars overturned. Swathes of street converted to mud where the paving stones had been torn up. The smell was burnt rubber. The sting in the eyes was sleeplessness; tonight it would be tear gas.

Álvaro had the map, so the group followed behind him in loose formation. Mimicking Álvaro, who himself seemed to be mimicking the spy heroes of Hollywood, or the guerrillas in the Vietnamese jungle, they moved quickly and kept close to the houses. When they heard a loud noise, such as a siren or a bang, they ducked into the doorways and crouched down. The intention was to obscure themselves and avoid danger, though it was uncertain what the danger was. As disorderly, as desolate as the scene appeared, it was not a war zone. There were no snipers on the balconies, nor mines buried in the ground underfoot, nor even a single *flic* to be seen. Instead there were bands of students lounging on the barricades, sharing pastries and coffee from flasks. Laughing couples sauntering past hand in hand. Old women walking their dogs. All the same, the group did not feel safe. They were foreigners. Not yet adjusted to events, they were vacillating now to confidence and now to fear.

—There's nothing to be afraid of, Eva would repeat from time to time.

The ultimate reassurance and the ultimate terror.

At Odéon metro station they turned off Saint-Germain and made their way through the Left Bank streets to the square of St-Sulpice Church. There, they took off their shoes and bathed their tired feet in the stagnant water of the fountain while they waited for Max. Their appointment with him was for ten o'clock. At twelve a man called Alain came. With brisk formality, he embraced each member of the group, repeating his name in turn so that everyone would know it.

—Max sent me to get you. He couldn't make it himself. He's wrapped up in something else.

—Where is he? said Eva.

—I couldn't tell you. By now, anywhere.

—Did he say where we should meet him?

Alain ignored her.

—Hop hop hop, he said, and set off in a hurry.

He took them to an attic room in a house a few streets away. The room — three paces wide and four long, without a toilet or a sink — was to accommodate the entire group.

—It's actually my storage room, Alain said. As a favour to Max, I've cleared it out so you can use it. Those are my boxes in the corridor, please don't touch them. I live downstairs, 5A on the third floor? Normally you'd be welcome to stay there, but I already have too many guests. I can't take in any more.

He suggested that they lay their sleeping bags out on the floor and take turns to sleep. When they needed to shit, they should use the cafés.

—Forget about washing, he said. This is no time to care about that.

Switching rapidly between French and English, he gave a brief history of the uprising, why it started, and how and when, and who were the people and the parties putting their mark on it. On Álvaro's map he drew red crosses on the centres of activity: Sorbonne University, the School of Fine Arts, the Odéon theatre.

—Is that where we'd find Max? Eva asked. At the Odéon?

—That's the last place I saw him, Alain said.

—So he isn't staying with you?

—Not this time. Max has so many friends. He could be staying with any number of people.

—How about Doris Lever, do you know her? The body artist?

—Of course.

Alain sneered.

—Everyone knows Doris. She's not staying with me either, unfortunately. I wish she was. Imagine having Doris Lever as a guest. That would be an experience.

—Do you know where we'd find her?

—Are you trying to get a meeting with Doris Lever?

—Well, she's one of our contacts.

Alain looked impressed first, suspicious second.

—Really? he said.

—Really.

Alain frowned, disbelieving.

—Well, if you do find her, good luck getting past her entourage.

—Has she been around?

—I saw her and Max together. I think they know each other from London? Maybe he could introduce you to her.

—I don't need an introduction to Doris Lever, Alain.

Eva spoke firmly, as a demand to be taken seriously, but also out of fatigue; she was worn out from years of being told how big, how talented, how *wild* Doris Lever was by people who had seen her work maybe once and did not know anything more than that about her. Eva — *yes, me, here, is anyone listening?* — had known Doris before she was DORIS, back when she was still a nobody. Her father's assistant at The East Wind theatre in King's Cross. The secretary. The dogsbody. The bit on the side. What distinguished Eva from other people was her unwillingness to broadcast this around or feel triumphant about it.

—Where did you last see her? she said.

—At the Odéon as well, said Alain. But, listen, that was yesterday. You never know where she might be today. People don't stay put for long. They hear something is happening elsewhere, and they go. Everything is changeful.

And nothing stopped. Throughout the days and the nights, it was going on. At any moment one could join in, and at any of the different cells. It would need a god outside time to see the plan of it, but somehow everyone knew to come together at six every evening at place Denfert-Rochereau.

—The demonstrations themselves begin at half past six, Alain said, but it's best to get there a bit early. I try to be there for six, and I recommend doing the same. You won't want to miss them. They're the main event.

He ran a hand through his respectable haircut.

—I guess I'll see you around, he said, and left.

*

Over bread and processed cheese and Pepsi and Marlboros brought up from a nearby supermarket, the group debated what to do next. Some suggested setting off straight away for the Odéon, to see what was happening there. Others objected to this idea. The Wherehouse collective was against the traditional theatre building. They deemed obsolete any efforts to bring people to the theatre. It was their conviction that the theatre today needed to go to the people. The street, because it belonged to everybody, was where performance belonged.

Another idea was to rest for a few hours and then join the rally that evening. But there was a problem with that too. In London, Wherehouse did not take part in rallies. They had not attended the big anti-war demonstration in March because such manifestations were for people who were already convinced. Useful as a show of force, perhaps, but incapable of changing people's minds. Wherehouse, on the other hand, reached very few people, but those they did reach, they changed. The group were not naive enough to believe that they alone would stop the war, but they had complete faith in their ability to destroy the values that caused the war and eventually destroy the culture that had created those values. Just as Mao, Eva reminded them, had done in China with his small guerrilla army.

As they conversed, the journey told in the group's voices. They were tired but trying not to show it. They presented optimism when in fact they were lost and unsure of themselves.

Wanting air, Eva detached from the circle and went to the window. Opened it. Leaned out. Maybe it was the lack of sleep, maybe the strangeness of being abroad, but the people walking in the street below appeared insubstantial, like shadows; the houses without depth. By contrast, the pile of uncollected rubbish by the side of the road looked solid, dense. Cats prowled around the bags which were overfilled and bursting. The breeze whipped at the bits of torn plastic, making them flutter. On a wall opposite, a Communist Party poster had been pasted beside some text about student power and a torn sheet calling for resistance against police oppression. Che was there, as were Mao and Ho Chi Minh, the tops of their heads stripped away to reveal segments of older film advertisements. Across their chests someone had sprayed:

LSD NOW

The scene reminded her some of home. The Wherehouse commune. The only difference being that everything had been turned inside out; the interior exploded outwards. That was what made it strange.

She leaned on the windowsill and sighed. As great as it all looked, she felt unable to connect. In front of her was actual, living revolution, yet in her mind she was replaying the conversation she had just had with Alain, seeing again how mention of Doris's name had made his eyes widen and his top lip shiver, and feeling the accompanying force of bitterness in her chest.

Doris Lever.

The Body Artist from Bethnal Green.

Or the Cockney Whore, as Uncle Simon called her, and as Eva sometimes called her too. *Doris Lever, the Cockney fucking Whore*, who had been just out of school, in her first year of secretarial college, when she met Eva's father. Not especially pretty, possessing no perceptible talent — what had her father seen in her that had impelled him to pick her?

Behind Eva, a discussion about whether performing ghost theatre on the barricades would work was descending into a vicious quarrel in which, in the same careful way, the opposing parties were not allowing an honest debate to begin because their real opinions had to be kept in reserve. The idea that they — her extended family, closer than blood — should sham in her presence, even in the slightest degree, was enough to make Eva despise them.

—Stop!

She swung round:

—Just fucking stop, okay?

With two powerful paces she put herself into the centre of the circle. Kicked away the empty cans and used wrappers to make space.

—Everyone get up.

The group mumbled and moaned.

—On your feet. All of you.

Slowly, sighing, they obeyed.

—We're going to scream this out, she said.

—Scream what out? someone said.

—The fear. The falsity. All of this bad feeling.

Clapping her hands as a signal to commence, she gyrated her hips, then swung her arms around, then inclined to the edge of her balance and back.

—You know what to do, come on.

—Is this really necessary, Eva? We're tired.

—This will revitalise you.

She executed the same actions in reverse, and added to them, and exaggerated them, and cut them short, and sped them up, and slowed them down, all the while trying to maintain gestural precision. The others tried to follow her lead. Once this became impossible, the choreography too frenzied, they made up their own moves and went with those.

—Come to grips with yourself, Eva said. Use the space.

With so many bodies in such a small room, they bumped and slapped against one another, which made everyone laugh. Eva took possession of their laughter and brought it low into her chest, transforming it into a yogic intonation. For a long minute they danced and intoned, their voice an extension of their movement: *oo, oh, aw, om, ah, u, er, oo*, a stream of vowels, and then consonants like sticks thrown into its flow, *ba, to, maw, cah, fu, soo*. As soon as the chanting started to feel too solemn, Eva brought the group's voice back up to a yell, then high, high to a howl. In capitalist society no one knew how to scream any more, to cry out. Having been told all their lives to keep their voices down, people had lost full use of their throats. If only they could see, as the Wherehouse collective did, that under the impulse to speak lay the deeper longing to exteriorise the inner scream: the only true truth.

Out of breath, throats raw, but feeling elated, the group collapsed back onto the floor. On her command — *Now show some love!* — they rolled about and hugged and kissed and begged each other's forgiveness.

Of its own accord, the circle reformed. The group joined hands. Eye met eye, and again there were smiles. Before, their appearances had been united but their spirits apart; now the inner and the outer were realigned. Restored was the hope that authentic meetings between human beings could still occur — a hope without which Wherehouse could not exist.

Eva suggested splitting up and spreading out, in order to gather as much information from as many different sites as possible. Then they would regroup, share whatever they had learned, and see what further action they would take on that basis.

—We're the Wherehouse performance collective. We seek the directly lived moment. We should feel at home wherever rebellion is living and being lived. So why don't we just go and enjoy the spectacle. Soak it up. Then we'll see what to do next.

There was resistance to the idea of breaking up the group, but in the end practicalities decided the matter: there were two keys to the room, so the group was divided in half. Eva, Álvaro and two others would go out now; the rest would get some sleep and join the action later. If the sub-groups did not see each other at the demonstration that evening, they would meet back at the room in the morning to discuss what they had seen and done. These discussions would form the basis of their work for the following day.

Eva's sub-group voted three-to-one to start at the Odéon. They took an indirect route there, along Saint-Germain, down Saint-Michel, then circling back, in order to collect some more impressions. Things were still quiet, with most of the activity focussed on rebuilding the barricades in preparation for the demonstrations. One arresting scene they witnessed was that of a motley gang of students and local residents carrying material from an adjacent building site — blocks of stone, planks, wheelbarrows, metal drums, steel girders — to reinforce a particularly large barricade at the crossing of the two boulevards. Álvaro took photographs of an older man who had come down in his dressing gown to help. Eva told him to stop. The worst thing was to be a revolutionary tourist.

In contrast to the calm of the streets, the Odéon was swarming. It could be heard from several blocks away: a thousand dreams of youth merging in the theatre square, and another thousand inside, bees in a hive, climbing one over the other, desperate to be in the middle; a deafening.

In the theatre, despite the glass chandeliers and the lines of white columns, which were cold and inhospitable, the occupying force created an atmosphere of domesticity. Over portable gas burners, people cooked. In the alcoves and on the couches, people slept. Upstairs in the offices, people worked. Backstage, along the corridors and in the dressing rooms, people fucked.

—What do you think? Álvaro whispered to Eva.

—I'm not sure yet, she said.

The crowd had its contingent of workers. In the foyer, a group of Renault employees could be identified by a banner calling for solidarity with their strike. And in the restaurant some cleaning ladies had used their mops and buckets to build a makeshift stall, where they were collecting signatures for a petition. The large majority of the occupiers, however, came from the professional classes. Most were students; most of those, by all appearances, snobs. Next, a few artists. Directors. Writers. Then the parasites: the fellow travellers, the voyeurs, the hippies, the exemplars of radical chic. Judging from accents and looks, there were lots of foreigners. Americans. Italians. Germans. Dutch. Very few British. Neither Max nor Doris were anywhere to be seen.

—Should we stay? Álvaro asked the others.

—We're here now. We might as well.

—Let's give it a few minutes.

They took a place upstairs in the dress circle, on the steps because there were no free seats.

—Oh, I see. They're making speeches.

—Is that all that's going to happen?

—God, I hope not.

The auditorium was functioning as a sort of general assembly. On the stage, behind a long table, sat a panel of young men. Each sported a variation of the same pullover. Each kept his hair untidy in the typical fashion. Cigarette in hand or on lip, eyes bulging with fatigue, face set in a perpetual scowl, scribbling on bits of paper and calling people up and sending people off — each was certain of his own indisputable usefulness. Every so often, young women would enter from the wings to deliver to the table a message in the form of a written note or a whispered word, which would be passed down the line, and then a response passed back up. How one won a place at the table, and what one was supposed to be doing while seated at it was not clear. Unless, that is, one occupied the middle place, in which case one had obviously succeeded, by whatever means, in becoming the chairman.

—All right, settle down. Thank you, Comrade. An insightful contribution, which we are grateful for. All voices welcome. Next up is—

Anyone, it seemed, could put their name on the list to speak at the microphone. Word was that a spokesman for the Occident movement had been allowed a slot that morning. Something Eva would have liked to see. Give her a fascist any day, over the creep in the Russian Army jacket that currently had the floor. *Fuck Russia. China is the only future.*

—I'm not sure I can bear much of this, Eva said.

—Me neither, Álvaro said.

—Shh, guys, said one of the other members. Give it a chance.

Posted on a board outside the auditorium were the topics of debate scheduled for that day: art and revolution, the colonial question, ideology and mystification, Marxism, Leninism, Maoism, anarchism, the ethics of violence. Eva was at a loss as to which of these subjects the speaker was meant to be addressing. Vague and convoluted, it was not Mao anyway. As she listened, the text of Max's telegram flashed in her mind:

WHAT ARE YOU STILL DOING OVER THERE IT HAS
STARTED COME

—Is he saying something interesting at least? Álvaro asked.

Eva shook her head:

—You're not missing anything.

Álvaro lifted his camera and pointed it at the stage.

Eva put her hand in front of the lens:

—Save the film.

Álvaro dropped the camera so that it hung by the strap from his
neck. Gave her an indignant look. He did not like it when she dictated
his behaviour.

—You'll thank me later, she said.

Someone had once said that revolutions could be recognised by
the volume of words they generated. If this was true, and if the Odéon
reflected what was happening in the rest of the city, then Paris was the
revolution to beat all others. There was no limit placed on how long
one could speak. If someone was talking then it was taken for granted
they had an idea or an experience worth communicating. One's turn
would come. In the meantime, it was *interdit* to interrupt.

Sighing extravagantly, she got up and kicked off her boots. Trod
barefoot through the sprawled bodies to the circle rail. Álvaro, loyal
Álvaro, followed her there.

—What are you doing? he said.

—Nothing, she said.

—Eva. You're planning something, I can see it in your face.

—What you see in my face is *ennui*.

Banners had been hung from the rail, one overlapping the other,
all the way around the front of the circle. The one directly underneath
them read:

ATTENTION! THE RADIO LIES!

Eva discovered that, by subtly dropping a hand over the edge and
tapping the surface, one could create a ripple which passed down the
length of the banner, and onto the next, and the next, reaching almost
the other side of the theatre.

—Stop that, Eva, Álvaro said.

—Stop what?

—I see what you're doing.

—I'm not doing anything.

—You're trying to distract the speaker. What's up your sleeve?

—Hold on to me.

—What are you going to do?

—I'm going to sit here.

She threw a leg over the rail.

Álvaro grabbed her jacket:

—Eva!

She laughed:

—I won't fall if you bloody hold me.

He flung his arms around her waist, and she lifted her other leg over.

—*Joder*, Eva! Don't do anything stupid.

—Stop resisting me, and just hold on.

The rail was sufficiently flat and wide to provide a comfortable seat for someone as lean as her. She kicked her feet out, far out into the air. Spread her toes.

—Wow, that feels good, she said.

—You're only staying there a minute, Álvaro said.

—Oh, yes! she said, taking her hands from the rail and spreading out her arms, as if preparing for flight. Ha ha, yes!

Álvaro tightened his grip on her:

—A minute and then you're coming back in. Do you hear me?

—I hear you, she said, I hear you.

But she was not really heeding him. Her mind was absorbed with the view between her thighs of the people in the stalls below, and with the accompanying question, *is anyone else fooled by this nonsense?*

In the seats below, the audience appeared drained of energy, listless. Heads resting on shoulders, legs draped over armrests, bodies slumped, looking this way and that, tuning in and out — they were intoxicated. Drunk on words. In love with the idea of communication while all around true meaning perished as plant life did in harsh climates. Words left their mouths, clean and hopeful, only to fall onto the carpet like dead things.

Stale seeds and rotten barley.

She bent her knees and, in a state fast approaching giddiness, brought her legs up to her chest, her heels to rest on the rail.

—*No me jodas!* What the hell are you doing?

She was now crouching on the edge, her bottom merely brushing against the rail. The whole theatre throbbed with a soundless vibration which, it took her a moment to realise, was the beating of her own heart.

—Take my ankles, she said.

—Are you fucking serious?

—Take. My. Ankles.

She sucked in a breath and held it. Álvaro had just removed his arms from her waist, so there was nothing supporting her. But she was all right. She was not going to fall. As long as her lungs were filled with air, she was weightless.

An instant later she felt Álvaro grasp her ankles, and her breath rushed out, and she was solid once more. Fixing her gaze on a single point at the back of the stage, beyond the panel of men — who by now had noticed her and were consulting with one another about what to do about her — slowly she began to straighten her legs. She felt firm. Riveted to the rail. Formidable. Until, halfway up, suddenly prey to nervous agitation, her muscles began to tremble inside her trousers.

Sensing this, Álvaro locked his arms around her shins and wedged his head between her thighs. Squeezing, she could feel the flesh of his face bunching forwards; his breath was warm on the inside of her leg when he said:

—*Me cago en la puta hostia!*

While rising to her feet, she had kept her arms outstretched for balance; now that she was standing straight, she found that she had come into a pose resembling a crucifix. Judging this vain, she lifted her arms over her head, as if to hold a globe.

She was guilty of it as well: the worship of self-expression. She had in her life spent many long hours analysing the past and building the future out of the sheer pleasure of words. But after a while she learned that this had its limits. People were too busy to listen. Events developed at such a speed that her declarations became instantly obsolete. Mao had a better way: do first, then speak. Only the voice of experience — of the revolutionary who had already made revolution — carried durable truths.

The speaker on stage, who until this moment had resisted giving Eva any attention, choosing instead to direct his remarks to the front row of the stalls, could resist no longer. He broke off and threw an arm out in her direction.

—What are you doing? he roared into the microphone. Get down from there! Somebody stop her, she's going to jump!

The panel members, previously uncertain of what course of action to take, rose to their feet and barked orders for her to get down. The heads in the stalls turned backwards and up. In the central aisle a group of anarchists heckled and waved their black placards. Behind her, the diffused chatter ceased and individual voices called out.

—Oh, just push her, for fuck's sake!

—Jump!

—Hysteric!

—Look at that bitch!

—It's not normal!

—Shake your ass!

—Tits out! Tits out!

Once in position on the rail, Eva's first idea was to keep her torso rigid and her arms held straight up, and to stay absolutely still, so as to create a kind of visual silence, such as a statue, but, fighting against the urge to manifest, she tired quickly. From a neutral standing position, she tested out some small movements while inwardly watching her centre of balance. She found that she could not safely tip forward or to the sides. She could lean backward, but only lightly, for fear that Álvaro would not be able to sustain her. Any slight rotation or undulation made her unstable and would have to be avoided.

Her limits established, she began to enlarge her gestures, to make them louder.

All right now, let me show you.

Her motion soon assumed a recognisable form, which, because determined by the need to keep balance, was rigid and precise and unsparing: technologic.

—Eva, what the fucking fuck are you doing?

—One more minute, Álvy. Please.

In time with the silent rhythm which pulsed about her, she hammered and churned and looped and jerked: arms like pistons and drills, hands like cogs, head like a robot's.

Ha ha, this is how.

Expelling all hesitation and deliberation, finding finesse even in the brutality, she mimicked the movements of machines on the factory assembly line and at the construction site. Then, without needing to modify much, she switched to mimicking the movements of police officers in a riot and soldiers in a war.

Look, look at what I'm doing.

For it took someone extraordinary to do it: to draw upon and express a reality that was physical but which transcended objects.

—Get down! Order please!

She raised her face to the roof, supposing that it was leaking and that rain was coming in, when in reality it was sweat. The beating in her ears dissolved into taunts and claps and cheers and the yells of the chairman.

—Order!

And now Álvaro, hissing:

—I'm finished with you, Eva. Do you hear me? It's over.

—Shut up and take some pictures.

—What're you talking about, I'm holding on to you.

—Let go then.

—You're out of your mind.

—Let go and take my fucking picture.

She could feel him disobeying her by tightening his grip on her shins and applying a backward pressure. Readying himself to pull her down.

—Now, Álvaro! Picture! Or we really are finished!

Her weight passed onto her heels. Álvaro's chosen method was to tip her back until she fell on top of him. It would have been dangerous to resist, so instead she concentrated her tension on the spot that he could not control: the mouth. It was decision time. In an instant it would be over. Was she going to speak?

—

As she toppled backwards, first she lifted up her arms, then her right leg, so that all of her weight pivoted on a single foot.

—

Now, with the air rushing past her, through her, she thought: no. Speaking would be a mistake. The physical quality of life, that was communicating.

Pain: her bones collapsed onto Álvaro's.

Pain: the back of her skull collided with his jaw.

Pain: her shoulder blades slammed against his ribs, and the impact cracked his camera.

A moment then, and she could feel Álvaro writhe underneath her, could hear him heave. Winded, he was in the panicked state of believing that breath would never return.

She rolled off him onto the carpet, which felt thick and soft, as welcoming as a mattress. Beside her, Álvaro turned onto his side and pulled his legs up to adopt the foetal position. She watched his face bloat and redden, his eyes balloon. A high-pitched wheeze issued from his throat.

When finally the first breaths of his restored life came, he used them to gasp:

—My Rolleiflex. My Rolleiflex.

Many times in the past she had wanted to smash that camera, for it seemed that Álvaro had grown dependent on it, unable to see the world except through its lens. But the real act of destroying it, however accidental, did not feel good.

—I'm sorry, baby, she said, and she really was.

—Fuck you, Eva.

The other Wherehouse members helped them to their feet and hustled them through the corridor of jeering bodies.

—Wait! My boots!

She ran back through the twisted faces, grabbed her boots, and then rejoined the others who were waiting for her at the top of the stairs. Together they went down and outside.

On the steps of the theatre, a group of students dressed in costumes stolen from the dressing rooms — Arab sheiks, Sgt. Pepper's Band, Batman, Martians — gave them a round of applause.

—Oh fuck you, Eva said to them in French.

Only idiots applaud. Real progressives rage.

—What was that? said one of the Wherehouse members.

—Know what you are, Eva? said another. An individualist. So bloody wrapped up in yourself, you don't care about the group.

—Bollocks, Eva said. I formed the bloody group. The group is my life.

—Then you should have told us beforehand what you were planning.

—I wasn't planning anything. It just happened.

Looking at their faces, Eva saw them changed. As she herself felt changed.

Everything you do changes you a little.

—Let me deal with this, guys, said Álvaro.

In his shivering hands, a bit of plastic that had broken off his camera.

—Deal with what? said Eva.

—Do you have the key? he said. To the room?

She took it from her pocket.

—Give it to them, he said.

She obeyed:

—I didn't want to be in charge of it in the first place.

—Keep it safe, Álvaro said to the others. Make your way back to the room whenever you want. We'll see you there later, or in the morning for the meeting. Me and Eva are going to go and have a little talk.

He turned and set off through the throng towards rue de Vaugirard.

Eva stayed where she was and watched him go.

After a few strides, he glanced back. Seeing that she was not following, he returned. Threw his camera, the main body of it, at her feet.

—Come the fuck on, Eva.

Sighing, she knelt down to pick the camera up.

—Leave it! he said. It's useless.

She stood back up and held out the camera, an offering.

He opened the flap of his satchel so that she could put it inside.

—There goes the photo exhibition, he said. None of the work we do in Paris will be documented. Are you happy?

—No.

—God, what a waste. What am I supposed to do now?

—We'll get you a new one.

—With what money, Eva?

—I don't know. You might have to wait till we get back.

He jammed his fingers into his hair:

—Fucking pointless being here now.

—Don't be like that. When we get back—

—What? When we get back to London, then what?

She could feel the other members, and beyond them the Odéon crowd, watching, relishing their quarrel.

—I'm sure our parents wouldn't mind paying for a new—

—Whose parents?

—Mine. We'll ask mine.

He laughed:

—Your father? He's broke.

—He's not *broke*.

—Only because he's a leech. Living off other people. First your mother. Now Doris Lever.

—Shut up. You know I hate when you use information I've given you in confidence as a weapon against me.

—What you don't like is hearing the truth.

—Look, I'll ask Mama for some money.

—Pah! You're too proud to ask her for anything. No, no. As always, we'll have to go to my parents—

—Correction. Most of the time it's *my* uncle Simon who bails us out.

—except this time it's not going to happen. I refuse to call them for more money. You broke my camera, so you're going to have to replace it. Now, come on.

He grabbed her arm and dragged her off.

—We'll see you guys later.

Although his grip hurt and his pace forced her into a trot, she did not fight him.

Further down rue de Vaugirard, when it was certain that she was submitting, he let her go. Released, she slowed her walk. Asserting his continued authority, he marched on, two steps ahead, all the while discharging an unbroken wind of Spanish curses.

—I should have known when the vote went against you—

—What vote?

—You voted against going to the Odéon. I should have known that, when it went against you, you were going to act up. You don't like—. Forget it.

—What, Álvy? What don't I like?

—You don't like losing to the group. You always want things to go your own way.

—Look who's talking.

—Eva, if you don't mind, we're talking about you right now. And I think you know why.

—For me it was just a stupid vote. And I wasn't acting up in the theatre, I'm not a child. I'm a performer. It was spontaneous. It just came out of me.

—What came out of you? I mean, what the hell was that?

—I don't know. What did it look like to you?

—Pathetic. Pathetic was how it looked.

—Now you're just trying to shame me.

—How can I shame someone who doesn't have any shame?

She folded her arms as a defence against this: it was not true. Shame was one of the few constants in her life. Regular and reliable, its attacks deformed even the undeformed joys. Often, when thinking about past performances, even the most successful of them, the shame was so acute that she could not bear to be inside her skin.

—Someone had to do something, she said. You saw what was happening in that theatre. I saw your face, you hated it as much as me.

—I didn't hate it as much as that.

—All of that spouting off?

—I've never seen anything like it before. You'd never bloody see it in London. In Spain you'd be arrested.

—And now that you've seen it, you're a believer?

—Jesus, that pisses me off.

—What?

—That you're always already past things. Like you've seen everything, done everything, and can only get excited about the next thing that doesn't exist yet. You've never seen a theatre occupation before either, or any other kind of occupation for that matter, so don't put on the blasé act with me.

—Oh do forgive me if I don't get misty-eyed about some people camping out. And a student debate.

—You're impossible. *De verdad.*

—Look. Álvy. As far as I could see, the yappers in that theatre were nothing but hypocrites. Did you see all of them sitting at that table? Pretending they're involving people in the revolution when in fact, with their little show, they're doing the reverse, inhibiting their involvement?

—The revolution wasn't happening in there, is that what you're saying? Where is it happening then?

—That remains to be seen. We've only been here a few hours.

—It's happening in your mind, by the sounds of it.

—In my mind, yeah. And in your mind. And in the people's mind.

—An illusion? Revolution is one big fantasy, is that it?

—No, it's life.

—Revolution is life?

—Yeah. If it's a real revolution, it doesn't just happen in theatres. It happens everywhere. On the streets. In people's homes. It's like the Wherehouse manifesto says, *Don't enact. Act. Don't imitate life. Live.*

They had reached the crossroads with boulevard Saint-Michel. Álvaro took her elbow before crossing through the debris on the road.

—More revolutionary than the revolution, he said. That's you, through and through.

—Well, more revolutionary than those men in there, I hope so.

—And me? he said. More revolutionary than me?

—I didn't say that, she said.

Her relationship with Álvaro was in its essential ingredients a competition between ambitious minds. *Am I able to form this man?* It was a question of personal success. At the end of an argument with him, her mind would be exhausted. But she rarely lost.

Álvaro had struggled through two years at the School of Economics. Ingrained in him was a Spaniard's reverence for loyalty as the highest of human virtues, and at the LSE he failed to find anything with which he could form a lasting attachment. In his studies he was easily bored. As soon as he encountered a difficulty with a subject, his interest wandered away to another subject, often in a different field, where it stayed until it met a problem there. In his social relations the pattern was similar. One person seemed to embody the ideal of friendship until that person showed himself to be anything less than devoted, at which point another person had to be found and another friendship formed. In this way, life at the LSE provided him with a series of frustrations which led him to cease attending lectures altogether and to join the Radical Student Alliance. When even this turned out to be a disappointment — radicals, it transpired, understood less than anybody the meaning of allegiance — he began to question the value of life itself and ultimately to condemn it.

After a string of bad grades in his second year, his parents procured, by unethical means, a doctor's letter which won him a year's leave of absence. Instead of catching up on his studies as they had intended, he spent the year running around with the theatre and film people, and dancing at the Ad Lib on Leicester Square — with such a lack of self-consciousness, Eva remembered, that he put all the professional actors in the shade. They met at a New Year's party there, and he joined Wherehouse soon after, at first as a chronicler of the collective's work, and subsequently as a full member. The following year, much to the outrage of his parents, he did not return to university. By then radical performance had become his employment; Wherehouse, with Eva at its core, his family; already in his relations with both, he had developed the angry loyalty of the old domestic animal.

When Eva met him, he was depressed and drinking heavily, sleeping all week and partying all weekend; his parents were threatening hospitalisation. It was Wherehouse that saved him. That got him off the drink. Gave him a purpose. Lifted his spirit. It was Wherehouse that built him up from the ruin the LSE had made of him. Yet the curious thing was, once he was better and happy, Álvaro began to speak of the LSE in the fondest of terms, nostalgically, as upper-class boarders sometimes came to speak of their alma mater: as a harsh and unforgiving environment, a kind of hell, but one which had made him what he was. Álvaro's commitment to Wherehouse had not expunged from his mind the dream of future success in the world — success which he could visualise in no way other than going back to a university he hated, to study a subject he had scant interest in, and to pursue a related career, as a journalist or indeed as an economist, which actually would succeed in hospitalising him. Before agreeing to participate in a Wherehouse performance, he gave serious thought to what damage it might do to these magnificent prospects. Alone in his room, the door locked, he made lists for and against participating. Would the performance take place in a public space? Would the media be present? Would masks or make-up be used to hide his likeness? Was there the risk of arrest or of a future employer finding out he was there? It made Eva sad to know he struggled with such questions; that still he feared being a failure in his parents' eyes. It was what made her pity him.

She herself had attended drama school. Which was an exquisite rebellion against her own parents, whose perception was that drama schools were merely dressed-up finishing schools. The only people that went to the Royal Academy, they said, were girls who would once have been debs, rich Americans desirous of an English accent, and the less able daughters of the bourgeoisie who needed to be kept out of mischief until marriage. It was an old-fashioned view, formed in their youth and barely modified since, yet it was not entirely false. Two girls in her class of sixty-six had indeed been titled. And most of the rest were only a couple of strata below: the pillars of society.

In common with her parents, Álvaro thought that drama school was a lesser kind of education. And she could not say that he was wrong. The Royal Academy did not have a system. A philosophy. When the teachers introduced the students to a method, they were quick to remind them that there was no single way to good acting; there was room for all kinds of approaches and for none at all. In class, references were made to Stanislavski and Brecht, but no one suggested a close reading of their theories. If so inclined, a student was expected to find out about them in her own time and decide their value for herself. It was Eva's first real encounter with English eclecticism, and she was astonished and maddened by it. Presented as an open-minded acceptance of the equal validity of all methods, in fact it concealed a hostility to any method in particular — and went some way to explaining why the individual excellence of England's actors was matched only by the general impotence of its theatres, which were the laughing stock of the continent.

Even so, she had not dropped out. This was something she could say in her favour. Unlike Álvaro, and unlike her sister Iris, she had played the game at the Royal Academy and had not been defeated by it. She had thrown herself in, and, in spite of the conservatism, the narrowness, the arbitrary standards, had come out on top. First in her class every year, the recipient of various prizes, a regular presence in the principal cast in school productions, after graduation she was offered a place in the Royal Shakespeare Company, which, as had always been her plan, she turned down. For that was what the true rebel did. She stayed the course. Learned the rules. Became the best, exactly as the rule-makers defined it. And then, just when they expected her to complete her integration, with a kiss and a wave, she turned and walked the other way.

—Listen, I love you, Álvy, she said now.

—Well, I can't say the same thing to you, when you behave like this.

They had reached place de la Sorbonne, which, like the theatre square, was filled with striking students. Some held placards: DOWN WITH THE CONSUMER SOCIETY and FUCK THE POLICE. Others wore t-shirts: I'M A MARXIST, THE GROUCHO KIND. Or handed out duplicated leaflets. Eva took one of these. Its headline was: VIOLATE YOUR ALMA MATER.

—There you go, she said, handing it to Álvaro. Some advice for you.

Refusing to get her joke, he threw the leaflet on the ground with the others.

Two women were sitting high up in a windowsill, legs open, no knickers, waving Vietcong flags.

—Look there!

He did not look.

Literature stalls had been set up on either side of the street, selling the works of Marx and Lenin, and Mao's *Sayings*, as well as old issues of journals, yellowed by the years. Enormous portraits of Trotsky and Fidel and Che had been pasted onto the walls. There was even a Stalin, though a black cross had been sprayed across his face.

—You know, I don't know why I put up with it, he said.

—Put up with what?

—People wonder, and I don't have a clue what to tell them.

—You tell them to fuck off.

—And then I find myself thinking—

—Oh here it comes.

—why did I leave university? For this? I should've stuck it out. I'm wasting my time with you lot.

—Are we going to have this conversation again?

—I shouldn't have let you convince me to leave the LSE.

—Earth to Álvy, leaving was *your* decision. You hated that place.

—If I went back, with what I know now, I'd get a first. I know I would.

—Why don't you then? Call your parents. Tell them you want to re-register. They'd be delighted.

—*They* would be. But you wouldn't, would you? That's the point. You wouldn't give me the support that I've given you.

At the junction with rue de la Sorbonne, a stall had been set out with notices and posters denouncing the French Communist Party, which was still in thrall to the Russians and refusing to learn the lessons from China. On the wall behind the stall was a large billboard on which was written every statement attacking the student revolution to have appeared in Party leaflets and newspapers. A man with a megaphone was decrying the Party's counterrevolutionary tendencies.

Eva stopped to listen for a minute. She translated what she heard for Álvaro, though he did not seem to be interested.

They moved off towards the Sorbonne Chapel, where they sat on the steps underneath big letters which read:

WE WANT SOMEWHERE TO PISS, NOT SOMEWHERE TO
PRAY

—So have you forgiven me? she said, taking Álvaro's hand.

He gave her an uncertain look.

—Eva, I want to tell you something.

—Sounds serious.

—Just listen.

—You're not leaving Wherehouse, Álvaro. Not now. Just when
we're finding our feet. Making progress. You promised—

—Shh. That's not what I was going to say.

—What then?

—What I was going to say was, you're not invisible, you know.

—Me? I know that.

—You have a—. You have a presence. People see you. You don't
need to do dangerous stuff like climbing onto balconies to get
attention.

—That's not what that was about. If attention was what I was after,
I'd be in the West End, or doing Pinter for the fucking BBC, like my
mother. If you knew me at all, you'd know I don't care what people
think of me.

—Then maybe I don't know you.

—Right. Maybe you don't.

Because the truth was, when she was performing, she became
nothing. She gave herself to her public. Her body. Her thoughts.
There was no Eva left. *No difference between me and them.* People
could think what they liked about her, because she was not even
there. The only relevant thing was the message she was carrying. *War.
Oppression. Injustice. Unemployment. Deportation. Workers' problems.
Race prejudice. Mao.*

—I think, said Álvaro, that what you want is for your indifference
to public notice to be universally recognised.

—Ah!

She drew fists to her face and turned away from him, exasperated.

—I could kill you. You say these things only to hurt me.

—I don't do anything to hurt you. I'm trying to help you.

—By hurting me. You've always thought that's the only way to win against me. You've never understood how wrong you are about that.

Álvaro touched her arm:

—Are you crying?

She glanced over her shoulder so that he could see her face: dry as a bone.

—All right, all right, he said and leaned back against the pillar.

His skin was pale. He looked drained. He was a man facing defeat in the final round.

—All I'm saying is, he said, that if you really felt you belonged in the group, if the group was enough for you, you wouldn't need to do this sort of thing. Do you feel the group is holding you back?

—From what?

—Doing your own thing.

She shifted back round so that she was facing him again:

—I don't feel like anyone is holding me back. Each member brings something different to the table. Everyone is valued equally. That's always been our ethos. What you're saying, I don't recognise it. It's coming from you, not from me.

—The group isn't blind, Eva. It's sees your ambition. It makes them nervous. They think you have your own plans.

—Plans?

—Like, are you in Paris for Wherehouse, or are you just chasing Doris Lever?

—Oh that's dense.

She got to her feet and began to pace a short path along the bottom step, two steps this way and two that.

—So bloody dense.

—They know about Doris and your dad.

—Hardly a secret.

—They know you've history with her. That when you were a child she lived at the theatre with your family. And that you and she were close.

—Close is pushing it.

—And that's she's been to China. Seen the real revolution, first-hand.

—So what if she's been to China? I'm going to get there myself one day. You watch.

—She has influence on you, Eva. She does all the things you want to do. The group are worried that you're scheming to get close to her again.

—Everyone needs to fucking relax. I'm not running after Doris.

—You *are* fascinated by her. You mention her a lot.

—I respect her. Her work can be interesting sometimes. But we're different. Doris calls herself an artist, and I don't see myself as an artist in that way. I'm a performer, one that can't work alone. I have to work with a group. Part of it is personal, I'd be lost without you guys. And part of it is political. A group can make work that's a hundred times more powerful.

—If that's the case, why is Doris Lever better known than Wherehouse? She's in galleries all over. And the papers. Isn't there a book about her now?

—Her thing is in vogue now, that's all. And she's been at it longer than we have. We just need a bit more time to figure out how to spread our message. When you look at it, we have an advantage over Doris. We have our methods. Our manifesto. We've got Vietnam. We've got Cuba. We've got *Mao*. She might've gone to China, but she doesn't really *believe* in China, as an ideal to work towards. She's all over the place. No system. No philosophy.

Álvaro held out his hand, as if to ask her to help him up. When she took it, he pulled her into him and kissed her. His goatee beard scratched her skin. She pushed his hair back from his forehead, then let it flop forward again. He pressed her breasts against his chest and rubbed her bottom.

—Come on, he said, getting up.

—Back to the room? she said, allowing him to take her with him. He shook his head:

—Let's stay out a while longer, just you and me.

—I could do with putting my head down for an hour.

—All right. Let's find a place.

Hand-in-hand, then with arms around each other's waists, they went up rue de la Sorbonne to the main entrance of the university. Eva translated the poster on the door:

THE REVOLUTION WHICH IS BEGINNING WILL CALL INTO QUESTION NOT ONLY CAPITALIST SOCIETY BUT INDUSTRIAL SOCIETY. THE CONSUMER SOCIETY IS BOUND FOR A VIOLENT DEATH. SOCIAL ALIENATION MUST VANISH FROM HISTORY. WE ARE INVENTING A NEW AND ORIGINAL WORLD. IMAGINATION IS SEIZING POWER.

Inside, posted on the corridor wall was a large hand-drawn map, beautiful to look at, with the important buildings and squares marked by intricate little illustrations. The streets shown were those of the Latin Quarter, but on the top it said, HEROIC VIETNAM QUARTER. The main Sorbonne auditorium was called CHE GUEVARA HALL. The Pantheon Square, HO CHI MINH PLACE.

Dormitories had been set up in some empty classrooms on the third floor. Finding none of the beds free, they pleaded their case to a number of couples and groups — they had travelled a long way, Eva told them, and had nowhere else to go — a tactic which eventually fell on sympathetic ears.

They climbed onto the mattress fully clothed except for their shoes. They embraced for a while under the sheet, and touched and felt and rubbed, but she found herself too tired to take it further.

—Do you mind if I just sleep for a bit?

—All right.

But he quickly became bored and started to toss and turn.

—You don't have to stay, she said.

—I wouldn't mind having another look around. Would you be all right? I wouldn't like leaving you.

—I'd be fine.

—Sure?

—Álvy, I said I'd be fine.

He kissed her:

—I'll come and find you shortly, and we'll go to the demonstration together, all right? Don't disappear.

—I won't move till you come.

—Good, he said. Get some sleep.

Contained within his departing caresses, their vehemence, was a brag about how long he worked and how late he stayed out; how little he slept; how self-denying he could be. They kissed for a long time, but she could sense that he could not wait to get away on his own. And when he was gone, she felt relieved. For a commune member, there was no way out of entanglement. The only responsible course was to ensure that, when the desire to be alone came, one satisfied it by giving it to others.

She flopped over onto her back, reached one arm into the liberated space and laid the other across her eyes. The room was noisy and stuffy. Around her no one was sleeping. Rather, everyone seemed to be smoking and talking and giggling and petting at once. Without being anything like boarding school, it reminded her of boarding school, which she had liked, not least because she had been liked there, so she quickly fell into a contented sleep populated by lots of laughing faces.

JIANG QING

1974

iv.

She raised her pass as she entered the outer gate of the Chairman's courtyard. The two sentinels did not take their hands from their sub-machine guns in order to do a full check of her identification, as they were supposed to. Wisely they did not move at all except to glance briefly out of the tail of their eyes. Wise indeed, these lowly boys; they knew not to cross her.

By contrast, in the porter's lodge at the inner gate, the more senior guards were slouched over chairs, their feet up, chattering loudly and freely. As soon as they saw her approach, they stubbed out their cigarettes and jumped up.

—Soldiers, she said to them, are your minds fixed on Mao Zedong Thought? Because it looked like you were gossiping like women.

She hummed, pleased with herself, while she filled out the visitor's form.

The soldiers listened in silence to her tune, which was 'Sailing the Seas Depends on the Helmsman'.

She handed the form back to be stamped. One of the soldiers took the seal out of the locked drawer and pressed it onto the bottom corner of the page. Then, completed form in hand, he came out of the lodge and accompanied her along the covered corridor running around the courtyard, and into the underground tunnel that led to the inmost place: Building 202, the Chairman's residence.

As they walked, she took the opportunity to examine the soldier's face. It had reached her ear that one of the Chairman's guards had done an imitation of her. According to the report, he had put on a straw hat of the kind she used in the garden, and had pranced about in it, twisting his body this way and that, shouting orders in a deep voice like a man. This news must have been relayed by a hundred mouths before coming to her; she had cried herself into fits when she heard it. She had not yet found the culprit. Was it this one?

—Was it you? she said.

—Commander? he said.

—Don't play dumb with me. You know what I refer to.

—Sorry, Commander, I don't.

The soldier pressed a button on the wall and a voice answered down the loudspeaker. The soldier stated their business into the grille as if broadcasting to the nation.

—Commander Jiang for the Chairman.

The door buzzed open and the soldier held it for her.

—Who are our friends, Soldier? she said as they climbed the stairs. And who are our enemies? This is a question of first importance for the Revolution.

—Yes, Commander.

—Have you ever looked around the Compound and asked yourself, can everyone who works here really be so revolutionary? Two-faced counterrevolutionaries that hold up the red flag while opposing the red flag could be sleeping right next to you. Even here, at the centre of operations, reactionary scoundrels could be skulking in dark corners waiting to jump out and act brazenly as soon as the climate is right.

—Yes, Commander.

—I myself have noticed a change in behaviour amongst many comrades in the Compound of late. They have started acting like grandees and have fallen into deluded and inflated notions, a consequence of living in such a cut-off way, no doubt. They are working hard, but their work is accompanied by steadily deepening cynicism. Have you seen it too? A slightly malicious tone? a sarcastic edge to a voice? those little things which so quickly develop into the cancer that eats a movement from the inside?

—Yes, Commander. This way, Commander.

The soldier conducted her through a door and round the corner of a modern white-walled corridor.

—And it's not just others we have to watch out for, is it? It's vital we remain vigilant about ourselves too. Counterrevolutionary influences are hidden in the most secret places of our own bodies. As communists, we have a duty to locate those influences and purge ourselves of them. Have you ever taken the time to wonder, am I as revolutionary as I claim to be? Do you keep an eye on what kind of jokes you make, for instance? Are your jokes contrary to what you say in Party meetings? Do they go against what you thought you believed in?

—I try not to joke, Commander.

The soldier opened a door and stood against it. Gave her the visitor's form and directed her into the reception hall of Building 202.

—I'll be waiting here to bring you back.

She folded the form in the middle. Ran the crease between two fingertips in order to make it permanent. All day she was treated with respect, but people's feelings ran as shallow as water; privately nobody cared about her.

—Soldier—

She lowered her voice so as not to be heard by the guard at the reception desk.

—piss a puddle and look at yourself in it. What is it that you see? Do you deserve to be where you are?

She brought her lips to his ear.

—What is that smell? Is it your soul? Stinking like your mother's cunt?

Smiling broadly — at the end of the day, if the choice was to imitate or to be imitated, she would always choose the latter — she came away. She gave the visitor's form to the guard at the reception, who nodded her on. As she made her way to the stairs, behind her she could hear him lift the telephone receiver and turn the dial.

Up the two flights, she was fast enough to catch one of the Chairman's minor secretaries with the telephone to her ear. Seeing her appear, the secretary said a couple of quiet words and put the receiver down. Jiang Qing stood in front of the secretary without speaking. The secretary put her elbows on her desk, interlaced her fingers and looked down at them. The two guards flanking the double doors behind stared at an uncertain point above Jiang Qing's head. After a minute, during which each actress in this tableau faithfully maintained her pose, the double doors opened and the Chairman's personal secretary, Zhang Yufeng, came out.

—Ah, Sister Zhang, Jiang Qing said.

—Commander, Zhang Yufeng said and made a ceremonious gesture: *Won't you be good enough to come in?*

Building 202 was brand new. Zhang Yufeng's office had acquired more furnishings since Jiang Qing's previous visit. Jiang Qing admired the choices that Zhang Yufeng had made, everything was rational and functional and modern, though the room still had the look of being on show. The open bookcases, which last time had been empty, were now filled with books and magazines. Narrow side-tables had been added, on which bowls and tea things and vases of flowers were arranged. Maps of China and the world, and an occasional scroll, hung on the north and south walls. Sitting against the east wall was a row of four big chairs, covered in old rose brocade, with footstools in front. Zhang Yufeng's worktable had been upgraded to a cloth-covered scholar's desk. In the corner of the room, resembling a still photograph, was a meeting space comprising two sofas and a coffee table. Zhang Yufeng conducted Jiang Qing there now. Patted a cushion as an invitation to sit down.

—Might I offer you some tea? she said.

Jiang Qing waved a finger:

—I won't take anything stimulating.

Zhang Yufeng sat down on one of the sofas, arranged herself neatly.

—If not tea, then you'll have some hot water?

Jiang Qing stayed standing:

—I'm not staying, Sister Zhang.

Zhang Yufeng pressed the buzzer and an assistant came in with scented tea already prepared. While the assistant laid the table, Jiang Qing eyed the door to the Chairman's bedroom, which was blocked by a guard whose hand clasped the handle of his sword as if about to draw it.

Zhang Yufeng poured tea into two cups. Took one for herself. Slid the other across towards Jiang Qing.

—In case you change your mind, she said.

Jiang Qing's armpits moistened, and she felt obscure emotions rise into her throat. In dealings with comrades, it was essential to assign positions. No useful interaction was possible without doing so first. If two revolutionaries talked to each other without knowing and honouring their respective ranks, they achieved nothing. She lifted her heels off the ground a little, and stood exactly where she was: eminent, dominant.

—This is for you, she said then, producing a gift from the pocket of her uniform.

—Oh, said Zhang Yufeng flatly as she reached across the table to accept it.

She opened the wrapping carefully so as not to tear it.

—Did you do this? she said once the gift was revealed.

—I pressed it myself, said Jiang Qing. But I can't take credit for the frame. That's my bodyguard's work.

—A chrysanthemum.

—If you like it, you might put it up somewhere. There's still plenty of space on the walls.

—A good idea.

—I also took a picture of the same flower, which I'm developing at the moment. On my next visit I'll bring you a copy. It might be tasteful to display them together, the specimen and the photograph, one next to the other.

—I'll certainly have a look. You are kind, thank you.

—It's no more than you merit.

Zhang Yufeng put the pressed flower on the cushion next to her and took up her cup again. Jiang Qing saw no hint of gratitude in these gestures, but rather a hardness towards receiving.

—Please, Zhang Yufeng said, gesturing to the platter of exotic raw vegetables.

—No, thank you, said Jiang Qing.

—Won't you sit down?

—I don't want to keep you.

—There's always time for you, Commander Jiang.

Jiang Qing, for her part, tried to remember to be kind at breakfast, kind at lunch and kind at dinner; she felt an urge to perform generous actions every day. Giving had its joy in seeing the joy of the receiver. To deny the giver this was a kind of cruelty.

—Really I just need to nip in to the Chairman, she said. Have a quick word. Then I'll leave you to your good work.

Zhang Yufeng sipped from her cup, then laid it on her lap and stroked it.

—The Chairman is getting his hair cut, she said.

Having his enema.

—He'll be glad of the distraction.

—Please don't disturb him. It took us long enough to coax him into the chair.

—I know exactly what to say to relax him.

—He'll see you another time. Send a note and we'll put you in the diary.

Ignoring this, Jiang Qing went to stand in front of the guard. Here, half a pace from his chest, close enough to smell his unwashed skin beneath the spotless uniform, she silently willed him to step aside. When he did not, she turned to Zhang Yufeng:

—Please. I'll only be a minute.

Zhang Yufeng drew a hand across her forehead in order to brush her fringe to one side. Underneath, her expression appeared gentle and kind.

—The Chairman is old and in poor health, she said. You show not one spark of consideration for him.

—And you, Little Zhang?

Jiang Qing turned back to the soldier and searched his eyes for complicity.

—You're treating the Chairman like a corpse at a funeral. The man is well enough to see his wife.

—He doesn't want any more quarrels with you.

—I'm not here to quarrel. I'm here to ask my husband for his advice on a political question. A matter of utmost importance to the Cultural Revolution. Am I the only one in Beijing who remains interested in what our Great Saviour has to say?

Zhang Yufeng slid forward on the sofa. Put her cup on the table, then her hands flat on her knees. With her eyes staring ahead and her back straight, she looked like one of the infinitely calm buddhas of the old China.

—All right, Commander, she said. If you insist. At ease, soldier.

The soldier saluted and stepped to the right.

Sighing out her residual frustration, Jiang Qing made for the door. Opened it a crack. A smell like that of a Russian hospital rushed out. She froze. Turned to Zhang Yufeng, who had not moved:

—Aren't you going to accompany me?

Zhang Yufeng was using a plump white finger to rummage around the raw vegetables, feigning to look for something in particular.

—You can go in, Commander. I can't stop you. But you must go alone. I won't facilitate this unwarranted disturbance.

Jiang Qing stiffened. Her grip on the doorknob tightened. She dared not go in alone. The Chairman's various diseases had left his speech so impeded that Jiang Qing no longer understood him. Whereas once, not even so long ago, his utterances had sounded like a war drum, as clear as the seasons and more precious than gold, these days he drooled uncontrollably, struggled for breath and communicated solely by grunts and croaks, incomprehensible to everyone except Zhang Yufeng. Zhang Yufeng, having been at his side since he first began to deteriorate, was the only one able to decode the sounds that he now made. She had become his interpreter. Jiang Qing would say his ventriloquist.

—Won't you help me, Sister? Jiang Qing said.

—I'm sorry, Commander, Zhang Yufeng said. The answer is no.

Jiang Qing let her chin drop into her chest. She would not enter without Zhang Yufeng. The risk of misunderstanding the Chairman, and of angering him thereby, was too great. She pressed her forehead against the door and composed herself. Then she closed the door and came away. Went to lean on the back of the sofa.

—Sister Zhang, I pray you—

Zhang Yufeng raised an open hand:

—Before you say anything more, Commander, please hear me.

She indicated to Jiang Qing that she should sit. Kept her arm outstretched until Jiang Qing had lowered herself all the way down.

—I would like to tell you how I spent last night, Zhang Yufeng said.

—What happened last night?

—Nothing happened last night, Commander, that does not happen every night. It was not an unusual night for me in that I didn't get a moment's rest. As you know, I'm expected to stay by the Chairman's bedside until he has fallen asleep. I'm the only one he'll tolerate. He refuses be left alone with any—

—Are you complaining, Sister Zhang?

—one else. Lying down, he finds it hard to breathe, so he must stay on one side. When he tires of that side, unable to turn over, he insists on getting up and doing a tour of the room—

—Yours is a most privileged position.

—for which he needs me as a crutch. Then he gets hungry and I must spoon chicken broth—

—The most privileged in all of China.

—into his mouth. Of course it's hard for him to swallow, and most of it ends up on his front, which means his pyjamas then have to be changed. He'll want to excrete after that, so I must hold him while he does so, and mop up—

—That's enough!

Zhang Yufeng fell silent.

Jiang Qing took up the tea, which she realised she wanted after all, and gulped it down.

—You exaggerate, Sister Zhang, she said, slamming the cup back down. This is the Chairman you're speaking about. Your tone alone is grounds for arrest.

Zhang Yufeng kept careful control over her features to stop them betraying her bitterness:

—People all over the world love our Great Leader, but no one loves him as I do. No one does as much for him as me.

—Is that what you believe?

—It is the fact.

Jiang Qing sucked in her lips and closed her eyes. In her life, there was only Mao. In his service, she had swept away her individualism as an autumn gale sweeps away fallen leaves, and now she was nothing. She accepted being nothing. *He alone existed. He could demand anything of me. The truth of my life is outside me, in him.*

—Sister Zhang, she said, opening her eyes again. I must ask you to stop this talk. I can't listen to any more of it. I prefer not to speak of him to you.

—In that case, Commander, I'll limit myself to the following.

Zhang Yufeng's mask had slipped, revealing a surface far less clean, far less smooth.

—I, Zhang Yufeng, have been chosen to look after the Chairman, therefore it is I, Zhang Yufeng—

She placed a hand on her sternum and beat it three times.

—who decides what's best for him. It has taken great effort to relieve the Chairman of his pains and to get him into a position in which he can rest. I've ordered the medical staff not to disturb him, and I must ask you, too, to respect that order.

Jiang Qing let her gaze roam around Zhang Yufeng's face. Dark peasant skin. Expressive eyes. Wide open features. Well-defined nose. And her body. Leather shoes. Four pockets on her uniform. Flat chest. Shoulders hunched as if trying to escape the scrutiny of a crowd; the stoop of a watched woman.

—Anything that is in the Chairman's hands—

Her fine lips were moving again.

—is also in my hands. Don't hesitate to tell me your business, Commander, and I'll make certain it reaches him. Why did you come here today?

For a moment Jiang Qing saw herself in Zhang Yufeng. Looking at her, a deformed reflection returned to her, and she was perturbed and embarrassed before it. Zhang layered over Jiang, and Jiang layered over Zhang: she was unable to make independent sense of herself. All the things that made her *I* were gone, and she was, momentarily, two extremely lonely people. We suffer, she thought, but we have no one to tell.

—Sister Zhang—

From behind a sofa cushion, Zhang Yufeng produced a notebook. Leaning forward, she opened this onto the table, flattened a fresh page, and took a pen from a special box. She was going to take notes. This was the signal she wanted to give. She was going to record everything so that if a different day ever came, she would be able to prove her innocence, or failing that, seek a tooth for a tooth.

—I've come about the forthcoming ballet performance in honour of Mrs Marcos.

—As I thought, said Zhang Yufeng as she scribbled into her book. I heard you've ordered an extra week of rehearsals.

—Nine days. As usual you've heard incorrectly.

—This decision has made many people unhappy.

—What gives you that idea?

—There have been complaints.

—From whom? My people are happy. Following my orders makes them so.

—Some comrades, I won't name them, fail to see the point of more practice. They think it unnecessary. They were under the impression that work on *The Red Detachment of Women* had finished. That the ballet had been perfected.

—Can I remind you, Sister Zhang, that the development of *The Red Detachment of Women* is in my charge? and that I, and only I, will say when it has been perfected? If it takes another eight years, so be it.

—Hasn't it already been classified as a model?

—Until I say so, definitively, we can assume that it's not yet a model.

—So it's not a model?

—To say the ballet is a model is to speak as though it's good in every respect. That is at variance with the facts. It's not true that everything about it is good. It still contains shortcomings and mistakes.

—You're going to make changes to it?

—If a room is not cleaned regularly, the Party's work collects dust. Constant motion prevents the inroads of germs and other organisms.

—The rumours are accurate then.

—Don't give your attention to rumours, Little Zhang. A rumour is but a wind howling about mountain peaks.

—The dancers are worried that you plan to change the cast.

—How the mouths have been working.

—All my information has come through the official channels.

—It can't be the dancers who are grumbling. The dancers know that being awarded a part is not a lifelong contract. They understand that they can't stay forever in one role. They must gain experience in all kinds of roles.

—They've been touring and are tired. They'd appreciate some consistency.

—They're young and trained to be athletes. They ought to be ready for change and welcome it when it comes.

—Is it true you're going to install a new principal dancer?

—For crying out loud, what business is it—?

Feeling hot and prickly, Jiang Qing rubbed her back against the cushion in an effort to itch an inaccessible part of it.

—If you must know, yes. The dancer who plays the role of ARMY CAPTAIN isn't up to scratch. He has the vitality that comes with youth, but he lacks the technical discipline that the role demands. I had a replacement in mind but unfortunately he's indisposed. I'll make my new choice known presently.

—Changing the lead at such a late juncture won't be popular, Commander.

—I take pride in unpopularity. What's right is rarely what's liked.

Widening and narrowing, Zhang Yufeng's eyes wanted to nail Jiang Qing into a single position. Failing, she looked down to write in her book.

—You must remember, Jiang Qing went on, that we've been sending out announcements about the gala performance on Radio Beijing. Next week the foreigners will be tuned in. They'll be watching Mrs Marcos, first and foremost, because they can't stop being fascinated by her. But they'll also be watching what she watches. They'll be waiting to see if she likes our ballet before deciding if they should like it or not, which is the way it works in the capitalist world. For this reason, Sister Zhang, the performance must be of a new order of superior. The best dancers must be chosen, and they must spare nothing of their talent to make this performance a sensation. Not for an instant must they be allowed to ease up. China is stepping onto a global stage, and she must shine as the sun which makes all things grow.

Zhang Yufeng looked up from her writing. Tapped her lips with her pen. When she spoke again, it was in the voice of the Chairman as he had been in his health.

—That may be so, Commander, she said, but you yourself must see that in your doings you provoke too much enmity.

Listening to Zhang Yufeng taking the Chairman off like this, Jiang Qing could hear her own self mimicking him.

—None of my decisions, she said, transgress the bounds of my authority.

—You possess many good qualities, Commander, and have rendered good service. You're respected by your team, quite rightly so, but this, yes, this sometimes leads to conceit. You must always remember not to become conceited.

—I take pride in my competence, which is different from being conceited.

—If you're not modest and cease to exert yourself for the common good, if you don't respect the cadres as they respect you, then you'll stop being a revolutionary leader, and become—. Well, you'll begin to inflict harm on the interests of the Party.

Jiang Qing's rage manifested itself in a full-toothed smile. She was well schooled in giving apologies at the very times when she ought to be demanding them. It was a skill that women in the Party learned early.

—I'm not here to defend myself, Sister Zhang. But I will say this.

Zhang Yufeng poised the nib of her pen over a fresh page.

—There are some in the Party who blame me for every odour that's not pleasing, for every darkening cloud. Given the chance, they'd gladly burn my flesh. They are not small in number either. Their spit combined could make a well deep enough to sink me. But is that justice? I don't deserve to be pilloried. I'm not really bad. Of the many virtues I possess, my number one is this: when I get my teeth into something, I persist, I follow through, I stick with it and get the damn thing done. Which is what I'm doing with *The Red Detachment of Women*. I'm getting it done. Perfecting it. This is my job. Should I be prevented from it?

Zhang Yufeng was in the final year of her golden age, which for a Chinese woman was between twelve and thirty. She had met the Chairman at eighteen and had given the rest of her good years to him. But that was nothing compared to Jiang Qing. Jiang Qing had been twenty-four when she was chosen by the Chairman to be his assistant, and she was now entering the cycle of sixty. When Zhang

Yufeng had completed forty years, as Jiang Qing had, maybe then she could claim to speak for Mao, but not before.

Zhang Yufeng dropped the pen into the crevice at the centre of her book and, with one hand, snapped it shut.

—All right, Commander. What is it that you want exactly?

Jiang Qing helped herself to more tea. Swirled it around in the cup. Swigged it.

—The costs of the extra rehearsals aren't covered by the Cultural Committee budget, she said. I was hoping to withdraw some money from the Chairman's slush fund.

—How much?

—Eight thousand.

—Eight thousand?

—I know this seems like a large amount, but in the context of mounting a ballet, it's a pittance.

—Fine. Anything else?

Jiang Qing had been raised in a poor peasant family. She had been given no formal education. When she arrived at Mao's countryside commune, her knowledge of Marxism consisted of no more than a few phrases and some militant opinions. Certainly she felt the passion and the sense of struggle, but she did not know the ideas, the history. Yet she had what most of the other peasant girls did not. She had spent five years in Shanghai trying to make it as an actress, which had conferred on her both a city style and a talent for getting men to pay attention to her. She was one of the few girls in the commune who could sing and dance and act. In the get-togethers, the senior officers vied with each other to dance with her. She was exuberant, and smiled a lot, and was sure to make it seem like the men were leading. One night a commune leader signalled for her to follow him. Willingly she went to his office, where he asked her, *Are you prepared to assume any role the Party assigns you? Are you prepared to perform any act unconditionally, no matter what it is?* And her answer, which came immediately, was yes.

—There is one more thing, said Jiang Qing. The Chairman's next private dance party is scheduled for two days before Mrs Marcos's arrival. This date interferes with my rehearsal plans. I wanted to postpone it until after Mrs Marcos leaves.

—This is a sensitive topic, Commander.

—Which is why I wanted to speak to the Chairman directly. To reassure him that his needs weren't being disregarded.

—Aren't they?

—Not in the slightest. I'm merely requesting to put his party off for a few days, so that we can focus our resources on our international dignitary.

—Aren't you already wasting your resources on unnecessary rehearsals? Why ought your rehearsals take precedence over the Chairman's relaxation?

—If the Chairman were to agree, to compensate we could plan a bumper party for a fortnight's time. Twice the number of girls.

—The Chairman likes things kept regular. Once a week, every week. He looks forward to his parties. In our conversations he mentions them often. They're one of the last remaining pastimes which, in his condition, he can wholly enjoy.

—I wouldn't ask if it weren't an emergency.

—It's you, now, who exaggerates.

—I can't ask my dancers to stay up late, spending their energies, and then expect them to be at their best at rehearsals the following morning.

—Cancel the rehearsal.

—I'm not cancelling anything.

—Then give them an extra hour in bed in the morning. That should be enough for them to recover. They're trained athletes, isn't that what you said?

Jiang Qing sat back and pondered. She had to try to persuade Zhang Yufeng by speaking words within her comprehension.

—Another option would be to do a round of the hotels where the foreigners stay.

Zhang Yufeng glanced sideways beneath her lashes:

—Out of the question. We tried that once and it was a disaster. The Chairman was appalled by our selection. The Central Ballet girls are what he likes. And there mustn't be any repeats either. Don't bring him anyone he's seen before. We can't keep serving him the same dishes and expect him to be sated.

Zhang Yufeng's face was mimed and meaningful as she took command of a situation which until now had placed her at a weakness.

—Instead of postponing the party we *could* bring it forward.

She reopened her book. Found a calendar on a page near the front.

—I imagine tonight is too soon for you. You'll need time to choose the girls and prepare them. So how about—

She put her finger on a date.

—tomorrow night?

—Tomorrow?

Jiang Qing sighed:

—All right.

Zhang Yufeng drew a circle on the calendar, and with tiny strokes wrote *party* inside it.

—That settles it then, she said. This way you'll get your rehearsals and the Chairman will get his party. Everyone wins.

She stood up and held out a cool hand:

—You see, Commander? Travelling together, the destination is never far away.

From the distance of her seat, Jiang Qing examined Zhang Yufeng's outstretched hand. Something sincere and dangerous had started up between them, for which Jiang Qing felt an acute intolerance. Only savages and animals were sincere. No actress ever forgot that she was actually on stage. What the actress hoped for, far from sincerity, was a part she could play better than anyone else. Jiang Qing would play the performance of Mao's wife until the day she died, and it was a performance she did not mind being disliked for.

She said nothing for several seconds.

As the time ticked by, Zhang Yufeng was becoming a stranger to her once again.

Finally, with a friendly laugh, she relented and gave Zhang Yufeng the Western handshake. But: *I determine its strength, I decide when it ends*, there could be no exchange between them on an equal footing.

—Please give the Chairman my special love, she said.

Strange noises were coming through the auditorium doors. She went in and found herself in the middle of an orgy. The dancers were lounging in the stalls, or leaning against the walls, or wandering arm-in-arm across the boards; their patter and their laughter resounded. Chao Ying was sitting on the stage with his legs dangling over the edge, expressing opinions on who-knew-what to a group of the girls crouched in a semi-circle below him. The orchestra members, too, were out of their seats and gadding about: two of the violinists were in the aisles, pretending to duel with their bows. The stage crew were scratching their arses in the wings. In the lighting booth, there was a game of mah-jong taking place. It was trivial and disgusting. All that was missing was fruit wine and caviar.

She clapped her hands once:

—What the hell is this?

An awareness of her presence gradually infected the crowd, and they, all three hundred of them, fell silent. Descending the stairs, she bored a hole through them as they moved away from her as politely as possible.

—What a picture you all make, she said when she reached the bottom. If I were new to Beijing, a peasant from the countryside, or a foreigner, God forbid, and did not know this to be the Great Hall of the People, I'd swear I'd just walked into a counterrevolutionary shithole.

—Commander, said Chao Ying, who had come off the stage and was standing in the pose of contrition, we weren't expecting you till this afternoon.

—I'd like to say I'm astounded by your complacency, Director. And by the idealistic bankruptcy of this environment.

She walked circles around Chao Ying, all the while looking him up and down.

—But I'm not in the least astounded. Everywhere I look these days, the idealism that has motivated the Chinese to work hard and to accept privations for the sake of the Revolution is being replaced by dubiety, laziness and only half-hearted compliance. Undeniably the Cultural Revolution is a great victory for us but, thanks to people like you, I'm constantly reminded it hasn't yet been completed. You remind me — and I thank you for this — that there can be no relenting, and that after a few years it'll have to be started all over again.

—We were just taking a break, said Chao Ying.

She stopped her circumnavigations in order to peer around the auditorium like a guest offended by a dirty house.

—A break, you say, Director? Good, good. The instruments will be tuned in that case? The dancers warmed up? We can get started straight away?

Chao Ying's face burned red:

—Without question, Commander.

She acknowledged him with a fierce little nod, and then:

—Women! Corps de ballet! Here!

The female dancers rushed down the aisles and out of the wings. She swept an arm across the stage as a sign for them to form a line. She waited, hand on her hips, while they assembled; and she waited again, tapping her foot, while the slouchers corrected their posture.

—Are we ready? she said. Have we all had our dumps? Is there anyone who still needs to perfume her arse? We're going to rehearse the target practice dance from scene two.

—But Commander, said Chao Ying, stepping forward, the plan was to rehearse the scenes in order, starting with the prologue. That's why the props are there.

She waved a dismissive hand at the lanterns and the whipping post that sat on the stage:

—Crew, remove those props. Bring in the rifles instead.

—With respect, Commander—

Chao Ying tilted his head forward, not quite a bow.

—the target practice dance is, in my modest opinion, as near to perfect as it'll ever be. If you intend to work on the group dances, there are others that need more attention. The dance of the Red Army men in scene five, for example, would not suffer from a little adjustment.

Chao Ying spoke as if he had never met her before, as if he knew nothing of her methods, which enraged her.

—I'm not opening a discussion, Director, she said without looking at him. In fact, I doubt I'll be speaking to you for the rest of the day.

She kept still, her gaze directed diagonally downwards, until she felt that Chao Ying had receded a sufficient distance into the stalls.

—Dancers, she said then, clapping her hands, I want you to start after the marching entrance and finish before the ARMY CAPTAIN's sword dance. Just that short section. Orchestra, please play this nice and fast. Don't let it run over two minutes, got that?

The dancers formed two rows of nine stage right, their rifles held against the outside of their legs, their faces displayed to the audience.

—We all know where we are? Now remember to subdue the old ways. Be joyful and dance powerfully. On three, and two, and—

She nodded to the conductor, the music started up, and the dancers began.

—No, no, no.

She stopped them after only a few seconds.

—That looked weak. Where's the positive emotion? From the top.

The dancers went back to their first positions and began again. This time they made straighter extensions and raised their rifles higher, but this did not eliminate the dreaminess, the aura of sadness which hung about them. Jiang Qing recognised their condition. They were thinking about other things, feeling listless, always on the point of dragging their feet, and, out of a fear of showing it, were pushing their energy out into their limbs, which got them through the steps all right, but which also made them look like wound-up machines.

Because they knew their parts inside out, they did not feel the need to go on feeling them anew. They merely remembered and repeated the external movements, recalling how they did them when they first got it right, refusing to call on any fresh emotions.

She let them finish the sequence, then sent them back to the starting positions. She had already picked out the two worst offenders, but she needed another round in order to make her final selection.

—You know, she told them while they waited for her cue, if you dance without realising who you are, where you come from, and, most importantly, what you want, which is to conquer society, you will be dancing without revolutionary spirit. Like that, you'll always fail to attain realism, and will be nothing more than automatons. Revolution, remember, must be always on your mind.

She raised a finger and the conductor raised his baton.

—This time, she said before giving the signal, check the falseness in your actions. Search for the true gesture of the Revolution. And consider this: sometimes enthusiasm is more important than quality.

On their third attempt, the dancers beamed and sparkled, trying their best to show the face of the Party, but real fervour was as red as fire and as white as cogon grass flowers, which this was not. Jiang Qing saw past their trained expressions to their thoughts. They were thinking of the hours they had worked. Of the days, the months, the years they had given. *Don't do that*, Jiang Qing thought in response. *Don't think of yourselves. The Party has the first and only real claim on your lives. If you let yourself think otherwise, you're finished.*

The sequence complete, the dancers looked to Jiang Qing for her judgement. She climbed onto the stage. Drew a line in the air with her finger, as if marking the boards, and the dancers lined up in front of her.

—Are you happy with how you danced?

She walked up and down the line as a company commander would at a practice drill.

—If a foreigner were watching you today, would you be able to tell her, *This is the best that China has to offer?*

The dancers breathed heavily through their nostrils, their chins and their gazes elevated.

—I urge you to think about how you might be viewed from the outside. You mustn't forget that we're the centre of the world's attention. Every single day, all the people of the world are watching China's development. Their eyes are on us. On you. Imagine that. How lucky you are. To be Chinese at this moment in history. And, what's more, to have been chosen to embody the beauty of the Revolution.

Going round the end of the line, she walked behind the dancers, touching the backs of those she had selected.

—The people in the West have to make do with a rubbish culture. In the cities of Europe, they're fighting in the streets for the right to live as you do. They would die for what you have. You should appreciate your good fortune. The struggle against the decadent and the cult of the ugly in art is your task, and it is a momentous one. If you succeed, the world will thank you.

She came back to stand in front of the line.

—This is why you should never be satisfied with your work because it's near perfect. You should always try to find faults with it. You must never slacken your pursuit of artistic and ideological perfection.

She planted her feet hip-width apart and clasped her hands behind her back.

—Now —

She spoke calmly.

—the dancers I have touched, please step forward.

Three dancers came out of the line.

—I touched four of you, said Jiang Qing. Who's holding back?

The fourth dancer stepped forward.

—Names?

Voices shivering and cracking, the dancers gave their names.

She stood in front of each them in turn and looked them over. Lifted their drooping chins. Turned their faces to view their profiles. As she did so, she was assailed by premonitions of the ephemeral nature of her own achievements. Would socialist art in China flourish when she was not around to oversee it? Would it keep its splendour? The Cultural Revolution was still on the march, it had not stopped, yet nowadays it was advancing only slowly, with small, uncertain steps. The present problem was that people considered it impossible to accomplish things which could be accomplished if they exerted themselves. Her first instinct was to strike these dancers across their cheeks in order to make an example of them, but, out of a greater wish to be seen to be magnanimous, she overcame it.

—Follow me, she said.

She came off the stage and went up the aisle through the stalls, with the four dancers trotting behind her.

—Director, she called out to Chao Ying who was brooding in row eight, take over from here. You'll have do without these four. They won't be back for the rest of the day.

She ordered the Volga, which took them via the underground tunnel to the Compound. Touring had given the dancers the experience of travelling in trains and buses, but this was the first time they had ever been in an official car, and it made them nervous. They fidgeted in the leather seats, and, feeling underdressed, tugged on the ends of their rehearsal shorts as if that would make them longer. She took woollen rugs from the cabinet and put them over their bare legs.

—Better? she said.

The dancers nodded in unison.

The smile that came to her now was a natural one.

—Do you know why you're here?

They regarded her as if trapped in a corner.

—You're here because you're idlers. Lazy little bourgeoises.

One of the dancers, who since leaving the auditorium had been visibly suppressing her tears, now let them up.

Jiang Qing raised her voice to be heard over her sobs:

—Ballet should be full of human will. To dance is to fight. In the target practice dance, the women soldiers are preparing for mortal battle, yet all you showed were glum faces and apathy. You moved as if your bodies had been drained of blood and energy.

Contaminated by the first's tears, now they all started up. Jiang Qing gave them tissues to wipe their faces.

—If you take only a desultory interest in your work, if you go about things casually and leave them as they come out, you won't make progress. The opposite: you'll retrogress. Have you ever heard the saying, *There are no poor soldiers under an able general*? As your leader, I'm responsible for your development. How you perform is a reflection of my own performance as your guide. If you are wrong, then I am wrong. Are you trying to mortify me?

—No, Auntie Jiang. We love you.

—If you love me, why aren't you showing it?

—We're sorry.

—Sorry is not going to wash the window. What are you going to do to improve yourselves?

The dancers smeared their faces with their hands and blinked though their wet lashes.

—Think of the song that is sung as you make your first entrance. What does it say?

—*Advance, advance*—

One of the dancers half-sang between gulps of air.

—*the burden of revolution is heavy and the resentment of women is deep.*

—That's exactly right. But in your work today I saw neither the burden nor the resentment which enables you to carry that burden. All I saw was indifference. If you're indifferent, if you don't care, you'll die a non-person, a no one. Is that what you want? In revolution, half-measures may as well be no measures. They lead to decline in a person, and eventually degeneracy. The apathetic person dies friendless and alone. No one attends his funeral.

The dancers sniffed and swallowed:

—Thank you, Auntie, for your teaching. To die alone isn't what we want. If we die, we want to die making revolution, surrounded by our comrades.

Jiang Qing took a piece of ice from the drinks cabinet, wet it with water, and gave it to the girls in a linen napkin.

—For your puffy eyes, she said.

Each of the dancers in turn dabbed their eyes with the ice cube, then passed it on.

Watching them, only with difficulty could Jiang Qing conceal the surging-up inside her, the discovery that she was happy, that this indeed was happiness.

—Here, give that to me, Jiang Qing said when the last dancer had had her go.

She threw the wet napkin containing the remains of the ice cube into a wine cooler.

—The question now is, are you prepared to make up for your errors?

Out of all the girls who had flocked to the countryside commune, she, Jiang Qing, had been chosen. She was, they said, the lucky one. But fate only led her to the starting line. Ambition got her on. The average Chinese woman had no ambition to be powerful, nor did she dream of changing her fortunes overnight. A husband, a son, food on the table: these things brought her contentment, and contentment brought her happiness. Jiang Qing was unique in setting no limit to her ambitions. Her low birth was a spur to future greatness. Her time in Shanghai, meanwhile, showed her what life was like for a woman who had not got there, and it was worse than not living at all.

—Are you prepared to undergo the form of rectification the Party has decided for you?

If Jiang Qing had remained content merely to be a secretary, the Chairman would not have tolerated her for long. He would have tossed her out and replaced her with one of the other ordinary girls that populated the commune in large numbers. He used the role of assistant as a form of initiation. Disguised in his orders was the question: *Are you driven and compelled, as I am, to keep at it because nothing else means enough?*

—Are you ready to perform any act unconditionally, no matter what it is?

He had not loved her at first. He was won over by her love for him, by a loyalty that implied something more than submission. She was prepared to love him with complete generosity, for what he was and not what she wanted from him. She poured all her care and attention in one direction, to the one man who was strong enough to take her at her fullest. She let him occupy her whole life. She took on his emotions and thoughts. Her decisions were based on his decisions, her existence on his. For she knew that only in this way could she live happily in his shadow, and that only by coming out of his shadow one day she would achieve success of her own.

—Answer me, she said now to the dancers. Do you trust that the Party has your best interests at heart? Do you understand that the People's Government is ungrudging and lenient? That its aim isn't to punish you for the sake of it, but rather to improve your world outlook, align it more closely to the Party, so that you can be of greater benefit to the Revolution?

The dancers bobbed their heads eagerly:

—We haven't raised high the banner of the People's Government, they said. We've let it drop. We'll do whatever is necessary to rectify our mistakes.

Smiling, Jiang Qing held out both hands.

They placed their hands in hers, one on top of the other.

—You're going to go through a special test, she said. Tomorrow night, you'll be brought to a place where you can be re-educated. Taken out of your normal routine and given a chance to learn, to be objective. Now I warn you, it won't be anything you've seen before, and you might suffer, but whatever suffering you do will make you a better communist. Whatever happens, always remember that with the radiance of Mao Zedong Thought lighting your forward path, you have the fortitude to pick yourself up and go on.

At the Compound, she signed the dancers in, and got them visitor passes. Two guards escorted them across the courtyard of the

Chairman's old residence. The dancers, as they peered around, looked shocked.

—Don't lose your critical faculties, she told them. They're only buildings.

They went up the marble steps, between the bronze dragons, to Apartment 118. The guards took up positions outside.

—This—

She opened the door and pulled back the curtains.

—is where you'll be brought tomorrow night. Come on in. Don't be shy.

She switched on the lamps. Opened the window drapes just a little, to let in some natural light.

The dancers stayed bunched at the door, terrified of venturing any further.

—I understand your fears, said Jiang Qing, you are young and this is new, but you must overcome them. Tomorrow this room will be your stage. This is your one and only chance to get acquainted with it.

Reluctantly, keeping close to one another, the dancers did a tour of the room. As they shuffled round, they fixed their eyes on the floor, not daring to stop and look at the wooden screens and the silk hangings. Jiang Qing physically had to stop them and turn them by the hip.

—For heaven's sake, she said, look! Your eyes won't burn out of your heads. You mustn't be stupefied. They're just objects.

At the bookcase, thinking she was obeying orders, one of them reached out for a volume of the *Encyclopaedia Britannica*.

—No, said Jiang Qing. Not that. You're not to touch any of the books. Unless, that is, he asks you to read to him. Which is unlikely.

The shock beat up in them so rapidly, their eyelashes fluttered, and they looked half-blind.

—Why the faces? Haven't you understood yet?

They had. But the immensity of the spoken words overwhelmed them.

—You're going to meet the Chairman. You're going to dance for him.

One of them clutched her mouth and started to cry again. The others just looked dumb, knocked out of themselves.

Jiang Qing laughed:

—Leaders are not emperors. They're functionaries of the Party merely. In this room, don't think of the Chairman as the Great Saviour. Think of him as merely a state official of the Chinese Republic. There's an expression: *To rule truly is to serve.* Tomorrow the Chairman will be *your* servant, come to kowtow before your bodies, your talent.

Even at the height of their sexual relationship, when they made love several times a day, the Chairman would turn to Jiang Qing and say, *I wonder whether the kind of love I've read about in Western poetry can really exist. What would it be like, do you think?* In those moments, she could see she was caught in a contradiction. On the one hand, she believed she loved her husband better than anyone, and triumphantly asserted that love to him — *I love you, I am the only one who loves you* — and on the other hand, she was often struck by the obvious fact that he was impenetrable, intractable, not to be found.

This was because he was two men: *husband and Chairman.*

The intensity of the love she felt for the husband was possible only in a world in which things were important, in which the words one spoke, and the actions one took, left their mark. Later, when the Revolution changed history, her love changed with it. From then on, she rarely felt the passion for the husband that she did for the Chairman. The Chairman became her first love, pure and innocent. However much she loved the husband, it would never be enough to last a life, whereas now she had a relationship that possessed the sanctity of worship and lifelong devotion.

She sat down on the bed:

—He'll be lying here.

She made a circle in the air with a finger:

—You'll dance over there.

She gestured to the other side of the mattress:

—And if he asks you to join him here, of course you're to do so.

She got up. Smoothed the sheets where she had wrinkled them by sitting. Opened one of the sideboards and began flipping through the record collection. A fearful silence enveloped her from behind.

—You'll see, she said without looking round. When you're with him, everything seems important. Living becomes a privilege. You feel twice as much.

She picked out a record of ballroom music. Removed the sleeve. Wiped the vinyl with the special duster.

—But he's an old man now. And, as when dealing with any man his age, one must learn to read the signs of his mood.

To speak before being spoken to is rash.

Not to speak when spoken to is to be evasive.

To speak without observing the expression on your face is to be blind.

Unless you've studied Mao Zedong Thought, you'll be ill-equipped to speak at all.

If you do speak, don't claim to know too much; he doesn't like girls who are too world-wise.

When you offend against him, there's nowhere you can turn to in your prayers.

She put the record on the player. Lifted the needle over. Waited for the music to start. Raised the volume. Lowered it. Raised it again.

—Do you recognise this music?

The dancers shook their heads.

—Do you know how to dance the foxtrot?

Again they shook their heads, and Jiang Qing laughed.

—You know the loyalty dance? The foxtrot is like capitalism's loyalty dance.

She stepped into the dancing space, and, holding an imaginary partner, demonstrated both the male and the female steps: *slow, slow, quick-quick, slow.*

—I'm teaching it to you, she said as she turned around the room, so that tomorrow night you can perform it for the Chairman. But, after that, you'll never dance it again. You'll forget you ever heard of it. You won't show the steps to anyone, or even say the word *foxtrot*, or even think it to yourselves.

She finished her demonstration and came to stand in front of them.

—You were never here, do you understand? You didn't meet the Chairman. This didn't happen. This will be your lifetime secret. One which won't be easy to keep. The ego is strong and will be tempted to divulge, but you must resist it. You must think of the greater contribution your silence is making. If you don't, if you give in and start squealing, you'll be found out, and the consequences for you will be most severe.

She split them into pairs, and set them orbiting around her, and criticised them until their execution was flawless.

—Remember, you're impersonating the dregs of the old society, so you can drop your revolutionary poses for now. Stick your chests out. Don't hide your legs.

She made them dance for five, ten, twenty minutes without stopping. *What are they thinking? Deep down, what are they really feeling? Tomorrow, with the Chairman watching them, will they feel what she felt: the distance and the enormous closeness?*

—The foxtrot is bad but giving to the Chairman is good. By turning the bad to good, you are making the future glorious.

Will they see the world as she sees it: filled with people with whom she has to share her love?

—Everything good has something nasty about its first origin. Think: did your mother not shit out of her arse at the same time she was giving birth to you?

The world: an obligation to share?

The world: a rival?

EVA

1968

<u>v.</u>

Coming out of sleep, sound by sound she became aware of the dormitory. Without opening her eyes, she felt around on the mattress beside her. Finding no one there, she bolted upright.

—Álvaro?

She had been dreaming about arguments she was always going to lose, and here now, unarguably, though no less dreamlike, was Paris.

—Álvy, are you here?

Her calls turned the heads of the students on the neighbouring beds. None of the faces were friendly. Some appeared hostile to this foreign voice. Most, indifferent.

—My boyfriend? she said to them in French. The guy who was with me before? Has anyone seen him?

The students blinked, shrugged, turned away. The boy on the opposite bed resumed his strumming; the girl her singing; the surrounding heads their bobbing.

—Fuck you all, Eva murmured in English as she put on her boots.

She searched the whole building, the corridors on each floor and in every unlocked room, but sluggishly and with only half a heart. Part of her was furious that Álvaro had not returned, and she had every intention of admonishing him for it when they were reunited, yet another part of her, the larger part, was glad to be alone. Washing her face at the bathroom sinks, she looked into the mirror and said to herself, *What are we going to do now?*

She found the Action Committee in a classroom on the first floor. The bust of a classic French philosopher had been placed on the ground to keep the door open. Desks were arranged in a large square, around which a number of men sat.

Let me do the talking.

She introduced herself.

—English?

—London.

—Alone?

—I'm part of a performance group.

In order to prove she was not a *flic*, she gave the names of some people that Max had instructed her to give.

—Your French is all right. Any other languages, apart from English?

—A bit of Spanish.

—Chinese?

—No. But I admire Mao. I've read his work closely and believe it shows the real meaning of things behind what is apparent.

While the men murmured amongst themselves, she gave them some information about Wherehouse, its history, its manifesto. The atmosphere was so tense — a phone in the corner was ringing and no one seemed interested in answering it — and the men so evidently unimpressed, she could not help exaggerating the group's size and importance.

—Have you been to the Odéon?

—We've just come from there.

The man glanced through the open door to see if anyone else was waiting outside:

—We?

—The group and me.

—Wouldn't that be a more suitable base for you?

—We feel—

She fiddled with the rings on her fingers.

—we feel we'd contribute more here. At the Sorbonne.

Again the men leaned in: more murmuring.

—We're here to learn, comrades, she said. We want to understand how you run things, what your methods are, to see if they would work as effectively in England. Our aim is to use your flame to light the radical fires at home. The revolution won't spread on its own. It needs people to carry it, in their fists and in their minds. We intend to be that people. We intend to be the carriers.

At this point, sensing that the men were wavering, Álvaro would have produced his address book from his satchel. The book, which he kept in a second bag of its own, sown to size in purple silk, contained the names of hundreds of kindred spirits across the world: people who had stayed at Wherehouse, and their friends, and friends of those friends. One of Álvaro's pleasures was to put these spirits in touch with each other. *Look*, he would have said. *Look here. I have people in England. Holland. Germany. Spain. Latin America. Cuba. You know, Cuba?*

—Trust me, she said in his place. We have ideas. And contacts. Do you know Doris Lever?

The men shook their heads:

—Where is your group now?

—Waiting downstairs.

—Do you mind being split up?

She pictured Álvaro swiping through the pages of his book in search of names that might convince them.

—No.

They assigned her to the communications room of the Propaganda Committee, the location of which they circled on a duplicated map.

—Go alone. If the rest of your group want to get involved, they'll have to come here individually to be screened.

—I understand, she said, folding the map into her pocket. Cheers, boys. You won't regret it.

As she made her way outside, she vindicated herself to herself: *Looks like I'm in. They didn't put us all together, which is a pity. I tried to convince them, but personal relationships aren't grounds for special treatment. They send you where you're needed.*

The communications office was in a modern building on rue Censier. It had glass doors and conditioned air and closed-circuit television. In the foyer she stopped to examine a machine selling food in sterilised containers. Masking tape had been stuck over the coin slot and a poster pasted on the front:

DON'T BE CAPITALISM'S GUINEA PIG: USE THE CANTEEN
She obeyed the order.

In a big hall with concrete walls, she ate sausage rolls and drank orange juice and chatted with the people who shared her table. On learning that she was English, they were quick to express their disgust with De Gaulle and to ask her, in hopeful tones, about the Labour government in Britain: were things any better under them? She took pleasure in enlightening them. Her interlocutors enjoyed her candour and expressed appreciation for her insights. It was refreshing, they said, to encounter a foreigner with genuine revolutionary principles, for they had witnessed over the previous weeks an invasion by the cynical and the unbelieving: those who had merely come to see. They deemed her a different breed, and, as a reward, let her in on some of the things about France that outsiders tended not to know, and gave her advice on getting by here. Then, when she had finished eating, they conducted her to the lift and pressed the button for the relevant floor, the eighth.

—Victory for Vietnam, they said as the lift doors closed.

She raised a fist in return:

—Fight to win peace.

At the communications office she was welcomed by a woman in a mini skirt and high boots called Kati, who presented her to the rest of the team. Right away Eva was in no doubt that the office was run by agreeable people. They embraced her and inquired into her circumstances and, seeing her puffy eyes and chapped lips, gave her water and coffee and sticks of make-up for her own personal use. With almost excessive patience they explained to her the purpose of the office, the roles they themselves carried out — phone operator, filing clerk, typist, translator, transcriber, illustrator, printer — and the tasks that each role involved. Kindly they gave her some degree of freedom in choosing the work she would like to do. They were respectful, they were serious, they were stylish, they were well-meaning.

Be that as it may, she was obliged to feel sorry and not a little embarrassed for them. For at the end of the day they were all women. Not a single man amongst them. Which could only mean that the power resided elsewhere, in the auditoriums and the committee rooms below, and that here, stuck up in the attic, they were condemned to observe and react only. The secretaries, the shit-workers, the movement chicks who clocked in and out and were rung for — that was who they were, and she, to her own embarrassment now, was about to become one of them.

She chose to assist in the printing of posters. On a large central worktable, a woman stretched silk screens across wooden frames. A second traced the designs on. A third blocked the solids out with gum and coated the surface with varnish. A fourth used the wooden plank to drive the ink across the screen. A fifth lifted the frame and pulled out the freshly printed sheet. Eva's job, as the sixth, was to hang up the damp posters to dry. EVERY VIEW OF THINGS WHICH IS NOT STRANGE IS FALSE, said one. WE WANT COMMUNICATION, NOT TELECOMMUNICATION, another. Skulls in police helmets. De Gaulle as an assassin. Barbed wire across a television screen. The media as a bottle of poison: DO NOT SWALLOW!

Eva had previously been dismissive of this kind of work. Her sister Iris, after dropping out of art college, had worked for a while at the Poster Workshop in London, which Eva had teased her about. *What a waste of time*, she used to say. *Why make everything by hand when you can produce it en masse on an offset press?* The refusal of political artists to avail themselves of the most advanced technology was, in Eva's view, conservative, bourgeois, pointless. Iris's counterargument, that production for use rather than profit had to be based on handicraft, failed to convince Eva. A paintbrush could never be a match for a printer. Drawing a picture of a bomb was an indulgent luxury when every night the television screen showed hundreds of bombs dropping on peasant villages. The media ruled the world now, and only radical performance, because it was live, the meeting of body with body, would ever be able to mount a real challenge to it.

But after a couple of hours working at the silk screen, Eva wondered if perhaps her past judgements had been rash. She was beginning to see the attraction of materials and of craft. Of having in one's hands a single object, and of changing it simply by changing it, and of never rushing but rather seeing each step through. Iris had been right. It was satisfying. There was dignity in it. And no small amount of peace. In the place of the noise of machines, there was the hush of concentration, and the smell of linseed oil and ink and white spirit and cigarettes. Was this not how the people in China lived?

At around four o' clock, a group of men came in, members of the Student–Worker Liaison Committee, five in all.

—Here they are, whispered her neighbour at the worktable. The cocks.

—Pardon me? she said, surprised, for until now she had not heard any cross words spoken.

—The cocks, her neighbour repeated, flicking an eye to the men by the door. The strutting roosters. The ridiculous bastards.

The men were crowded round Kati's desk. They had drafted a short text, which they wanted typed up, illustrated and duplicated as a leaflet. Kati read it and handed it back.

—We don't just put any old thing into production, she said. What's your aim with this?

Visibly taken aback, unused to having to justify themselves, they passed the text around in order that each man in turn should check that this was not some inferior earlier draft, that indeed it was the version that they had agreed upon, before placing it down on the desk and smoothing it out in front of Kati once more.

—As the Student-Worker Liaison Committee—

The man who spoke was handsome enough for Eva to want to be noticed by him.

—our aim is to make contact and establish links with the proletariat. These leaflets, which you *will* produce, mademoiselle, will be distributed in the first instance to the striking workers at the Renault plant, and thereafter to any group of workers who share our general libertarian-revolutionary outlook. This text was drawn up in committee, following many hours of discussion, and subsequently submitted to general criticism. It has attained majority approval. Neither you nor anyone in this office has the authority to censor it.

Kati was not intimidated. She picked up the text between thumb and forefinger and shook it in the air while she calmly sketched out the process of printing a leaflet, the expense of it, the number of people it required, the time it took. Did the men honestly think this was worth spending so much of the revolution's limited resources on? Listening to her, Eva was confident that eventually Kati would accept the text. Her show of resistance was intended to make a point only: it was all well and good to spend your time in committees and public debates, but the real work was done here, behind the scenes, in offices like this, by women like us, toiling day and night, and it was about time that men like you — handsome, idle men — took notice.

The man rested his fingertips on Kati's desk and began to argue with her, rationally. She responded equally rationally. Eva's impulse was to intervene, but she held herself back.

—You're right, she whispered instead to her neighbour. Quite ridiculous.

At six, the men came back, more of them this time, to accompany the women to the demonstration. One or two of the women put on their jackets to go, but the majority did not move from their stations. Diligent, dedicated, they were forgoing the excitement of the march in favour of the relative quiet here, a decision they made not out of modesty, Eva thought, but rather in acknowledgement of their own importance.

—You coming?

The handsome man grinned at her.

She shook her head: no. She would stay.

She was kept on the silk screens until around midnight, at which point the focus of the activity in the office switched to reporting on the demonstration, and she was assigned to turning the handle on the printing press. The temperature in the room rose sharply as people rushed in with reports and missives to be typed, and rolls of film to be developed. Animated discussions took place about which line to take in the forthcoming bulletins. The phone rang and the wire rapped. Somehow spirits remained festive even as orders were shouted and bodies rushed about from one post to another. When things calmed down again at five a.m., she was sent off to get some sleep. When she returned soon after nine, the office was empty except for a couple of women in the back room manning the radios. She volunteered to take over from one of them and spent the rest of the morning transcribing the French transmissions from Radio Beijing.

This rhythm — busy nights at the worktables followed by quiet mornings at the radio — became her routine over the following days. She adapted swiftly and learned to enjoy herself in it. The people she came into contact with metamorphosed automatically into friends. They were for the most part of a plain and sensible sort, untheatrical, but she respected them because they did things well. They applied themselves to their work without a divided mind, and in their relations with each other they engaged neither in flattery nor in unkindness — an efficiency which sprang up when women had an industry and were left alone to organise it, and which was no different from love.

After four days — an eternity, the longest period she had been separated from the Wherehouse group since its establishment — Max appeared. Even in his French clothes and after years of foreign living, he looked red and Londonish. A pair of fashionable glasses did not fully conceal the white discs that encircled his eyes. The thinness of his limbs accentuated the fat which had collected at his stomach, bloating out from his bones like an oversized cyst. He came in accompanied by a Frenchman two decades his junior: thick-haired, unshaven, not unhandsome, evidently Max's boy because he had on a variation of the same thin silk scarf as Max, and was wearing it in the same mode, one end thrown loosely over the shoulder.

In his initial scan of the room, Max did not see her because she was concealed by a line of drying posters. He went to the desk to enquire and quickly got into an argument with Kati about whether or not he had the right to ask her who she was and what authority she held.

—Now it's the pederasts, whispered her neighbour. The tough men have given up on us, so they're sending in the fruitcakes.

The woman chuckled to herself and was still chuckling to herself when:

—Never mind, there she is!

Max broke away from his altercation and came over to Eva, embraced her.

—I knew I'd find you eventually.

Her cheek pressed against his, she glanced past Max's ear. Her neighbour was once again engrossed in her work, her face set in a bare expression which said: *I have not seen you, I have not heard you, what you do is your business.*

—What a ball breaker, Max said, referring to Kati. How in Christ have you been putting up with that?

—She's nice, Max, if you don't act the dickhead. And I've been enjoying it here actually.

—Really? Wouldn't have thought the typing pool was for you.

She took his arm and pulled him away from the worktable to the social space by the window.

—Not so bloody loud.

With an open palm, she invited him to sit down.

He looked at the dirty old sofa and laughed.

—Stop being such a little prefect, Eva. Trying to control everyone. It's a revolution, or haven't you noticed?

Max's boy, who had been perusing the posters on the walls, came to join them:

—Eva, isn't it? I'm Cyril.

—Cyril, Eva, said Max. Eva, Cyril.

—Enchanted, she said as they kissed.

Max took a photo of them.

—Not here, she said. Please.

—In that case, let's get out of here.

—To go where?

—Place de la Sorbonne. There's a special march planned. You can't miss it. Come. I'll explain on the way.

—No, Max. I can't. It's busy here.

—Shh-shh-shh—

Max pressed a finger against his own lips.

—I want you to listen to me now, Eva, okay?

His voice was curt and stern, insisting on compliance.

—The rest of your group, whatever you're called, are waiting at place de la Sorbonne. I'm going to meet them there at six, as I said I would. And you'll be coming with me. You and I both know that's what's going to happen, so let's drop the interim dramatics and just cut to the inevitable outcome, shall we?

—So you've seen them?

—Alain hosted an artists' meeting at his flat this morning, and I went upstairs to the room to invite you all down. It seems you haven't been sleeping in the room. Álvaro tells me you haven't been back there since you arrived.

She sighed.

—What're you playing at, Eva?

—None of your business, Max.

Max took off his glasses so that the solemnness of his grey eyes would travel to her unobstructed:

—And Iris? You left London without your sister.

—She wasn't around. We needed to leave. In your telegram you said to hurry.

—I've told you before, you undervalue your sister. Which is the same thing as mistreating her. All you see is a hippy, and you think hippies are—

—The new snobs.

—Right, which means you miss how interesting she is, and how capable actually, more capable, I'm absolutely positive, than any of the other little darlings in your groupuscule.

Cyril put a hand on Max's arm:

—Please, Max. Go softly.

She wanted to slap the boy, softly, about the face.

—I'll need to apologise to Iris when I get back, she said. I know that.

Max blew onto the lenses of his glasses and wiped them using the end of his shirt.

—And Álvaro? he said. You're going to lose him, you know. He's a good bloke, and you're going to chase him away.

—Max, said Cyril. Be soft, I said.

Max ignored him:

—This grouplet, they're your people, Eva. You handpicked them. You have a basic duty not to desert them.

—Please don't give me a lecture, all right? How are they?

—You mean what remains of them. Half of them have gone back to England.

—Shit.

Tension shot up her back and neck. She closed her eyes and rolled her shoulders.

—D'you blame them? D'you care?'

She paused. Then:

—Yes. I do care.

—Álvaro thinks you might've gone back to London too. I told him he was wrong. I knew you'd never bail out.

—Thank you.

—My guess was, after the stunt you pulled at the Odéon, you'd just want to be keeping a low profile.

—They told you about that?

—Yes. But the Odéon's not what Álvaro's angry about. He's angry you disappeared, obviously.

—Some of *that* is his fault. He left and didn't come back.

—Getting separated isn't the problem. He's angry, they all are, that you didn't rejoin them at Alain's room. That was your meeting place. They were waiting for you there.

She pictured all their bodies crushed into that room, gone stale and smelly with the days.

—Now it's time for you to make up with them, said Max. To salvage what's left of your collective.

Over the previous days she had thought constantly, and with a deepening sense of concern, about her people. Iris. Álvaro. The other Wherehouse members. *Where are they? What are they doing? Are they angry with me?* She had abandoned them, so they had reason to be. Yet she was angry with them too, and had her own reasons for being so, and for doing what she did. They might well be the abandoned ones, but she was the lost one — *is that not what everyone thinks?* — and it was not clear to her who was worse off.

Being lost was for her not a straightforward feeling, nor did it necessarily contradict the feeling of being home. She had grown up in the old servants' quarters above her grandparents' hotel in Bloomsbury. At that time her parents were struggling actors and could not afford a place of their own, and as long as they insisted on calling themselves communists, her grandparents would not pay for one. She had a false memory of wandering freely in the hotel, from guest room to guest room, gaining access to all kinds of human stories, when in reality she had been confined to a cramped flat and subject to a hundred rules about where she could go, what she could touch and what she could ask of the staff. And although she followed these rules obediently, still she never definitively figured out what was by rights hers and what was *for the paying guests only*, whether she should go up the principal staircase or the workers' ladder at the back, or if a given corridor was public or unfrequented.

After the hotel, there was a series of flats around London, and then, when her parents joined a travelling theatre troupe, a string of boarding houses and, for a time, a camper van, and, as before, a hundred rules designed to keep her — the child of parents who had themselves driven out of the mainstream — from going missing.

She was convinced that any problems she had came from that time. Her unhealthy desire to belong. Her fear of being in the wrong place or of not arriving at the right one. Her morbid fascination with the new. Her belief that the present could only be made tolerable by the future. A recurring nightmare she had saw her at risk of losing her part in a plan and compensating for that by making endless plans — which was precisely what she found herself doing when she was awake.

It was not until boarding school — insisted on and paid for by her grandparents — that, for the first time, she felt immersed in a flow whose course she did not want to swim against. There, on the Sussex coast, in the Victorian mansion and the surrounding grounds that they called Mountfield, everything was in tune with nature and God's command, and was leading to a pleasant conclusion: popularity, success, association.

The girls' dormitory was the first place she felt truly lost, that is, truly at home. There, her parents had no authority over her. She was outside the control of boys and men. There were many rules, but the teachers who policed them — by constant surveillance, including spying through peepholes — did so with the understanding that their own behaviour, as the only adults in this little realm, was also under inspection by the pupils and liable to be reported on in the larger world, so they were surprisingly generous in the amount of leeway they gave to the girls to mould and to adopt their own personalities.

The Mountfield girls — whom the office girls at the Sorbonne reminded her of — were used to a higher standard of comfort at home than she was. They thought the beds and the bathrooms and the classrooms were crummy; she found them quite pleasant. Having been well fed at regular meals, they were unaccustomed to feeling hungry, whereas she, whose mother never ate enough, had always been underfed, and so did not feel the bad food as much. With one side of herself she was ill at ease with the girls because they were so middle class and she did not want to accept them. But with another side she admired much of what she found in them. They were reserved but they were also rude, often in exactly the same moment. They were polite and courteous in manner but shot through with aggressive insolence. Puritan yet with their own kind of sex and style. Her plan was to ignore their contempt for foreigners and the working class, and their neurotic dread of poverty, and to work to bring them nearer to the type of middle class that she had decided to be: a player in the roaring, drinking, book-lined and magazine-discussing division; the people who knew what life was really for.

In this way she became popular. She learned, once a girl had shown an interest in friendship with her, to turn up her nose just enough, to be the right amount of superior. Then, while the girl was working to gain her approval, she turned on her charm, what the teachers called *character*, which in practice simply meant the power to impose her will.

Life at Mountfield was hierarchical in the sense that whatever happened was right, so she had to ensure that she decided what happened, even if it meant she sometimes had to be cruel. Leaving aside a couple of bitchy rivalries, on the whole her relationships, once they had settled into the right pattern, were cooperative and considerate, sometimes fascinating, always affectionate if never literally sexual. She and the girls helped each other, both in being good and in being errant, and together got a huge amount done. Without their favour, she would not have made house prefect, nor later school prefect, nor then member of the first fifteen. She adored them, they were her people, and she dreaded the thought of having to leave them.

The one thing that prevented her from entirely losing herself at Mountfield, and thereby making it her home, was Iris. To the same extent that Eva was welcomed and taken in, Iris was rebuffed and kept out. She was an alien in the halls. A visitor passing through. Around her there had hung an aura of otherworldliness; in her eyes a look that denoted a migration to another plane. Her demeanour was dejected. She was a being with its spirit subtracted. A weirdo. Sometimes, during a normal conversation, her eye would start to twitch, or her lips to smack. When called upon to speak in class, she would repeat the same phrase over and over, or say it backwards for no good reason. If she managed to form a friendship, she would then ruin it by lying. Her fabrications were so extravagant, so stunning in their lack of realism, that the girls found it impossible to get close to her, though their shunning of her was tempered by the suspicion that Iris herself could not determine where fact and fiction met. Worst of all, she wet the bed. The matron put plastic around her mattress but did not allow her sheets to be washed more regularly than the weekly standard. As a result, she went around smelling of piss.

Eva had a duty to defend her younger sister, to help her assimilate, to be with her so that she was not so much alone. But in truth Eva was as wary of Iris as everybody else. When the girls made wide, careful arcs around Iris in the halls, Eva followed their lead.

—That's your sister, isn't it? they would say.

—Unfortunately, Eva would say, striding onwards, not looking back.

At home Eva could tolerate Iris, but at Mountfield she found that she despised her. For Iris was holding her back, keeping her from getting properly in. Iris was a link to the chaos that was their parents' life. She had to be got rid of.

One morning the prefect from Iris's house woke Eva up to say that Iris had fallen out of bed, a common enough occurrence, only on this occasion there was blood on the sheets.

—I think she's had a nosebleed.

When Eva went there, she found Iris sitting in the bedside chair, dazed, her tongue swollen in her mouth, and with blood smeared around her chin and on her nightie, and on her pillowcase and on the sheets.

—What on earth have you done now, Iris?

Eva went closer to inspect her.

—That's not a nosebleed. You've gone and bitten your bloody tongue.

Iris looked blankly at her for a moment, then vomited down her front.

Eva and the prefect stood back so as not to get splashed. Turned away so as not to have to see.

—What'll we do? asked the prefect.

—Leave it to me, said Eva.

It would not be possible to hide the stains on the sheets, but a story could be invented to excuse them. Her first period, for instance. Ten was not too young for that. It would be difficult to explain how the blood ended up on her chest and on the pillowcase, but, with a little imagination, it could be made fly.

But in the end when Eva went to the teachers, she did not tell such a story. Rather she gave them the truth. Her sister had bitten her tongue in her sleep, she said, which could only mean one thing.

Once Iris was expelled — *Iris is a kind girl who, when she applies herself, does well, but she has become a risk to herself and others, a liability that the insurance won't cover, she'll have to be sent home and kept home* — everything at Mountfield that had not quite fitted Eva started to fit her. In this big world, there was home. Finally she could relax. She was alone with her people.

Wearily, Max rubbed a finger across the wrinkles at the corner of his eye. Examined the grains of dried mucus that had transferred to his fingertip. Brushed them away with his thumb.

—So?

An image of the handsome man's smile flashed in Eva's mind.

—I don't think I can go back to the group, she said. Not yet. Can't they do without me for a couple of days more?

Cyril tapped his watch, calling time.

Max nodded and put his glasses back on.

—Look, Eva, I get what you're doing. Don't think I don't. You got caught up in the events and you didn't want to sacrifice your experiences for the others. But you must see that once you start a thing, especially if you pose as its leader, you have to follow through.

—There aren't supposed to be any leaders.

—But there are, aren't there? And you're it, I'm afraid.

—Maybe I don't want to be.

Max waved a hand at her dismissively:

—Opff!

He paced to the window.

Eva and Cyril looked at him looking out at the rooftops.

—Every time I see you, he said without turning round, you get more like your mother, you know that? She was the same. Started wanting it both ways. *I'm in and I'm out. I'm top and I'm bottom. I'm rich and I'm communist. I'm West End and I'm radical.* But it's not possible, don't you see, Eva? Front or back, *avant* or *arrière*, you can't be in the two places at once, you have to make a choice. I used to say to your mother, *This won't always be your place, things change, but right now you have to understand where you are, and be there. If you don't—.* Well, Eva, you know what happens if you don't. Don't forget the lessons of—

—My parents' marriage?

—I was going to say your parents' theatre. But, now that you mention it, their marriage too. The games we play can so quickly and so easily fall apart.

Get lost, Max, she wanted to say. *Fuck off and leave me here where I'm happy. Tell Wherehouse to go their own way. Tell them they'd be better off without me.*

Instead she took her jacket off the hook, looked around the office sadly, thanked the women for having her, and followed Max out the door.

*

The march was to go from place de la Sorbonne to the Renault plant at Boulogne-Billancourt. What started as a strike at Renault had developed into a full-blown occupation. In the Latin Quarter discussions abounded about how best to support the Renault workers, and multiple propositions were drawn up, but no concerted action was taken. Finally, in response to a rumour that the *flics* were planning to smash the Renault occupation that evening, the Student-Worker Liaison Committee put out a call for an international brigade to go and relieve the strikers and if necessary fight alongside them.

—I don't know, said Eva as they made their way to the meeting point. Is our place really in the factories? Are we deceiving ourselves?

—Whatever do you mean? said Max. Aren't you supposed to be a Maoist?

—Yeah, I am, but—

—Isn't going into the factories what people like us should be doing, according to the man himself?

—It's hardly the same thing.

—Why not?

—Because this is Europe, isn't it? When the rich in China are sent to the factories, they stay in the factories! Their wealth is stripped from them and they become workers like everybody else. Change in China isn't superficial like it is here. It's systemic. Total.

Max was walking with an arm around Cyril's shoulder. Now he put his other arm around Eva, forming an advancing line which negotiated the busy path with difficulty.

—That may well be, Eva, but what's happening at the Renault plant *is* significant. For our lives here. In Europe. It would be a crime not to make contact.

—Right. I'm just not sure if it'll really change anything.

—You don't really think that, do you?

—I think maybe I do.

Álvaro and the three other remaining Wherehouse members were waiting by a shuttered kiosk outside Luxembourg station. Only the male members were there. None of the women had stayed, and

Eva did not blame them. This revolution, like every revolution before it, was men's play. To belong here meant being a man's woman.

On noticing Eva approach, shiftily the group muttered warnings to each other, and looked away.

—Hi, she said.

Half-turning, Álvaro's face, which spoke for them all, was cramped with rage.

—I know, said Max, stepping in, that you've some stuff to sort out. I've been speaking with Eva about it, and she has promised to explain herself and atone for her sins. But can I suggest we hold off until after the march, or at least until we're on our way? We're already late, the Renault factory is in the back of beyond, I've no idea how to get there, or which route they're going to take. I don't want to miss them or get lost.

Playing at indifference — sniffs and shrugs — the group set off at Max's pace. Álvaro stayed a step behind, Eva two steps behind him. Arriving at place de la Sorbonne, at the edge of the crowd, at last she found the courage to touch Álvaro's back.

—Hey, she said.

He recoiled. Swiped away her hand.

—Don't.

—Sorry.

—Save it. You know it's over.

She hesitated: did she know? Maybe she did.

—For good this time, he said.

—Oh Álvy, you always say that.

Detaching from her, Álvaro pushed into the mass of bodies, in pursuit of the white handkerchief that Max had raised over their heads, weaving its way to the centre. Reluctantly Eva followed the line that Álvaro carved.

The throng, which numbered a couple of thousand, was overwhelmingly male and overwhelmingly juvenile. One or two girls had been hoisted like mascots onto their boyfriends' shoulders. Amidst the dancing and saluting, there was the odd flash of a woman's

face. Erupting occasionally from the sea of nice haircuts, an adult man.
But the rest: all boys. Tender boys, nice boys, bad boys, wayward boys,
awestruck boys, terrified boys. Boys who wanted to forget about being
grown up. Maoist boys. Trotskyist boys. Anarchist boys. Libertarian
boys. Cliques of anything from two to twenty, swaying arm-in-arm.
Calling at each other across the square, or through the open windows.
Elated, but with anxious expressions. Loudspeakers boomed. *Action*
newssheets flew from hand to hand. Placards waved. Posters went up
and came down. And at the heart of it all were the boys chanting:

—Professors, you are old!

And:

—We exist! We are here!

And though it felt to them spontaneous, they did not for a
moment forget the audience for whom they were acting: the eyes of
their peers, the photographic lenses, the television cameras towards
which, naturally, they directed their spontaneity, reflexively aware of
the symbolic potential of each gesture they did not make as well as
each one that they did. Impressed by seriousness, warned against too
much laughter, on their lips lay unspoken questions.

It was the best-looking political occasion Eva could imagine
existing. It was like a golden age. Once she had seen it, she never
needed to see anything else. Gorgeous. Yet outside the frame, in the
sky above, the black clouds of nuclear apocalypse had not gone away,
and below, in her belly, she could feel a sort of shame at seeing herself
here: neither a student nor a traditional worker; too old to be the new
guard, too young to be the old; one of only a handful of women: was
this her place? She was a Maoist, so she knew how she was supposed
to look, what she was supposed to be doing, but, if she were to join
in, *If I were to do the chants and shake my fists, would it really be me
doing those things?*

Watching the back of Álvaro's head — a small disc of sallow skin
where the hair on his crown had prematurely begun to thin — she
thought about how often she had lain with her nose rubbing against
that head, smelling the oil and the musk and the almond from his

shampoo. Holding him from behind like that, a position which he said gave him comfort, they would talk for hours into the night. In their intimacy, they modelled themselves on high-powered French intellectuals. When speaking about art and literature and film, they were careful always to use a political lens. They understood that their lifestyle and their views placed them, in the eyes of most, on the left side of the left, yet they could not pinpoint *precisely* where on the spectrum they belonged, which was why they talked so much. They had not read any Lenin and had not got further with Marx than the *Manifesto*, but they did know their Mao; she made sure of that. They had learned from her parents' mistakes not to join the official Communist Party, or fall for anything the Russians said, though they did follow closely the pronouncements of the smaller political groups, the Maoist cells, and adopted any articulations that sounded about right for now.

Fixed, however, was their fury at the Labour government in Britain for its refusal to implement any socialist policies and for its support of America's war in Vietnam. They dreamed of opportunities to give vent to this feeling, and to turn it to good use, which was what Wherehouse was all about. Yet now that they were part of this great happening, in France of all places, they felt disappointed. At least she did, and she imagined Álvaro would be feeling similarly. They could not blame the revolution itself for this. It was bigger and more beautiful than anything they could have wished for. It could only be that they were disappointed with themselves, with each other.

Are we really who we think we are?

After a short speech about the Renault occupation given by a man standing on a box and roaring into a megaphone, the crowd moved off, funnelling into a stream as they crossed boulevard Saint-Michel onto rue Vaugirard. They walked behind a single banner prepared by a Maoist faction:

THE STRONG HANDS OF THE WORKING CLASS MUST NOW TAKE OVER THE TORCH FROM THE FRAGILE HANDS OF THE STUDENTS

When they passed in front of the occupied Odéon, several

hundred more joined, eliciting loud applause.

—The streets are ours! Come with us to Renault! they cried at the onlookers as they proceeded down Vaugirard towards the working districts of the south-west.

Eva felt alone in the carnival. Deliberately she walked at a distance from Álvaro and the others, though she made sure not to lose sight of them. To those marchers who approached her, offered her fags, flirted with her, tried to sell her *Humanité Nouvelle*, she responded politely but firmly:

—No, thank you.

Every so often Max dropped back and said something like:

—Do you see the man there with the nose? No, don't look now! That's the film director Guy Ernaux. He has some cheek being here, with the kind of films he makes.

By the time they had marched the seven kilometres to Issy-les-Moulineaux it was already dusk. They went through poorly lit streets, avoiding the mountains of uncollected rubbish, covering their noses against the smell, calling to the people who congregated in the doors of the bistros, singing with added vigour to the Algerians who lined the path.

—Long live the Algerian Liberation Front! the Maoists shouted.

The Arabs watched apprehensively, some smiling or nodding in an embarrassed way. None joined in.

The marchers crossed the Seine, and as they approached the square beyond which lay the Renault plant, their hearts were pounding like doubled-up fists. Eva was not immune to the excitement; even in her solitude, slowly it had infected her. Duly she did some cheering, and sang, and sometimes called out incoherently because it felt good to do so.

Parked across the square, obstructing the way, was a lorry fitted with a loudspeaker. On top stood a Communist Party official.

—Thank you for coming, comrades, he was saying into his brand-new microphone. We appreciate your solidarity. But please no provocations. Don't go too near the factory gate. If the police come, do not antagonise them. And go home soon. You'll need all your strength in the days to come.

Taunting and jeering the man, drowning out his words with bursts of the 'Internationale', the marchers moved past the lorry, flowing around each of its sides.

—Fuck Stalin! a man near Eva shouted as they passed.

Eva liked that. She laughed and clapped and joined in for a round of:

—Fuck Soviet repression! Long live Chairman Mao!

Reaching the factory entrance, the marchers banged on the metal fence and shook the chains that kept the gate bolted. From the outside, two buildings were visible: three storeys on the left, two storeys on the right. Lights were on in the taller building. Groups of workers could be seen moving about in the windows and on the roof. Some were sitting on the sills with their legs dangling over.

—Factories to the workers, the marchers shouted, raising their clenched fists.

The workers began to wave and shout in response.

Ten, twenty times the slogan reverberated around the square, and when finally it died out, a huge cheer arose, for contact had been made.

A number of workers came to the fence to talk. Using Max's camera, Álvaro took photos of the students as they passed bottles of beer and fags and copies of *Servir le peuple* through the bars. Eva was happy to see him engaged in this task. She thought he looked attractive doing it and felt a bit less sorry for him.

The marchers asked the workers about what the men inside needed most, and how they could help. They wondered why the gates were locked when at the Sorbonne the doors were always kept open, to everyone. Would the workers allow a student contingent to enter? The workers refused, saying the machines had to be protected. The marchers insisted, saying that a few students, escorted by the strike committee, could not possibly damage anything. The workers, hesitant, agreed to put the idea to the occupation leaders.

Keeping an ear on these discussions, Eva turned her attention to the shorter building to the right, which was in darkness. The lamps on the factory grounds had been kicked out or smashed in order to hinder a police raid, so things were hard to make out, but what looked like two large screens had been hung on the front of the building, and a structure of some kind had been built onto the roof. Dark figures could be seen moving about here and there.

—What's that? she said.

—A surprise, Max said.

She looked at him:

—What kind of surprise? Let me guess, something to do with Doris.

He put a finger to his lips:

—Shh. Just wait and see.

Max had lost all his hair on top. What remained on the sides he had grown long and brushed into an S-shape that went over his ears and curled upwards midway down the neck. To Eva it was as if he had aged before his time. A Peter Pan whose accumulated years had been added suddenly. Perhaps he appeared this way to her because, seeing him now — upright, dignified, standing abreast of boys half his age and shouting slogans of which he would once have profoundly disapproved as a Party member — he could not but represent the incompatibility of the old and the new generations of the left. In his interactions with the younger militants, Max went out of his way to demonstrate that not all socialists from the preceding generations were hostile to them. He, for one, claimed to be on board with the counterculture and its war against a corrupt technology which was enslaving people in a cycle of production and consumption. He had left behind that old brand of left politics which fully accepted the principle of more consumer goods for everyone, and the deadening assembly line which produced them. Unlike most of his former Party comrades, he no longer believed that the existence of elites was a fact of life. He was one of the few of the old guard who carried a book of Mao's *Sayings* and publicly called for the outright victory of the Vietcong, rather than just expressing a wishy-washy desire for a peace accord.

But — it did not go unnoticed by her — his views betrayed a deeper conviction. Which was that Europe since the war was the land of the blessed. Which meant that if Europeans were unhappy, it was just that they had not yet realised their good fortune. A region without conflict, a level of comfort, a range of choices and a degree of social security beyond the reach of all but the wealthiest in previous epochs: Max quietly believed that, for as long as this situation lasted, major social upheaval would not be on Europe's agenda. Behind the mass demonstrations, however impressive, there would not be revolution.

—Max? Why don't you ever work with Wherehouse like you work with Doris?

—Wherehouse doesn't need me, Max said. You're doing fine on your own.

—So Doris needs you?

As Doris's collaborator, Max spent most of his time scouring Europe for places — galleries, squares, trains, public toilets — for Doris to mount her performances in.

—Doris doesn't need anyone. It just so happens that we see eye to eye, artistically, and work well together. It's just the way it's worked out.

—But why, whenever we've asked Doris to work with us, has she refused?

—I can't tell you why. She makes her own decisions.

—I'm sure if you told her it was a good idea to collaborate with us, she'd do it.

To warm himself, Max crossed his scarf over his breastplate, and wrapped the lapels of his jacket over it. He put an arm around Cyril's waist and tried to pull him closer. Blushing, Cyril batted him away. Max stuffed the rejected hand into his pocket.

—To be honest, Eva, you exaggerate my influence over Doris. She has her own mind. She's the artist, I'm just her, what would you call me?

—Mentor?

—I wouldn't go that far. I'm closer to being her helper.

—But she listens to you.

—Not in everything. She discards as much as she takes on.

—Do you think it's a good idea? A collaboration?

Max was keeping an eye on Álvaro, who was standing with his back to the railings and taking pictures of the tumult.

—I hope your boyfriend is looking after my camera.

She poked Max in the ribs:

—You didn't answer my question.

He put an arm around her. Kissed her on the side of the head.

—Dear Eva. You are a sweet one.

—Max!

—What Wherehouse does and what Doris does are different. Groups aren't Doris's bag, and to be honest they're not really mine any more.

—That's a pity. And a bit unfair if you ask me.

—There's nothing unfair about it. If something doesn't happen it's because it isn't meant to be. You can't force people to be in your gang. I thought you hated Doris anyway.

Eva watched Álvaro turn his lens on the other Wherehouse members, who turned their backs so as not to be captured.

—I'm not a kid any more. The days of hating Doris are long gone.

Max showed her a sincere smile.

—I'm glad to hear you say that, Eva. Your parents' theatre, those days, they were messy, undeniably so. It can't have been easy for you. Doris has to take responsibility for her part in what happened. And I think she does, honestly. But remember Doris was young then too. Basically still a child like you and your sister. If you can learn to meet Doris today not just as—

—The Cockney Whore?

—Right. If you can get past that and meet her as a person in her own right, a contemporary, one of your peers, you'll see what a fascinating person she is. And how talented.

—I've tried to make contact with her. Numerous times.

—Through your father? I imagine he's banned her from going near you.

—She doesn't return my calls. When I go to see Papa, she leaves the flat, or goes to another room.

—I'll talk to Paul. It's probably his fault. Left to her own devices, I doubt Doris would have any qualms about meeting with you.

The first time Eva had met Doris was in fifty-six. At Victoria Station on a Saturday morning in late July, the day she returned from boarding school for the summer vac. She was not looking forward to coming home, if indeed home was what any sane person would call what she was returning to. She had received letters from her mother telling her what to expect. A factory in Somers Town. A boarding house for drunks. Her family and an ensemble of actors living together under one leaking roof. The East Wind theatre, they were calling it. She destroyed the letters and dared not tell any of her friends, not even to prove to them how *crazy* her family truly were — *no wonder her sister had problems!* — for she had already decided to hate her new home, and, as soon as she saw it, to demand that she be sent to stay with her grandparents in their new house in the suburbs: the suburbs whose bare mention made her parents apoplectic.

She got off the train and dragged her own suitcase down the steps behind her, *thunk, thunk, thunk.* She left the suitcase on the concrete where it landed and looked up and down the platform's length. The crowd around her shifted, then began to move; at first as separate little cells, now as a single unit. She stayed where she was, facing the back of the train, her body open to the stream of people — the other Mountfield girls marked out from the rest by their bright-blue blazers — coming towards her; going past her. She perceived as a physical sensation their vast reserves of indifference: it was like cold water running over her skin.

She made the long journey to the turnstiles in a state of dread of the inevitable. In the station hall she could not see her family anywhere: not her parents, not her uncle Simon, not Max, no one. She walked in little circles, peering about; her suitcase scratched the ground as she went around. It did not occur to her to read the signs with names written in large print that the cabbies and the chauffeurs were holding up; these signs were not intended for her — she was a Mountfield girl but not *that* sort of Mountfield girl — so they were invisible to her. It was not until someone tapped her on the shoulder:

—You ain't Eva, is you?

that she became conscious of the letters E-V-A-T-H-U-R-L-O-W drawn in thick black lines across a square of brown cardboard, and a woman, a girl really, waving it up and down, in order to draw her attention to it.

—I *thought* it might be you, you look just like your mum, d'you know that? I's Doris, your dad's assistant at the theatre.

Eva had closed her eyes and turned away a little, so as to conceal what might be showing on her face. Opening again and turning back, she realised she had noticed Doris before, as she was coming up the platform; a number of times her gaze had been drawn to her, and now that she was close up, she could see that Doris was beautiful. From afar, she had not promised to be; from over there, her lustre had been wrapped in shadows, which made Eva think how unjust it was that fair hair was preferred to dark, for it drew us to a dull thing called beauty and blinded us to the brighter thing that lay far down. Black, jet black, Doris's was, and cut into a fringe that sat just above her eyebrows. Dark lines underscored her eyes, making them look unslept. Her nose was prominent, with the slightest of ripples. She was not wearing any ornaments but she was wearing make-up, too much of it, which was a pity because she did not need it. Perhaps she was unaware of her looks; perhaps she refused to believe in them. Eva thought she probably lacked a woman in her life to advise her.

—Your mum and dad told me to tell you they's sorry they couldn't come themselves. They's in rehearsals all day today.

She was a Cockney, and one of her front teeth protruded so that her sibilants came with a lisp. This touched Eva, and aroused, also, a swelling up of indignation and hatred.

—Don't take it personal, yeah? They just couldn't get away.

Despite the pressure of her feelings, Eva managed a casual shrug that said, *I don't care who picks me up. I'd have been just as happy to make my own way back.*

—How are we getting there? she said. A cab? I'm not getting the bus.

Doris picked up the suitcase and made a mime for how heavy it was.

—Don't you worry, I's driving. This way.

Doris conducted her out of the station. Eva kept herself a pace behind and examined the movement of Doris's buttocks underneath her light summer skirt and the small muscular changes that took place on her bare calves as she walked. Over the years Eva had witnessed her father in the company of a number of different girls. In her memory were glimpses of him getting out of taxis with them, or passing through rooms, or going through doors, his hand on their elbow, his lips close to their ear. At parties and pubs, in foyers and dressing rooms, he would accidentally touch them with his feet and his hair and his sleeve and even his lap, which would generate responses in them — laughter, blushes, gentle digs, *Behave!* — to which he then pretended to be oblivious. From a young age she was aware, without ever being told, that these were her father's girlfriends. Instinctively she knew her duty was to hate them. Yet hers had been an abstract kind of hate, something on which she had not been able to get a full grip, for she had never been introduced to the girls, she did not know where they came from or what they were like, they were ghosts, blurred and weightless, wafting out of her vision as quickly as they had wafted in; when they disappeared, always her hope was that they would not be coming back, and they never did. Now, though, she had a clear face to hate, and that face was beautiful, and coming from it was a voice that was simple and strong and natural, and what it seemed to be saying was, *Your papa has given me a job so I'll be sticking around for a while, whether you like it or not.* She felt a rush of painful emotions that must have been what hating in the concrete was like; more complicated than could ever be anticipated, and more overpowering.

Doris took them onto Lower Belgrave Street where, parked

parallel to the path, dwarfed by the cars on either side, was an orange Messerschmitt.

—Is this it? said Eva.

—It ain't a Jag, said Doris, but it saves on the petrol.

—Nope, uh-uh.

—What's the difference as long as it goes?

—The difference is, I'm not getting into it.

Doris lifted open the roof and gestured to her to get into the back.

Eva stuck her tongue deep into her cheek and looked up and down the road. It was as if her parents *wanted* to humiliate her. Sighing loudly, then making a spectacle of sucking in her belly, she climbed in. The cramped space obliged her to sit in such a way that her skirt rode up her thighs and her knees almost touched the seat in front: it was mortifying.

Doris lifted Eva's suitcase onto her lap. Climbed into the driver's seat.

—Ready?

With the roof closed over, Eva kept her head bent sideways even though there was no real danger of banging it. When they started moving, Doris told her to be careful how she sat: too much to one side and the car would tip. In that moment Eva thought she would like to be dead.

As an extra torture, images came to her of how thrilled her father would be to be seen being driven around in such a contraption. What was shaming for another man would be delightful for him; he would revel in the attention. She pictured him sticking his hand out the tiny window to give pedestrians an aristocratic wave: *Yoo-hoo! So long, chums!*

—Mama can drive, Eva said to Doris now, but Papa can't.

—Yeah, I know, said Doris. He'll have to learn one day.

Then after a minute of silence she said:

—It's only recent that me own old man has started to allow me to drive this thing. With me job at The East Wind, the late hours and that, he thought it were safer for me to have it. *You want it, you have it,* he said. Before, though, he'd only ever take me out on the weekends, give me a few minutes at the wheel, then wash it and put it back in the garage. Men and their cars, eh?

Eva listened to this with her arms folded across the top of the suitcase and her face towards the window:

—Huh, she said. Well, Mama drove a van during the war. That's how she knows how.

—So I believe, said Doris. She's something, i'nt she? your mum.

—Huh, said Eva again.

The Messerschmitt was like an oven. Doris put the window down to get some air inside. In the breeze, moisture that had brimmed threateningly at Eva's hairline duly began to trickle down.

—Eva, darlin', said Doris, is there something lying by your feet, can you see?

Keeping her right hand on the steering bar, Doris used her left to rummage blindly through her bag, then to feel around the floor.

—Me dad keeps a pair of shaded specs here somewhere. Can you see them, love? The light is bloody merciless.

Eva did not move to help her. Noting this with a sigh, Doris gave up her search and turned her attention to a matter more immediately tractable: an itch on her neck where her collar was chafing. She leaned forward, arched her back, and with a clumsy shrug liberated her shoulders of her cardigan. The blouse she was wearing underneath was sleeveless, allowing the rubber of the seat cover to scorch her skin.

—Ay, filthy fuck, she said.

—What's wrong? said Eva, who was getting nervous.

—Nothing, she said.

Then:

—Swine, you! to the 513 to Holborn Circus which had taken advantage of her fluster to pull out in front, causing her to swerve.

A stop light at the junction of Pentonville Road and King's Cross gave Doris a chance to collect herself. Eva watched her examine herself in the visor mirror: the discs of rouge blended high onto the cheekbones were resisting well, but the lines cleverly drawn some distance from the eyes were now blurred at the edges. Doris licked a finger and ran it beneath, labouring with rising aggression at the spots that would not rub out. Reciting quiet apologies to her father, she wiped her blackened finger on the side of the seat.

—Oof, I hate make-up, she said, don't you? It makes me feel dirty. Does nothing for me except have me wanting a good clean. Once it's on I can't forget it's on, d'you know what I mean? It's there, on me, like a greasy cloth over my face, and all I's doing is waiting for the time to cream it off.

But Eva's father would have insisted. *Well, you needn't imagine you're going to go without, Doris*, he would have said. *Not while you're working for us. No, no, you must make a bit of an effort. No need to slap it on or anything, that's not what I'm saying. Just a stroke here* — he would have run a finger along her cheek — *and maybe here* — her temples — *and here* — her lips — *to demonstrate that you're conscious of yourself, that's all, and that you're willing to prove your worth.*

A horn blast from the black Alvis in the queue behind jolted Doris out of her mirror-reverie and into the performance of those gestures, precise and brutal, that machines

—This fucking machine!

demanded of their operators: plenty of revving before the brake came off; full throttle and straight into third to clear King's Cross and join Euston Road; fourth gear then and fairly zipping — Eva closed her eyes and unconsciously began to talk to her God — until they were caught by another light on the western corner of St Pancras Station as they prepared to turn right onto Midland Road.

As they braked, Eva was thrown so far forwards that she nearly knocked the front of her head against the back of Doris's.

—Oh balls it, Doris said.

She drummed out her impatience onto the dashboard, jigging her legs so wildly that her knees knocked.

—Hot, innit?

She stretched her neck out of the open window and sucked in what she could.

—Ugh, said Eva. Yuck.

—You know what, said Doris, you's right, and yanked the window shut.

Behind glass now, yet all too palpable still: the city. Given up to heat and welter, and to flies that refused to be waved away, and to a thirst that could not be quenched. The rise in temperature had not been sudden. Little by little, over the course of days, the light had brightened and the winds had warmed, as the forecasts had promised, yet the change, now fully experienced, took Eva by surprise. Life at Mountfield was built on routine and dates and timetables, yet everything passed so quickly — every day a thousand miles covered, life rolling on at the rate of a tempest — that the slow world of winter followed by spring followed by summer got passed over and forgotten. Yet now on Euston Road, in her father's girl's car, the real rate of things returned to her consciousness. Summer and sky and brick and stone, they were not going to change for her. Nor was her life going to become another's simply because she was willing it to. Nor indeed was time going to stop so that she could be in two places at once: both here and anywhere but here.

When finally given way, they swung at full tilt onto Midland Road, scattering the gang of boys who had spread themselves in a loose line across the street in order to taunt them:

—Oi, missus! Come on then! Hit us with your hairdryer!

With a clear road ahead, Doris pressed the pedal to the floor, and they flew through the long shadows cast by the station, under the bridge, past the coal depot and into the terraces of Somers Town, where they soon got lost.

Doris slowed the car to a crawl and squinted about.

—Sorry about this, she said. I's still finding me way.

She asked directions from a band of young men who were hanging around at the entrance to an alley. Once they had finished laughing and whistling, they, all five of them, accompanied the car by running alongside and banging on the roof when it was time to turn. Eva sank down into her shirt collar and hid her face behind a hand.

Scaffolding covered two-thirds of The East Wind façade. Men in helmets and overalls moved among the forest of metal poles, with the largest number congregated on the first level, drilling long panels of red plastic onto a metal frame to make a canopy above the main door. Home, it seemed, was a building site.

Doris jammed on the brakes, lifted open the roof of the car and stood up inside it.

—Oi! she called up to them. Simon! You up there?

—Jesus H Christ, Eva whispered to herself.

The young men from the courts, their cortège, stood around, watching, wanting to know what their business was. Doris did not send them away, and Eva would have been afraid to.

—Over here, Simon. Yeah, hi!

The drills stopped. The workmen turned to look. Simon stood up from kneeling and came to the edge of the wooden plank. To Eva he was recognisable from the manner in which his appearance diverged from her father's. A nose that spread sideways rather than pointing out. A cleft chin instead of one that slackened. In the place of fleshy pouches, sad valleys running down his cheeks. He was wearing jeans and a vest, which she could not imagine her father in, and had a hefty, built-up frame, one simultaneously enhanced and undermined by his war injuries: his left arm severed at the elbow, an intricate web of scars on his neck and shoulders.

—Doris? he said. And look who it is! Eva's back!

Unlike her father, Simon had retained his Yorkshire accent, which Eva thought he played up a bit too much.

He waved his stump:

—Back for the vac already, is it?

She flashed a hand, then quickly hid it away.

—Yeah, Uncle Si, hi.

—Simon, said Doris, can you do us a favour and open the warehouse door?

—All right, he said. But—

He drew a circle in the air around the King's Cross boys.

—who are your friends here?

—These fine gents showed us the way.

He used the drill bit to push his helmet a little further back on his head.

—Yeah? Well, the gents will have to wait outside.

He gave his drill to one of the other workers and passed on some quiet orders. Came down the ladder two steps at a time, his stump running down the outside rail to keep his balance. Once on the ground he took his helmet off. A tuft of brown curls sprang upwards, which he rubbed with his palm in a quick circular motion.

—That's it, boys, he said, approaching the King's Cross posse. Show's over.

When he walked, he landed more heavily on one foot than the other, as though his body were no longer at one with his will.

—I'll take them from here.

—Thanks, fellas, Doris said. You's have been a smashing help.

The young men shuffled about but did not retreat. Accidental witnesses to an uncertain scene, they nevertheless felt entangled in it, and thus obliged to accumulate their impressions, lest they be called upon for them in the future.

With a jerk of his head, Simon told Doris to follow him. She drove behind him in first gear into a lane that ran between the factory building and a piece of wasteland next door. Scaffolding overhead gave the effect of a tunnel. Doris turned on the headlamps. Ahead, it was as though Simon were emitting his own light; his strange contours appeared precise and sharp and close by. Eva did not like when her father expressed pity for Simon, she thought it a terrible emotion to feel for one's brother, yet it was what she felt for him now. She challenged herself to feel something else. What materialised was a mounting sentiment of revulsion.

They came out into a courtyard bounded by the rear walls of the factory, the wasteland hoarding and the backs of two terraces. Simon guided her past a bank of skips and crates to a wide metal shutter, which, roughly but also with remarkable dexterity, he unlocked and pulled up. He went in and turned on a light, beckoned her to follow.

—Easy does it! Valuable stuff in here.

Scattered about inside were more crates, along with various cardboard boxes and tin trunks and empty costume rails. Leaning against the walls: flat wedges of scenery, and lengths of plastic and Essex board. From racks of steel piping, lanterns hung, their gaze lowered, extinguished.

—Put yourself in there, he said, pointing to a space between a fake fireplace and an old sofa.

There was enough room for the car, but not to open the roof all of the way, which made it difficult to get out. Simon had to hold the top while they squeezed themselves, one leg at a time, through a narrow gap.

Simon took Eva's suitcase.

—Come on. I'll bring this in for you.

They followed him through a low door, down a dark corridor, up a flight of steps, and finally into a large, high-ceilinged room with bare brick walls and a mezzanine. Doris ran straight up the mezzanine stairs and disappeared into the third of the five doors. Simon conducted Eva over to a bar that had been newly built along the back wall. He dusted off the only stool.

—Sit. And don't touch anything.

She watched him, now, ascend the stairs and disappear through the same door. When the door opened, voices rushed out; when it closed, the sounds became muffled.

A matter of seconds and Simon was coming back down.

—I've told them you're here, he said. Good luck. We'll catch up later, yeah? All good at the school?

She nodded.

—Glad to hear it.

He left by the same door they had entered.

Alone, she sat in a profound silence. The sound of drilling outside encased the room and made it seem even larger than it was, and overwhelmingly quiet. She had expected lots of people to be here, a community of actors filling all of the spaces and being annoying, so to find herself on her own instead, in this vast empty room, cold and damp in spite of the weather, well, *that* was annoying.

—Eva?

Her mother was leaning on the mezzanine rails and staring down at her.

—You got home all right?

Her mother's voice sounded unreal after such loud thoughts in such a silent place. A clean blade of sound in the air. No echo. Nothing wasted. The actress.

—Mama?

Her mother closed her fingers over twice in quick succession, as if clapping with a single hand.

—Up you come, darling.

As she climbed the stairs, the blood in her body drained slowly downwards; her head grew lighter and her feet heavier with every step. When she reached the top, her mother said:

—This way.

And disappeared through the door, leaving it ajar behind her.

With hands that were icy and perspiring at the same time, Eva knocked.

—Oh, do come in, Eva, for goodness sake.

The rehearsal studio, into which she now soundlessly passed, was a large rectangular room, one wall of which was almost entirely taken up by windows, which magnified the sun and made it hard to make anything out at first. Once she had adjusted, she saw temporary markings in yellow tape on the floor. Judging from the shine and the smell of varnish that hung about, the boards had been recently sanded. Chairs were arranged around the walls and a large noticeboard had been hung up, and various notes and sketches pinned to it. In one corner was a rail of clothing and a box of props; in another, a refreshment table. To the right side, looking across the acting space towards the window, was the director's table, on top of which sat several ashtrays and a clock and a roll of coins and foolscap pads and pens, and behind which sat her father and Max and, in between, Doris. Opposite this, against the wall by the window, was an upright piano, whose low stool was occupied by her sister, Iris. Her mother was standing on one foot beside Iris: her arm outstretched, a hand gripping the corner of the piano's top board, her left foot held in her left hand and pulled behind her in order to stretch out the muscles of her thighs.

In the centre of the room, a masked actor was standing on a chair. Kneeling on the floor in front of him was a second actor, a grown adult man, wearing a brightly coloured silk shift over his civvies and a pair of heeled shoes strapped over his socks. The masked actor was declaiming a sort of poetry; his supplicant was emitting a sort of whimpering. The rest of the ensemble — about twelve or thirteen others, the women dressed in light shift dresses and short-sleeved blouses, the men with their trousers rolled up and handkerchiefs tied around their heads and ovals of sweat under their arms — were scattered around in various postures of observation; a number of them had lifted masks off their faces and had them sitting on top of their heads. After glancing at Eva when she came in, they did their best to disregard her, but she had already infected the atmosphere. A second then and the actors fell out of the roles. A collective moan was released.

Too enthusiastically, she said:

—Hi!

Everyone turned to take her in, properly this time. What did they see? In comparison to them, even after her journey in the heat, she was tidy and ironed and well arranged. Her blazer had not been unbuttoned at the front, nor had her tie been loosened. Her socks were staying up at her knee and had no wrinkles. Her loafers had little by way of marks or scuffing. The only disturbance, which Eva had noticed while staring at her own reflection in the car window, was some frizz in her hair which formed a delicate crown of light around her head.

—You're here! her father said.

Purposely not rushing, he pushed his pen into the central fold between the pages of his script and dropped it — *slap!* — onto the floor beside him. He got up. Yawned. Arched his back. Ran a hand down the front of his trousers to smooth them. All of which delayed him in saying:

—Everyone, this is my elder daughter, Eva.

The group murmured.

—Sorry, said Eva. I don't mean to cut in.

—No, darling, said her father. We're glad to see you.

—Oh? So what's all this then?

On *this*, Eva cocked her head towards Doris.

Doris shifted in her chair.

Eva's father wrapped his arms around his body, embracing himself.

Her mother finished her stretching by dropping her leg and shaking it out:

—Welcome to your new home, my love.

—Some welcome.

Her mother was dressed entirely in grey, not that of drabness but of carefully adopted simplicity. Her silk blouse was collarless and had a loose body that hung low over a tight pair of slacks. She wore no jewellery except for a silver wristwatch and a slim wedding ring. A band kept her hair pulled remorselessly back. The effect was to exhibit the full, difficult shape of her face.

—Come here, darling, and sit with your sister by the piano.

Eva did not move, so her mother went to her. Pecked her just beside the mouth. Eva tilted her head to one side. Rolled her shoulder across her cheek to wipe it.

—Please, she said. You don't have to.

Her mother stood in front of her and scanned her down. Eva squinted away her mother's scrutiny.

—What, Mama?

—I'm just looking at you.

—Well, don't.

Her mother hated — and Eva *loved* that she hated — that other people were raising her child. Her mother hated, too, that her parents, Eva's grandparents, were paying the fees; hated that they had made boarding school for the children a condition of their financial investment in The East Wind theatre, as if they were buying Eva and Iris passage from an unsafe environment. But more than anything, her mother hated that Eva liked boarding school. That she thrived on all of the rules.

—Mama, you're crowding me.

Eva stepped round her mother as if round a bothersome obstacle.

—Pickle, her father said, we must have a party to celebrate your return.

—Oh Papa, let's not.

—Do you like the place? he said.

She shrugged:

—It's all right.

—Nearly there, eh?

—Is it?

Max intervened:

—Look, Eva, it's my fault. You can blame me. Your mother was on the way out to get you, but I insisted she stay and work on this silly play of mine. I'll make it up to you, if you promise not to hate me.

—I was *lit-er-ally* the only girl not met.

Her mother laughed:

—Honestly, I doubt that.

—The only one. Orphan bloody Annie.

Eva turned to Doris for backing. Doris looked at the floor. Eva dismissed her with a swipe of her hand, and turned back to her public:

—Though, of course, I half-expected it.

—It was good of Doris to go when we asked, said her mother. You should thank her, Eva.

Eva took hold of her skirt and, as if a gown, swished it across her thighs, and in an accent taken from the American pictures said:

—Thanking you kindly, *Daw-ris*.

As she grew into the room, her sister shrank even further back. Which made it easy for Eva to leave her unnoticed.

—Aren't you going to say hello to Iris? her mother said.

Eva turned, as if under duress, in the direction of the piano. Seeing Iris as she was, slouched forwards, a bruise on her face, her hair unbrushed, her clothes not quite clean, Eva felt a kind of shame. And also a sharp stab of envy.

—Hi, Eva said.

Iris lifted her eyebrows briefly in response.

Alissa tried again to usher Eva over to the piano, this time by taking her arm.

—Unfortunately, Simon is busy with the building work today, so he can't look after you. You'll have to sit here with Iris and be quiet. And I mean, *quiet*. We'll have lots of time to catch up at supper. I bought a cake.

—Hang on. You want me to sit there and mind Iris? Is this what you expect me to spend my summer doing? *Bay-be-sittin*?

Eva shook off her mother's hold. Glowering in mock seriousness, she sauntered through the acting space and wove her way through the actors. She looked over the shoulders of those seated to read what was written on their scripts.

—Eva, said her mother, don't be a pain.

Eva picked up a spare script from the table.

—May I, sir? she said to her father.

—Go on, you goose, he said.

—Put that down, said her mother. I'm sorry about this everyone. It won't be like this all summer. We'll find an arrangement that works.

—Look, just ignore her, okay? said her father. Eva, sit where you like. Let's get back to work. We're wasting time with all of this.

Eva flopped onto her father's chair and opened the script.

—As the man says, she said, time is *moan-ay*.

Her father took up his own script from the floor and put it under his arm. Then he cast around for a place to put himself. Eva did not move, nor did her father ask her to. He went to lean against the back wall. Raised his hands and held them frozen a few inches apart. Once everyone had settled, he clapped them together.

—All right, let's move on to scene four. That's you, Alissa. You must know these lines by now, so try without the script. From the top.

The play they were rehearsing obviously had a Chinese theme, for the things pinned onto the noticeboard all related to China. Pages of Chinese calligraphy. Photographs of Chinese cities and Chinese communes and Chinese opera. Posters of Chinese propaganda. On the table was a pile of anthologies of Chinese poetry and Laozi and Confucius, and a book on whose spine a single word was printed: MAO.

Eva turned the playscript over. THE SING-SONG TRIBUNAL was the title on the front. Underneath it said: AN EPIC. A superfluous bit of information, she thought, given the size of the thing, the weight of it on the lap. She flicked through it to the end: over two hundred pages. Which explained why Max appeared even thinner than usual; why the tendons of his neck were prominent, as were the bones at the base, and why there were dark depressions in his cheeks, and why a new hole had been punched into his belt and the buckle fastened a long way to one side and the unused length of leather hung down his front to his mid-thigh: this was how Max looked after one of his bouts of intensive writing.

Alissa took a mask from the props table and came to stand at the edge of the acting space.

—No, not that one, Paul said, taking the mask from her and giving her another. Try this one this time.

Eva had not seen these masks before. They did not belong to her parents. Most probably they were Max's. Recent additions to his ever-expanding collection of precious things. They certainly conformed to his taste. Hewn from single blocks of wood and painted in swirling colours that made the human face look like a butterfly wing, simultaneously inviting the gaze and warning against the touch; they had an unnerving beauty. The one her mother was now holding had a gold forehead and nose. Black cheeks. Frowning red lips. Holes for the eyes, just big enough to poke a finger through. But closed at the mouth; no opening. An impediment to speech. Chinese.

Her mother took a moment to study the design of the mask and to feel its texture. Then she pressed it against her face. Eva was startled by the change: her mother had disappeared into her eyes, which, wet and shining, seemed to bore into the world.

Her father came around and tied the straps at the back.

—Not so tight, her mother said, her voice audible behind the wood but changed; deadened.

Her father, having checked how the mask looked and nodding his approval, went to stand behind Doris at the director's table. From there he said:

—Right, Alissa. In your own time.

By wagging its chin, her mother adjusted how the mask was sitting. She rubbed her fingertips over its front, as if memorising its lineaments and adopting them as her own. Peering down through the eye holes, she ran a toe along the line of tape that marked the acting space. She withdrew her foot and paused. Then took a stride inwards.

—No! said her father. Go back. In order for there to be theatre, a second is all that's needed. As soon as the tip of your nose, or your toe, enters the stage, the story is already being told.

Her mother stepped back out. Recomposed herself by shaking out her arms and legs. Then launched herself forward exactly as before.

—Again? You're waiting till your entire body is already on before showing us who you are. I want to see your character right away. Before you enter, the lines of your body should already be showing a specific state.

Her mother returned to her starting point. Her limbs had visibly begun to twitch.

—You mustn't think, said her father, addressing the entire group, that to come into a space, and to go out again, is an easy thing to do. It requires a huge amount of imagination. And with a mask on, a hundred times more again.

Her mother went again and this time round managed to complete the scene. Eva could not fathom what story was being told, or what sort of personality her mother's character was supposed to have; all she could gather was that her mother was playing some sort of Chinese prostitute, and that this prostitute had some grievances she wanted to vent.

—All right, Alissa, her father said, that was all right. Now I want you to do it again, only this time I want you to forget being realistic. Naturalism, remember, is for fakes.

Her mother went again. The same lines. The same gestures. Making, as far as Eva could see, no substantive changes to her previous performance.

Once finished, her mother stood outside the space with her hands on her hips, awaiting judgement. Her father fixed her with a solemn look. Bowed his head, ceremoniously, as towards someone very slightly higher than he.

—Alissa, he said, if I may?

He approached her mother and took her mask off. Made a tour of the acting space with the mask facing outwards, so that the group could see it and take it in.

—A mask is not make-up, he said. You don't just put it on to go down the shops. Nothing about a mask will impress anyone unless you meet with it, join with it. Make it part of you, and you part of it. Inhabit it! A mask is artificial, so be artificial! Are you understanding what I'm saying? A mask is not there for you to hide behind. It won't allow it. It's a dictator, you must yield to it. Everything you do is at its service. If you don't respect it, or if you use it incorrectly, it will reveal all your weaknesses, and denounce you without pity.

Reaching the director's table, he put his right hand on Doris's shoulder. Leaned in to get a better look at the girl's notebook.

—Did I forget anything?

Doris held up the notebook and pointed at it with her pen. Max tipped sideways, also to look, though in his case with folded arms and a sceptical frown.

—Hmm, her father said. Hmm-hmm—

—What? said her mother, her hands still welded to her hips.

Her father was rubbing Doris's back.

—Doris has made some quite, well, astute, I'd say, observations here, he said. Would you like to take a look, Alissa?

Eva craned her neck to try and see what Doris had written, but there were too many heads in the way.

—Yes, her father said, this is indeed very interess—

Crack!

First Eva's attention flew to her mother's face, which was red and enraged, and then to the mask, which her mother had just taken from her father's hand and flung to the floor.

—My mask! Max said, jumping to his feet. What did Paul *just say* about respecting the masks?

Her mother ignored him.

—Can I have a word, Paul? she said.

Still leaning forwards, and keeping a hand resting on Doris's shoulder, her father had tilted his head, as if to get another angle on his wife:

—What on earth is the matter with you?

—I need a minute. In private.

Her father straightened his posture. Curled up one corner of his mouth.

—There's only one kind of business in this theatre, Alissa. And that's public. Anything you'd like to say, you shouldn't be afraid to say here, in front of the group.

Her mother laughed a sarcastic laugh, and then said:

—All right. We'll do it your way.

She sauntered out to the centre of the acting space and, from there, turned to face the director's table. Fleeing her gaze, Max suddenly became interested in his nails. Doris put the head of her pen into her mouth and sucked. Paul took his hands off the girl and folded them across his chest. In Eva's stomach, there was the swirl of nerves that is the anticipation of an incident.

—I have some questions about this approach you seem to be

taking, her mother said. You know, China. The masks.

—Are you worried about the masks? Or are you worried about your performance just now?

—The masks.

—Because, honestly, you shouldn't be worried about your performance, my dear. The English have always worked primarily with the voice. It's a challenge for us to engage our entire body, as I've been asking you to do. The problem goes far back. To our schooling.

—I'm not worried about my performance, Paul. It's this China stuff that's bothering me. What's the point of it? I mean, if the radical transformation of the theatre is our goal, it can't be the result of some artistic whim. We're sailing very close to chinoiserie, aren't we? To the kind of cultural imperialism we're supposed to despise?

—No, no, Alissa. You mustn't—

Max stood up. Came round the table to lean on its front edge.

—You mustn't think that. Our aim is to assimilate some facets of the Chinese approach, right, but for a distinctly Western purpose. We're not trying to make counterfeits of Chinese art. Rather we're isolating a number of devices used in Chinese theatre, and adapting them, developing them.

—Look, Max, her mother said tiredly, I'm not trying to undermine you. I think highly of you and your work. I'm just not convinced that your motivations are wholly aesthetic. Your political sympathies with China aren't a secret.

—They're not a secret, Alissa, because I don't make a secret of them. We're all communists here, aren't we? Or at least we're meant to be. We should all be happy there's a place in the world where communism hasn't degenerated. That place happens to be China. I think we should be talking about it. Nay, shouting about it!

Nodding forcefully, her father took over:

—Listen, darling, I understand your concerns. We, you and me and Max, we belong to the generation for whom the Soviet Union represented the hope of the world, the quintessential locale of revolution. It is hard for us to imagine another in its place. But

Doris's generation, Eva's, Iris's, they won't be able to rely on Russia for direction in the same way we did. Not after everything that's gone on. They're going to have to open their minds to other examples of communism in practice, in different places around the world. So maybe it's time for us, too, to make a leap of imagination. To go elsewhere for inspiration. Maybe that's the test of what it means to be a revolutionary today.

—Is your aim to stir up public opinion against Russia? Because I think that's what we ought to avoid, especially now, with so many people leaving the Party.

Max shook his head sadly:

—Condemning Russia isn't our intention, Alissa. Not at all. But it's true what you say, I do see China as the only way out of the terrible logic of the blocs that we're stuck in. This two-camp notion of society: America versus Russia.

Alissa folded her arms against him.

—A third way isn't what I signed up for, Max. When Paul and I first talked about establishing this theatre, the banner we imagined hanging on the front was bright and distinct. Red. Communist. And that meant, and I think it still means, friendship with Russia. If, amongst yourselves, you've come up with an alternative position, then it's only fair that I, we, all of the ensemble, know what it is.

She tossed her chin in Doris's direction.

—Wouldn't you say so, Doris?

Doris pointed her pen at the space between her flat little breasts:

—Me?

—Is there someone else here with that name?

—Ahm—

—What's your view on all of this?

—Well, I—

—Put yourself in my shoes. If you were running a theatre, and performing in it besides, wouldn't you like some clarity on the political attitudes that were going to be adopted, on the stage and, it seems, off it as well?

Doris nodded slowly.

—I suppose if I was you, yeah. I'd want to know.

—Thank you, Doris.

Alissa turned a hand towards the girl, as if to present her.

—You see, even—

—Personally, though, Doris broke in, I don't see how wearing Chinese masks in a play means rejecting Russia. Necessarily.

Eva caught her breath.

Her mother gave Doris a strained smile before turning on her heels and going slowly to the refreshments table, as if to pour herself something. Instead she pounded a fist on top, making all the cups rattle.

—You can all go and fuck yourselves, she said. I've had it.

—Alissa, said Max, going to her, you've got to calm down.

—Don't come near me, Max, she said, holding up an open palm to stop him. Not a step closer.

—All right, all right, said Max, halting where he was.

—Just tell me this, she said. The character I'm playing, this Chinese prostitute, LIXIN. What does her name mean again?

—*Embrace the new*, said Max.

—That's right. Well, I think something new here is what she's calling for. A new vehicle to carry her.

—What do you mean?

—I mean, I'm not playing her.

—What? It's the main part! I wrote it for *you*!

—What is it with you men and your fascination with prostitutes? And why are men who don't frequent them the most fascinated? Queers above all?

—Christ, Alissa, said her father, get a hold of yourself. Listen to what you're saying.

—What I'm saying is that LIXIN is a role that is itself about the struggle for a role, is it not?

—You could say that about any great role, said Max.

—Well, I'll just come out and say it then. I don't care how big the role is, I'm not playing the fucking prostitute. She's not right for me, I'm not right for her. I want another part.

—Oh God, oh Lord, said her father. Which one?

—The narrator figure, THE JUDGE.

—What? No, said Max. That's a male role.

—So? You have men running around in women's nighties all the time.

—That's not the same, said her father.

—I'm not saying it's the same, said Alissa. Nothing's the *same*.

—You're serious? said Max. You've thought about this?

—Yes, I've thought about it.

Eva watched her mother move to the window, where — framed by the blazing white of the day — she uttered the simple words that would bring the final storm:

—I want to be THE JUDGE. So I'm going to be THE JUDGE. And that's the end of it.

—In which case—

While the adults were arguing, Eva had come out of her seat and picked her mother's mask off the floor and brought it to the acting space. The room, all the faces, now turned to look at her there.

—In which case, *I'll* play the prostitute, Papa. I'll show Mama how it's done.

Shaking his head and tutting, her father advanced towards her with an arm outstretched:

—Stop it, Eva. This isn't a game. Give me thaa—

Her mother froze him by raising her voice.

—Paul! For Christ sake. She just feels left out. Let her do it. It'll only take a minute. We could all use the break, wouldn't you say?

Her father inflated his cheeks and blew through his lips:

—All right, all right.

Eva found her mother's face, and their eyes locked, and an understanding passed between them. When playing the prostitute, her mother had done whatever she had wished to do, and so had created nothing. Now Eva would do only what she could and would therefore accomplish what was demanded.

Her mother helped her on with the mask. Its insides rubbed against her cheekbones. Her lips, when she moved them, brushed and kissed the wood. Her breaths returned amplified. In the space for the nose, odours of men.

Her mother stepped away and gave her the floor.

—Do you want the script?

—No, I'll make up my own words.

Standing on the yellow line, Eva became conscious of the gallery of actors. And of Simon, who had come into the room and was standing with a foot against the back wall. And Doris, the assiduous note-taker. And Max, dear old Max, whom Eva probably wanted to please most of all. What were they expecting of her? A prostitute, that was all.

So she entered as that.

And she did the legs.

And she did the hips.

And she did the mink stole and the high heels.

And by fluttering her hands in front of the mask's eye-holes, she did the eyelashes.

But she could sense that this was not impressing anyone.

By looking around at the faces, she could see it.

So she switched.

Go inside. Locate a feeling. See the character. Make the character appear. Her father's past instructions materialised in her body as intentions, if not exactly as conscious thoughts. *Draw a picture of the body in space. Freeze for a fraction of a second. Give the audience time to receive the image. Here, in stillness, make the character live. Then complete the gesture. Give it rhythm, balance. Avoid the slowness that tries to be profound. But take the time to finish everything.*

Exit.

There was silence where she expected applause.

Her father helped her off with the mask.

—Well, my love, wow, that was, that was—

She wiped her forehead, pressed her hands onto her cheeks. Her face felt altered, as though it had metamorphosed to fit its disguise, and was now, as if registering its freedom, reverting to its habitual arrangement. *What must I look like?*

—Was I any good, Papa?

With a little grimace she deflected the oncoming praise.

—Why, yes, darling, you were very, how shall I ss—

—You were fine, said her mother.

—Max? said Eva. What did you think? I'm in the drama club in school. I've been practising.

—And it shows, sweetheart, said Max. You gave us detail. Nuance. Truly, you captured the psychology of—

—Ha ha—

Eva started, as if she had just heard the noise of bullets.

—ha ha ha ha—

Behind her, Iris was laughing.

—ha ha ha ha ha ha—

And she was not even trying to conceal it.

—ha ha ha ha ha ha ha ha—

Mentally, Eva went blank, but at the same time she could feel the sensations of her body moving across the room and lunging at her sister.

—ha ha ha ha ha ha ha ha ha ha—

It had to be stopped. It could not be allowed to go on.

—ha ha ha ha ha ha ha ha ha ha ha ha—

But not even when she kicked Iris's shin and pulled Iris's hair did it cease. Rather it ascended into a terrible, hysterical, silent howl.

—

She caught hold of Iris's wrists and tried to wrench her off the stool, but Iris resisted by planting her feet, leaning back and hurling her arms about. As they fought, their four arms appeared as two, like the moving pistons of a machine. They continued this quiet dance — the breath of one against the breath of another — until their mother came between them and slapped at their arms, and pushed Eva away, and somehow in the confusion ended up assuming the same position that Eva had just been in, grasping Iris's wrists and trying to control her movements, but to no avail, so as a final gesture, designed to extricate herself, she threw Iris's arms back into her chest with such violence that Iris had to rub the place where they had struck.

A moment then and Iris was crying.

A pace away, Eva watched.

A further pace to the left, her mother breathed.

In time with one another, they watched and breathed and watched.

And running between them now: Doris. Her father's girl. Who, embracing Iris, said:

—Is you people mad? It could be one of her fits!

And allowing Iris to weep into her breast, said:

—It's all right, petal. You's all right. It'll pass. There, there.

Boom!

A firework. A single explosion over the darkened Renault factory building, leaving a puff of grey smoke in the navy sky. The demonstrators, thinking it was the police firing, began to swing about themselves in panic. Álvaro drew straight lines in the air with the camera lens in search of the source. Max took Eva's hand and squeezed it: *Here we go.*

Boom! Boom! Boom! Boom!

Four more explosions in quick succession. The workers in the neighbouring factory building came to the windows. More bodies appeared on the roof. The marchers, now understanding that something was about to happen, turned towards the factory gates, peered through the railings, rose onto their toes to see over the heads in front. Around them a deep quiet gathered, one which threatened to last — ten seconds went by, twenty seconds — until it was excised by music coming from a hidden stack of loudspeakers, the volume slowly edging up.

Classical music.

And up.

Choral.

And up.

Sung by boys.

Up and up: the music played in the darkness for a long minute.

The waiting made the students restless, and they began to heckle and jeer. A group of workers sitting on the ground outside the factory building began a football chant.

—What's going on, Max? Eva said.

—Shut up and watch, said Max.

At a point when the music rose to a crescendo: light. A pair of projectors came to life. The screens hanging on the front of the factory building glowed a brilliant white.

The crowd cheered: something at last.

The white turned to flashes of grey and brown, four-three-two-one, then two separate films began to play. On the left, images of bombs falling on Vietnam. On the right, a silent instructional video on how to build a Molotov cocktail. The juxtaposition evoked a predictably dual response. There was booing and hissing when an American bomb struck a peasant village, laughter and clapping when the homemade bomb was tested against a city wall.

When the films simultaneously ended about three minutes later, to the applause of the crowd, the screens went black once more, the music changed to an unvarying mechanical beat, and a spotlight came on, illuminating the top of the building. A wooden structure in conical form, like a megaphone sitting on its lip, had been placed on the roof. Winding around the wall of the cone, from the bottom to its apex and back down, was a flight of steps.

A female figure emerged from the darkness to stand at the base of this structure. Her appearance prompted hooting and whistling from the workers, and laughing and booing from the students, for what they saw first, and what momentarily blinded them to the rest of her accoutrement, was the brown sacking she was wearing, which was tied by a rope diagonally between her breasts, leaving one of them uncovered.

—As I thought, said Eva.

—Shh, said Max. Watch.

As Doris came more fully into the light, the crowd's focus moved away from her naked breast to the load she was carrying, and their heckles and their boos turned to gasps and shouts of alarm. Across her shoulder lay a metal pole of the kind used to construct scaffolding. Hanging from each end of the pole was a medium-sized car door: one plastered with the face of De Gaulle, the other with the face of Lyndon Johnson. At first Eva thought that the doors were props made of cardboard; the strain on Doris's face and in the muscles of her limbs she presumed to be an act. But as Doris made her way towards the cone's first step, her knees bending under the burden, her bare footfalls leaden and deliberate, Eva understood that the doors were real. The towel placed at the base of Doris's neck was not just for show, it was there to protect her shoulders from the pressing weight of the bar.

—Are those doors from one of the factory's cars? Eva said.

—No, said Max, unable to conceal his delight. Look at the rust. The broken windows. They're from the barricades in town.

Doris passed in front of the cone in order to reach the steps on the opposite side. As she did so, the car door on the left end of the pole — De Gaulle — reached out over the edge of the roof. Eva held her breath. Were Doris to lose her grip, the door would plunge to the ground and probably bring her with it.

Doris mounted the first three steps quickly, then stopped. Took a breath which, even from this distance, could been seen to expand her belly. Puffing out her cheeks, she released it and took the next two steps. Paused again. The steps got narrower as they went up, so this was as far as she could go with the pole held as it was, perpendicularly in relation to the structure. By degrees, inch by inch, she twisted her body at the waist, anticlockwise towards her audience, until the pole was pointing in her direction of travel. Acting as a central balance, she pulled down on the pole's left side in order to tilt its right side upwards, so that the forward-facing door was not hitting against the higher steps. Eva watched Doris undertake these manipulations with increasing distress. If she lost her footing, chances were she would tumble down to her death.

—She's out of her fucking mind, she said.

—Not at all, said Max. She's the sanest person here.

In this contorted pose, wincing against the strain, her forehead already wet with sweat, Doris climbed the final steps. The diameter of the platform at the top of the cone was no larger than that of a car wheel. She placed her right foot on it and waited. Only when she was sure she could complete the action did she bring her left foot up to meet the right. Standing on the summit now, she untwisted her body so that she was facing the crowd. The doors, attached by ropes to the pole, rocked slightly, requiring her to plant her feet, squat a little and hold still while they settled.

Half of the crowd cheered at Doris thus presented on her plinth. The other half, which by now had turned against her, taunted and jeered.

—What the fuck is this? a nearby Maoist cried. Decadence. Pornography.

—Art, Max said under his breath. The future of art.

Once her load had stabilised, Doris performed the twisting action in reverse in order to go down the steps on the other side of the cone. Descending was even more perilous because she had to resist the downward pull of the front car door. If she were to give in to it, even a little, it would rush to the earth and she would topple forwards after it. As she came down, she touched each step with her toes, as if testing the temperature of water, before trusting her foot to it.

In the time it took her to reach the base of the cone, those in the crowd who had not become hostile to her had lost interest in her. All around, people were returning to their little groups and their prior conversations.

—Is this all she's going to do? said Eva, glancing around.

—Christ, Eva, said Max. Stop worrying about what other people think.

Once down on the roof, Doris paused once more, staring out into the light, her skin bright red and drenched. Eva felt the desire to climb up there and embrace her and sponge her head and say, *You can come down now, it's over.*

But it was not over. Doris was making for the steps to climb them a second time.

—Oh God, said Eva, she's going again.

—Ahuhn, said Max.

—Is she going to keeping going?

—For as long as she can, I think.

The group of workers who before had given a football chant were now shouting:

—Get them off or get the fuck off.

Some students began to throw bottles through the fence.

Álvaro buzzed around the bottle-throwers, snapping pictures of their angry faces.

—Why isn't he shooting Doris? said Max. Doris is the one he should be getting.

—He's getting the audience. Aren't they part of it?

Max flapped his lips irritably:

—He shouldn't be flattering those idiots.

From the loudspeakers the drumbeat continued to pound. Doris, on her second lap, tried to keep her steps in time with the beat, and mostly succeeded. But on her third lap, and her fourth, exhaustion forced her to let go of any idea of synchronicity and to follow her own disjointed rhythm. Now one foot forward; now, sometimes as long as a minute later, the other foot.

Eva looked at Max.

—What's she going to do if she loses her strength and can't go on?

Max bit the skin around his thumb:

—I've no idea.

—There's no plan?

—In her work there're just two things: the starting point and the performance. No rehearsals. No prescribed endings.

—But when will she know to stop?

—She'll stop when she's stopped.

—By us?

—Or by her own limits. Whichever comes ff—

Sirens.

Screams.

Shots fired into the air.

What came, in the event, was the *flics*.

They attacked at two points at once: from behind, in order to concentrate the crowd into the area immediately in front of the factory gates; and from the east, in order to scoop the crowd out of the square and into the streets to the west. There, the fleeing students were met by vans, which screeched out of the cross-streets and came to a halt across the road. A trap.

A wave passed through the crowd as the *flics* drove into its extremities. The bodies around Eva lurched forwards. In order not to be separated, she locked arms with Max and Cyril.

—Álvy! she screamed. I can't see Álvy!

A violent surge ripped Cyril away. Max let go of Eva in order to push forward and grab him, leaving her alone, facing against the stream. A body slammed against her, sending her careening forward. So as not to fall and be trampled underfoot, she reached out, grabbed the army jacket of the boy in front, and dragged him to the ground.

—Max!

—Don't get arrested, Eva. They'll deport you. And don't go to the hospitals either. They check there too.

From behind, someone put her into a stranglehold and screamed senselessly in her ear. To free herself she bit into the bare skin of the forearm. Whirling round, she tried to make sense of what was happening. In a spot where the crowd had thinned out, she could see the *flics* charging, their capes flaring out behind them. Some of the students were running away, some were holding their ground.

Terrified, she fought through the crush laterally towards the fence. She could feel her shoes sink into flesh as she went. Gripping the bars, she looked up at the factory roof.

Doris had not stopped her performance. The spotlight was still on, and, as if nothing had changed, she was making her way up the steps of the cone.

—Doris! Eva yelled, but her voice was lost in the din.

She raised herself up by standing on the fence's low rung:

—Doris!

Out of breath — it was pointless — she put her back against the bars and searched the herd for Álvaro but could see him nowhere. The *flics*, armed with batons and bayonets and rifle-butts, were storming the marchers with a ferocity that she had not fully believed when she had read about it in the bulletins. They were charging indiscriminately into the students. Hurling them through the air. Battering them. As she watched, ten metres from where she stood, two seized a young girl, tore her skirt, and then jumped on her stomach and chest until she vomited blood.

—This is what you wanted, isn't it, you bitch? they shouted as they did so.

To her left, a group of about fifteen students had linked arms to make a defensive line. The *flics* were kicking them and jabbing them in an effort to break the chain. The students appealed to the *flics* to back off, to join them, to behave as human beings. Enraged, the *flics* hit them around the head. Those that fell they dragged away to the vans.

She jumped off the fence and allowed the current to carry her towards the streets to the west. Ahead of her a small gang broke away, making for a second, quieter exit from the square, and she followed them. The *flics*, spotting them, launched gas grenades — Vietnam mace — into their path. Rather than double back, which risked their being caught, the gang decided to run through the smoke. She went with them. She covered her face with her jumper and breathed only through her mouth. Coughing and gagging, eyes streaming and mucus gushing across her cheeks, she ran. Hands outstretched, she bumped into people and trees, and was saved from tripping and falling by a boy who held her up by the jacket.

—Thank you, she said.

And then:

—Oh God sorry, for in righting herself she caused him to stumble.

As she hurried on, she rubbed her eyes even though she knew she was not supposed to. The stinging became so intense that all she wanted was to sit down and put her jacket over her head and sob, as some others were doing. But she kept going. As she came out of the gas cloud, stepping over the fainting bodies, she saw through the blur in her eyes a boy waving a red flag, directing her into an open door. She lumbered towards it, under what felt like rain, but which was in fact water being thrown from the windows of the flats to clear the atmosphere.

—Go inside! the boy was shouting. Get in before we have to shut the door!

At the door, she leaned for a moment against the wall and dared to look around. Where the street met the square, yellow smoke. At the next intersection, a line of vans into which students were being pulled. On the other side of the street, Álvaro, yes, it was him, being beaten. His head was seized, his neck twisted. He was being hit on the head and in the stomach. Blood poured from his mouth and nose.

—Shame! she began to scream. Shame! Shame!

She pushed herself off the wall and began to run in Álvaro's direction, but in that moment a line of *flics* emerged from the smoke, charging up the street, and the boy with the red flag hooked her arm and pulled her inside.

—My boyfriend, she yelled. That's my boyfriend! as she let herself be taken.

The door was slammed shut. About twenty students were crowded into the staircase, coughing and spitting and slapping each other's faces and putting their heads between their legs to keep themselves from fainting.

—We should barricade this door, she said. They'll knock it in if we don't.

Half-heartedly, the students glanced around. There was nothing to build a barricade with.

The boy with the red flag went up the stairs and she went after him. He was banging on the flat doors and ringing on the bells.

—Water! All we want is some water for our eyes!

But nobody answered.

On the top floor, she sat down on the stairs and the boy joined her. They sat in silence, coughing and catching their breath. It did not matter that no one had opened their doors to them. In a flat they would be no safer. She had learned from reading the reports that there were no sanctuaries. Any moment now the *flics* would batter down the door and search every flat in the house. Anyone with black hands or gas spots on their clothes, anyone bruised or cut, would be arrested.

—It's inevitable, she said. They're going to get us.

—Fucking fascists, said the boy.

She stood up:

—I'm not going to cower in here like a rat.

She ran down the stairs.

—Wait! Where are you going! the boy called after her.

Pushing through the bodies in the hall, ignoring their protests, she opened the front door and peeped out. Seeing no *flics* in the immediate vicinity, she made a dash for it. To her left, a crowd of students were rocking a stranded police van.

—Down with the police state! they were shouting.

Álvaro was no longer there; just spots of blood on the ground where he had been. She located a clear path back to the factory square through the small groups of fighting bodies. On either side as she ran, the *thuck-thuck* of the club on skull.

She entered the square through a gap in the line of *flics* created by an altercation with a group of black-clad anarchists wielding sticks. The square had been cleared of students. She ran towards the gates, making wide loops to avoid the scattered groups of *flics*, mostly occupied with checking each other's wounds and talking into handsets.

The factory gates had been forced open. *Flics* were swarming the grounds. Workers were being arrested, though there appeared to be less violence inside the fence than out. The spotlight had been turned off. But Doris —Eva could not believe her eyes — was still standing on her cone. Three *flics* were on the roof, holding the structure steady, and ordering her down. She was ignoring them. Motionless, facing proudly out, the pole still lying across her shoulders, the car doors balanced on either side, she appeared a figure of justice for the machine age; one that was about to be toppled.

—Doris! Eva called out and waved both her arms. Then:

—Doris! again, as if to warn her, though perhaps her real motivation was to let her know that someone was watching, and to tell her, *I'm here, watch me too.*

A pair of *flics* were stationed at the factory entrance. Eva approached them with hands raised, saying:

—I'm a foreigner.

—Yes, said one of the them. Come to shit on us in France.

The other waved her away:

—Get lost.

—Didn't you hear me? I'm a foreigner. A troublemaker. Take me in.

—Fuck off, slut, the first said, touching his rifle as an expression of his seriousness.

—Aren't you going to arrest me?

The second laughed. Then raised his visor so that she could see his sneering face.

—You'd like that wouldn't you, you little tart?

Eva held his eye. Stepped forward.

The first pointed his rifle at her:

—Don't move any closer.

Defiant, she moved forward again.

The second laughed at her stupidity and raised an arm as if to belt her.

Anticipating his blow, she sidestepped, and, from that spot, in front of an audience of one, if she was lucky two, she performed the most beautiful act of her life: a light, almost playful slap on the *flic*'s cheek.

She was taken to the detention centre, a requisitioned athletics stadium in Clichy. Inside the barbed wire fence, under the rain, she was made to wait on her feet for hours. Then her hair was cut off, and she was taken to the cell, a converted changing room, four metres by six, containing about thirty foreigners awaiting deportation. There was so little space everyone who could had to stand. Buckets in each corner served as toilets; already half-full, they clogged the air with their awful smells. A small window gave onto a courtyard where the French students were taken to be beaten. Every so often a boy would go by half naked, legs lacerated, holding his stomach, pissing everywhere.

She found Álvaro crouching under the window. His face was bruised and swollen, his right eye sealed shut. She pushed the surrounding bodies back, much to their displeasure, and knelt before him. Embraced him. Touched his head. Kissed his forehead.

—Ow. Watch it.

He squinted at her with his good eye:

—Are you okay? Did they hurt you?

—I'll live, she said. You?

He dropped his head into his hands:

—I just want to get out of here.

—You and me both.

A boy behind her started to complain about the space she was unnecessarily taking up.

—Oh fuck off, she said but then did stand up. Put her back against the wall. Spoke down to the top of Álvaro's head.

—Max's camera? she said.

—The *flics* took it. He knew the risks when he gave it to me.

—Where are the others?

Álvaro nodded over to the spot in the centre where the three remaining Wherehouse members were sitting together.

She waved over but they made as if not to see her.

—Are they all right?

—They're fine.

—Are they going to come back with us?

—Back?

—To the commune in London.

—I don't know. We're not talking. We had a fight.

—About me?

—Not everything's about you.

—

—But, yeah, the fight was about you. They can't blame you for everything, that's what I told them. No one forced them to come.

In the cell there was the kind of quiet fostered by people who knew how to go forward when the time came to go forward, and to keep still when the time came to keep still. The exception was a group of Maoists who were making the rounds, getting into arguments, searching out errors in people's attitudes. Eva could not see them through the multitude, but judging from the accents of their English, there were four: two American men, an Indian man and a German woman.

—*Mao's peasant army have taught the Vietnamese what they need to know. Vietnam is a people's war. If you want to support Vietnam, then you have to support China.*

—I wish they'd shut up, said Álvaro.

She fiddled with Álvaro's ear:

—Don't be such a grouser. That's what *we* should be doing.

He flicked her hand away.

—What's wrong? she said. Isn't Mao still our man?

He shrugged:

—I don't want to talk about politics right now.

—All right, no politics.

—*In China people have ideals. There are no drugs. No prostitution. People are honest. They get worked up over a little event and start crying. They're so sincere. It's great.*

—But we should talk, you and me.

—About what?

—About us.

—I've got nothing to say.

—Want to hear what I have to say?

—No.

—*In China hundreds of millions of people responded to a single command. If people are all of one heart and mind, they can accomplish great things. In the West it's different. A man can barely speak for himself, never mind for millions. Nobody listens to anything anyone says.*

She slid her back down the wall so that she was squatting beside Álvaro.

—Can I just say one thing?

—I can't stop you, he said. No one can stop you doing anything. If you decide it's time to do something, you don't take no for answer.

—You're right. I'm sorry.

She put her arms around her shins and her chin on her knees. Looked out through the forest of legs.

—Anyway it's over now. Once we're in London it'll be back to normal.

She plonked down on the floor and sighed.

—Then we'll miss it.

—*Mao has done so much for China, it's amazing. He fought to win peace and won.*

After about an hour the cell door opened and, in defiance of the pro-testations of those already crushed inside, more people were thrust in. A burst of applause followed by whistles and insults and sneers suggested that Doris was amongst them.

Eva's heart started to pound. Having sunk into the deathly exhaustion that was the atmosphere of this place, suddenly she felt awake again, restless, hot and cold by turns, unnaturally excited.

—Is that who I think it is? said Álvaro.

—Stay here, she said, standing up and brushing herself off.

—Where the fuck would I go?

It took her a minute to shove through the bodies, some of whom deliberately blocked her way.

—Stay where you are, British. There's no room. You're making it worse for everyone.

In a state approaching giddiness, she poked and nudged and muscled through, and only barely felt the jabs she received in return.

—Excuse me. Out of my way. My friend is over there. Let me pass.

By the time she'd made it to the other side, the Maoists had formed a close circle around Doris, encasing her. Under the pretence of initiating a debate about art, they were launching a verbal attack on her.

Eva jostled her way to the Maoist wall. Knocked on it.

—She's my friend. Let me through.

The Maoists turned their heads.

—That's right, she said, I'm talking to you lot. Let me in there.

Doris peered out over the shoulders:

—Eva, it's you!

Unlike the other girls, whose hair had been roughly chopped, Doris's head had been shaved like the boys'. There were bruises about her face and neck. Her performance costume had been replaced by a man's prison tunic. On her feet, a pair of white plastic slippers. It was a shock to see her so changed, yet as much had been added to her as had been taken away. With the dark frame around her face stripped away, her features stood out.

Squeezing through a gap between the two Americans, Eva put her arms around Doris. Doris, surprised by this embrace, did not enter into it the entire way. Eva, as she drew Doris towards her, was aware of the distance remaining between them and could sense, now, Doris's desire to be released. Yet she hung on an instant longer. After these long days spent dancing around the periphery, this felt like reaching the centre. Everything that happened from here on in — *why think of what's finished instead of what's beginning?* — would flow from this point.

—I knew you'd come, said Doris.

—Papa didn't want me to.

Doris laughed and shook her head:

—I's glad you didn't listen to him. Been worth it, has it?

—It's been—. I don't know how it's been really.

—A good sign.

—Is it? It feels a bit, I don't know.

—Like an anticlimax?

Eva shrugged.

—Don't beat yourself up about it, said Doris. Takes practice to be able to figure these situations out. Did you see Max while you was here?

Eva nodded sadly:

—He isn't in this place, though. They mustn't have got him.

—Course they didn't. Max'd do anything not to get nicked. If they did get him, he'd bribe someone or find some other way to get out. He dreads having to go back to England too much to let it happen.

—And you? You're happy to go back?

—I ain't like Max. End of the day, England's my place. I like being away, but I couldn't stay away for good.

—So you're going to go back to Papa?

Doris ignored her question:

—England'll always be England, and it won't ever be better. For that, we've only ourselves to blame. But when I's abroad I do miss the feel of the place. I's accepted the fact that I's gonna spend my life grumbling about it.

—Papa's worried you're not going to go back to him.

—Don't, Eva.

Eva rubbed her newly cropped hair and blushed.

—How long's you been here anyway? said Doris. You come with your group? Did you put anything on?

Eva had to choke back a wave of nausea that threatened her:

—Bits and pieces only. Nothing like yours.

—So you seen it?

—You were incredible.

Doris smiled:

—Don't know about that.

Doris turned round and brought Eva in to huddle beside her.

—It were the best I could do in the conditions I found and with the materials available. If I's honest, the factory workers and the union bosses were a fucking nightmare to deal with.

—We can hear what you're saying, said the Indian Maoist behind them.

—Ain't none of your business what we's saying, said Doris.

—Oh no? We were the ones watching your little show. Don't you want to know what your public thinks?

—Not particular.

—Typical bohemian attitude. Desperate for an audience for your crap but not interested in hearing what the people think about it.

He was a bearded Sikh. Navy turban. A Mao badge on the lapel of his military tunic. Both his sleeves and his trouser legs rolled up like a peasant soldier. He and Doris began to bicker.

—Stop! Eva said after they'd gone on for long minutes and did not show signs of stopping. Quit bickering and listen to me.

—And just *who* the fuck are you? said the Maoist.

Eva did not wear a Mao suit or carry Mao's *Sayings* in her pocket — putting on the costume was not her way — but she knew her Mao, and she knew Doris too, better than most did, and if anyone was going to bring them together, it was her.

—You're both right, she said.

—Two opposing opinions can't both be right, said the Maoist.

—Trust me, said Eva, you agree on the fundamentals. I mean, for fuck's sake, man, this is Doris Lever you're talking to. She's *been* to China.

—Bullshit. She hasn't been anywhere near the place.

—Seen it with me own eyes, said Doris.

—Prove it.

—Ain't gotta prove shit to you.

The Maoist laughed a self-righteous laugh:

—See? You're full of it.

He made to turn away.

Eva grabbed his arm:

—What's your name?

He looked at her hand until she removed it.

—I'm Sunny.

—Sunny, listen, she said, you've got to understand, we're not the enemy. We're your comrades. Doris as well. From where I'm standing, I see a lot of common ground between us. We should work together.

—No way, said Doris.

—Not a chance, said the Maoist.

Around them, some people had begun to jeer. The Maoists were responding with middle fingers and name-calling.

—Listen, said Eva. Everyone!

She had to raise her voice to be heard over the din.

—All of you, please! Can I have your attention? I have a proposition to make.

Everyone in this cell was living proof that revolutionary energy was international. The fire passed around the world, mind to mind, to make one mind; fist to fist, to make one fist. The Revolution would not spread on its own. It needed people to carry it. The Chinese flame had been lit in Paris, and the aim now should be to use the flames to light the radical fires elsewhere. They, all of them, should be the carriers. They needed to come together. Collaborate.

—I'm Eva Thurlow from the Wherehouse theatre collective in London. All I ask is that you hear me out.

IRIS

1968

vi.

Her father lived in a basement flat in a terrace off the Caledonian Road. It took them half an hour to walk there, during which time Keith, who had been good all day and had not complained, began to speak of stomach cramps and weakness in the legs.

—Don't start, she told him.

Her father answered the door with his usual air of mild regret. He was wrapped in a grey cardigan with holes in the elbows. He looked pale, thin, pouchy under the eyes; what remained of his fine hair was sticking up, suggesting a recent stint on the pillows.

—Who's this? he said, nodding at Keith.

—A friend, she said. Keith, this is my dad.

—How's it going, said Keith.

Her father raked a look down Keith's front.

—Is he one of those Black Power heads? he said, addressing Iris.

He turned to Keith:

—Are you one of those—

—No, sir.

Her father, while he thought about this *no*, gave the impression that the sun was dazzling his eyes.

—Are you two—?

—Papa!

—All right, all right.

He turned to go back down the sunless corridor.

—Close the door behind you.

They followed him up the short flight of stairs to the kitchen. The television had been taken from the sitting room and put on the counter by the sink.

—Is that safe there?

—It's fine.

He turned it off and sat at the table in front of a cold mug of coffee. The table was sticky with cup marks and scattered sugar granules. As a centrepiece, a dirty frying pan sat on top of a folded copy of *The Catholic Worker*.

—Sit down there, Keith, she said, indicating the chair opposite her father.

She found the crusts of a sliced pan in the bread bin and put them on to be toasted. In the fridge was an old courgette, which she chopped and fried, and eggs, which she beat to make an omelette. She made a strong pot of tea, five spoons.

—D'you need a hand? said Keith.

—Sit there and relax.

Keith sat back and avoided looking at her father by staring out the window.

—You all right, Papa? she said.

Her father was alternating between clenching and unclenching his fists and brushing imaginary things from his sleeve.

—Papa?

—What?

—I said, are you all right?

—Fine. D'you have everything you need?

—I've managed with what you've got. Are you hungry? You want some?

He shook his head distractedly.

She made room on the table and put the food down, invited Keith to help himself.

Keith arranged his plate and cup neatly, thanked her, and began to eat with surprising restraint, smiling encouragingly as he chewed.

The table, with the three of them sitting at it, felt tiny. Underneath, if any of them moved a foot, immediately it came up against another and had to be retracted.

—So Papa. What's going on?

Her father did not answer right away. He was swirling around the liquid in his mug and looking at it with eyes whose gaze had turned inwards.

—Have you been going to work, Papa? Did you call them at least? Did you tell them you were sick, or something? Anything?

Her father taught speech and drama to primary school students, a job which he carried out reluctantly and with cynicism, but which he pretended to be passionate about when he bumped into people from his past and they invariably asked, *Oh, you enjoy doing that, do you?*

—Papa, are you listening to me?

Eyelashes fluttering, at last he came out of himself. He studied her clothes, as if she had just made a wardrobe change.

—Iris, he said, you're in a—. What is that you're wearing?

She put down her fork.

—In common English it's called a kaftan.

He swished his hand effeminately.

—Oh stop talking like the telly.

She gulped down a mouthful of tea. Over the top of the cup, she glared out of the window.

Faced with the side of her head, her father now appealed to Keith:

—What do you think, Mister Keith?

Keith stopped chewing.

—Can you see what I'm saying?

Keith shrugged.

Her father nodded as if receiving Keith's accord telepathically.

—You seem like a nice chap. Come to this country to make a

better life. I for one am glad you're here because I have a question to ask you. Do you see my daughter? You see her there?

Slowly Keith slid his eyes towards Iris and swallowed.

With a shake of her head, Iris instructed him not to humour her father.

—Take a look at her, please, Mister Keith, and tell me, from your perspective, what do you see? The hair. The clothes. What do you make of it?

Her father's rejection of communism, which was late but sudden, coincided with his conclusion that his daughters were sloppy and immoral. It was not a great distance to travel from there to guilt, and from guilt to an embrace of Catholic Christianity. As for Iris, she would have liked, once in a while, to be to blame for her own life.

Keith cleared his throat:

—I, uh—

—Do you have girls like her where you're from? I'm guessing not. I'm guessing there's nothing of the sort. And there wouldn't be any here either, not a one, if we, in our ignorance, hadn't raised them the way we did.

He pointed a finger of one hand at Iris, a finger of the other at himself, in accusation.

—They're the way they are because that's how *we* made them.

Then he extended his arms out wide, as if to invite the whole world into them.

—*We* did it. Us. It's our fault.

She banged down her cup:

—Papa, look at me.

Her father turned, his maniacal face now framed between outstretched hands.

—What happened with Doris?

Hearing the name, and instantly weakened by it, he let his face slacken and his arms fall to the table.

—What do you bloody well think happened? She went to Paris.

—Did she invite you to go with her?

—Not with so many words.

—With any words?

—I could tell she didn't want me to go. She doesn't exactly make it difficult to understand.

—What did she say?

He rubbed his eyes with a savage force:

—She said she can't work when I'm around. That I'm a weight on her. I'm suffocating her. She has to go away, on her own. Her opportunities lie elsewhere, and I'm keeping her from them.

—So, the usual.

He pressed his temples as if trying to remember:

—No, no. This time she had something new. Let me think, what was it now? *Your egocentricity is beginning to threaten my capacity for work. I have to remove myself from your influence.*

Iris had to fight back a smile. Everything considered, she liked Doris. Or rather she liked her for her father. She could not advise her father to stay in a marriage that was not working, yet she knew that if he lost Doris for good, that would be the end of him. He would use religion to take his suffering away, and eventually, with no one there to hold him back, would surrender his whole self to it. That had to be prevented.

—She's done this before, Papa. She probably just needs some time. Are you sure she's not just taking a break?

—Did you hear me? *I have to remove myself from your influence.*

—I doubt she meant, you know, permanently.

—She broke up with me, Iris. This is it. *Fin.*

Iris pushed her plate away and tapped the table impatiently:

—You've got to lay off with the God shit.

He shook his head solemnly:

—That's not it.

Iris leaned back on her chair and reached for the packet of cigarettes on the counter.

—Well, if you ask me, Doris will stay in Paris only until the party ends. Then she'll be back.

—No, not this time. She's always wanted to get out of England. This is her chance. She'll meet someone, a Frenchman, and that'll be it.

Iris lit a cigarette. Then pocketed the packet and returned the lighter to its place in her pouch.

—If you really didn't think there was a hope of her coming back, why did you send Eva and the others to find her?

Her father's face arranged itself into a look of anguish:

—God, I wish Eva hadn't gone.

—What're you talking about? You were at the commune a few days ago, telling her to go. Too scared to chase after your own wife yourself.

—I went to the *commune*, as you call it, because I knew Eva would be tempted to go, and I wanted to dissuade her. I was trying to stop her!

Iris gave her cigarette to Keith to drag from.

—Simon told me a different story.

—Simon? He wasn't even there. He was hiding upstairs in his lair.

—That's what he told me.

—And you believe him over me?

She waved away the smoke that Keith blew over the table:

—I suppose I do.

There was a long silence then.

Eventually she said:

—You should visit him more often.

—He could come here too, couldn't he? What's stopping him?

—Papa. He's your brother.

—Look, I know. I will.

He bowed his head.

—I should be more Christian. When you think about it, Jesus himself was a madman.

Straightening up, he spoke now with practised smoothness.

—Do you believe in God, Keith?

Keith finished the cigarette and stubbed it out in a pot on the windowsill: no plant, just hardened soil and a hoard of fag ends.

—Sure, I believe.

Her father gave her a look of triumph, as if in that moment he personally had instilled in Keith the Spirit of the Lord.

—Iris thinks the Catholic Church is against progress. Against the twentieth century. And I say, so what if it is? So am I, if the twentieth century means the crazy world I see about me.

Like a holy simpleton, he signed himself with the cross.

—Oh for fuck's sake, said Iris.

Her father patted the pockets of his cardigan, looking for his cigarettes. Not finding them, he went glum.

—You know, I worry about you, Iris. The drugs and the places you go at night.

—Drugs? I don't know what put that into your head.

—It'll be the end of you. I hope you're careful.

—I can look after myss—

Abruptly Keith stood up and began piling the plates. Took them to the sink and turned on the tap.

—Yeah, we should go, said Iris.

Her father accompanied them down to the front door.

—Thanks for the food, said Keith, and went up the area steps to wait on the street.

Her father hugged her.

—You're good to come round.

He pressed a banknote into her hand.

—You know, don't you, that you won't be able to stay in that building much longer?

—I know, Papa.

—They mean to put up flats. Your mother is serious about selling it.

—Have you been speaking to her?

—I had to let her know Eva had gone. In case anything happened.

—Nothing's going to happen.

She crumpled the money and put it away.

—See you, Papa. Take a walk or something.

*

—Your dad is heavy, Keith said on their way back down Caledonian Road.

—What he needs is a trip and a fuck.

When they reached King's Cross, Keith said:

—Well, it was nice, thanks a lot.

—Where you off to now?

—Back to the Hill.

—This about my dad?

—Nah, I just need to get back. Got my own shit going on.

—You can sleep at mine. My dad gave me some cash. We can get chips on the way. And go out for breakfast tomorrow.

—More food? You starve me for hours and now—

—Come on, Keith. Just tonight. Then you can go back.

Keith shrugged, okay.

They had chips from a shop opposite the station and bought two more bags to take home. At the theatre lodging house, the Indian students, Neel and Sid, were cooking in the kitchen. The corridors were filled with smoke and with the smell of spices. Iris and Keith went straight up to her room. Iris locked the door and jumped into the bed. Lit the candle in a lantern, one that her mother had given her years ago, which instantly heated the air.

—Home sweet home, she said.

In contrast to her own careless appearance, she put a lot of thought into her living space. She enjoyed the small, well-defined limits of her room, and she liked to have it neat. Keith ate from his bag of chips as he inspected pictures on the walls and the objects on the shelves; her personal archaeology. He brought his nose close to the psychedelic posters and the framed pieces of Chinese calligraphy. Lifted the minerals and the crystals to test them for their weight. Fanned through the pack of tarot cards. Iris welcomed his attention. She recognised herself in her objects. They were materialised bits of her soul.

Keith took her doll from the shelf.

—That's Mao, she said. I made it when I was a kid.

—You said Mao was a bloke. This looks like a girl to me.

—It is a girl. But I called her Mao.

He put it back:

—Freaky.

After putting more chips into his mouth, he ran a greasy finger along her line of books. Overlooking the Confucius and the *Tao* and the *I Ching* and the early leather-bound edition of *The Idiot*, he went straight for *Capital*. He put the chips down on the shelf so that he could use both hands to flick through the book.

—Where'd you get all this? he said, putting the book back.

—From Uncle Max, mostly. Who's not really my uncle.

Keith pointed at the framed professional photo of her mother:

—Who's this?

—My mother.

—Wha!

—I know.

—What you said about her before, at the party—

—I don't remember what I said.

—Probably for the best. What happened to her?

—What do you mean?

—When did she, you know, pass?

—She's not dead.

—Oh. I got the impression.

—She's dead to me. That's the impression you got.

Suddenly tired of talking about her things, she rooted in her stash box and found a leftover morsel. She broke one of her father's cigarettes into a rolling paper and began to burn and crumble the hash on top.

—Come here, she said as she rolled.

Keith transferred his unfinished bag of chips from the shelf to the desk and came to sit on the rug by the bed.

She licked the paper, smoothed the finished joint and handed it to him with the lighter.

—You light up.

—Nah, thanks.

—You don't smoke?

He shook his head.

—What's your weakness, then? You're not into junk, are you?

—Fuck off, I don't do junk.

—Yeah, stay away from junk.

From kneeling, she fell onto her back, stunned:

—Hold on, you're straight?

—These days, yeah.

—I don't believe it.

—I take a drink, but I try to stay away from everything else. I'm on a new leaf. Keeping the head clean. Staying out of trouble.

—But how d'you do it, being straight at a party like that?

—I like people who are high.

—You do?

—When you're there, and everyone's tripping, it's like a closed world. A no-sense world. Maybe if you're someone who needs people to say the same things all the time, or if hearing fucked-up things makes you nervy, maybe it's not for you. But—

—You like it.

—Yeah, I like it. I like to listen. And look. And think.

He smiled:

—I got plenty of thinking done over you.

She sucked on the joint and thought about this.

—I dig it, she said.

In San Francisco, everyone would be just as they were now: no one forcing them into doing what they did not want to do, no discrepancy between rich and poor, black and white, the freedom to do what you wanted, to take drugs or not, to stay up all night, to work your own hours, to be non-regimented, not to have to prove one's worth by dressing a particular way or catching the seven forty-five to Waterloo.

—So why do you take acid? Keith said.

—Insight, she said, pulling in some more smoke. You got a guru?

Like, someone who you get completely, and who gets you?

He thought for a second:

—Not in one person.

She nodded her head for a long time.

—Yeah, man, I hear you. Not in one person. Fragments. Here and there. That's what it's about. Like flashes when you're listening to music or reading a poem, and something flares up and that's you.

She put the joint in the ashtray and lay down on the pillow.

—You're cool, Keith, you know. All we've got to do is make you so that you know what's happening.

Without taking off her clothes, she pulled the blankets over herself.

—That reefer made me sleepy. You want to share the bed?

—You don't want me kicking you.

—I don't care. Kick all you like.

—I'm fine here on the floor. Plenty of cushions here that I can use.

She curled up. Moaned with pleasure.

—I always look forward to sleep because I'm going to dream.

—D'you have nice dreams?

—I don't know.

—You don't know?

—I mean, I know I dream because everyone dreams. But I never remember them.

—Why d'you look forward to them then?

—I guess I like knowing *that* I dream. It doesn't matter that they don't stay with me. Will you watch me?

—While you dream?

—I don't mean all night. Just if something happens.

—Is something going to happen?

—Probably.

—What am I to do?

—Watch I don't fall. Or bang my head.

—All right.

She blew out the candle and closed her eyes.

—Does it hurt, he said after a while, when it's happening?

She opened her eyes for a moment and looked into the dark.

—When I wake up I feel strange, but when it's happening, I can't feel anything.

—Am I to wake you?

—Just let it waste.

—There's nothing I can do to stop it?

—Nothing. So don't bother trying. It's useless to interrupt.

After her expulsion from boarding school, she was made to sleep in her mother's bed, supposedly so that her mother could keep an eye on her, though in reality it was Iris who ended up looking out for her mother. Her mother's routine, on waking in the morning, was to roll over and write her dreams into a journal she kept by the bed. Then she got up and prepared a bowl of hot water. Sitting at her dressing table, she covered her head with a towel and breathed the steam into her lungs. When this got too much, she tilted back and doused her throat with a prescribed spray. Then, sucking on a Nigroid tablet, she massaged her neck, seeking herself.

Iris, woken by her mother's movements, would go to rub her shoulders. She did not say a word while she did this, for mornings were meant to be mute; no chatter. Through the mirror in front, her mother would blow her a kiss, which was a sign for Iris to dip her index fingers into a tub of hot ointment and draw circles with it on her mother's temples, applying as much pressure as she could, following an instruction once given her. When her mother had had enough of this, she would take Iris's hand and put it over her nose and mouth, and breathe in its smell.

After a light breakfast — toast without butter and no milk in the coffee because it produced phlegm — they went to the piano. Singing was something they did together every morning since Iris began to be schooled at home. During the refurbishment the piano had been kept in the bedroom, but as soon as the new rehearsal studio was completed, it was moved there: a much larger space which required her mother to increase her range if she did not want to sound diminished; and a more public space, too, more exposed, which demanded that Iris overcome her impulse to sing in a half-voice out of fear of being overheard. Here, they had to perform.

By the time they arrived, Simon would already be in the studio, preparing it for that day's rehearsal. He would have already cleared away yesterday's mess, mopped the floor, checked the markings, polished the windowpanes, arranged the chairs, tidied the noticeboard, set out the props; or, at least, on the morning that Iris remembered more clearly than any other, he had already done all of this, and was now preparing the refreshment table in the corner.

Iris ran over and gave her uncle a brief hug, before going to the piano, lifting up the keyboard cover and sitting down in front of it, ready to be directed, eager to get it over with. Her mother put the final duet from Monteverdi's *L'incoronazione di Poppea* onto the rack, and took her place to Iris's right, facing the room. As Iris played the first notes, her mother's mouth dutifully opened, and an unbelievable sound came out.

—*Pur ti miro*, it sang: full-bodied, exquisitely pitched and of a timbre whose quality sometimes seemed to shock even her.

Iris responded with:

—*Pur ti godo*, a beat too late, fine, but flat, coming only from the larynx.

Her mother ran a clenched fist down her front as a signal to her daughter to press downwards to find depth. Which Iris wanted to obey but she was distracted by her uncle. Eyes flicking sideways and over her shoulder, she could not forget that Simon was present.

At the end of the first verse her mother knocked a knuckle on the top of the piano and Iris stopped playing.

—Simon, sweetheart? her mother said. Can you give us a few minutes, would you mind?

Simon mumbled something to himself. Put the cigarette he was about to light behind his ear and went outside with his coffee. Kicked the door shut behind him.

—Now, Iris—

Alissa pulled on the child's shoulder in order to turn her round on the stool.

—do me a favour and have a look. The whole room, take it in. The height. The length. The volume, do you see the *vol-ume* of this place? Your voice ought to fill it all. By not even trying, you're being mean, nothing more. Keeping yourself for you alone and not sharing out. Denying us the gift that only you can give us. Your voice. Your expression. Nothing less than who and what you are.

Iris sat on her hands. Looked down at the space between her thighs. Jigged her knees from side to side.

—I mean, you're only ten years old, for God's sake, what could you possibly possess that's so precious that you should keep it locked away?

Her mother put her hands on her hips:

—Hmm. Let's do something else.

They tried 'Abends will ich schlafen gehn' from Humperdinck's *Hänsel und Gretel,* which came out better. Not great; better. Iris's voice carried further this time, but in her rush to get from one note to the next she was over-modulating, which resulted in loss of breath and some unnecessary swallowing. Her mother exaggerated the movement of her lips and jaw and emphasised the consonants in an effort to tell Iris to slow down. *Enunciate,* she mouthed while Iris was singing, *e-nun-ci-ate.* For more than anything else what people loved was a sharp voice which left each word distinct. *If one wanted to be respected in this world, one had to become articulate; one had to master speech.* And the most effective way to do that was to learn how to sing.

—Was that all right, Mama?

Her mother pulled down both ends of her mouth.

—You look tired, she said, loath to praise her daughter for doing what she ought to be capable of. Her rule was never to reward half-efforts or flukes but only advanced work achieved through diligence and graft. *As a child one heard so many lies.*

—I'm fine, Mama.

—Did you sleep?

—Ahuhn.

—Were you reading?

—Ah-ah.

—You know you shouldn't get tired. The doctors said.

—I have to read for my lessons. I'm not going to stop reading.

—Just not so late.

—It wasn't that late.

Her mother put the sheet music back into the folder.

—Have you taken your tablets?

—At breakfast. You saw.

—Tone, Iris.

Iris inflated her cheeks in frustration:

—Mama!

—All right, madam, we're finished.

Jumping up, Iris tucked the stool under the piano and stood before her mother for the final inspection; an advertisement for filial obedience. Her mother fixed her collar and picked a loose hair from her front.

—Don't forget to wash that face of yours before you present yourself.

Iris nodded dutifully, though she did not quite understand this need to be clean, when her tutor Miss Fletcher seemed permanently to be three days after a wash.

At this point, when her mother normally tapped her on the chin and sent her away, she did something different. She knelt down in front of Iris and gripped her arms and said:

—One moment, my love. Before you go. Tell me. How has it been since your sister got back?

Iris shrugged: fine.

—Are you getting on all right, the two of you? Are you fighting?

Iris shook her head: a lie.

—You know your sister means well, Iris. You must try to

understand where she's coming from. It's not all roses with her either, though she tries to give that impression.

Iris sucked in her lips and looked at the floor.

Her mother let go of her, suddenly, and went to the window.

The distant sound of traffic.

Rain on glass.

Room.

—And what do you make of the new girl?

Iris stopped scratching the itch under the elastic of her knickers.

—The secretary, I mean. Doris. Do you like her?

Iris thought about this for a while, looking for the trick.

—She's nice, she said then.

—Nice?

Her mother came away from the window. From the props table she took a package wrapped in brown paper and brought it to Iris.

—Listen, Iris. This is for you. A gift. But first I need to tell you something.

—All right.

—It's an adult thing, so it's not easy for me to say. Can I ask you to be mature and to listen and try to understand?

Iris nodded. Her throat had gone dry, her hands cold.

—Have you noticed that Doris and your father have a close friendship? Hmm? Well, the fact is, you see, they're sort of girlfriend and boyfriend. I don't think this should be kept from you because over the coming weeks you're going to see certain things and I don't want you to be confused by them. You aren't stupid, children aren't. I don't think pretending is fair on anyone.

—You're not Papa's girlfriend any more?

—I am. I'm still Papa's wife, and I love him very much. And he loves me. That hasn't changed. That *has not* changed. It's just that sometimes life is complicated, more complicated than in story books and magazines, and people don't like to talk about it, but it's quite common, actually, that mothers and fathers have other friendships, with people from the outside. We've just decided to be more open about it than some others are, that's all.

—Do you have an outside boyfriend?

Her mother actually smiled.

—No, darling. I have the theatre, my acting, and that's enough for me. But your father is different. He has, what'll I say, a bigger appetite. When my mind is on my work, I'm distracted, you see, I can't give him everything he requires. Someone else is needed to, as it were, make up the shortfall. Can you comprehend that?

Iris nodded: she could.

Her mother kissed her on the cheek.

—Good girl. Now open your present.

Iris knelt down and put the package on the floor between her thighs. Began to tear off the paper.

—Hold on, her mother said, crouching down and halting Iris's actions by laying a hand on her arm. There's one more thing. You're not to get too close to Doris. Her job here is just a temporary arrangement. She's not going to be around for long. You can see yourself, she's young. With us she'll grow a bit and then she'll leave. I can't allow her to overstay. Her friendship with your father, it has a beginning and an end, do you understand?

Iris nodded.

—And when she has to go, her mother said, it might not be pleasant either. I want you to be prepared for that.

—All right.

—Good. That's all I wanted to say. Finish opening your present.

Beneath the wrapping was a Chinese lantern of carved red wood and glass panels painted with mountain scenes. Long red tassels hung from the mouths of four dragon heads that pointed out of the top.

—Do you like it? You put a candle in here, you see—

Her mother opened the front panel.

—and it all lights up. The whole room. Do you see the pictures on the glass?

Her mother held up the lantern and turned it round.

—We're going to hang a few these around the theatre, to give the place an Eastern feel. But this one is all yours. No one will be allowed to touch it without your permission. We'll put it by the bed. It'll be perfect for reading. Late, too, if you can't sleep. All right?

She woke on wet sheets and surrounded by a barrier of cushions.

Keith, who was still there, said:

—How you feeling?

Then he wiped her forehead with a damp cloth, and, when she got up, helped her to heat water for a bath and to soak and scrub the sheets. He stayed with her all of that day and slept at Wherehouse that night, and the next night, and every night following. Though he did not say it expressly, it was clear he liked the set-up. The factory-cum-theatre barely seemed plausible to him as a place of habitation. The space was so large, so sparsely populated, its angles and volumes so improbable, it was like a stage within which a second stage had been built merely as an amusement. He felt like an actor in a film.

—We're like something off the telly, he would say when they sat on deck chairs on the roof, drinking cider and looking out over King's Cross.

Or:

—Is it the candid camera? when Iris would suggest a game of water pistols in the auditorium.

Notwithstanding the dirt and the draughts and the fact that at night the local children threw stones at the boarded-up windows and tried to break in and had to be chased away, in almost every aspect Wherehouse beat what he had before. There was no landlord breathing down his neck. No one stealing his things. No one waiting to jump onto his mattress as soon as he rose from it. On a couple of occasions he took the bus back to the Hill *to look after some business*, but Iris did not worry that he had gone for good. He would come back, she knew, and loyally he did, most recently accompanied by two Negro acquaintances of his, these ones real Jamaicans.

—This is Glen and Eggie, he said, my neighbours from up the

road. They got into a spot of trouble, went behind on their rent and got chucked out. Can they crash here for a few nights?

She could not say no. The previous day someone from Álvaro's international network, a Swede, had arrived on the doorstep, and she had allowed him to stay. Never let the record show that she let the blond stranger in and barred the London blacks.

—Are you drawing Security?

—Yah, that's right, miss.

—Good. Because you'll have to pay a pound a week into the house fund.

—A pound for two of we?

—All right, a pound for you both. The rooms in the lodging house are locked, so you'll have to bed down in the common room. I'll show you the way. Got sleeping bags? All right, we'll find you a blanket or something. There's a Swede sleeping in there at the moment. Per is his name. It's up to you to get along with him. No messing, yeah? Smoke your reefers on the roof. And keep a watch out. In this country you go to jail for a joint. Don't go into the upstairs rooms. My uncle lives up there and he doesn't appreciate visitors. No touching the artwork. I mean hands fucking off, you understand me? And you can only stay until the collective gets back from Paris. Not a day longer. As soon as they're home, you're out.

—We get pounce on?

—Don't rule it out. Have you got political opinions?

—Nah, miss, us don't fill our heads with that fuckery.

—Fine by me. Just don't tell them that. Clear off when they come and there'll be no aggro.

The Jamaicans were in windcheaters and long t-shirts and broken jeans. They wore knitted globes to hold in their hair.

—Now Keith, do me a favour, can you? said Iris. Look at your friends.

Keith looked at Glen and Eggie.

—Now look at me.

He looked at her.

—Now look at yourself.

He looked down his front.

—Notice the difference?

He put his hands in his pockets and, from there, pulled up his sagging trousers:

—What?

—We've got to get you some new threads, spade! You're in gainful employment now. You can't go around looking like you've been dressed using coupons. You'll chase off the punters. They'll think you're a snitch.

She did not want him to look fake, so she decided against Carnaby Street and took him instead to the market at Camden Lock.

—These clothes are cheap, he said.

—That's the point. You wear one rig-out this week and a different one the next. Life is change, man. A flux. You going to ride it? Or resist?

It was what Eva called the peaceful production of the means of destruction; the perfection of waste. It was what Iris called being alive today.

She picked him out a bright yellow shirt and pair of flared jeans.

—Try these on.

—You ragging?

—All I'm asking is that you open your mind.

—To yellow?

—To beauty. To self-expression.

—Is this part of the deal? I try these on, I get my slice of lunch?

—Give and take, the only two forces in the universe.

He went to change in the corner of the stall.

—If you're trying to make me believe London is swinging, he called out from behind the curtain, and that I can be a swinger too, it ain't going to work. Don't look so bloody swinging to me.

He pulled the curtain across and stepped out.

—Fuck yeah! said Iris. Do you dig it?

He looked into the mirror:

—Yach!

—The important thing is that you're not plastic. That you feel yourself.

He wiped his hands down his front. Burrowed a finger into the crease in his crotch in order to adjust how his testicles were sitting.

—I don't feel meself.

He looked like someone madly normal dressed up as someone mad.

—We'll take them.

The batch of LSD was large — two hundred paper trips and a hundred sugar cubes — so they had to work the days as well as the nights to shift it. The late mornings were for sleeping. The afternoons were for the squats and the party flats. The evenings: Scotch and Mason's Yard and Speakeasy and All Nighters. The nights: the dance clubs and the afters. Such a full schedule gave no leeway for nursing hangovers. Iris had to stay sober. Failing that, she had to limit herself to a quarter-tab or a few tokes of a joint. Which was not easy. Being lucid at the midweek house parties was tedious; being so at Middle Earth on Friday night was a horror show.

Having Keith there helped. He was hungry for the money promised at the end of the job and so did everything to ensure the operation stayed on track. When she felt tempted to dabble, she would turn to him like a child seeking permission from an overseer, and he would shake his head and say:

—Let's get this job done first. Then you can switch on all you like.

On their travels around the city, she had a number of seizures in inconvenient places, like on the stairs of a squat, and in the aisle of a supermarket, and on the floor of Flamingos, and on the first Tube. On each occasion she woke up to Keith fussing over her. Kneeling beside her. His face in hers. One hand resting on her forehead to keep her head steady. The other hand stuck in her mouth to free her tongue from her clenched teeth. Observing him in her stupor, she wondered if he existed, he was so unlike anyone she had met before. He was not fearful of her. He did not feel sorry for her. He did not hesitate to reprimand her.

—I thought I told you to take your meds, he would say. Next time I'll put them up your arse meself.

Sometimes during the onset of a fit, she received warnings. She started to notice bad smells like charred meat or burning rubber. Or she became dreamy and saw bright auras around objects. When this happened, she would alert Keith, *I'm about to*, and he would grab her and shake her by the shoulders and scream *No!* This was the startle-and-shake response, which in theory was supposed to halt the oncoming seizure, but which in practice rarely did, leaving Keith to push any furniture or bodies out of the way, and to help her onto her back, and to put a gag between her teeth, and to loosen her clothing, and to lay her head and her arms and her legs firmly on the ground and put pressure on them for the duration.

Once, when they were alone on the roof after a long day of work, Iris lied to Keith that she was about to have a fit because she wanted to see his actions with clear eyes. She let him shake her and shout at her. She watched him clear away the chairs and make a space for her on the ground. She gave him her body to be laid down. And there, prostrate beneath him, overcome by feelings of tenderness and gratitude towards him, as well as tinglings of passion running from her throat to her vagina, she reached her head up and kissed him on the lips.

He recoiled. Wiped his mouth with his sleeve.

—What was that? he said.

—Oh, she said, her feelings plummeting.

—You're not having a fit?

—It must have gone away.

—You sure?

—I think so.

—Jesus. You keep me on me toes.

—Sorry.

—It's okay.

—Come and lie beside me.

—On the ground? No. It's dirty.

He went back to sit on the deck chair.

She sat up. Tucked her feet behind her.

—You think I'm ugly, don't you?

—No. Get that out of your head.

—What is it then? Are you queer?

—What? No! Your mind is a sewer.

—Well, are you?

—I said, no! Can't there be anything else between a normal man and a normal woman? An innocent friendship?

She pointed at her can of beer on the low wall by the roof's edge.

He got up and brought it to her.

She took it from him and swigged from it and did not say thanks.

Simon had been against allowing someone from outside the family in on the job, and a Negro at that, but once he saw how well Iris and Keith worked as a team, how much they were selling, and how quickly, he ceased his objections.

—Your Man Friday can come in on this one, but then he has to fuck off, that clear? As soon as the backlog is moved, we're going back to the old way, just you and me.

—All right.

—Just tell me you're not fucking him.

—I'm not.

—Didn't think so. You're too smart. Come to me if he tries to touch you, and I'll sort him out. All right? I mean it.

Sober, or close to it, Iris joined Keith in his natural habitat: on the margins of the parties. From there, she scrutinised. Noticed what she had not noticed before. Understood what one had to be lucid to understand.

—Tell you what though, she said to him, it's better when you've dropped.

—Reality isn't enough?

—Or maybe it's too much. That might be why.

She was being drawn into friendship with Keith by swift, imperceptible stages. Because she had warned him not to ask her about her personal affairs, and because he had the irritating habit of respecting her wishes, they shared quite a lot of silence at first. She did her best to welcome this: the global sum of evil would be diminished if people learned to sit together quietly. But, over a stretch of days, the quiet became harder to sustain.

They began to talk, and she learned a few facts about his life. His father had been an American GI stationed in Portsmouth during the war. His mother was a local girl, a waitress. They met at a dance and walked out for a year before he was transferred to France, where he was killed. When Keith was born, his mother resisted the pressure to send him to a children's home and raised him on her own. It was from her that Keith got his love for Simon and Garfunkel. (*Don't worry*, said Iris, *we can change that.*) He telephoned her every week and sent her cards and, whenever he came by it, money.

—Are you going to send her some of your earnings from this job?

—Probably.

—Are you guilty? Is that why you do it?

—Do what?

—Send your mother money. Phone her.

—Don't know. Don't think so. Anyway, what do I have to be guilty about?

—D'you love her? I mean really love her, exactly as she is?

—She's me mam, so yeah.

—Then you're not like most people. Most people can't accept their mothers for who they are. Not really.

—It's sad you don't love your own mother.

—Sad? No. The best day of my life was when I learned that love isn't a duty, that I didn't have to love anyone, including my mother. Loving only who you want to love, that's freedom, man.

—You think you're free?

—In that sense, yeah I am.

—Not sure about that. You're still busy with your mam in your mind, i'nt ya? It's natural you still have feelings for her. They never go away.

—I have feelings all right. I won't deny that.

—What did she do, anyway, to make you hate her so much?

—I don't hate her. I just don't want anything to do with her, for my own personal reasons.

—The divorce?

—Cliché, right? But, yeah, that's part of it.

—Was it your mam's fault?

—Suppose so. Partly. Papa wasn't innocent either.

—But you don't hate him.

—I know what that sounds like. It's not easy to explain.

—All right.

—What do you mean *all right*? I don't like how you said that.

—I just said *all right*.

—Look, it's like this. They both made mistakes. But Mama was the one who walked away, you know? They could have worked it out.

—She might've had her reasons.

—Their theatre failed. That was her reason. She liked working with Papa more than she liked being his wife. Their collaboration was what kept her with him. Her the actress, him the director, you know? A double act thing. They'd still be together if their theatre had taken off. That's my reading, anyway.

—Why did it fail?

—The East Wind?

—Yeah. Was *that* your Mam's fault?

—No. To be honest, if anyone's to blame for that, it's—

She turned to face into the flashing lights and the music, where everything was simple and stable, where the people — the seekers and the heads and the hippies and the junkies and the tourists — existed for sensation, and that alone was what united them.

—It's all right, Keith said, his breath on her ear. We don't have to talk about it any more.

*

The bomb site beside The East Wind theatre had changed little since the day soon after the war's end when a lorry came to take away the larger pieces of debris. After that, once the advertising hoardings went up, the site was left to harden into its current form, and to settle into the environment as a permanent ruin. Its central area, where four terraced houses had collapsed in their entirety, was a wasteground of interconnecting mounds of earth. Folded into these mounds, like raisins into a cake, were bits of masonry and glass and metal and wood. Telegraph poles, snapped in the middle like matches, stuck out and lay around. Rough grass pushed through the cracks. Dock and nettle insisted on a life, undeterred by dog shit, littered packets and old ashes. At different places ivy, privet, elder, and rosebay willowherb had taken hold.

Marking the limits of the site were the side walls of the surviving terraces, onto which the remnants of the neighbouring houses still clung. Visible against the brick were the outlines of a staircase and parts of the internal floors and walls. On the patches of plaster that had not fallen away, one could just about make out where wallpaper might have been or a picture might have hung. To Iris, from her vantage point on top of the highest mound, it was reminiscent of a doll's house that had been opened out, the fourth wall removed.

Beside her, Simon kicked the mound with the toe of his boot. Struck it with the sharp end of his shovel.

—Don't look promising, he said. I doubt we'll find much that'll be of use to us. But seeing as we're here, we might as well have a root round, see what turns up.

Now that the refurbishment of the theatre was all but done, Simon had let the building team go. He would do the last jobs himself. From time to time, he brought Iris and Eva to the wasteland to help find materials for the stage set of the theatre's first play, *The Sing-Song Tribunal*.

—Any loose bricks you find, pile them there.

He used the shovel to point to a flat circle of ground by the hoarding.

—Metal, put it there. Wood there. Any junk or bric-a-brac, anything intact, anything shiny, bring to me, and I'll make a call on it.

In the area where the second of the four houses had fallen, the ground had sunk to form a crater. This was the sisters' favourite spot, to which they ran now and into which they slid on their arses. They began to rummage and dig. Iris was the first to find something interesting, a bit of a window frame, which she took back to Simon to inspect.

Up the side of the mound, she ran, and took hold of the back of Simon's shirt in order to keep her balance on the uneven summit.

Dropping the stub of his cigarette, Simon trod the embers underfoot. Stood the shovel so that it rested against his chest. Wrapped his right arm around the handle to free his good hand. Then took the window frame from her.

—Hmm, he said, throwing the frame into his wheelbarrow. Maybe.

From the pocket of his overalls, he took out Max's drawing of the set. Holding a corner of the page, he unfolded it with his teeth. As he examined the sketch, he was careful to keep his fingers off the pencil to avoid smudging it further.

—Can I see? said Iris.

Her cheek brushed against his arm as she leaned in to get a look.

—Hang on, he said. I'm thinking.

She made an attempt to handle the drawing.

Simon lifted it out of her reach.

—It's the only copy. I can't get it mucked up.

She filled her cheeks with air and released it through her lips.

—Where's Eva? said Simon.

—Over there. She's cut herself.

—Blinkin Mavis, that didn't take long.

Simon slung the shovel over his shoulder and went down the side of the mound, allowing gravity to pull him into a run.

Iris chased behind him:

—Don't tell her I told you.

Locally the bomb site was called the Patch. The children of the area were warned by their mothers not to go playing in the Patch — *I'll belt you if I see you in the Patch, they'll have you up if they catch you in the Patch* — even though there was nothing especially dangerous about it; the Patch posed less risk to a roaming child than the gang-infested streets surrounding it. These warnings were the consequence of a superstition people had that when the past returned, it would come in the same form, to the same place, which was a stupid thing to believe, Iris thought. How could people be afraid of what *has* happened? It was not possible to tell the future from the past like that. The things that were going to happen would not be anything like the things that had happened, and, if her parents were to be believed, would be much worse. After the next war, it would not be just a terrace but London itself, the whole of Europe, that the children would name the Patch.

Approaching, Iris could see that Eva had her right hand pressed under her left forearm.

—You all right, toots? said Simon. Let me see your hand.

Eva glared at Iris.

—What? Iris said. I didn't say anything.

Simon knelt down beside Eva.

—Show it me here, he said. Come on. Give.

Eva released her hand and held it out. Simon took her wrist: an open cut on her finger, blood rubbed over her skin, stains on her sleeve and down the side of her dress.

—You've got it all over yourself. Your folks'll have me guts.

He whipped out his handkerchief. Flicked it in the air to unfold it. Wrapped it around the cut.

—Ugh, said Eva.

—Ugh nothing, he said. Just out of the wash.

He held the wrapping in place with this thumb.

—Iris, I'll press here and you tie the knot.

As she did so, Iris avoided Eva's glare.

—How's that, Eva? said Simon. Better?

Eva nodded.

—I should get you both out of here before you do yourselves a real injury.

—No! said Iris.

Simon stood up from kneeling:

—Come on. I've got a thirst anyway.

—What, the pub again? said Eva.

—We'll get some grub at a caff, what d'you say? Aren't you hungry?

—I'm covered in blood, said Eva. I can't go about like this. We shouldn't even be out here. Why can't we go back in and watch the rehearsals?

—You need to learn to know, child, when and where you're not welcome.

The Tube took them to Notting Hill Gate, then they walked south towards Kensington High Street.

—Where we off to? said Eva.

—What're you in the mood for? Egg and chips?

—Long way to come for egg and chips.

—I've a message to run as well.

—Thought so. You see, Iris? We're never just brought to a place. It's never, *I'm taking you here because I think you'll like it*. There's always another reason. An *ulterior* motive.

—Don't be clever, Eva.

Kensington, according to Simon, was a sordid and miserable place. *Drab and patched and tired out. Not old like Italy was old; just old-fashioned.* He knew a few men who had ended up in these desolate bedsitters, with their indoor dustbins and their dry rot. He claimed not to be surprised by the frequent news of their suicides.

—In fact I'd say the real number is higher. The families hide it, you see.

On the High Street, near the corner with Allen Street, was a newspaper shop. An advertising board outside showed a headline from the *News of the World*. In the window were sweet bottles gone sticky and packets of Players faded by the sun. On the wall by the door someone had pasted a poster, which Iris read aloud:

—PEOPLE OF KENSINGTON ACT NOW

And underneath:

—NIGGER LEAVE OUR GIRLS ALONE

Inside was gloomy and smelled of stale tobacco smoke and glue and liquorice allsorts.

—Can we have chewing gum? said Iris.

—No. Pick out something to read.

The only good light was provided by a bare fluorescent bulb above the register. The shopkeeper, Arthur, sat illuminated there, his pale skin turned near to green. When he saw Simon coming in, Arthur got up and went through a curtain of red-white-and-blue ribbons. Simon waited for him at the counter.

—Can I have this? said Iris.

She was holding up a *Woman's Own*.

—No, said Simon. Something else.

—Exactly, said Eva. You're ten.

Arthur came back in with two items. A magazine concealed in black plastic. And a block of something, the size of a book, wrapped in green paper and string. Only years later would Iris understand that her uncle was buying a girly mag and a kilo of hashish.

—One and two, said Arthur. Anything else?

Arthur had a soft voice and in everyday conduct was kind and gentle. When Simon first met him, soon after landing in Salerno, he had said to himself, *This one won't last. It's blokes like him that get popped.* But then one night, under long bombardment, Simon saw Arthur's other side.

—What was his other side like? Iris once asked Simon.

—Dark. Like the bit of the moon you don't see.

—Simon, mate, Arthur said now. Anything else?

—Eh yeah sorry, Arthur.

Iris had chosen an edition of *Amazing Stories*. Eva an out-of-date *Everywoman* discounted to half price. From the rack, Simon snatched a *Sunday Pictorial* and an *Observer*.

—These as well. And a packet of Du Mauriers.

Simon tried paying with money crunched up in his fist. But Arthur did not care for that, and counted it out in the open, flattening each note on the counter. And it was a lot.

—Uncle Simon? said Iris, wide-eyed.

—Shh.

Arthur did not open the register but put the cash straight into his pocket.

—All there? Simon said.

—All there, Arthur said. Let me know how you get on.

For food, as promised, Simon took the girls to a caff near Kensington Station. There were motorcycles parked at angles on the path outside, and a group of Teddy Boys was standing about. One of them — drape jacket, drainpipe trousers, Tony Curtis quiff with plenty on the front — stepped in to block the door.

—Scuse us, said Simon.

—Scuse you, said the Teddy without moving.

Instinctively Simon pushed the sisters back so that they were behind him. He had put the girly mag and the hashish, too big for any of his pockets, inside his jacket and zipped it up. To stop them falling through the hem, he was holding them in place with his good hand.

The Teddy took a step forward:

—You gonna show what you have there, geezer, or'll I have to make you?

Gaze locked to his adversary's, Simon breathed.

Iris could hear his breath in her ears: in, out, in—

Feigning to check on the sisters, Simon turned his head so that the scars on his neck would be visible. Then he folded back his cuff to reveal the smooth head of his stump.

The Teddy flinched.

Simon met his eyes again.

The Teddy stepped aside.

Inside the caff, Simon guided the girls to a table and went to order at the counter. Silent, suspicious, Iris watched him unload the plates and cups from the tray to the tabletop. He pulled a second table over and joined it to theirs. Went round and sat on the same side as the girls, facing out.

—Iris, you come here and sit beside me.

She dragged her chair closer, and Simon put his bad arm around her shoulder.

—Eva, you go sit over there, he said, nodding at the empty chair on the opposite side of the table.

Back in the war, it was the calm and quiet ones, the undistinguished people who withstood the pressures and could be relied upon, whereas the extroverts, the people who showed great bravado — *My God I can't wait to get at those Jerries!* — crumbled in an instant; the moment they were fired on, they froze or ran away or exploded in a puff of smoke. It was for this reason, Simon once told Iris, that he could not love the sisters equally.

—Eat up, he said now. And you know the rule, no noises.

While Iris played with her chips, dipping them into the eggs and watching the yolks spill over, afraid to scrape her knife on the plate, Simon slurped from his coffee, which, while paying, he had surreptitiously dashed with some brandy from his flask. She could smell it.

Simon laid out his newspapers on the empty bit of table.

—Uncle Simon?

—Ahuhn?

—What is it anyway?

—What?

She prodded the bulge in his jacket:

—That.

—Shh. Enough talking. Read your magazine.

He went through the *Sunday Pictorial* without stopping to read below any of the photographs. Thinking back on this, Iris supposed that he was probably distracted, now that he had the hashish on his person, by the numbers in his mind. The calculations. He would have learned the economics of it from Arthur, and it would have boggled him. In The East Wind he had access, Arthur would have told him, to a ready market. He was sitting on a goldmine. Actors, you see, when they were not working, had lives so monotonous, so painful that the urge to escape themselves led them beyond the everyday staples of coffee and drink into the darker realm of powder and pills. And when they were working it was even worse: during a long run especially, longing each night to beat the heights of the previous performance, they chewed all kinds of stuff, mostly Benzedrine, to get themselves through it. Half of The East Wind were probably already addicts. And how did addicts, brought to be so alert, get to sleep at night? How did they calm down and switch off? More and more it was to hashish they were turning. *Haven't tried it myself*, Arthur would have said, *but this is what the freaks are after these days, and it's supposed to work a dream.* If Simon played his cards right, he could clear this kilo-block in a couple of weeks, which would bring in more than a bank clerk earned in six months. The numbers would have looked wrong to him, they were so high, but once he had gone over them and over them, and made sure there was no catch, he would have begun to believe that, actually, contrary to what was popularly said, there was nothing easier to get than money, nor was there anything in the world more important. Once he had realised this, there would have come to churn constantly in his mind the thoughts of saving and accumulating, saving and accumulating. Cash, brass, wonga, swift dinero: he was panting for it, all the time. And, you bet you, it had to be swift. For, in fifteen years maximum, the H-bomb would have disposed of them all, and there were things he wanted to do first. Get away from England, for starters.

—What have you got?

It was Eva this time.

—Hmm? Simon glanced up. Oh, nothing astonishing. Talks at Number 10. A thing on what the Jews believe. You?

—*How to make an asset of your shortcomings.*

—And?

Eva shook her head.

Simon yawned an artificial yawn. Folded up the *Pictorial*. Threw it on an unoccupied chair. Waved at the woman behind the counter to fill up his cup. Tilted another swig of brandy in. Opened up the *Observer*.

—Do you know something, Uncle Simon? said Iris.

—What?

She looked distastefully at his coffee cup:

—Alcohol contains no proteins or vitamins. All it provides to the body is heat energy. And calories.

—Did you get that from your magazine?

—Miss Fletcher. She gave me a book.

—On fermentation?

—On *intoxication*. The problem drinker is a sick person who needs a hospital. Medical science can cure him. There were diagrams.

—Your parents'll be glad they're getting their money's worth.

—My parents? Not their money, is it? Grandma pays the tutor.

—Who told you that?

—Grandma did. She says I'd be illiterate if it weren't for her.

—That's enough of that.

—What?

—Talking about money.

—Why?

—You're a child. Children shouldn't.

Simon put his elbow on the table and supported the side of his face against the palm of his good hand. Iris watched him read the *Observer* headline. And reread it. Again. And again. His eyes moving across it, until:

—May I drop on this spot.

With a sudden focus, he scanned down through the article.

—May I get run over and smashed.

—What? said Iris.

—Finish up, we've to get back.

—So it's home now, all of a sudden? said Eva. We've half our chips left.

—Move now!

Back at the theatre — a rush to the Tube, and a rush from it — Simon opened the rehearsal studio door only a crack, and passed soundlessly in. The sisters, heeding his order for quiet, crept after him. In the centre of the room, their mother was sitting behind a table, dressed in a judge's scarlet gown. Sitting in a line in front of her were four actors in Chinese masks. Their father mouthed something to Doris — Iris could not make out what — and Doris jumped up and gently herded the newcomers back outside.

—Sorry, Doris said, softly closing the door behind her. You's have come at the bad moment.

—I need to speak with Paul, said Simon. Urgent.

—Ain't a good time.

Doris ushered Iris and Eva further away from the doorway.

—We's in the middle of something tricky, and you know your brother when he's stressed. Can't it wait till tonight?

Doris touched the crook of Simon's elbow, as if to herd him off. Iris watched her uncle look down at Doris's hand. If he wanted to, with just a twitch of an arm, he could have swatted her aside. A flutter, a jerk, a bark and she would be out of his way and disposed of.

—You're right, Doris, he said. I do know my brother. And I know he'll want to see this.

From where he had it, pressed against the side of his thigh, he raised up the *Observer*, held it out to the side so that he could look at it too; displayed it as a barrister might a damning piece of evidence to a jury.

—Oh that, said Doris.

—So you've already seen it?

She dove her hands into her pockets and pouted:

—Ain't exactly a surprise. We's been hearing about it for a while. We knew it'd be published sooner or later.

—And now here it is. In all its beauty. Not just gossip any more. The whole thing, printed out, start to finish. Worse than any of your lot would've imagined, I'd say.

Doris withdrew her hands from her pockets in order, self-protectively, to fold her arms:

—A difficult development. But nothing we can't get over.

Iris could not take her eyes off the line of fine dark hair above Doris's lip, where there was dampness caught.

—A difficult development? Simon said. That's all you're going to say? You're a communist now, aren't you? Like the rest of them? You must have a proper opinion about it.

Doris turned to the sisters:

—Girls, d'you mind going to your rooms? Me and your uncle need a minute for some grown-up talk.

Iris did not move, Eva neither, and Simon did not order them away.

—They're not doing any harm and have as much right as you to be here.

—Ahuhn, Eva said. That's right.

This made Simon laugh.

Doris's eyelids shivered as his breath hit her.

—I'm ending this, she said and made to walk away.

He caught her wrist.

She tugged herself free.

—He hasn't seen it yet, has he? I think we should get him out here so we can show it to him. I'm sure he wouldn't like to be kept in the dark.

Doris did not move:

—Don't show him that paper.

—Hmm?

—Don't, Simon. Keep it away from him for now. Rehearsals are already tense enough. That article is the last thing he needs to see. Word'll reach him soon enough, and we'll deal with it then.

Doris held her hand out.

—Can I have it?

Her mouth was open, her cheeks were aflame. She grasped the edge of the paper:

—Simon? Can I have it please?

—*Chat-a-nooga-choo-choo,* Simon began to sing (which was something he learned to do while charging towards the enemy; it helped to block out the mind, he said. *There's very little difference as to the sensations in the body before pulling a trigger and before stealing a kiss*).

—What's the matter with you? said Doris. Let go.

She began to pull on her side of the paper. He did not resist her totally, rather just enough to keep a handle on his side, and to have her pull him towards her.

—For fuck sake, Simon, this is getting—

He let go of the paper, knowing that her own force would propel her backwards, and that, thus positioned against the wall, all he would have to do in order to fondle her breasts, and to rub his groin against her V, and to have the taste of her neck in his mouth, was to feign a trip and to stumble forwards.

—ahh!

She pushed him away. Gave him a furious glare. Then rushed back into the studio.

The newspaper lay on the floor at Iris's feet. She reached down and picked it up.

—Here, said Eva, give me that.

Iris clasped her arms around it:

—No, I got it first.

—Uncle Simon, tell Iris to give me the paper.

But Simon was already on his way down the stairs.

—What are we supposed to do with it? Eva called after him.

—It's a newspaper, he said. Read it.

—Which part?

—You're a smart girl. Figure it out.

—What's it about?

—It's about Russia. Your parents' god. And how it has failed.

—Shall I give it to Papa? said Iris.

—You want him to see sense, don't you?

They were outside the London Carlton on St Martin's Lane waiting for the evening performance to end. The plan was to try and sell paper trips to the theatregoers as they came out.

—So? said Keith. I don't see the point of the story. What did you do wrong?

—The point, said Iris, is what I did next. I knew I shouldn't have. Even Eva warned me, *Don't dare show that paper to Papa.* But I didn't listen. That same evening I went and gave it to him.

—And?

—All hell broke loose. The beginning of the end.

—End of what?

—The theatre. My parents' marriage.

—Over a thing in a newspaper?

—It was the first domino. I knocked it over.

The path outside the London Carlton was illuminated by the lights on the building's façade. The theatre's name was written in red neon. The sign board and the posters for the current production were framed with yellow bulbs. Standing in it, the light felt unnaturally bright: daytime forced into the night.

—The article must've been important, then, said Keith. What was it about?

—Oh God. Believe it not, I can remember the headline exactly. KHRUSHCHEV'S EXPOSURE OF STALIN IN FULL. RUSSIA'S 20 YEARS OF TERROR.

—What? That's all it was? I thought you were going to say it was about your family. Like, dirt someone had dug up.

—Nah, spade, you've got things the wrong way around. For my parents the state of the world was more important than anything else. Family dirt would have been nothing. And actually, now that you mention it, the article *was* about family. It *was* our dirt. My parents had been Party members for more than twenty years. They'd joined when they were students and had stayed in through all the bad years. Even when every week there was a new report going around about the abuses in the Soviet Union, they'd stayed in.

—So this article finally made them leave?

—No, not even then. You have to understand, my parents' dream had always been to open London's first communist theatre ensemble, and they were on the verge of realising it. They couldn't bring themselves to leave the Party just a couple of months before opening night. Instead, they called this big meeting and told the actors that they'd read the article and had decided, despite everything, to stay in. Then, typical of my parents, they gave the actors an ultimatum. Anyone who wanted to continue working at The East Wind had to stay in as well.

—What happened? Did they?

—Half of them did. The other half tore up their Party membership cards and refused to continue to work with anyone who didn't do the same. They gave my parents an ultimatum of their own: if *they* didn't leave the Party immediately, they'd walk. My parents probably thought they were bluffing. What actor would walk away from a steady paying job? But that's exactly what they did, leaving my parents with only half an ensemble.

It was now half past nine. The woman in the London Carlton box office had said the play would finish at thirty-five minutes past. Keith dropped his load of *IT* magazines onto the ground by the theatre's left-hand corner. Their idea was to set themselves up as sellers of the magazine. Size up the people who bought a copy and, if they judged them to be genuinely tuned in, offer them a trip as well. Iris, tired of standing, sat down on the stack.

—You know, she said, I've thought about it a lot, and really there's no getting away from it. It was me who showed my parents that article, so it was my fault those actors left.

—You blame yourself? said Keith. Your parents would've seen the article sooner or later, right?

—Yeah, but timing is everything, isn't it? Maybe it wouldn't have mattered so much if they'd seen it later. After opening night. What actor would leave a successful production?

—Ah, that's some mystical shit there. A load of what ifs. You'll drive yourself crazy with that shit.

—Part of me thinks that, subconsciously, I planned it. That I wanted to destroy my parents' theatre.

—That doesn't make any sense. You told me you enjoyed living in the theatre. You said you was proud your parents was theatre people. That you liked being around the actors.

—But I was never allowed to be fully part of it, was I? I was always kept on the sidelines. The spastic child.

—Could've been much worse.

—It wasn't that bad, you're right.

She had been happy enough while she had everyone, her parents and the actors, all to herself. But then Eva came home from boarding school, and from the moment she walked in the door, she started getting in on the act. Ingratiating herself with everybody and making it obvious she wanted to be part of the theatre. And Iris could not let that happen. She had to stop her.

—If I couldn't be part of the theatre, then I wanted no one else to be. So I got what I wanted, I suppose. But it didn't look like that at first. When the actors left, the theatre didn't just close right then and there. My parents didn't give up on it so easily. They tried to salvage it. Did this frantic search for new members. Ran last-minute auditions. And guess who got a part.

—Your sister?

She nodded.

—So, hang on, said Keith. You wanted to *stop* Eva getting a part, but instead you ended up *getting* her one? Fuck, girl, you was stung.

—We were all stung, we just didn't know it yet. The truth is, the moment my parents gave Eva that part, they kissed their theatre, and their marriage, goodbye.

Keith arranged his face in a confused expression:

—It's all fucked up. But you know something? Somewhere I understand why you did what you did. And why your parents did what they did. It's Simon I can't figure out. Why was he so eager to show your parents the article? Wasn't he living in the theatre and drawing a wage there? What would he have gained from blowing everything up?

—Simon? He's the simplest part of the puzzle. First off, he hated communists. Still does. He'd do anything to prove them wrong. Second, he only has one thing on his mind. Money. He has this idea, you see, of leaving England and going to live in Italy. He says he wants to buy a house in this little village he passed through during the war. Maybe he met a girl there or something. The point is, he's short on prospects, so he got it into his head that because my mother's family is rich, my mother must know how to make money, and that, if my parents were raking it in, he'd benefit from that somehow. He knew, though, that a communist theatre wasn't going to make anything. He thought my parents should be putting on popular shows that'd bring lots of punters. For that to happen, he needed to turn my parents into capitalists, which first meant convincing them to leave the Party.

—Easier just to get a job.

—And it's same with Wherehouse. He doesn't care about what we do. For him, we're just a means to an end. A place where he can live rent-free and save all the takings for his big move.

—Will he ever go, do you think?

—To Italy? Who fucking knows. I'd be surprised if he hadn't saved enough money by now. Don't know what's stopping him.

Iris got up and went to the line of black-and-white rehearsal photographs on the theatre wall. Pressed her finger against the glass behind which the photograph was mounted.

—If you ask me, she said, the really tough one to figure out is *her*.

—Who?

Keith bent forward and brought his nose close to the photograph.

—Is that—

—The one and only. Why did *she* allow Doris to work in the theatre? None of Papa's other girls were ever given a job like that. And why did she let Papa give Eva a role in the play? What sort of mother does that? Do you know what the role was? A fucking prostitute. Her own daughter.

Keith listened with narrowed eyes:

—Iris, what are you up to? Is there some other reason we're here?

—We're here to sell the *International Times* to London's hip and happening theatregoers.

—Don't bullshit me.

—All right, maybe I wanted to show you.

—Show me what?

—Where the demon woman works.

Keith walked out to the kerb. Looked up at the sign board.

—*Miss Julie*?

—That's the play.

—I know that's the play. Alissa Thurlow. Is that her? The name sounds made up.

—It's not. It's hers. Ours.

—You use your mother's name?

—It's what happened after the divorce.

—Ah, right. Money. Your mother's the rich one. It's always about that. You hate her, as well, for having money?

Iris sucked in her lips: yes.

Keith came back to stand beside Iris.

—So let me get this straight, Miss *Thurlow*. First you take me to meet your Holy Joe father. Now you want me to meet your famous mother who you hate and don't even talk to?

—We're not going to meet her. I just brought you here to show you what she does.

—Why?

—You're right, who cares.

—You care. That's my point. I've seen the scrapbook you keep with all her reviews and interviews. You hate her because you care. It'd be easier, you know, just to talk to her.

—Easier? To be at each other's throats all the time? To have a shit relationship like everyone else?

He shrugged:

—Yeah.

The theatre doors opened, and people began streaming out. Iris picked up three copies of the magazine. Turned them to face outwards and held them by the edges so that the cover was visible.

—Can I interest you in an *International Times*? she said. All the inside news from the underground?

Most ignored her. Those who bought a copy looked too old, or too suburban, or too stiff, or too perfumed to be interested in what else she was selling.

—Can I have a couple of those?

The voice came from behind her. She turned to see a young couple, mid-thirties. Him: a suede-silk shirt and round glasses with tinted lenses. Her: a pink headband, black eye make-up and a PVC mackintosh bunched at the waist. They were smiling and holding hands.

—Sure, said Iris. I'll give you two for one. That way you'll have no arguments about who gets to read it in bed tonight.

Keith, who was holding the drugs, was a hovering presence two paces behind.

—How much? said the man.

—Bob and sixpence.

While the man rummaged in his pockets, Iris folded two copies and handed them to the woman.

—I love this magazine, she said.

Iris observed the woman's fake eyelashes fluttering, and the gloss on her lips spreading into a smile, as she scanned the cover. Iris thought of Eva, who disdained *IT* magazine because the only politics it had was: *Smoke anything, inhale anything, inject anything, it's your life, baby, do it.*

The man gave Iris two shillings.

Iris searched her pouch for the change.

—Were you at the show?

—We were, said the woman, putting the magazines under her arm. I enjoyed it. Him, not so much.

—Not my thing, the man said. Got the tickets for free. Didn't want to waste them.

Iris put the change into the man's hand, which he had kept open to receive it.

—How about Alissa Thurlow? Was she any good?

The couple glanced at each other, amused.

—Well, I just love her, said the woman. I always make sure to watch her when she's on the telly. The dramas. And the costume stuff. Personally I think she's one of our best.

—How did she get on as MISS JULIE? said Iris.

—Well, she's the best ever MISS JULIE, isn't she? She's the, what's the word—?

—Definitive? said the man.

—Yes, the definitive MISS JULIE. No one can do MISS JULIE like Alissa Thurlow. When you think of MISS JULIE, you think of her.

—Shit, though, how old is Alissa Thurlow now? said Iris.

—I don't know. Forties, fifties?

—Isn't MISS JULIE supposed to be a young woman?

—Honestly, that doesn't really matter. Alissa Thurlow is so good, she just pulls you in and takes you away, and you forget about her age and all that. That's my opinion anyway.

The man chucked his chin at Iris:

—I'm with you on this. She's way too old for that part.

Iris let them walk away without offering them trips.

Keith came to stand beside her again:

—No?

She shook her head:

—You're right. We shouldn't have come here.

—I didn't say that.

—So I'm saying it then. We shouldn't have.

They walked back to King's Cross. Bought wine at an off-licence near the station.

—Your uncle won't be happy that we haven't sold everything.

—We've had a good run. He can't complain. I won't let him.

The streets were quiet. The after-work rush long over. In Somers Town the sitting rooms were occupied and the television sets were on:

squares within squares of light. Muffled bursts of gunfire and laughter came through the glass in the windows. Making their final turn, Iris saw a white van parked at the Wherehouse entrance, and a group of figures standing nearby. She pulled Keith into a doorway.

—Is that them? he said. Your group?

She squinted into the gloom. None of the body shapes appeared familiar.

—There's a van. But I don't recognise the people.

One by one the figures disappeared inside the lodging house door.

—Are they breaking in? said Keith.

—They could have forced the lock.

Once the coast was clear, Iris ran up and checked the lodging house door. The lock was intact. Inside, the lodging house was empty, the only sound was The Doors' new album, *Waiting for the Sun*, coming from the Indian lodgers' rooms downstairs.

They went through to the theatre. They could hear voices coming from the auditorium.

—Hello? Iris called out before going in.

The figures were scattered around the room. Two butch-looking men were examining the half-finished lanterns on the worktables. On the stage, a pair of blond men in army jackets were talking to Per, the Swede. Nearby, an Indian in a turban was peering into the wings. The Jamaicans, Glen and Eggie, were smoking by the second exit. Álvaro was next to them. His head was wrapped in bandages, and he was obviously excited to be in the Jamaicans' company, and he was obviously telling them how *amazing* Paris had been, for his voice was raised and he was gesticulating wildly.

—Álvaro? said Iris.

Everyone stopped talking and turned towards her.

Eva appeared from behind the rack of moveable seating.

—What the fuck? said Iris.

Eva ruffled her own hair:

—The fascist cut. You like?

—Who are these people? said Iris. Where is everyone?

—There's been a change of guard. This is the collective now. Everyone, listen up. This is my sister.

The bodies shifted around and waved.

—You look well, Eva said. You've put on weight.

—I've been looking after myself.

Eva gave her a wide smile. Her face was dirty and her breath smelled, which did not suit her.

—I see you've let some people stay, she said.

—I didn't know when you'd be coming back.

—It's all right. As long as they contribute, and they're good.

It took a moment for Iris to realise that the man emerging from the workbenches was Doris. Her head had been completely shaved. She wore an oversized black leather jacket, an old check shirt, blue jeans and flat black boots. A borrowed look. A man's silhouette. In this guise, she was — it sickened Iris to admit — spectacular.

—Hi there, Doris said.

—So you came back, Iris said. Have you seen Papa yet? You need to phone him. He's climbing the walls.

Doris pushed her hands deep into her pockets:

—I like your lanterns. Eva tells me you've been working on them with the local kids.

—Just call him. He's your fucking husband.

—I see you bought wine, said Eva. Here let me.

She took the bottle out of Iris's hand.

—We got rice and vegetables. I was about to cook a stir-fry. A celebratory first supper. You and your friends will join us of course.

Iris switched her gaze between Eva and Doris, then ran it along the new faces arranged in a row behind them. Perfect. A picture postcard. Eva had it all now. Her detachment of politicos. Her loyal boyfriend. Her mother's theatre. Her father's lover.

Eva took a step forwards:

—Also—

She lowered her voice, though not enough to be unheard by the others.

—I wanted to say that we're sorry we left like we did. The clock was against us. You'd have hated it anyway. Definitely not your thing.

Iris had been playing with one of her pendants, running it along its chain so that it made a noise like a zip opening. Now she dropped it so that it fell against her chest:

—It's not your place to decide what's my thing and what isn't.

—You're right, you're right. Can we call this a new start?

—That depends.

Iris directed her words at the men in the army jackets and Mao pins, who, like so many of their kind before, would be interpreting her appearance as a sign of weakness.

—I want to know everything that happened while you were away. Where everyone is gone. Who these people are. What your plan is now.

—We'll tell you everything. Over dinner. But first things first. Do we have any money?

—We're there already?

—There's no time to waste.

—What do you need money for?

Doris touched Eva's shoulder as a request to take over.

—Listen, Iris, she said, a lot has happened, but the long and short of it is, I's agreed to collaborate with Wherehouse, on a—. You's would call it a happening, I call it a performance. We's still at the initial stages, chucking ideas around. Before we go any further, but, we need to know if there's funds. Ain't much point planning something if we can't afford to do it.

Iris put a hand over her pouch:

—Money? Not a lot. Some.

—Smashing, said Eva. That's smashing. Now the other thing. The film projector. Is it with the props in the storage room?

—I think Simon has it upstairs. What do you need it for?

—After dinner I was going to show the group the film of *The Sing-Song Tribunal*.

—Why?

—I was telling Doris about it, and she thinks it might be a good starting point.

—I don't want people seeing that, Eva.

—Oh come on, Iris. There's nothing to be ashamed of.

—I'm not ashamed. I just don't want it dredged up again. It's history. Over.

—*The Sing-Song Tribunal*? said Keith. Wasn't that your parents' play?

—Butt the fuck out, Keith.

Doris came forward a second time:

—It's all right, Iris. I understand. I were there, remember? It weren't an easy time for any of us. So how about this. Me and your sister will watch it alone. Just me and her. None of the others. Would you mind that?

—I don't see why you want to revisit all of that.

Doris looked at an ill-defined point over Iris's head.

—I can't really explain why. Except that I's got memories from that time, and I want to put them up against the evidence. To see if I can do anything useful with them.

—You're not going to use the film in a happening, are you?

—We's not thinking that far ahead yet. For now we just want to watch it.

Iris sighed:

—Set your world alight. I can't stop you.

—Good, said Eva. I'll go and ask Simon for it now.

—No, said Iris. I'll go.

Upstairs, Simon was pacing his room, from the desk to the wall and back. The fluorescent light overhead was on and the wireless was switched off, as he needed them to be in order to obsess about something. Iris put the drugs money and the remaining trips on the desk. Normally Simon counted the takings immediately but today he paid no attention to them.

—Who are those freaks downstairs?

—Been spying?

—I saw them come in. I don't like the look of them. Who are they?
—New friends of Eva.
—Is that Doris I saw? Got up like a bloody man? She can't stay here.
—Relax, Simon.
—Did you hear me? She can't stay.
—What's got into you?
—What's she doing here?
—I've just got back. I know as much as you do.
—You have to get rid of her.
—I know you don't much like her, Simon, but I think you might be overreacting.
—No cut for you till you get her out.
—Oh piss off. What's wrong with you?
—Today. She needs to go today.
—You never visit Papa, so when was the last time you saw her? Years, I'd say. She'll hardly expect you to be mates all of a sudden. Just stay up here and ignore her.
—I repeat, no cut for you till she's gone.
—Oh, look, whatever. Once I call Papa and tell him she's here, he'll come for her, and she'll go with him. That'll be the end of it.

She went to the corner cupboard and opened it.

Simon stopped pacing:

—What're you looking for.
—The projector. She wants it.
—Who does?

She twisted round.

Simon met her eyes, then let his face drop into his hands.

III

EVA

1956

<u>vii.</u>

Simon came up behind her and tapped her on the shoulder. She jumped.

—Only me, he whispered.

—Jesus, Simon, she said.

She was at the rehearsal studio door, waiting to be called in for her audition.

—How you feeling? he said.

She shrugged. The nerves showed on her skin, which was pale.

—You know, Eva—

—I'm going over my lines, d'you mind?

—Sorry, yes, I'll leave you. I just wanted to say, you don't have to go through with this, if you don't ww—

Her father opened the door.

—Simon, do you mind staying outside? We want to keep this strictly between—

Simon waved away her father's explanation. Disappeared down the corridor.

Paul ushered Eva in:

—Small change of plan, darling. I know you've prepared a couple of pieces to present to us, and you'll get a chance do that in a minute. But the group thought it'd be good idea if you joined a game first. To see how you cope with improvising and free work. Nothing complicated. Just imagine you're back in the schoolyard, okay? Follow the instructions and be yourself.

A circle of actors was an aggressive thing. It trapped the tension coming inwards from all those egos and magnified it. Put a chair in the centre, as they had done today, and demand that the actors take turns to sit in that chair, and an already aggressive thing became savage. Eva felt the back of her neck tingle, and her armpits prickle, and drops of water run down her sides, as her father led her to the space in the circle beside her mother. The game, which was called *The Chair of Questions*, began, and the actors took their turns. When it came time for Eva to enter, she hesitated. She felt watched, and she felt they did not want to be watching her. Her name was being called, but, playing deaf, she was refusing to go to the chair.

—Eva? Eva? Eva? Eva?

Until, maybe ten seconds later, her mother put a hand on the small of her back as if to comfort her, and, unseen by the others, gave her a little push—

IRIS

1968

<u>viii.</u>

She brought the film projector and the screen to Eva's room. Eva and Doris had thrown the cushions from the bed onto the floor to sit on and had hung a sheet over the window to prevent the city lights from polluting the dark. While they unfurled the screen, Iris put the projector on the desk, which had been pushed against the back wall.

The projector, a Kodak, had been purchased by her father to show recordings of performances. He had taught the young Iris how to use it. That was a long time ago, machines had moved on, but she remembered what to do: open the sides of the box, attach the spools, wind the film around the sprockets, flick the switches.

Due to the expense of camera film, in all only nine minutes of *The Sing-Song Tribunal* had been recorded, divided into three spools: Act One (three minutes), Act Three (three minutes) and Act Five (three minutes). On the spool covers, written on a length of masking tape, were the words OPENING NIGHT, 6 NOV 1956, the only night the play had ever been performed.

While Eva and Doris settled onto the cushions on the floor, Iris made to leave.

—Don't go, said Eva. Stay and watch it with us.

271

Iris hesitated and then, against her truer wishes, said:

—All right.

She did not know what to expect. Her parents had never prohibited her from watching the film. She had often thought about doing so, but in the end she never had. An inner guardian had always protected her from it, as from something harmful.

She turned off the light and set the projector rolling.

They were quiet in the dark, which was absolute.

Out of that then, a square of white light appeared on the screen, then silent moving images—

JIANG QING

1974

ix.

She led the four dancers down the corridor to Apartment 118 and knocked on the door. The dancers, dressed in their costumes, were fighting off temptations to see that their shirts were sitting flat, and their pocket-flaps tucked in, and their shorts not riding up.

—Just do what we rehearsed, she told them, and you'll be fine.

Zhang Yufeng opened the door and beckoned them to enter. Jiang Qing stepped out of the way, and they filed in, one by one, as instructed. Once they were all inside, Zhang Yufeng nodded to Jiang Qing, an officious gesture, before closing the door.

Jiang Qing put her ear to the wood a moment. Waited for the music to start up. Then made her way down the corridor and round the corner. Using a master key, she unlocked the storeroom. Inside, she turned on the fluorescent light just long enough to map out a path through the broken and unused imperial furniture.

In the dark again, she made her way to the opposite wall. Took down the scroll. Licked a finger and pushed it through the rice paper that she used to cover the peephole. Then she brought her eye to the hole, allowed her vision to adjust, and watched—

THE
INTERRUPTION

I must write to you, dear Mao, here in this room, to inform you of my progress. There is not an hour in my days when I am not engaged in the struggle against myself. And my nights, do not ask me about my nights, for they are immersed in dreams in which I am judged by monstrous figures masked as me. In darkness and in light, both, I slave at it, an ideal condition for a Communist, a state of grace, yet it has not always been easy, and I have suffered much, sometimes to the point of despair. Still, revered husband, I have persevered. I have gone back over every event. Retraced every action, every bad thought. And now I can name ninety-nine occasions when I feel I may have impeded the Revolution. Do you see the list here, Red Sun in my Heart, unrolled under your light?

But this morning, just as I was penning my last item, a banging started which forced me to interrupt my work. The door swung open — I heard it — and the outside air rushed in — I felt it — and then there was light, bright light, with five figures emerging from it, and I am eager to describe to you, Supreme Teacher, what happened next.

The figures had white outfits on, but they were not doctors; all were known to me as Party members. They dragged me by the hair to the centre of the room and kicked me in the back of my legs so that I would fall down to a kneel. Then they made a circle around me and began to taunt me. They called me *ox demon*. They called me *snake spirit*. They called me *high-class whore*. They called me *Empress Wu*. They, who had once allied themselves with me, produced hand-drawn posters in which I appear as a witch, a rat, a jackal, a tart with a siren's tail and with knives sticking into my body.

—What do you think of that? they asked.

To which I said:

—I think it is a good thing that young people should rebel against the older generation.

But perhaps they were not really looking for a reply, for, instead of listening to my generous words, they slapped me in the mouth and told me to shut up.

The door opened again, and a record player was rolled in on a trolley. The extension cable was plugged into a socket in the corridor, which prevented the door from closing fully. Out of a fear that we would be heard through the open door, they put on 'Men with Fine, Loyal Hearts', and turned up the volume. Bellowing to be heard over the music — these are the comical touches that I know you will appreciate — they proceeded to read my indictment. The inventory of my so-called crimes was so long, its outlandishness so tediously familiar, that I could not refrain from yawning as it was enumerated. When they were finished, they asked:

—Do you still deny these charges?

To which I replied:

—Is it a crime in China to make Revolution?

This did not make them happy.

—Stand up! they said. Stand up when you speak!

When I did so, they knocked me back down, and, with a hand gripping the back of my head, forced me to kowtow in such a way that my forehead was hitting the floor like a pestle pounding garlic.

—If you have done nothing wrong, why would you be here?

—I do not know why I am here. I always tell you, you have the wrong person.

At that, they beat me across the back with a brass buckle.

—Stop playing the bloody fool. Confess now and we will be lenient.

—Everything I did followed Mao's line. What you are doing is asking a widow to pay her husband's debt. To you all, I say I am happy and honoured to pay this debt.

Still unsatisfied, they tied my hands behind my back and pushed them up to my ears:

—Once and for all, you must plead guilty in front of the revolutionary masses.

I could hear the sound of my tendons tearing and the blood vessels bursting open:

—My only error was to be more radical even than my husband, more Mao than Mao. Such an error can only ever be judged by the Chairman himself. I will plead guilty in only one hall of justice, and that is his.

Confounded by my indifference to their cruelty, they then tied me to a chair with iron wires, tightening and tightening the binds until deep furrows formed in my skin and blood poured down.

—You have been tried by the people and found guilty, yet you continue to profess your innocence. The masses think one thing about you, while you think another. When are you going to align your mind to theirs?

They told me that even my daughter had denounced me. They said Li Na was in agreement with China's guilty verdict in my case. They lowered the volume of the music and brought my attention to the sounds coming from outside the room, saying that Li Na was next door, but I would not see her unless I wrote a confession. They play-acted so convincingly that, for a mad second, I thought I really did hear Li Na's voice. Even so, instead of giving them a confession, I sucked the mucus out of my nostrils and spat it into their faces.

This gesture, capturing the sum total of my feelings, did not put an end to their pantomime. For then they brought in a woman, her identity obscured by a headscarf and dark glasses, and put her sitting in a chair a couple of metres away, and said:

—Look, here is Li Na. Do you want your darling daughter to witness your humiliation?

This made me laugh so hard that one of my teeth actually fell out. The useless motherfuckers. Did they truly think I feared getting rid of my pride and dignity in front of this impersonator? To remind them who they were dealing with, I released the internal muscles which until then I had been contracting, and the contents of my bladder rushed out of me, through my clothes and onto the concrete.

—That one was for the cameras, I said.

Now it was their turn to laugh. They could not help it. But laughing did not make them happy.

—Jiang Qing, they said, we have added up the bill for your life. It is time to settle accounts.

They freed one of my hands and put a pen in it, then held out a document and ordered me to sign it. When I refused — by dropping the pen and, with magical timing, just as it hit the ground, farting loudly — they went into a rage. They put my hands in a basin of black ink and ordered me to smear the ink over my own face, which I readily did. With only one hand, however, I could not apply ink fast enough for their liking, so they splashed it over me until it was dripping from my eyes and my nose and my mouth, long strings of black reaching all the way down to the concrete. Deciding that even this was not enough, they poured it down the neck of my shirt so that it oozed out from my waist, ran along my legs and came out the end of my trousers. Then they poured what remained down my actual neck until I vomited it back up.

One would think that these events move fast, but actually they are slow with lots of pauses to change the music and to convene.

How far was too far?

I had time to think and plan my responses. They were using techniques that I myself had perfected, so I often knew in advance of their orders what they wanted me to do. This allowed me to perform reactions before actions. I answered before I was asked. I sneered before I was jeered. I suffered blows before I was hit. I passed out before reaching my limit and came back to consciousness before any cold water touched my skin. In this way I felt I was performing at a great distance from my torturers. I was playing here, while they were playing way over there.

Thus detached, I turned to concentrate on myself, and found that I gradually separated from the person I was familiar with, and, according to the law of one divides into two, multiplied into many foreign-seeming forms. One of these forms was particularly startling, and my purpose in writing to you, Great Leader, is to describe it as best I can to you.

In my place, on the chair in the centre of the room, was a woman

I had once struggled against, the wife of a shoe seller who had been caught possessing foreign products. Her face was streaked with lipstick. Clumps of hair had been pulled from her scalp. She was wearing a necklace made of ping-pong balls. High-heeled shoes had been strung together and looped around her body. Broken bits of Western junk, like playing cards and aluminium cans, dangled from her clothes. She had been forced to sit on a burning cigarette and was being made to recount over and over again how she had come to commit her crime. During the pauses between her phrases, a crowd shouted slogans and jeered, and at the same time pressed forward, convulsed in an agony of impatience, longing to drag her down from the stage, and beat her with fists and broomsticks, and parade her through the streets, thereby upholding justice on behalf of themselves, the people.

All the while I was in the wings, directing the torturers' every move. Although I was hidden from the masses by a screen, I knew the woman was aware of my presence, for occasionally she would turn her head a little and glance in my direction. And what magnificent eyes she had now that she was suffering. She had let go of defiance, had embraced hardship and trauma, and as a consequence the lines of her face had softened and her natural beauty had returned. Her honour was gone, her self-respect with it; all she had inside now was a nucleus, a hard kernel of hate: the pain of the oppressed that has existed since our ancestors' times, the hatred of thousands of years — and it made her glow.

Her acknowledgement of this hate at her soul's core meant that she could truly empathise with her torturers. Like her, hatred was the only satisfaction they had left, it was their final identity. All they were doing, she recognised, was looking for a punishment that would make punishment unnecessary, a violence that would end violence. They believed that the only way to be understood was to hurt, and perhaps they were right: she would show her mutual understanding by not resisting. When they came hard, she gave them soft. Their blows she met with humbleness, gentleness, then let them go. And while she said:

—Good people, I kowtow to you, I was wrong in the past.

And she said:

—I am guilty, I committed crimes against the Revolution, I lower my head and admit it.

And she said:

—I must be obedient, I am not allowed to speak or act without permission, if I do so, may you beat me and smash me.

She was in fact thinking: *I am justified. I am the winner if I give way to you willingly. Your cruelty arises from your greater misery. You are doing nothing but cleansing me for my forthcoming mission to save China. I, the victim, am on the right side of history, and will be remembered, not merely memorialised. My hate will outrun yours; it is the water that cannot be mopped up, the fire that cannot be put down.*

So I ask you, wise husband, to tell me please, when I describe this to you, what do you see? You see more than I, and further, so perhaps you can clarify these happenings for me. This woman, whom I remember from my past, was she me? Or was she not-me? Was she a ghost, come on an evil wind?

The living dead, the texts of literature say, are by nature reactionary. They insist that the world return to the way it was for them. Is that why she appeared to me? To demand that I give her back her China? If so, hers was a wasted visit, for that is not something I can do. I could not even give her *my* China, if she should want that, for my China no longer exists either. The China of today is neither hers nor mine but belongs to others.

And now I ask myself:

When I die, whom would *I* visit? Whom would I break in upon to demand the return of my world? Who is to blame for stealing the Revolution from me? On whom could I bear down to take revenge in my name? I would not even know where to start. After so long a fight one loses the capacity to distinguish who has done what to whom. When the mantis catches the cicada, the finch is right behind. One thing overcomes another, and eventually we all get even.

Your leading lady,
Jiang Qing

III

JIANG QING

1974

<u>X.</u>

—and what she saw turned her blood, as though she had stumbled across a snake in the middle of the road.

She reeled back from the peephole and, feeling her legs weakening, groped about in the dark for somewhere to sit down. The sensation was that of a heavy bag of rice suddenly being placed on her shoulders. She clung to the wall to steady herself, nearly taking down a court robe that hung there.

As she staggered around, she hit her head on an empty bird cage, and knocked over a spittoon with her foot. Cursing, she ventured away from the peripheries towards the centre of the room and located the area where gifts from foreigners were stored: boxes of Cuban cigars from Castro and aged brandy from Ceaușescu. She sat atop a case and breathed deeply, filling her senses with the sweet smell of camphor wood.

Blinking into the black, she had the impression that for the first time since her childhood she was seeing objects clearly. Life was suddenly present, in all its meaning. She was in it, not looking through a window at it. Thoughts which she had had before, but which she was prohibited to think, were now visible in her mind and demanding her attention:

Mao is dying. You're going to lose him.

IRIS

1968

<u>xi.</u>

—then the third spool of film abruptly ended. The final images flickered and were consumed by white light. Blinking into the glare, she listened without emotion to Eva, who had started to cry, and to Doris who was rubbing Eva's back and saying:

—It's all right, let it out. If I was you, I'd do the same.

Out of nothing, then, Iris felt all the frustration, the agony, the despair of a childhood spent in her sister's shadow. *What the fucking hell is she bawling about?*

—What is with you? she said.

—Shh, said Doris. Don't.

—No, I'm serious. I want to know. Are you crying because I took your place in the stupid play? That you didn't have your big fucking moment? You've had plenty of moments since then to make up for it, haven't you?

—Shut up, Iris, said Eva.

—I mean, you're not going to start pretending, now, that you had it harder than me, are you?

—I said shut up.

—Papa's little actress. Dry your bloody eyes, please, and give us all a break.

Eva wiped her face and glared at her with red eyes:

—You're a monster, you know that? How can you speak to me like that after what we've just watched? What gives *you* the right to be angry with *me*?

—Maybe it has something to do with you going off to Paris without me.

—Oh God, is this going to be your new weapon?

—It's the truth of what happened, isn't it? You went off and left me here. Your sister. A full, voting commune member. And now, as a stinger, you come home and dredge up this family crap. For what purpose? You haven't learned anything.

—Enlighten me, Iris. What am I supposed to have learned?

—You honestly still think you're the victim, don't you? You don't get it at all. I did it for you.

—Excuse me?

—I took your place in *The Sing-Song Tribunal* because I was trying to save you.

Eva grimaced:

—Save me? From what?

Yourself.

—From nothing. Forget it.

Eva was a girl with a bit of talent, but not enough talent, and it haunted her. By taking her place in the play, Iris had protected her from the mortification of exposing herself to the world at too young an age. A mortification from which she would not have recovered. A mortification which would have destroyed her ambitions of becoming an actress. In point of fact, if Eva was able to call herself an actress today, it was owing to Iris's intervention. By rights, she should be *thanking* her. Down on her hands and knees.

—I just can't believe you continue to blame me for what happened, said Iris.

—Who else is there to blame?

—You know, it's not all about you, Eva. When I did what I did, I wasn't thinking about you. You were the furthest thing from my mind.

—That's for fucking sure.

—The only person I was thinking about was Mama. Isn't that obvious? It was *her* I was trying to get at. *Her* I was trying to show—

—Show what? What were you trying to show her exactly, Iris? You'd nothing to complain about. All the woman did was spoil you.

—Spoil me? Is that what you call how she treated me? She did terrible things to me. And the film proves it.

Eva had stopped crying. Her face was stone.

—Are you out of your mind? she said. The film proves nothing of the sort. What it shows is a dirty brat marching into a place she shouldn't have been. Taking *my* stage. Stealing *my* part. If I was your mother, God forbid, I'd have done much worse.

At that, the fury got too much. Iris closed her eyes and allowed it to consume her.

Keith was right. How could a ten-year-old be to blame for so much? Could nobody else see with whom final responsibility lay? Who the puppet master behind it all had been? Eva could cry all she liked, but it was not going to do them any good. This pain was the kind caused by a mother's hand, and the honey of revenge was the only medicine for it.

EVA

1956

<u>xii.</u>

—once it was over, she left the chair in the centre of the circle and joined her mother.

The same arm which her mother had used to push her into the circle, she now put around her waist. Eva read this as a consoling gesture. *Hard luck. You did your best.* Which even Eva, who did not yet know a lot about techniques, could tell had not been enough. She had been exposed; she had humiliated herself.

Iris, who was sitting on the piano stool, started to cry. It was something Eva would never forget: the moment her sister shed real tears for her. Doris comforted Iris by taking her hand and squeezing it, and by rubbing her back

Max stood up and began to gather his things from the director's table, as if signalling that that would be it for the day. Rehearsals would resume when an adequate actress had been found.

Well, that settled it, Eva thought. She had been given her chance, and she had blown it.

But then came the sound of a single pair of hands clapping. Which became an applause that spread to the circle, made its way round like a ring of fire igniting. Animated by it, Eva emerged from her hiding place in her mother's embrace and took a bow. Her mother, her hands freed, began to applaud with the others. Eva turned round and, with little waves of her hand, told everyone to stop, but they did not stop. They went on.

Truth stood in contrast to falsehood, did it not? Beauty in contrast to ugliness? Fragrant flowers to poisonous weeds? These people, these professionals, were clapping for her, which could only signify that she was good.

Her mother led her outside so that the members could vote.

Once they were alone on the mezzanine, Eva said:

—What did you think, Mama, really?

Her mother brushed a hair from Eva's cheek.

—Art, she said then, especially the theatre, is a realm you can't enter without the odd stumble. Don't be too disappointed if the group decide you're not ready.

After only a short minute, her father opened the door and stretched out his arms:

—Eva, darling.

Eva went in and accepted what she assumed to be her father's condolences.

—It was unanimous, precious, he said. You're in.

JIANG QING

1974

<u>xiii.</u>

A bright moon was in the sky, and she could not sleep. Her pills and drops did not help; her *qigong* breathing techniques neither. Wound up, head throbbing: it was as though her system was running on chicken blood. The left side of the bed was as inhospitable as the right. Closing the shutters stopped the cool air from coming in; opening them let the darkness out. Her eye-mask gave her an oppressive feeling like that of a vice gripping her temples, and she had to tear it off. Her thoughts were in a whirl, orbiting the subject of death without ever facing it. It felt like her mind was preparing to say goodbye to Mao — by saying everything once more, all that there was to say, all that she had left unsaid — while her heart was refusing to contemplate a life without him.

Exhausted, finally, by these rotations, she got up while it was still night, and washed. Sat at the table by the window, drinking boiled water and scrunching the curls of her perm back into her wet hair.

During her entire life with Mao, she had never given any proper thought to death in relation to him. To do so was a crime, one of the few she was genuinely afraid to commit, so she had refused to let it cross her mind. Normally death starts a long time ahead of when it arrives, yet out of duty to the Revolution she had declined to detect its advance on Mao. The Chairman, although obviously old, had not aged in her eyes; although obviously sick, he had not succumbed. When she looked at him, she saw the face of embalmed youth: not a wrinkle, not a crow's foot marring the carefully massaged flesh. He seemed always to be just now rising and not yet stopped.

Such a loyal refusal to see could no longer blot out what had been seen, however. Viewed through the peephole last night, Mao's aspect had changed. The face to which she had hitherto been blind became available. For the first time she saw Mao's glaze crack, and this shell, grown as thin as rice paper, crumble to dust, and the effigy of an old man emerge, complete in every detail, with wrinkles, yellow eyes, large brown moles, green-coated teeth, swollen veins, knotted fingers, tissue invaded by disease, insides black, death embedded.

Her first instinct had been to blame the dancers. Was it not their job to help Mao recover lost vigour, to freshen him up? But in truth they could not be faulted. They had put all their youth and vitality into their performance; with their smiles alone they had brought five lights and ten colours to the scene, and still they had not been able to puncture the shadow of dusk which was over all. Mao, once the Red Sun in the East, China's Star of Salvation, was a burnt-out man. His embers were dying away to ash. The cold was gathering around. It was the almost hour.

Now, alone in her own room, she thought she might cry, for her thought was: *When you, Mao, are dead, will I dare to be alive?*

Clasping a hand over her mouth to prevent the liberation of her grief, she scrabbled for the lamp switch and flicked it on. Dazzled, she covered her eyes with her other hand, and, her entire face covered like this, collapsed forward onto her lap. In a matter of months he would be gone, she knew it, and she was frightened by this foreknowledge, and reminded of her own mortality, and angry about being left to face the future on her own. She shuddered: no tears, just a silent wail.

But then it came to her: *No, no, Mao, you won't die. You won't have to. You'll go on, as an anguish inside of me.*

And this brought her round. Her inner noise quietened, the convulsions ceased, and she parted her fingers to look out again. The lamp was reflected in the window glass, preventing her from seeing out, so she switched it back off. Visible now, marked out by the moonlight, was the garden: rock and water and earth and plant. Her feelings departed her and attached to these forms. *There is nothing to lament,* she thought, rubbing her face with her hands, and her hands on a nearby cushion, *for Mao cannot die. He has become installed in my heart, has taken root in me. He is my life-force, my oxygen. As long as I am alive, he will endure.*

She wrapped herself in a blanket and went out onto the veranda, where the breeze had a bite, and where the vast landscape managed also to be private. She leaned on the veranda wall, and, aided by her knowledge of the meticulous planning that went into this wildness, picked out the path that led to the pavilion where, in another life, she used to sit with Mao and view the moon. Now the pavilion was empty, so she had to be his eyes, ears and voice:

The lonely goddess in the moon spreads her ample sleeves
To dance for those good souls in the endless sky.
Of a sudden comes word of the Tiger's defeat on earth
Tears stream down like an upturned bowl of rain.

Before dawn, at the first whistles of the birds, she ordered the car, and arrived at the Central Ballet compound in advance of the morning gongs. She ordered the driver to park in the central concourse, and, without waiting for her bodyguards to secure the area, went by herself to the women's dormitory block.

The dancers were still asleep, so the halls were empty; silence was conveyed by the squeak of her plastic shoes on the washed floors. Entering room six on the second floor, she turned on the light and took the gong from the shelf. Stuck it three times.

—Everybody up! An early rise this morning! Come on, up! Up!

The dancers groaned and peeped out from under their blankets, indisposed to renouncing any of their sleep allowance. As soon as they realised who was there, however, they sprang up and stood to attention.

—Don't just stand there, hurry! Into your exercise clothes and out for your jog. We have a lot to accomplish today.

Tong Hua, whom Jiang Qing had come to see, began to undress with the others.

—No, Jiang Qing said to her. Not you. You stay where you are. Sit down.

Tong Hua, gone white, perched her hard little arse on the edge of the mattress, fearful of committing more of herself to the command. Jiang Qing sat down on the neighbouring bed, facing her. Tong Hua was not one of the prettier girls, having marks on her cheeks from a severe bout of adolescent acne, but she had a melon-seed-shaped face and a pursed cherry mouth which were likely to make men want her nonetheless. While the other dancers changed, Jiang Qing poured Tong Hua a cup of tea from a flask which she had brought and set it down to cool on the side-table. From her uniform pocket she produced a boiled egg, cracked it against the iron bedpost, and peeled the top third of the shell off.

—There you go, she said, handing it to Tong Hua.

Tong Hua received the egg with the fingers of both hands. Then bowed her head in gratitude. The dancers nearby glanced at Tong Hua and exchanged, with their eyes, feelings about her.

—What are you gawping at? Jiang Qing shouted at them. Get out. Ten laps of the concourse, and no slacking off. I'll be counting from the window.

When the dancers had left, Jiang Qing said to Tong Hua:

—Do you need to piss?

She nodded.

—Can you hold it in?

She nodded.

Jiang Qing leaned over and removed the hardened mucus collected in the corners of Tong Hua's eyes.

— Tong Hua. I suppose your parents gave you that name. The Chairman gave me mine, would you believe?

She traced out the characters of her name on her open palm.

—*Green river* like this, but also, by virtue of its sound, *pure waters*, do you see? Do you like it?

—Yes.

—So do I. I sometimes say it to myself, out loud, just to hear it. Jiang Qing. *Jiang Qing*. I like the feel of it in my mouth, and I like hearing it in the air around me, you know? There are many things one can do to feel close to one's husband. Some day you'll see for yourself.

Tong Hua met Jiang Qing's eye, then immediately lowered her gaze again.

—I'd like to give you a name, Jiang Qing said. A stage name. A revolutionary name. I was thinking about *Wenge*. Do you like that?

Tong Hua nodded.

—Wenge it is then. Say it.

—Wenge.

—It suits you. A strong name. A warrior's name. Say it again. My name is?

—My name is Wenge.

In the short time they had been speaking, Wenge's posture had deteriorated into a slouch, a common problem amongst these young girls, in spite of their training. Jiang Qing moved to the bed beside her and ran a finger up her spine in order to correct it.

—So tell me about yourself, Wenge. Your family. Where you come from.

In a low voice, cautious and rehearsed, Wenge told a familiar story about being raised in poverty in a provincial village, before, at the age of ten, being selected by a group of visiting Party officials to attend the Academy. She was at pains to explain that her family background had been checked, and that it contained all three of the good classes: peasants, workers, and soldiers.

—How fortunate you are, said Jiang Qing. Do you feel special?

Wenge shook her head vigorously once, which made Jiang Qing smile.

—I'd be surprised if you didn't feel, well, if you didn't feel just a little bit special.

Wenge was turning her half-eaten egg around in her fingers.

Jiang Qing touched the girls's quivering leg to steady it.

—Go on. Eat your egg.

Wenge nibbled off the white at the top, revealing the hardened yolk: a sun peeping out of clouds.

—Have some tea.

Wenge blew on the tea, then sipped loudly.

—Listen, Wenge, said Jiang Qing, I know I promised you an extra hour in bed this morning after your late night last night. I hate to deny you that. But I have news that couldn't wait till later.

Using the knuckle of her index finger, she pushed Wenge's chin up.

—I watched you last night, child. I wasn't in the room, but I could see you, do you understand? I can always see you. I'm always watching.

Wenge had let her back hunch again, and her shoulders jut forwards, as if trying to hide her heart. Jiang Qing righted her once more.

—The dancer has only her body. And the body isn't an opinion. It's a collection of physical laws. The dancer explores the limits of what these laws allow. Either she can touch those limits, and traverse them, or she can't. The audience can see if she's good from tens of *li* away. If she's bad, she's immediately exposed.

Wenge's lips, which had been drawn into her mouth, unfolded outwards, and her tongue slid out to wet them; then she sucked everything back in.

—What I'm saying, Wenge, is that your performance last night impressed me. It was clear to me that you're better than the others and deserve to be seen.

Wenge closed her eyes and released a breath through her nostrils.

—Now you mustn't misunderstand what's happening here. It isn't the Chairman who has picked you out for special attention. The Chairman is—. Well, it's doubtful he'd have been able to distinguish you from the others. Luckily for you, I have excellent vision.

Jiang Qing tapped the frame of her spectacles.

—Don't let these ugly things fool you. My eyes are like a hawk's. Nothing escapes them. And, as I say, they liked what they saw.

Jiang Qing rubbed the girl's neck and shoulders. Mention of Mao had clearly overloaded her.

—There's a girl, Jiang Qing said. Eat up.

It took Wenge a long minute to finish the egg. Once she had done so, Jiang Qing took the shell from her, dropped it into the unfinished tea, and took the cup to the window. Outside, the entire troupe of dancers, male and female, were jogging in a circle around the edges of the concourse. Parked in the centre, next to the Volgas, was the line of buses which would transport them to the Great Hall for rehearsals. Jiang Qing opened the window and flung the unfinished tea and the shell out.

—Do you want to be the best, Wenge? she said, coming away from the window.

—I, I, I don't know, Auntie Jiang.

Jiang Qing twisted the cup back onto the top of the flask and gave it to Wenge to hold. Wenge gripped it in both hands as though it were a precious relic.

—This is a private conversation, strictly between you and me. You don't have to be modest. Do you want to be the best?

—Ahm—

—Silly goose, do you trust me?

—Yes, Auntie Jiang. I love you.

Jiang Qing took Wenge's rehearsal clothes from the drawer and dropped them into Wenge's lap. Without waiting for the order, Wenge began to change.

—Then you must trust me when I tell you that you're extraordinary, and that you deserve this promotion.

Wenge paused with one leg in her shorts and one leg out.

—You heard me, said Jiang Qing.

Wenge turned away to put on her bra.

—When someone appoints you to a high position, said Jiang Qing, that someone is assuming responsibility for your actions. You mustn't let them down.

—I wouldn't, ever, Auntie Jiang.

—Then you must follow my lead and do everything I say.

Wenge pulled her jersey over her head:

—Everything. I understand.

Jiang Qing took Wenge's bag from her hook and began to fill it with her personal things: dancing slippers, long trousers, coat, hairbrush, bar of soap.

Wenge put the flask under her arm and held out her hand for her bag, now full.

Jiang Qing indicated that, no, she would carry it.

She made to leave the room, and Wenge followed her.

At the door, she paused:

—Do you grasp what is happening to you, Wenge?

Wenge nodded but looked bewildered.

Jiang Qing pulled her in to her chest and clasped her tightly. The child's arms, wrapped around the flask, were crushed between their breasts.

—You're going to make a great ARMY CAPTAIN, Jiang Qing said.

She released her embrace but kept hold of the girl's shoulders.

Wenge's eyebrows were knitted. She was worried.

—You should be happy, said Jiang Qing.

—I am, Auntie Jiang. But, but why me?

Jiang Qing smacked Wenge on the side of the head:

—In Revolution, people don't choose jobs. Jobs choose people. This is called being obedient to the organisation.

Jiang Qing watched Wenge fight not to bring her hand to the place where she had been struck; and fight to prevent tears from coming to her eyes; and fight instead to summon the look of defiant radiance worn by the female soldiers in *The Red Detachment of Women*.

Good girl.

Wenge was allotted five days in which to learn the role of ARMY CAPTAIN. She was given lodgings in a room attached to Jiang Qing's own Separate Apartment, removed from all contact with the rest of the troupe. At five each morning she was woken by Jiang Qing herself, plunged into ice to sharpen her mental awareness, and sent to the garden for a jog. For breakfast, in addition to the regulation rice porridge and pickled turnips, she was allotted eggs and soy milk and wonton soup. After that, she was escorted to a secret room in the Compound, within the headquarters of the Central Garrison Corps on the east side of the lake, where she was drilled in male ballet steps till noon. At lunch she was served an extra bowl of rice and expected to eat it. The slot allocated to her midday sleep was half an hour longer than the norm, and, again, she was expected to use it. This was because, instead of the usual three hours of role-building in the afternoon, she had five; and after dinner, when ordinarily she would be let off to study, she had a further two hours of marching, rifle practice and martial arts: for such a strenuous routine, she needed to be well fed and rested. Jiang Qing conducted this training according to the ideal of Lei Feng: to go up mountains of knives and swim through seas of flames; to have one's body smashed to powder and one's bones crushed to smithereens. To this, Wenge submitted unquestioningly. Her reward at the end of the day was a full bath of hot water, for which she was provided with an extra bar of soap. The soap was jasmine, and Jiang Qing insisted that she come to her room, smelling of this, before going to bed.

—Have a seat in the big armchair, Jiang Qing would say, and after much goading Wenge would oblige.

—Are you tired? Jiang Qing would ask her.

—Not really, Wenge would lie.

—Nonsense, Jiang Qing would say, you've been dancing for ten hours.

She would order a basin of warm salted water to be brought in, and would herself kneel in front of the Wenge, and lift her feet into the basin. While Wenge's feet soaked, she would rub the girl's thighs and calves with tiger balm. Then she would lay a towel across her own thighs and place Wenge's wet feet onto it. She would dry Wenge's feet carefully, cut any broken nails, reapply the bandages on her toes, and perfume the skin with rose water.

—My dear Wenge, Jiang Qing would say in an effort to relax her, do you think I believe myself above this?

Once the treatment was finished, she would put a fresh pair of socks on Wenge's feet and bring the portable radiator closer to chase away the chill. Then they, both of them, would sit with their feet up on stools, drinking lotus brew and watching banned ballet films: of Fonteyn and Ulanova and Plisetskaya and Alonso and Kirkland and Nureyev and Baryshnikov.

After the film ended, and they had exhausted their criticisms of the state of dancing in the world today, Jiang Qing would order a second pot of tea, which was the signal that it was Wenge's turn to be criticised.

—I fear, Jiang Qing would say, that I lack the lion's voice for commanding. I can see that my instructions don't always reach you. I want to fire you up, to bring on the necessary storm, but at the same time I'm scared of inhibiting you, with the result that I end up serving you half-measures. This is my error. In committing it, my name falls behind Sun Shan. I can only hope that still words, shared here in private, will succeed where my former commands have failed.

One expected all the dancers at the Central Ballet to be talented. *Talent high to the extent of eight dou* was the unwritten standard. In Wenge's case, unusually, talent was accompanied by a high capacity for concentration and a quiet composure. She had developed a sense of dignity and responsibility and made no displays of temperament. At all times, she was serious, composed and completely absorbed in the work. In her technique, foreign conventions had successfully been broken down and subdued. She had mastered all the classic movements without letting them enslave her. Her limbs were beautifully trained. Her feet well arched. Her extensions high without any apparent forcing. Her back was supple enough that she could bend backwards to the floor ten, twenty, thirty times in a row, without wobbling or losing form.

In short, she was a ripened melon. So it did not surprise Jiang Qing that Wenge picked up the ARMY CAPTAIN's steps with ease. For a female dancer, these steps demanded a different kind of precision, one derived from commands and salutes, the language of military parades. To Wenge's credit, she realised early on that the challenge was not that of compensating for a perceived lack of strength by overreaching herself; the opposite, it was that of discovering a new kind of strength by limiting herself. To this end she restricted her bends. Straightened her limbs. Cut the temptation to point the toe, extend the leg, bend the back all the way. Rather than push beyond, she pulled back, garnered her energy inwards, to her centre, and from there, when the cue arrived, erupted into the required shapes.

And yet, and yet — it pained Jiang Qing to see — in the last resort, Wenge was not convincing. She had mastered all the different components of the role but was unable to assemble them into a complete performance. In her execution of the individual steps, in finding and holding the forms, she outdid even Song Yaojin, the best ARMY CAPTAIN there had ever been, yet she was unable to inhabit the role as he had. She had what it took to be the upright soldier, the perfect man, but appeared scared of herself as such, intimidated by her own abilities, and was therefore not entirely persuasive.

At first Jiang Qing thought Wenge was being hindered by vanity.

—Are you worried that portraying a man is ruining your appearance? she said to her. Are you afraid of not being pretty? A dread of losing men's regard, is that the reason you're messing up like this?

By and by, however, she realised that the problem went deeper than this. She noticed that Wenge's difficulties were most pronounced in those moments in the ballet when the ARMY CAPTAIN was on stage but not dancing, that is when Wenge was expected to replace ballet steps with the gestures of the dramatic theatre. In scene three, for instance, the ARMY CAPTAIN, disguised as a rich merchant, sits on a chair, watching an entertainment and fanning himself with a large white fan. Amusing, technically untaxing: it had been Song Yaojin's favourite bit to perform; he used to brag about being able to upstage all the other dancers with a single beat of the fan. But for Wenge it was different. The scene gave her terrible trouble. No matter how many times she practised it, she could not get it right. She was unable simply to sit for any stretch without seeming tense. Her attempts to use the fan according to the rules of men's conduct — gripping it from underneath, beating the air upwards, never bringing it to the face — led to her mishandling or dropping it. Because the ARMY CAPTAIN is in disguise in this scene; because the character himself is performing, his expressions and gestures are deliberately those of a suave and effeminate man. Wenge's failure to convey this effeminacy made her cry out in frustration.

—Wenge! What on earth is wrong with you? What are you doing with your hands? Are you playing a soldier or a faggot? Choose!

Jiang Qing hoped that being in costume would help. She had ordered the ARMY CAPTAIN's five outfits in Wenge's size, and when the outfits arrived, on the fourth day of their private rehearsals, she hung them on a rail and invited Wenge to get acquainted with them.

—What do you think?

Wenge stroked the material:

—They're—

—High-grade, I know. I thought you'd like them.

Jiang Qing picked out the military uniform and helped Wenge into it. Although Wenge's breasts were small, barely there, Jiang Qing thought it best that they be out of the way completely, and so bound them with a large bandage. Onto the front of Wenge's underwear she taped a small paperweight, so that Wenge would feel a load there. Extra padding had been sown into the sides of the jacket, and the belt fastened high across her ribs, in order to straighten Wenge's silhouette. Wenge had big thighs, which had previously prevented her from doing principal female roles, and around which she usually wrapped plastic so that they would sweat and become thinner; for the part of ARMY CAPTAIN they were an advantage, for they filled out the shorts without the need for stuffing. Her shins, on the other hand, were as thin as sticks; four pairs of leggings were required to broaden them. The last element, the cap, had been designed with a wire frame to add height. Jiang Qing pinned it to Wenge's hair, and stood back to look at the result.

—Yes, she said, and turned Wenge by the shoulders to face the mirror. Hmm? Am I right?

Wenge examined her reflection carefully, as though it was not hers, as though it belonged to someone else. Jiang Qing smiled, remembering the sensation of seeing oneself in costume for the first time: the mental switch which occurred that permitted one to shed one's common habits and to make the shapes of a character who looked like that.

—I don't recognise myself, Wenge said.

—I recognise you. You're the ARMY CAPTAIN. The body and the voice of China.

They practised in costume for the rest of the day, until Wenge got it right, that is until she stopped making the mistake of trying to play a man, and instead learned to forget that she was a woman.

That evening in Jiang Qing's room, for the first time Wenge admitted to being tired.

—Today, yes, she said. Today I feel it.

They were sitting side by side, facing the window. Between the armchairs, on a side table, their lotus brew was cooling. Jiang Qing wafted away the rising steam. Reached across and fixed Wenge's blanket, which had come down on one side. Tested the heat of the cups with her fingers. Judging them cool enough, she handed one to Wenge.

—Do you happen to know the story of Meng Lijun? she said.

Wenge shook her head.

Jiang Qing took some tea into her mouth and sloshed it about, for the taste, before swallowing it down.

—Watching you today reminded me of an actress I used to like when I lived in Shanghai. There was a specific theatre I used to go to, where this actress was employed. In all of Shanghai, she was the best at playing Meng Lijun.

Jiang Qing paused as her mind became filled with the memory of sitting amongst the bourgeois housewives and their daughters in the Great Chinese Theatre on Fuzhou Road, where, together, in a state of almost unbearable agitation, they would watch the red curtain rise and witness Xiao Dangui embodying their ideal man.

—The actress's name was Xiao Dangui. What made her great was that she didn't try to copy the style of other men to convince us that she was a man. Her words, her impulses, her actions told us, simply, that she was being a real man. If you ask me, in her place, a man wouldn't have done such a good job.

Smiling — it was secretly exhilarating to be speaking openly about this — she took some more tea, then put the cup down and pulled the blanket up to her chest.

—A woman is more capable of representing universal man. When a man plays that role, he ends up imitating great men in history and ends up feeling inhibited in their presence. He compensates for his own weakness by overacting, and that always ruins things.

Wenge was staring into her empty cup, aware that they had entered dangerous territory.

Jiang Qing lifted the lid of the pot and stirred the remaining tea, tapped the pot with the spoon. She poured Wenge another cup.

—The curious thing about Xiao Dangui was that, on stage, she barely seemed to do anything. I don't think she ever tried to be anyone else than a slightly subtracted version of herself. It was as if she believed that the less she did to make us believe, the more we would believe. And it was true, it worked.

Wenge brought her newly filled cup under her nose and breathed in the scent.

Jiang Qing did the same.

—In a couple of days' time, Wenge, you're going to dance the role of ARMY CAPTAIN in front of the entire Beijing Party apparatus, ten thousand people, and of course Mrs Marcos, who, owing to the outside attention she attracts, counts for ten thousand more. I can see you're scared. You don't believe you're up to the task, so you're finding false excuses for yourself. But that's the easy way. Where you find one excuse, you'll find a hundred. The hard thing is to run towards the difficulty, to go more deeply into what you've learned.

Wenge's hair, lustrous as ebony, had been cropped in such a way that it could be oiled and parted. Jiang Qing smoothed it where it had become tousled.

—I've told you what's right, child. All you have to do is move now to where it is.

She reintroduced Wenge into the troupe on the first day of full dress rehearsal, two days before the gala performance. At the auditorium door, Wenge went rigid and refused to budge like a stubborn ox at the bank of a fast-flowing river. Jiang Qing literally had to slap her on the bottom to get her across the threshold. The unit of Red Guards, which Jiang Qing had brought as backup, she ordered to wait outside in the corridor.

—Keep the doors ajar, she told them, and listen for my signal.

Inside, the house lights had been switched off. On stage, the troupe were well into scene one, by Jiang Qing's estimation about five minutes from the ARMY CAPTAIN's first appearance. As they descended the central aisle in the semi-darkness, Jiang Qing took Wenge's hand, which was cold to the touch, the palm moist. Wenge let out a whimper, which Jiang Qing answered by pulling down hard on her arm:

—None of that. I want none of that, do you hear? This is real life. You must face it.

From their seats in the fourth row of the stalls, Chao Ying and his assistants glanced over their shoulders:

—Shh!

Resting a calming hand on Wenge's back, then creeping it up to grip her collar, Jiang Qing shepherded the girl the rest of the way down. She decided against joining Chao Ying, opting instead for the seats directly in front of him. She waited until she was standing in Chao Ying's line of vision before taking off her scarf, then her cardigan, then, as if noticing a draught, putting her scarf back on. She did not sit down, either, until she had wiped the dust off the cushion and checked the floor for anything that might obstruct the comfortable placement of her feet. Protocol prevented Wenge from sitting until Jiang Qing had, which afforded Chao Ying ample opportunity to take in the cut and quality of the girl's ARMY CAPTAIN costume. The seats creaked, first for Jiang Qing; second, though less so, for Wenge.

—Commander—

Chao Ying leaned over their shoulders and hissed,

—what the hell is this?

Alarmed, Wenge tried to retract her head into her body like a turtle.

Jiang Qing put a hand on her knee: *just ignore him.*

—First you take Tong Hua away without any notice, and with no indication of when, or whether she'd be coming back. And now, whole days later, you saunter in here, as if nothing has happ—

Jiang Qing seized Chao Ying's nose between her thumb and forefinger and used it to propel him back into his seat.

—Son of a bitch! she said. I'll fuck your grandmother!

Chao Ying's assistants, both women, one to either side, the skin on their young faces reflecting the colours of the stage lamps, sat as though petrified, their mouths covered. Chao Ying himself appeared to be feeling in a single blow the sum of all the little corrections that Jiang Qing had been forced to give him over the course of his career.

—Remember yourself, Director Chao, she said.

—I have it very clear, Commander, who I am, and what my job is.

—In that case, you'll be able to count the number of ranks which divide us—

—There aren't as many as you seem to think.

—and you'll be careful how you comport yourself for the rest of the day. I'm here to make the necessary final changes to our gala performance for Mrs Marcos, which my position in the Propaganda Committee authorises and demands. I'll be watching to see how well you adjust to those changes. Anything less than your full compliance, I'll mark as insubordination.

Distracted by the talk coming from the stalls, the dancer playing the SLAVE GIRL missed her mark in a jump, and stumbled a little, putting her behind the beat for a number of steps. Jiang Qing called a stop to the music and told the dancer to start again at the beginning of her solo. The performance recommenced. Under Jiang Qing's gaze, the energy of the troupe flowed unforced, always moving forward, the thread unbroken. She could not find much to fault. The dancing was good, light. The poses exact. The performers accomplished what they set out to do, they were exposed and honest and alive, no one disgraced themselves. The ARMY CAPTAIN, whom she had criticised in the past for a range of bad habits, and on whom she was now keeping a particularly close eye, did not do anything that was radically unsound. But this did not bring her to question her plan to replace him. Her purpose remained fixed. Behind her, Chao Ying and his assistants were scribbling notes, tearing them out and passing them around, whereas she was calm and unstirring, in a state of assuredness, her arm resting on the armrest, her hand hanging off the end, her fingertips suspended centimetres above Wenge's knee; when the chosen moment came — in the sixth and final scene — she would simply tickle the girl, or pinch her, and that would be their cue to move.

When that scene arrived — the TYRANT's courtyard, an overcast sky, a huge banian tree in front of which the ARMY CAPTAIN is about to be executed on the burning pyre — she rose out of the seat and took Wenge up with her. As they climbed the temporary steps to the right of the orchestra pit, and as they crossed the stage, the ARMY CAPTAIN was holding his last pose: standing rigid in the flames, his right fist raised, looking defiantly out over the motherland.

From the stalls came Chao Ying's screaming:

—What on earth? How dare you! No, really, this is too much. Stop right there! Come down immediately! You're making a mockery of our work and destroying morale in the process. Really, I've never —. Come down! I mean, this is —. I can't go on like this!

Disdaining Chao Ying, Jiang Qing occupied centre stage and waited to be acknowledged by the cast. After a few seconds, the ARMY CAPTAIN dropped his pose, a reluctant relenting, and the TYRANT and his GUARDS followed suit. The music separated into discordant parts, then droned to a halt. In the wings, the RED DETACHMENT OF WOMEN, who had been poised to rush on and take their revenge on the TYRANT, folded their arms and exchanged confused looks.

Jiang Qing gestured to the ARMY CAPTAIN to join her. She applauded him as he made his way down from the pyre and approached.

—Bravo, bravo, she said.

The rest of the troupe clapped with her, hesitantly at first, but with increasing vigour.

—Bravo, bravo, bravo, bravo—

A full minute of this, Jiang Qing allowed, during which time the dancer stared furiously, first, at his own feet, then, gaining courage, at Wenge, who was squirming, shamefaced, at the stage edge.

Jiang Qing cut off the applause by slashing the air with her arm.

—Zhu Xi, she said, for that was the dancer's name, for two years, since the retirement of the great Song Yaojin, you've played the ARMY CAPTAIN with skill and delight. You've been an inspiration to ordinary people across the country, and a model of behaviour for Party members. I don't exaggerate when I say that, in your efforts to be an exceptionally good dancer, you've come exceptionally close to success. The Revolution thanks you.

She applauded him again, turning round on her heels, nodding and smiling. Then she went to Wenge, took her arm, and conducted her to centre stage. Put her standing to her left, a pace away. The girl's face was white and wet with sweat.

—As revolutionaries we have to go through a long process of tempering before we can grasp and skilfully apply the laws of Revolution. All of us, without exception, carry with us remnants of the various ideologies of the old society. In order to cleanse ourselves of these leftovers, besides learning from Party activities, we must participate in contemporary revolutionary practice, out there in the world.

Positioned like this between Zhu Xi and Wenge — their costumes identical, their meanings disparate, the old and the new manifestations — Jiang Qing felt a heightened sense of power; the happiness which came when resistance was overcome.

—On no account must we isolate ourselves or give ourselves airs. We might have come through the top academies, but we mustn't pretend to know when we don't. In order to preserve our purity as vanguard fighters of the proletariat, it's essential for us to go out and meet the people and to work hard at their side, and to use their wisdom to temper and cultivate ourselves in every respect.

She turned to Zhu Xi now, smiling at him in such a way that he could not doubt her sincerity.

—For this reason, Zhu Xi, I'm rewarding your hard-won achievements at the Central Ballet with a period of rehabilitation on a model farm in Inner Mongolia.

A collective gasp blew out from the wings. Zhu Xi stumbled backwards, as if falling against it.

—There, Jiang Qing went on, you'll have the opportunity to learn from the peasants and selflessly work the fields. It'll be a chance to get out of your own life, to put aside your personal ambitions, and to think, to study, to be objective. You'll return to society a new man, enlightened, with a deeper love for your country, ready to make an even greater contribution to its greatness. I dare say you'll come back as a living Lei Feng.

—No! No!

Zhu Xi was swinging around, flailing, in search of someone or something that might help him.

—You cannot do this. Help me someone, please!

He appealed to Chao Ying, who was now on the stage and coming fast towards them.

—It's all right, Zhu Xi, said Chao Ying. Calm down.

He gripped the dancer's arms in an effort to tranquillise him.

—You're not going anywhere.

Jiang Qing laughed:

—You think you know better than me what this man needs? What this man needs, what all men need, is someone who'll command great things of them. Not someone who has the power but, unpardonably, will not command.

Chao Ying placed himself as a barrier between Jiang Qing and Zhu Xi.

—That's enough.

With his feet planted wide, and his hands clutching his hips, Chao Ying probably thought he looked tough.

—You've had your moment, Commander Jiang, we've all seen you, we've all heard you, we all love you, deeply, and I must now ask you to leave the stage.

Jiang Qing laughed again, this time into his face:

—Director Chao, it's nice to see you show some proper interest in the work, at last. Now please let me explain what's happening here, for it seems you're failing to understand. I'm recommending Zhu Xi for a course of rehabilitation, in accordance with Party policy.

—Over my dead body.

—So you're against it? Zhu Xi doesn't need it, is that what you're saying? He's above it?

—That's not what I'm saying.

—Would you prefer to go in his place, is that it? I understand why you'd be eager. I'd go myself, in a shot, if I weren't tied to my duties here. By stepping down from our privileged positions and returning to poverty, we come to understand what the world is really like. Or have you forgotten, Director, about the world?

She turned to address the other dancers on stage, and the troupe in the wings, and the orchestra in the pit.

—Am I right, comrades? Do you all have fond memories, as I do, of the times you've been away? I learned some of life's most important lessons in the countryside. Above all, I realised that my real comrades, and the best communists, were the ones I worked with in the fields, not the people I typed with in some office. Or performed with in some theatre.

—*Some* theatre?

Chao Ying bellowed like an animal in order to seem bigger than he was.

—This is the Great Hall of the People. I am the Director of the Central Ballet of Beijing. It's in that capacity, on this stage, that I declare to you, Jiang Qing, that I won't allow you to send me or Zhu Xi or any of my dancers anywhere, now or at any time in the future. I'll denounce you!

—People denounce me every day, Director. I could hardly be called a real communist if someone weren't denouncing me.

—I have the ear of higher powers than you, and I'll make sure any directives you make, regarding the re-education of any dancer in this troupe, will have to pass through me. And you can be sure that I'll veto them.

Sneering, Jiang Qing turned to Wenge:

—Do you see what I mean, young Wenge? Are you watching this? It's always interesting to see how men who claim to be radical treat women.

—Oh, don't give me that, said Chao Ying.

—It was women who gave birth to human history, and all of its labour. Men's contribution has been nothing more than a drop of sperm. Yet men can't bear to move aside and let us take over the management of things.

—You'll have to step over my grave.

—Do you hear that, Wenge? This man doesn't want you to have

the leading role, even though, of all the dancers in the troupe, you're the most suited to it. He's still got one foot in the old society. He'll do everything to seal off a woman's force. To tame it. To bind it. I wonder, has Director Chao ever read what Mao has written about the importance of women? Does he even know what the *Sayings* say about our equal role in the Revolution?

—I'm not getting into a quotation war with you, Commander.

—He won't, Wenge, because he knows he'll lose. He's so busy upholding Mao's principles on stage, he never bothers to actually look at them.

Wenge, cracking, put her hands over her face and began to cry.

A dancer ran in from the wings and put an arm around her.

—Do you see what you do? said Chao Ying, addressing Jiang Qing. The mess you make?

—Women are the only true proletariat left. It's right for us to rebel. To unhorse the tyrant, wherever he's found.

Jiang Qing's whistle was on a cord around her neck, hidden in her shirt. She now pulled it out and brought it to her lips.

Chao Ying glanced up at the auditorium doors and saw the slits of light where they were being held ajar by Jiang Qing's Red Guards.

—All right, Commander. All right. Let's go to my office and have this out. It's not good for the troupe to see us argue. I'm sure, after some rational discussion, we can reach a solution.

—I'm not interested in private committees, Director.

Jiang Qing put the end of the whistle between her teeth.

Chao Ying threw his arms up in exasperation:

—Why? Why are you doing this?

—The reason is quite clear, Director.

Jiang Qing took the whistle out from between her teeth and tapped her chin as she spoke.

—The pure essence of Revolution is concentrated in women, and Chinese women are the most numerous in the world. They are the motor of global rebellion. Is that not the very message of our ballet?

Chao Ying was no longer agitated, he now appeared serene, but it was a serenity as hard as iron, he was not giving up.

—Tong Hua isn't ready for the role you want her to dance. Forcing her to do so would endanger the entire production. What if she makes a mistake? Do you want to embarrass her in front of our foreign guest? Do you want Mrs Marcos to see Chinese women as weak?

How exasperating it was of Chao Ying to put himself in a position where she had to injure him.

—Director, let me ask you a question.

She pointed the end of the whistle between his eyes.

—Have you ever given any thought as to why, when we were creating *The Red Detachment of Women*, we decided to have the ARMY CAPTAIN burned on a pyre, as opposed to having him shot or hung? Why did we choose death by fire for our hero when, historically, that has been a woman's punishment? I've been thinking a lot about this of late. Why didn't we have the ARMY CAPTAIN shoot himself, or put a sword into his own heart, given that those are the masculine methods? And I think I may have figured it out. The role of the ARMY CAPTAIN has always been a female one.

She paused to allow the silence which had formed around her words to deepen.

Then she blew the whistle.

For the rest of the day and the next morning, she worked to reconcile Wenge to the idea of playing the ARMY CAPTAIN in public, and to integrate her performance into the ballet. The other dancers put up little resistance to their new lead. Having witnessed the Red Guards chase Zhu Xi through the auditorium, then break his little finger as a punishment for his recalcitrance, the other dancers understood that this was the turn things had taken, and that it was in their interests to go with it. The strongest resistance came from Wenge herself, who had trouble believing in her right to be the centre of attention and had to be pressurised into it. Jiang Qing sympathised with her. It was hard to have confidence as a woman. One was on one's own.

Chao Ying, when threatened with arrest, agreed not to impede Jiang Qing's vision, nor to escalate the row, but he declined to partake further in the rehearsals, choosing instead to lodge himself in the back row of the stalls, and from there to sulk. His assistants were more helpful. They offered their services to Jiang Qing, who rewarded them with responsibilities beyond their experience. And why not? There was a female chivalry, too: woman for woman, sister helping sister.

Time was short. If they wanted the performance to be correct, a model, they would have to work until midnight tonight, and then do at least two run-throughs tomorrow. Jiang Qing did not like to rehearse on the same day as a performance, she thought it brought bad luck, but these were exceptional circumstances, in whose advent luck had played no part. Strength of will had got them to where they were; now all the stops had to be pulled out to reach the end. The dancers were on lock-in. The physiotherapists on call. The musicians and the crew had been told that they would not see their families until after the performance. Her message to her assistants: absolutely no disturbances.

—Commander—

—Comrade Shit-tank! What did I tell you?

—I'm sorry, Commander, but I thought you ought to know, she's here. The First Lady of the Philippines has arrived in China.

Jiang Qing rushed from the auditorium to a nearby office, the Sichuan Room, where a television had been set up on a sideboard and a single armchair placed in front of it. She put herself behind the armchair, leaning on the backrest. On screen were pictures from the airport: an aeroplane parked on the tarmac, a mobile staircase creeping towards the plane door, and two thousand children in formation, dancing and waving pom-poms.

—Live, said the assistant. Can you believe it?

—Shut up and hand me that phone.

The assistant brought the phone from the desk, careful not to get the wire caught in the furniture, and put it down on the arm of the chair.

—I'll put it here for you, shall I?

—Stop talking, you insect, and get out!

Once alone, she called Li Na.

—Daughter, are you watching this?

—Yes.

They did not say any more, but they kept the receiver to their ears, so they could hear the rhythm of each other's breathing change as the aeroplane door opened and Mrs Marcos stepped out dressed in a white gown that reached all the way to the ground and that shimmered in the sun: a sun which, on this autumn day in Beijing, was the whole sky. Mrs Marcos descended the steps as if from a high temple: floating. At the bottom she accepted a bouquet of flowers, waved east, waved west, and waved east again, before being accosted by the official welcoming party: the Vice-Premier, some Central Committee members, various mid-level diplomats.

Jiang Qing put the phone receiver to her chest to muffle it and shouted:

—Someone!

The same assistant came back in.

—Look, she said, pointing to the screen. I was told only ranks above nine could be at the airport. Nobodies, the lot of them. B-listers. Hangers-on. I'm mortified. Are you mortified?

—Yes, Commander.

—I should meet Mrs Marcos today as well. She deserves to have someone important shake her hand. Let's arrange to have her brought to me before she's taken to the guest villa.

—The schedule has been decided, Commander. You'll have a chance to greet her tomorrow before the performance. And you'll be at the same table at the banquet afterwards.

—That's not good enough. Why should I have to wait? And why should Mrs Marcos be snubbed in such a manner? It's outrageous.

—Courtesy and protocol require that the First Lady be given time to rest before starting formal activities.

She thought about this a minute:

—You turtle's egg. I hope you get pockmarks all over your head. Get out.

Mrs Marcos walked the path between the assembled children. At one point she stopped to appreciate the dancing, and the camera went in close, cutting off the pack of panting men that surrounded her, and giving the viewers a proper look at her face.

Jiang Qing swallowed.

On the other end of the line, Li Na was holding her breath.

It was an Asian face, but it had an expression which had disappeared from China. One could walk the streets of Beijing for a lifetime and never find an expression like it. Serene and gentle and kind — and satisfied. In China, to be given responsibility, one had to suffer, to starve, to work oneself to the bone; Mrs Marcos appeared never to have worked a day in her life. She glowed, not with the vigour of revolutionary struggle, but as though transfused with Western blood. She shone, she burned, dangerously so, in the style of high-class productions, of colour films, of millionaire's magazines, of Toscanini.

Jiang Qing froze: Mrs Marcos was looking into the camera, as though straight at her. It was only a second, yet in Jiang Qing's mind it lasted much longer; a protracted instant in which the world turned inside out, and Jiang Qing became the watched, Mrs Marcos the watcher. The television was Mrs Marcos's own camera. China, which before had not been lit, was now lit, the sun from the West had come out, and Mrs Marcos could see everything for herself.

What will she make of us?

How will she judge us?

Jiang Qing longed to hear her praise. And also feared her criticism. Even a mild objection, coming from those eyes, would break her heart.

IRIS

1968

<u>xiv.</u>

Downstairs in the basement flat, Sid gave her a Dexedrine from his hospital stash, which she swallowed then and there without water. Neel and Sid were studying on opposite sides of their little table, text-books open in front of them, sharing a single oil lamp. She sat down on the stool between them, eliciting grumbles and moans, but they would put up with her for a few more minutes, she knew.

She popped and chewed a second pill, which she demanded by opening her palm like a beggar on the street.

—Don't look at me like that. It's an emergency.

She despised the bourgeois housewives who took uppers to reduce their waists nearly as much as she despised the plastic hippies who took them for the illusion of power they gave. When she met anyone who was on uppers, she tried to get them off them. Uppers removed the worry of sleeping and eating, which was an advantage, but they did not do enough for the mind, and it was the mind that most people wanted changed, which was why, more often than not, uppers led to junk.

—You know me, boys. I don't normally do this shit. But I need something right now. It's fucking crazy up there.

The commune was overfull with the new heads from Paris. The Maoists.

—We're supposed to be collaborating on a thing. I don't know, a happening, an anything. Not much activity going on, though. Just lots of talk. And you wouldn't believe what these Mao freaks are saying.

Violence is an antitoxin. You have to fight to win peace.

—I tried arguing with them, but they don't listen to me. They only listen to one person. Doris. Because *she's* been to China.

As she spoke, Iris peered into the dark corner, trying to make out whether the movement of the little curtain hung across the coal heap was caused by a draught or by vermin. The only light that reached the room came through the bars of a small window set high in the wall; the bottom of the window frame made a precise line with the path outside. Iris's attention was drawn there now by a further darkening caused by the wheels of a passing pram, and a pair of stocky, stockinged legs following after. The legs halted to the left of the frame, where the lodging house steps began, and a woman's voice could be heard responding to a man's.

Iris broke off and rushed to the window, her bells jingling as she went. Looking up at an angle, she could see the bonnet of a police car parked on the road outside, and, through the woman's legs, a couple of paces further along, a pair of brightly shined shoes.

—Had any trouble, have you, madam? the copper was saying.

—Ow yeah, the woman was saying, awful nuisances, i'nt they? Darkies and aggro and loud music at all hours—

Iris made for the door:

—Sorry, loves, gotta handle this. Adore you as ever.

She went up to the main door. Before opening, she breathed into her hand, smelled her breath. Nothing bad came back: after a while the body began to clean itself.

She opened the door and stepped outside. The woman was Iris's age, though she looked twice that, with her three-quarter-length coat, worn as a fingers-up to the warm weather, and her backcombed hive held in by a floral scarf, knotted at the chin, a single curl springing free at the fringe. Her name was Jackson, which Iris knew because her son, Derik Jackson, was one of the local boys whom Iris brought into Wherehouse to make art from time to time.

—Can I help you, Mrs J? Iris said.

Startled, Jackson's eyes widened first, then slowly narrowed as she wiped a look down Iris's front. She seized the pram handle and jammed a foot on the low bar in order to lever the stiff front wheels into the air and get the back wheels moving.

—I'll leave you to it, officer. Just don't forget who you's here to serve.

—Who'd that be, Mrs J? said Iris.

—Who? said Jackson as she set off down the path, the joints of the pram squeaking. The real people of this area, is who.

—My love to the real people, Iris called after her. Especially that lovely son of yours. Tell him we'll have him in soon, to make some things, he does so enjoy it.

Iris waited until Jackson had turned the corner, before acknowledging the copper.

—Fine day, officer, she said.

Further down, amongst the rubbish which had not been cleared, a second copper was pasting bills onto the factory walls.

—Or offic*ers*.

—Do you live here, miss? said the first copper.

—Can I help you with something?

—Just answer the question.

—This building belongs to my mother. I'm here with her permission.

A burst of yells coming from the rooftop brought the copper to peer up, shielding his eyes against the brightness of the day.

—Having a party up there?

—Would it be a crime if we were?

—Would we find drugs, if we was to come in?

—Officer, I'm only twenty-two, my whole life ahead of me. I, too, have goals and ambitions. I wouldn't want to ruin them by getting addicted to drugs.

—Goals and ambitions, you say?

—That's right.

Iris scratched the burns on her bare upper arms, got from sitting out too long.

The copper consulted a paper on his black clipboard.

—You've been ignoring notices from the council. Been too busy with your goals and ambitions?

—We haven't received anything.

—Course you haven't. What's your name?

—Iris.

—Iris what?

—Thurlow.

—Spell that.

She spelled it, and he wrote it down.

—Are you paying your mother rent to be here?

—It's a family arrangement, officer. My mother has no use for the buildings. If we hadn't moved in, they'd have been left neglected.

—You might've saved yourself the trouble. These two buildings, the factory and the old temperance house here, are scheduled for demolition.

Iris felt a strong emotion that was the sum of many:

—When?

He handed her a notice in red print.

She scanned it quickly and stuffed it into her pocket.

Now, from the black clipboard, came a second paper, an official form in pink.

—Just sign the bottom of that.

—I'm not signing anything.

—Prefer to go down the station and sign it there?

—We'll apply for a reprieve.

—Too late for that. If you'd read the council notices, you might've had a chance.

She returned the pink form unsigned. Put her hands on her hips and glared down the road.

The copper shrugged and scribbled on the form himself:

—Don't matter. It's enough that I's talked to you.

—How d'you live with yourself?

—Fairly well, I'd say, miss.

—What you're doing is a cultural atrocity. An unjust seizure of artistic space.

—Best to take that up with your mum, I'd say.

—Soon there won't be any places left in London for artists to vibe in.

—Vibe, miss?

—A London devoid of artists, is that what you want? Must profit always come first? Who's the city for anyway?

The copper glanced up at the roof:

—For hardworking English people, I reckon.

—These buildings are already populated by hardworking people. This is their home. This is where they make their livelihoods.

—As I say, Miss—

He looked at his notes.

—Miss Thurlow, I'd take that up with your mother. Ten days to vacate. That's one zero. You have a lovely day. Stay out the sun.

Back inside, she met Keith coming in from the outside toilet, carrying an old *IT* he used to wipe his arse.

—How's it going up there?

He scratched his head:

—I've had enough.

She mounted the stairs:

—Come back up with me.

—I ain't going back up there. Was thinking of going for a wander.

—Hold off.

She gave him the notice from her pocket.

He opened out the scrunched-up ball.

—You worried about this? he said. I thought you got these all the time.

—We do. But this one is different.

Every once in a while her mother would send word, through her father, that the building was to be put on the market and that the Wherehouse group should therefore not delay in looking for alternative accommodation, which for a time would generate much anxiety among the members and difficult discussions about the future. But then nothing would happen. No FOR SALE sign would go up. No eviction notice would be sent. The police would not come to order them out. And eventually her mother's message would be written off as an empty threat, the turmoil would come to rest, and normal commune life would resume. Be that as it may, Iris never entirely dropped her guard. She knew her mother and what, in a critical moment, the woman was capable of. It was only a matter of time before she followed through on her warnings.

—This isn't just another one of her threats. This is curtains. It's happening.

—What're you going to do?

—Fight back.

—How?

—Don't know yet.

As they went up the lodging house stairs, Iris perceived the first pulsations of the Dexedrine in her nerves. Her legs were heavy despite a sudden feeling of energetic excess. Jumping over a cat shit on the third-floor landing sent needles up her legs, as if she had just come down from sitting on a high wall. In the bathroom on the top floor, standing on the edge of the bath to access the trapdoor in the ceiling, she thought herself lucid and coordinated, even though it took her several attempts to get through, and in the end she had to climb onto Keith's shoulders and, for the last push, stand on his head.

Returning to the roof, the whack of reefer came with fresh force. Glen, Eggie, and Álvaro were sitting on the ground with their backs against the low wall at the rooftop edge.

—You faggots, Iris said, the Bill just came knocking. Didn't you hear?

She came to stand in the clearing where everyone was throwing their joint-roaches and fag ends and used teabags and empty peanut packets.

—Where are the others?

Álvaro shrugged:

—Got too hot. Went back inside.

Iris took the joint from him but went off the idea as soon as it touched her lips. She was just coming up on the pills, and grass would take her back down or turn her green.

—Listen up, she said, handing the joint back. Get your minds together and come inside. Group meeting.

—Aw what?

—Come on. Some serious crap has come up. Anyone skips out, they'll be thrown out.

One by one they slid back inside and searched around until they found the rest of the group in the old rehearsal studio. Eva, Doris, and the Maoists were congregated around her father's directing table, which they had moved so that it sat under the bare bulb hanging from the ceiling. Per was sitting on a scrap of carpet, his back against the boards where the windows had once been, his legs crossed in the lotus position. Álvaro joined the Wherehouse members Rolo, Jay, and Stewie who were lounging on some foam rubber. Glen and Eggie went to sit on top of the broken piano, their feet resting on the closed fallboard. Keith hovered by the door.

—What're you all doing in here? said Iris.

—Working, Eva said. This happening won't plan itself.

Iris crossed the creaking floor to its sagging centre.

—Well, you'll have to put that aside for now. There's news. The bill has paid us a visit.

She unfurled the demolition notice and passed it around. Explained its significance as succinctly as she could. Time was short. A state of unity needed to be reached and a plan agreed, fast. Which would not be easy, given this combination of people.

—I want to fight this, she said, but I can't do it alone. It has to be a group effort. A unified front. All of us signed up and pledged. We don't have a lot of time. Ten days is tight. But we shouldn't let that put us off.

—This certainly puts a new face on things, said Doris, flicking the ends of her shirt back in order to plant her hand on her hip. What kind of fight are you talking about? A picket?

—Maybe, said Iris. We could lie in front of the bulldozers or—

—No, said Eva, assuming an authoritative pose of her own by resting half her weight on the table edge. We're a street theatre, but we're against picketing and marching. Those tactics are for genteel ladies who only take the sort of action that's guaranteed to be ineffective.

—We could take a legal case, said Rolo. How long have we been living here? We must have rights.

—No, said Eva, that's not the route we should be taking either.

—Why not? said Álvaro.

—Because the legal system doesn't exist. It's what the landlords and the bosses say, that's all.

As a sort of memento, Eva had kept her Paris cut, she had not been to the hairdresser to have it evened out, so when she shook her head now, clumps of different lengths moved on various parts of her head.

—If we go at this head-on, we'll be crushed and will end up being punished ourselves, for the very good that we do. We have to find a smarter, stealthier way. The Mao way.

With a sweep of her arm, she invited the others to come to the table.

Doris and the Maoists shifted around to make room.

Iris, Álvaro, and the old Wherehouse members joined her; Keith, the Jamaicans and Per hung back, half in and half out.

Spread on the table was a map of London. Red circles had been drawn around the BBC Television Centre in White City, Broadcasting House in Portland Place, the LWT studios in Wembley, Alexandra Palace in Muswell Hill and the Riverside Studios in Hammersmith.

Eva passed a hand over the map to smooth the creases out.

—Can everyone see?

Iris was jammed between the corn-fed hulks of the American Maoists Tray and Joshua. Across from her, Doris was not looking at the map itself but at everyone looking at the map, which seemed to interest her more.

Eva pointed at one of the circles on the map: Broadcasting House.

—So far, all of our happenings have taken place in the streets. Person-to-person. We've attached special importance to human contact, the meeting of bodies. And that's been great. But now, in this time of crisis—

—Global crisis, said Doris, but also local crisis. *Your* crisis.

—we need a change of tactics. We need to be more ambitious. Instead of trying to change the minds of a handful of people on the street, we should be thinking about changing popular opinion. And that means taking control of the media.

The Indian Maoist Sunny began to feel the chest of his military shirt with one hand and tap a red marker on the table with the other.

—That's right, he said. The biggest mistake the Paris rebels made was to fail to take ownership of the most powerful weapon available in our society: the television. If they'd seized the television headquarters, they'd have been able to broadcast their messages right across the country, into the majority of homes. Instead they took over the university and the Odéon theatre, where they could only speak to the people gathered there, the already converted. Rather than spread their message far and wide, they created a ghetto, a bubble.

—Mao didn't use the telly for his revolution, said Iris.

—You're right, he didn't, said Eva. But China is at a different stage of development than here. Think about how our society is now. We're controlled by the telly. The telly tells us what to do and how to do it. What to buy and how much we're all worth. We accept whatever the flashing images are saying. Mao's word-of-mouth approach isn't going to work in these circumstances. What we've got to do is find a way of transmitting Mao's message in a way that is at least as powerful as the telly. And, really, the only thing as powerful as the telly is the telly itself.

Listening to her, Sunny assumed a mask of great seriousness.

—You see, he said, the television just obeys whoever's in charge of it. In our control, the same television that today parrots the official capitalist line would be transformed into a tool of liberation.

Álvaro had rolled up the sleeves of his t-shirt to expose his upper arms and the black hairs on his shoulders. Arms folded, he was searching Sunny through:

—We need to get ourselves on TV, is that what you're saying?

—It isn't simply a question of getting on television, Sunny said. We couldn't just join a panel show and expect to be taken seriously. It'd be naive to accept whatever slot the capitalist ringmasters would want to fit us into and answer whatever moronic questions they'd decide to ask us. They'd manipulate everything and make us look like clowns. The aim should be to control when and where we appear, and get our message across without interference. We ourselves should strive to create the conditions that'd make that possible.

—So your plan—

With a finger, Iris flicked the map where Broadcasting House was marked.

—is to take over all of these TV studios?

—Not take over, said Eva.

—What then? Break in?

—Infiltrate.

—Okay. So you want to *infiltrate* all of thh—

—Not all of them. We don't have the resources for such a large operation. We'll have to choose one. Scope each of them out and come to a decision, collectively, as to which would be the best location for our intervention.

Iris laughed a mocking laugh:

—You're insane.

—Insane? said Sunny. No. *Capitalism* is insane.

—You're on board with this gaga shit, Doris?

Doris's features were still, her forehead quiet:

—Wherehouse is small, Iris. But sometimes the smallest things can change the course of history.

—Exactly, said Eva. Mao won the revolutionary war with a small peasant army. If we create disturbances, push the system, they'll have to hit back. Once they do, then revolution starts.

—What has any of this, I mean *any* of it, got to do with saving Wherehouse? said Iris.

—The only way to stop the demolition of this place, said Doris, is to make it indestructible. Something becomes indestructible when enough people put a value on it. By getting on the telly, you'll be convincing people that this place, and what you's do here, has too much value to be torn down.

—Right, said Eva. If nothing else, it'll give us a name. Once we have a name, and people are talking about us, they'll think twice before making us homeless.

—A name? said Iris. Are you talking about a *brand*?

Iris enjoyed watching Eva's face go puce and the rest of the Maoists squirm; it annoyed her, though, that Doris appeared unbothered.

—And TV studios? she went on. You don't think that's a bit, I don't know, out of our league?

—If the enemy doesn't hit back, said Sunny, there's no revolution. So we've got to provoke it. We're not going to do that with a picket. Or little bits of street theatre.

—Little bits of street theatre?

Iris turned to Eva, incredulous:

—Are you listening to this blow-in? Aren't you going to defend your collective?

—The point Sunny's making is a valid one, said Eva. We've got to use the enemy's own weapon against it.

—So that's what you all learned in Paris?

—More or less, yeah.

Sunny began to say something but Iris cut him off:

—Look around, Sunny. Look at us. D'you really think that we, us here, would be able to plan and execute a break-in at one of the big

TV studios? How is that even within the realm of possibility for you?

—I know it sounds ambitious, Sunny said, but you must remember England isn't a country in open revolution. There are demonstrations, sure, but no one is expecting actions of the kind we're talking about. The powers that be are off-guard. Security will be lax. I have a strong suspicion that, once we've accessed our chosen site, we'll find sympathisers inside who'll be willing to collaborate with us.

—Uhuhn, that's true, said Eva. Coming back here after Paris, you can really feel the insularity of the place, the triviality. London is asleep.

—Asleep?

Iris whipped off her headband and clasped a hand over her overheating forehead.

—The filth aren't asleep. Our friends, the Beecham's Pill, are as awake as ever, and breaking up every party they can find. One phone call, one alarm bell, and they'll be all over us like a rash.

—Have you given up wanting to defy the laws? said Eva.

—No. But I don't want to be stupid about it. I'm not going to walk myself into the chokey.

—There's nothing stupid about what we're suggesting. Stupid would be to continue planning actions that make no impact.

—Try making an impact from a prison cell. Will Wherehouse survive if we're all locked up? Will there be a revolution?

—Maybe, said the German Maoist Barbara. Getting incarcerated shouldn't be our aim, but if it happened, it could be the spark that starts a movement.

—With respect, said Iris, what you've just said shows how little you know about England.

—Look, said Eva, if we really want to be noticed, we have to draw the fire of the authorities, which means performing acts that people get arrested for. When people hear about us, they should think, *Is what they're doing really a crime? Or is it in fact a rebellion against the injustice of an oppressive force?* Being relevant, that's what'll save Wherehouse.

—*Oh my, how relevant!* said Iris. That's exactly what people will be thinking when we're caught breaking into the BBC.

—Breaking in? said Doris. We can be cleverer than that. More, what's the word, *subtler*. We have to appear natural, even if what we's doing is drastic and pushing a situation to the limit.

In frustration, Iris put her headband into her mouth and bit down on it:

—All right. Suppose, by some miracle, what you're saying happens. We walk *subtly* and *naturally* into one of these studios without getting arrested, and a kind stranger agrees to film us and put us on air. What're we going to do? The camera is pointing at us. Then what?

Together, the Maoists all looked at Doris.

Doris looked at Iris.

Iris's vision went blank with anger.

—You fucking crazy bastards.

She walked away. Punched the boarded windows. Pressed her forehead against the wood a second before turning back to the room.

—It has just dawned on me what you're up to. For weeks now, all we've been listening to is Doris talking about China and the public trials she saw there. You want to do the same thing, don't you? You want to put someone on trial. You want to kidnap someone and try them on camera.

The Worker's Stadium, capacity sixty thousand, a stage with portraits of Mao and slogans written in big letters, and the enemies of the revolution standing in a line with signs hanging around their necks, and a long table of Party men shouting out the crimes of the accused and calling on the public to name their punishment for each, and the crowd screaming *Shave her head* and *Smear ink on her face* and *Make her sit on a cigarette*, and the Party men ordering the Red Guards to carry the punishments out: Doris had described all of this in detail, had marvelled at the sheer *performance* of it, and Eva and the Maoists had thought it was wonderful, an effective technique of persuasion, of bringing the unjust to task, of making it so that injustice does not return.

—You're seriously thinking of doing that sadistic shit? said Iris.

Doris, now, was the only one brave enough to speak up.

—That's the idea, she said. A televised struggle session. Our version of the Chinese tribunals.

Iris was unable to disbelieve what she was hearing; these people were serious.

—Who? she said. Who were you thinking of? To put on trial?

—It doesn't really matter who, said Eva.

—What? Of course it matters who! *Who* is the whole point, isn't it?

—Well, we haven't settled on who yet. That's something we should decide all together.

There came a lull, then, during which everyone present looked at everyone else present and wondered what they were thinking, because they themselves did not know what to think. *Who? Who? Who? Who?* Then everyone, at once, told everyone else what they themselves were not thinking, which they believed everyone else should be thinking.

A clamour.

An outcry.

Mayhem.

Tying her headband back on so that it covered her ears, Iris left the room. Keith came after her but she told him to stay.

—Keep the peace here, she said as she aggressively tightened the knot at the back of her head. I'll be back in a minute.

She left the theatre through the knocked-out scullery wall and went up the lodging house stairs to her room. Made straight for the framed headshot of her mother. Took it off the wall. Looked at it. Wiped the dust away with her sleeve. Looked at it again. From her mother's eyes there came a kind of pleading.

Relax, Mama. Just play along and you won't be harmed.

She removed the photograph from the frame, and put it under her arm, threw the empty frame on the mattress. From the shelf, she took down her copy of *Miss Julie*, the scrapbook of her mother's articles and reviews, and her doll Mao, and returned with them to the rehearsal studio.

It'll look like punishment to you, Mama, but you'll be fine, I won't let them hurt you, all I'll be asking from you are new memories as recompense for the old ones.

The group was still gathered around the table, and still arguing. Iris squeezed in and threw the photo of her mother on top of the map. Everyone fell silent and looked down at it. In the face, there was some Iris and there was some Eva, and at the same time there was no comparison. The woman in the photo represented what everyone desired most: the otherworldly, the inexplicable.

—All right, Iris said, addressing Eva and the Maoists. I fucking hate to admit it, but you might be right. About the telly thing.

She flicked her hair over her shoulder, nervily, and took her headband from over her ears, tucked it behind them. She felt light in the head, high on the uppers and stirred by senses hard to control.

—But let's face it, cats, kidnapping a stranger, anyone, bigwig or small fry, will put us behind bars for life. Breaking and entering, put ten years on top of that. A job like the one you're suggesting would take months of planning, years maybe, and even then we wouldn't get far. We'd be in the back of a Black Maria before you could say Yoko Ono. But—

She caught Eva's eye, in which there vibrated a faint mistrust.

—but, if you ask me, there's a better way.

—You've got something in mind? said Eva.

Iris rotated her shoulders and jabbed sideways with her elbows so as to impel the neighbouring bodies to make more space for her at the table.

—We're thinking about the problem arse-up. Why go to the media when we can make the media come to us?

—What d'you mean? said Álvaro. The BBC are hardly going to come here. To some squat in Somers Town.

Iris shook her head and pointed at her mother's photo on the table.

—That there is the woman who owns these buildings. The one who's kicking us out. She's my mother.

She wagged a finger in Eva's direction.

—*Our* mother. You don't look like the kind of people who read the Sunday supps, but if you did, you'd know of her. She's an actress, a big one.

Iris dropped the scrapbook onto the table and opened it on a random page. An interview with their mother in the *Telegraph*. The headline read:

I CRIED WHEN STALIN DIED

Then underneath in smaller letters:

NOW I CRY FOR THE CHILDREN WHO SUFFER UNDER COMMUNISM

—She was a communist in the good old days. A full-on, card-carrying politico. But then she went full circle, and now spends her time telling the world that socialism is awful, and nuclear bombs are the business, and America can and should win in Vietnam. Like those ex-drug fiends, you know? who sign up at the enemy camp just in case anyone might think they hadn't seen the light.

Iris placed the doll Mao on the map roughly where Wherehouse was located. Using the red marker, she drew a line from Mao through the streets of King's Cross and Bloomsbury, into Soho and then the West End. On St Martin's Lane, she drew one, two, three circles around the London Carlton.

—This is the theatre where our mother is performing at the moment. About an hour from here, walking at a slow pace. Me and Keith have already checked the place out. Very little security, except for, maybe, an old fart at the stage door round back. It'd be easy enough to get backstage during the show. Or, if we wanted to, onto the stage itself.

She threw *Miss Julie* onto the table so that it landed beside the photo.

—This is the play she's in. She's the lead. Which, for those of you who don't know Strindberg, is a bit of a joke. Our mother was already too old for the role of MISS JULIE when it made her famous back in the fifties. Now she's reprising it, she says for the last time, but who fucking knows with that woman. The media seems to be swallowing it because there's a quite a bit of buzz surrounding the production. *Alissa Thurlow's last MISS JULIE*, they're saying. My guess is, if we planned a happening that interrupted one of her performances and alerted the journos in advance, maybe drop Doris's name as a bit of extra bait, they'd come and film whatever we wanted them to.

—A struggle session against your mother? said Sunny.

—In her own theatre? said Keith.

—On camera? said Tray.

—Is that what you're suggesting? said Eva.

Iris — Dexedrine flowing, heart pumping — nodded slowly.

Later, when they were alone, Eva asked her:

—Why are you doing this? You seriously want to interrupt Mama's play?

—That's the idea. That's what we voted to do.

—I don't care about the vote. No vote can change the fact that your so-called idea is shit. It isn't art. Isn't protest. Isn't politics. It has no message. Makes no challenge to the system. All this is, is your problems. Your own unpleasant feelings dressed up as something more.

They were in Iris's room. Eva was by the door, holding on to the knob in case Keith, whom she had ordered out, tried to get back in. Iris was on the bed, covered in a blanket, smoking, coming down, numb, impervious, wanting sleep but hours away from it. With her smoking hand, she gestured to her bookshelf where Mao's *Sayings* stood between De Beauvoir and R.D. Laing.

—You call yourself a Maoist, don't you? she said. Isn't it Mao who says revolution should explode in every heart and in every home? No true Maoist should be afraid to rebel against her own family.

—You might have the books, Iris, but that doesn't make you a Maoist. You're not interested in political change. You're just building a cover for a personal attack.

—It's personal only if you choose to look at it that way. We wouldn't be attacking Mama personally. We'd be undermining what she represents.

—You don't give a fuck about what she represents. You're just stuck in anger, and you want to make yourself feel better. You believe she hurt you, and you want to go back to a time before you were hurt. Because that can't happen, you want to punish her.

A person was not free until she got clear of the family: this was what Iris believed. It was what the counterculture was really about. The hippies got it, the freaks got it, even the politicos got it, when they put their money where their mouth was. The only decent kind of family — she did not know if it existed or would ever exist — was one which permitted each member to lead an independent life. Brothers who were free to wander when they were restless always came back. Sisters who were free to change remained interesting. Children should not feel obliged to swear obedience to their parents. Husbands and wives should not deprive themselves of possible happiness elsewhere if they grew weary of one another's company. It ought to be made easy that all family members part and reunite indefinitely, as often as they liked. Her own parents had had the right idea. They had taken a chance, had demanded freedom for themselves within their own family, and she was filled with indignation for their having given up that freedom, for their own reimprisonment in the old ways.

—Mama's not going to get hurt, she said. It's not going to be violent.

—It's not going to be anything, Eva said. Because it's not going to happen.

—We're a collective. We decide things together.

—This, I do get to decide alone. We're talking about my mother.

—Let me get this straight. You're worried about Mama's feelings all of a sudden?

—Yes.

—Well, I'm sorry about that. But we've had a vote. You can't overrule it.

—Watch me.

—Fundamentally, it's still your plan. All I did was improve on it. Make it workable. In my version, no one gets harmed. In yours, lots of people, maybe even lots of other people's mothers, would've got hurt. If you got off your high horse for a second, you'd see Mama's a fair target. She's also our only ticket for getting onto the telly and putting our message out.

—You do what you like, Iris, on your own time. Whatever makes you feel better and helps you to cope. But I draw the line at attacking my own family, whatever they believe. Your idea has nothing to do with class, or helping families, or transforming hearts—

—Or saving Wherehouse?

—Or, yeah, saving Wherehouse. You just want revenge, and revolution isn't about revenge.

—Revenge has nothing to do with it.

She said this easily. It came from her mouth effortlessly. So from where did this other idea draw its power: the idea that her injuries had their equivalent and could be paid back through the pain of the culprit? Why did she feel justified in wanting to experience, if only once, the exalted sensation of being allowed to despise and mistreat her mother as beneath her?

—You wear the clothes, said Eva. You do the drugs. You have the lingo. But you can't stand the fact that you learned everything you know from Mama and Papa. They taught you how to be a rebel, and you hate it. Deep down, you'd prefer if we'd had a conventional upbringing. Mama in the kitchen with an apron. Papa driving home from work in his car. It'd have been easier, wouldn't it? to fight against that.

—Once and for all, this isn't about what I feel. Or my childhood fucking traumas.

—Come off it, Iris. This is about one thing and one thing only.

Shivering in Eva's eyes, trembling about her mouth, was the thing.

—Don't say it, said Iris.

—I will, said Eva. I will say it. Because clearly it needs to be said. This is all about The East Wind, isn't it? Mama and Papa's play? What you think Mama did to you on opening night.

—Shut up.

—But what did Mama do, actually? I'll tell you what. Nothing. You don't have anything to hang on her. You just focus on her because you can't bear to look in the mirror at yourself and come to terms with what *you* did. Yes, you. To the play. To the theatre. To Mama and Papa's marriage. To me.

—I was a child.

—That's right, you were. Ten years old. And still you did it. Planned and executed it. Timed it all perfectly. Not Mama. You.

—It wasn't me. It wasn't my fault.

—For fuck sake, Iris, take some responsibility for onn—

There was a knock on the door.

—Wait a minute, Keith, said Eva.

—It's me, came Doris's voice.

Eva opened up.

Doris came in accompanied by Simon.

Iris glanced from one to the other:

—So you two are friends now?

—I was telling Simon about our plan, said Doris.

Iris stubbed out her joint on the lid of an empty can (*do what the fuck you want*) and wrapped herself tighter in her blanket.

Eva, who had gone to the window, stayed facing out while she said:

—And what do you think, Simon? I hope you've come to talk some sense into Iris.

Simon had his artificial hand pushed into his pocket, which he thought made it look less conspicuous.

—She can't just chuck us out like this. This is my home as well. We have a duty to fight back. To stand up for our rights.

—Rights? said Eva, turning now into the room. What rights are *you* worried about? You'd be bloody fine. With all your dirty money, you could buy yourself a house tomorrow.

She shook her head in Doris's direction:

—Excuse my family, Doris. I don't think they're anything at the moment, ideologically. Which would explain their confused state.

Iris, who had been turning her Zippo lighter around in her hand, now opened and closed its lid in quick succession.

—And what about you, Doris? she said. What d'you think? You didn't raise your hand in the vote.

—Not being a member myself, I didn't think it were my place.

—You're collaborating with us, aren't you? Your vote is as valid as anyone else's.

Doris frowned evasively:

—It ain't straightforward for me neither. I knew your mother. I worked with her.

Tucked underneath Doris's arm was Alissa's headshot. She now held this out to inspect it. Took a few steps closer to the lamp and tilted the photo towards it.

—Celebrity culture is right baffling to me. Is it the same for you?

She was staring into Alissa's headshot as if it contained hieroglyphics that needed working out.

—You know, when I were in China, I weren't sure how much of the real country I were seeing because I were escorted everywhere. But one thing I did notice was that they don't have a celebrity culture. They only have Mao.

Then she held the headshot up, Alissa's face facing out.

—Like, imagine if Alissa was England's Mao and hers were the only face you'd see, printed everywhere. Just hers, no one else's.

She turned the headshot round and looked at it again.

—Still, I guess celebrities have to be rare in every culture, right? There can't be too many or the whole house would come crashing down.

—Aren't you famous? said Iris.

—Me? Not really. Not at Alissa's level anyway. But I ain't immune to fame, the draw of it, despite what I tell meself. I don't think anyone is, really. We's all victims of it, and we's all supporters of it.

She folded the headshot twice and put it into her pocket.

—Can I keep this?

—Take whatever you need, said Iris.

Doris smiled then, first at Iris, then at Eva.

—So, Eva, what's your objection to Iris's idea exactly? It ain't political enough? Too personal?

—Basically, said Eva.

Nodding, as if agreeing, Doris moved to the wall to examine Jim Morrison's naked torso.

—I see what you's saying. But I disagree.

Eva's left eyebrow rose a fraction. It was not a secret that she looked up to Doris and wanted to be recognised by her. An excruciating moment passed in which she obviously wanted to move or talk and could not do either. Iris offered Eva a smile that had a boast in it. Once she was sure this had been seen, she hid it.

—I actually think Iris's idea has a lot of potential, said Doris. Does it really matter if it ain't the result of fixed political opinions? It's the result that counts. The impact it has. A struggle session against Alissa Thurlow? That can't be ignored.

Flushed, Eva searched for an empty place into which to pour her gaze:

—We're supposed to be a political performance group. In my book, being political means setting out your tent and saying, *This is the issue we want to address, and this is where we stand on it.* Involving our own mother muddies the waters. Makes things too individual, too messy.

—You know, said Doris, in the past I made the mistake of thinking that art had to be one-dimensional. It had to contain an unambiguous message. But that ain't how it goes any more. What does being political mean in nineteen-sixty-eight? It ain't just one thing, or one-sided.

—It might look like Iris is taking a stand, said Eva, but she isn't. Getting back at our mother is the same old shit. She's afraid of taking a real stand against the system because she's frightened of the consequences. She's frightened of being responsible for it. Struggling against Mama won't get her into trouble. It's safe. Easy.

As she listened, Iris stared into the flame of her lighter. Now she extinguished it by shutting the lid over it.

—Oh Eva, she said. Such discernment. Such discipline. How about cultivating some emotion while you're at it? A little emotional misconduct? Maybe my idea is wrong. But I'm not interested in being right all the time. I'm only interested in expression. Perspectives. I refuse to have a predetermined programme. I want to go on saying exactly what I think when I think it.

Doris raised a hand and undulated it, as if to smooth a crinkle in the atmosphere.

—Listen, she said. Maybe you's both right. Or maybe, as Iris says, you don't even have to be right. Maybe this conflict you have is what'll make the happening interesting. Who knows, maybe by working together you could put things back together in the family. Make things right again. Ain't nothing stopping our work being political and personal at the same time.

Standing separate, Eva looked like she was peering out from behind a fog.

Iris, so as not to see her and feel pity for her, lit the lighter again and put her focus there.

—If we truly want to be free in the free world, said Doris, we's to break some laws. To be individuals, we's to stand up to other individuals we's supposed to be indebted to. The more I think about it, the more sense Iris's idea makes. When I look back on my career so far, what strikes me is, I's always sought permission to do what I do. To perform where I do. I fill out the forms. Inform the relevant people. I make sure it's all above board, so that the authority's feathers won't be ruffled. I get fucking permission, don't I? Why's I so cautious all the time? Why do I need Big Daddy's say-so before proceeding?

Iris blew out the flame at the precise moment that Doris smashed her right fist into her left palm.

—If we don't go beyond the limits imposed on us, whatever the law says, if we don't trespass, we can't be free. To free ourselves is to trespass. All of you, are you listening? To trespass is to exist.

*

In the headshrinker's office where her mother took her twice a week — because *maybe they can do something for you* — a question Dr Kellendonk liked to ask her was:

—Can you remember a recent time when you were happy?

At first Iris did not answer, she was too terrified, but when given another chance, and then another, she finally did. Slowly, over the course of several sessions, she told Kellendonk about Doris.

—Does Doris make you happy, Iris? Is that what you're telling me?

She told Kellendonk — not all at once but in fragments, for in their talks he would return to it often — about the day when Doris took her in her Messerschmitt to Bethnal Green. That day, yes. That day Iris had been happy.

—Do you want to tell me more about that day? You don't have to worry, it'll just be between you and me.

It was towards the end of the rehearsals for *The Sing-Song Tribunal*. The ensemble had moved from the rehearsal studio to the auditorium. Time was running out and everyone was stressed. Her father was being a despot, her mother was overshadowing everyone else, Max was depressed, Eva appeared always to be on the point of tears — and Iris, who was forced to sit in the corner of the auditorium and sew her dolls, was miserable.

Then, at one point, Doris, who was photographing the rehearsals for the brochure, accidentally walked into her father's sightline, and he began to shout at her:

—Do you mind, Doris? You're in the way! Get out of the acting space! That's it, I've had enough of you. Fuck off and find something worthwhile to put your mind to. No, Doris, don't say anything. I'm sick to death of your pathetic, fat-arsed excuses for your own inadequacy.

At this, Doris dropped the camera on the stage floor and stormed out of the room, the first time she had ever done such a thing.

Iris dropped her sewing and chased after her.

In the bar, Simon was on a stepladder fixing the Chinese lanterns to the wall.

—What the hell's wrong with you? he said to Doris as she rushed past.

Doris headed straight for the passage to the storeroom.

Simon came down the ladder and followed her, and Iris followed him.

In the storeroom, Doris had opened the top of the Messerschmitt.

—What's cooking? said Simon

Doris threw her bag and cardigan onto the back seat.

—Doris? Did you hear me?

—I heard you, Simon, she said, climbing into the front. Leave me alone.

Over the course of the summer Simon's face had turned brown from taking sun baths on the roof. When he smiled — as he now did at Iris who had come to his side — his teeth were especially white. He kept the smile on when he turned back to Doris:

—Where you off to? he said to her.

—Mind your own fizzing business.

—You all right? You-know-who giving you a hard time?

He meant Iris's mother.

—No, Doris said.

Which was the truth. Iris had been watching, and lately her mother was making a special effort with Doris. It was Eva, actually, who was the getting the brunt of their mother's moods.

Doris pulled the car lid over.

Simon grabbed the edge of the lid, preventing her from closing it.

—You want some company?

—I'm going home to see me dad, Simon. You hardly want to go there.

—Why not?

Iris jigged from one foot to another:

—Yeah, can we come?

Simon raised his brows: *Well?*

—Sorry, Iris, Doris said. Not this time.

—You don't want your father to know us, Simon said, is that it?

Thinking back on this in later years, Iris would judge this a cruel thing for Simon to say, for he knew that Doris wanted nothing better than to introduce her first love, Paul, to her own father, but Paul had always refused. That was not part of the deal.

Simon put his good hand on Iris's head.

—You ever been to Bethnal Green, Iris?

—Dunno, she said. Have I?

—No, you haven't, he said.

And now to Doris:

—You don't want to show Iris where you're from?

Iris clutched the car at the precise place where her fingers would be cut off if Doris and Simon let go of the lid.

—God, all right, Doris sighed. But you's will be bored out of your senses, don't say I didn't warn you.

She let go of the lid, and Simon threw it open.

—Come on, tots, he said, helping Iris into the back seat.

—She'll have to sit on your lap, said Doris.

—I wouldn't mind having a go at driving it, said Simon.

—You don't know where the line is, do you?

Doris got out of the car and, as a kind of revenge against Paul, handed Simon the key.

—There's some tricks to it, I'll have to show you. And you mustn't overwork it. It'll only go so fast.

On the drive to Bethnal Green, Iris felt lightheaded. Opening night was next week. She had seen a lot of the rehearsals. Without even wanting to, she had learned some of the lines. Sometimes she was able to tell when the actors forgot a passage or fell to improvising. Without having to check the script, she could feed a corpsing actor — Eva mostly — her line. She was capable of seeing from a distance if someone's costume was not sitting correctly, or if a prop had been improperly placed. *The Sing-Song Tribunal* had become her universe. The totality of her experience. So this sudden escape, this act of unmooring, did not feel quite real; moving through the outside world was disorientating.

She felt Doris, on whose lap she was sitting, put her arms around her and squeeze hard.

—Ow, she said.

—Your father is something else, Doris said. What'll we do with him?

Simon took risks with the Messerschmitt. At difficult junctions. With cars much bigger than this one. All with only one hand on the steering bar. Iris understood that Simon wanted those around him to be a bit afraid, but she refused to be.

On Voss Street, he pushed the car backwards into the garage. Then they crossed Weavers Fields to Doris's tower block. Took the lift to the seventh floor. Though Doris had a key, she rang the doorbell to give her father some warning.

—Oh hello, love, Mr Lever said, opening. I weren't expecting you. I's got the rabbits out.

He left the front door open and went back inside, scooping rabbits off the floor as he went. Iris, enthralled, ran straight in, wanting to pet one, but Doris pulled her back.

—They'll piss on you if you scare them. I'll take you to their hutch in a minute.

Doris took her hand and led her down the hall. Simon followed. They loitered at the sitting room door while Mr Lever put the rabbits back in their hutch on the balcony.

Coming back in, he said:

—I'll make some tea.

—Don't bother yourself, Dad, said Doris. We ain't staying long. I'm just dropping by in case you needed the car.

—You want it, you have it, as long as you's looking after it?

—Not a scratch on it, Dad.

—All right, then, I'll put kettle on.

Iris jigged her leg, both excited to be here and impatient to go and see the rabbits.

They arranged themselves around the table and waited. Simon sat in a sort of religious stillness, his good hand resting on top of his stump, a look of serene contentment on his face.

—Does it talk? Iris said, pointing at the budgerigar in the cage.

Doris called into the kitchen:

—Dad, can you get the budgie to talk?

—What, love?

—The budgie. Can you make it talk?

—He's in a huff today. Won't say a word. Temperamental little bastard.

Doris winked at Iris, but her attention was already elsewhere.

—Who's that? she said, this time pointing at the large silver-framed photo of the Queen on the wall.

Simon burst out laughing.

—Shh, Iris, said Doris.

Mr Lever came back in with a tray of tea things, sliced pan, butter and jam.

—D'you see the view? he said.

—Fantastic, said Simon.

—South-facing. Sun all day. On a day like today, you can see the whole way to the City. Go out and have a look if you want.

—Can we? said Iris.

—In a minute, said Doris.

—They wanted to put me down on second, said Mr Lever. Or was it third?

—I think it was the second, Dad.

—I insisted on going up here.

—You're better off, said Simon.

—There's noise comes in from the neighbours, but at this point—

He put the tray down and took a seat himself.

—at this point I's past getting involved.

The tea was poured out, and Doris buttered a slice of bread for Iris.

It was the best tasting slice of bread she had ever eaten.

—The place needs a clean, Dad, Doris said, looking around. I'll come by again a day this week and do a runaround with the cloth.

—As you like, love.

Mr Lever was spreading jam but his attention was on Simon.

—Once upon a time people lived in a house full of family and friends, di'nt they, sir?

—That's right, said Simon. They did.

—These days, though, you'd lie on the staircase, your hip broken, and they'd step over you. Kuckers and shiksas, the lot of them.

—All right, Dad, said Doris. There's a child here.

—I can see that.

Keeping his gaze on Simon, Mr Lever cocked his head at Iris.

—She yours?

—Ahunh, said Simon, she is.

Iris glanced at her uncle but did not contradict him. Rarely was she allowed entrance into grown-up games, so she was not going to give up this chance. This was already her best day.

—Where's her mother? Mr Lever said.

—Dad, said Doris.

—It's all right, said Simon. Her mother, unfortunately, is unable to care for her. So it's left to me.

—Hmm, Mr Lever said, stirring his fourth spoon of sugar into his tea. Like meself. Except mine died. Sounds like yours doesn't have the same excuse.

—Afraid she doesn't.

—Some women are just born wanton, i'nt they? They'd be the man and defeat you without paying for it.

—We know how women are supposed to act. They themselves don't have a clue. Not any more.

Iris could see what Simon was doing: he was pretending to be her father by playing himself with total accuracy. She was so thrilled by this that she began to receive warnings of a fit. She noticed bad smells like charred meat and burning rubber, and became dreamy and saw bright auras around objects, but then all of this receded and she was back here, in the midst of things.

Mr Lever produced a gurgling sound in his throat: his approval.

—A child needs a mother.

—Aye, Mr Lever, said Simon, that's true in an ideal world.

—Is the mother what you want my Doris to be?

—If she'll have us, said Simon.

—Not sure how she'd be, said Mr Lever. You're sort of throwing her into the deep end there, i'nt ya?

—Dad.

—The situation is as it is, Mr Lever, said Simon. I can't do nought to change it. It's up to Doris to decide if she wants to be part of us. We're not forcing her. It'd only be if she said yes.

Doris burned red:

—All right, that's enough now of that.

—Ain't sure how good she'd be at it, honest to God, said Mr Lever. She's the last in the litter herself and never had anyone younger to look after. She ain't had much practice.

—She's good with Iris. And Iris loves her. Don't you, Iris?

—Ahuhn, said Iris.

Iris caught Simon's eyes, which did not show any suggestion that he ought not to be doing what he was doing. She looked away again in case she might laugh. Buried her nose in her cup.

Mr Lever drank some tea to wash down the bread he was still chewing:

—Doris said you was a Yorkshire man. I can hear it when you talk.

—Oh, aye. What else did she say about me?

—Not much. She's played it close. I know you're a commie, though. She told me that much. You didn't get her into it, that's her own doing, so I ain't going to blame you. But I do hope you see sense and get out of it soon.

—We'll see. The times are all change.

—And not getting any better, far as I can see.

Mr Lever glanced at Simon's injury.

—That, though, is an important thing she didn't tell me.

—Oh aye, said Simon, rubbing the end of the stump.

—Where did you fight?

—Italy.

—Well, look, I'm sorry for you.

—No need, Mr Lever.

—No man should have such a period of his life interrupted. Or have to live with the consequences, as you do. It can't be easy, it can't. But you did what you had to, di'nt ya?

—Dad, said Doris, I'm sure *Paul* don't want to talk about—

Iris giggled again. Her father had spent the war in a camp for conscientious objectors. The lies were piling one onto the other and getting more elaborate, and it was fantastic.

—What's up with her? said Mr Lever.

—Nothing, Doris said. Come on, Iris, let's go feed the rabbits.

Although a sunny day, there was a bracing wind on the balcony. Doris gave Iris a carrot and a leaf of lettuce from the box of old vegetables and opened the door of the hutch. Iris knelt down and tried to entice the rabbits out.

—Can I hold it? she said.

A rabbit had come out of the hutch to nibble on the lettuce leaf. Doris picked the animal up by the scruff and put it into Iris's arms.

—Bring it inside, Doris said. It's nippy out here.

Back in the sitting room, Simon was saying:

—All I'll say about that, Mr Lever, is that it takes a long time to understand a war.

Mr Lever had pushed his chair back from the table and was sitting with his legs spread wide and his hands gripping his knees.

—It ain't that hard to understand, he said. There's only one way to look at it. Nazism is a natural expression of the German character.

—I don't know, said Simon. There was some good in the Nazi regime. If we're to learn anything, that has to be admitted. Nothing in the world is entirely bad.

—But the Nazis! I'nt they the exception?

—The Jerries fought because they had a duty to, just like us. I never hated them just because I was shooting at them. I respected them. I hope I might live to have a German friend or two one day.

—Mercy be, I ain't never heard the like.

Doris began to clear the table, loudly stacking the plates on the tray.

—Iris, don't listen to these silly old men.

—It's okay, said Iris, who was rubbing her nose in the rabbit's fur, I know all about the Nazis.

Doris lifted up the tray to take them to the kitchen:

—It's terrible that you have to know about them things, Iris. But the war won't have been in vain if mankind begins to understand the price of resignation and selfishness. If we take our fate in our own hands and win peace and freedom everywhere on earth.

Mr Lever growled.

—Don't listen to that tripe, child. No one never succeeded in ridding the world of evil, and it won't be got rid of soon, not in our lifetime anyhow. Take the Germans—

—Dad. Stop.

—Me stop? Your man here's got a blue vein for the Nazis.

—Don't get the wrong end of the stick, Dad, said Doris.

—I was making more of a philosophical point, said Simon.

Doris went into the kitchen. Iris could hear her washing the dishes. The men's debate went on. Iris petted the rabbit and listened. Then Doris came back in.

—Oy Dad, she said, I wanted to remind you—

—About next week? Mr Lever said. I remember. I's got it marked on the calendar.

—You going to come then?

—Still thinking about it. Plays and all that ain't my cup of tea. And there'd only be commies, wouldn't there?

Doris took the rabbit from Iris and went to put it back outside.

—No obligations, Dad, but there's a seat booked for you. I'll leave the ticket behind the bar with Si—. With *Paul*.

Doris put the rabbit in the hutch, came back in, locked the balcony door. From her bag she took an envelope, which Iris immediately understood to contain her wages, and put it on the table. Mr Lever watched her doing this and said nothing.

Iris, her hands now free and roaming about, had located a stack of magazines. She was leafing through one containing lurid pictures of the home life of the Royal Family.

—You can take that with you, if you like, love, said Mr Lever. I'm long finished with it. It's only collecting dust there.

Doris snatched the magazine and threw it back on the pile:

—Leave that rubbish here.

At the front door, Mr Lever said:

—Come back again, Paul. You'd be welcome.

—Thanks, Mr Lever, said Simon, I'll take you up on that.

Then Mr Lever knelt down and touched Iris's chin and said:

—As I said, little Iris, I'm not sure what my Doris can do for you, but I hope it's some good.

EVA

1968

<u>XV.</u>

Miss Julie had been required reading at the Royal Academy, and she had seen two productions of the play, both starring her mother — the first at the Edinburgh Festival in fifty-nine, which had won Alissa blanket praise from the critics and imprinted her as MISS JULIE in the minds of audiences and casting directors alike; the second in London in sixty-six, a more expressionistic production and more controversial on account of its sadomasochistic costumes and imagery, which subsequently got a run in New York and put her mother's face into the American magazines — so she was not unfamiliar with it. She knew how it went, more or less. Yet only now, lying on her mattress, reading by torchlight because the electricity had been cut off that day, did she quite comprehend what a horrible piece of rot it was.

Strindberg, you lech.

She had read the first half leaning on her right elbow, while keeping the book open with her right hand and holding the torch with her left. Coming now to the part where the valet, JEAN, humiliates MISS JULIE — *Servant's whore, lackey's bitch, shut your mouth and get out of here* — Eva dropped onto her side and rolled over, swapping elbow and hands, but not before taking the opportunity to scratch an itch on her arse and to mumble to herself:

—Ach. Disgusting. I can't believe my mother got famous on the back of this crap.

A few pages before the end, Álvaro came in. Felt around the wall for the light switch, flicked it, and when it did not work, said:

—*Ah, mierda. Claro.*

She lit his path across the room by shining the torch on the floor and wagging it rapidly left and right, as an usher might for a latecomer in a dark auditorium. As he stumbled his way over, she dropped the book in order to fix her hair and plump her breasts. Reaching the mattress, Álvaro knocked a shoe against its edge; to save himself from tripping, he keeled over sideways, with enough precision to land with his cheek on the pillow, his back to her. He used his toes to kick off his shoes. Fiddled with the button of his jeans and managed to zip down the fly but ran out of energy before he could take his legs out. His shirt and socks still on, his white underpants poking out of his fly, he pulled the sheet over himself.

Silently Eva punished herself for being the plain Jane of the family, and longed to be beautiful like the girls in the French pictures or even just fascinating like her mother; it nearly made her cry, then and there, to think she was not. She pointed the torch back on her book, found her page again, cleared her throat, blew a lock of hair out of her eyes. *Don't. Don't say it. You're not that person. You don't own him. He's an autonomous being, and you want him to be free.*

—Where were you? Don't tell me. On the roof. With Iris's blacks.

He grunted:

—I was telling them about Frantz Fanon. They didn't know who he was.

—Been smoking again? You know what I think about that. You were doing so well with your drinking. Now it's this.

—If you've a problem with drugs, Eva, stop living off the proceeds.

Stung, feeling her face flush, she returned to her book. Allowed her eyes to run over the text without taking in its meaning. *You can't get angry. If you get angry, you'll be called angry.*

—Have you read this yet? she said, pinching the book by the spine and waving the pages so as to produce a sound like the beating of birds' wings. We're supposed to read it before the next meeting.

—Another one? I'm getting sick of all these meetings. Let's just do the thing already.

—This isn't your average happening, Álvy. It has to be planned properly. You'd be a better help if you weren't stoned all the time. Tell me, are you going to read the play or not? It's important that you know it.

—I'll read it tomorrow.

—The meeting's tomorrow.

—I'll do it in the morning.

—You'll sleep late. Then you'll be hung-over. When was the last time you had a morning?

—Eva? Leave me. The fuck. Alone.

She sighed and flipped back a page and began to read, at first with scant concentration — *I don't know why I should care if you read it or not, I've been against Iris's crackpot idea from the start, no skin off my nose if it all goes pear-shaped* — but she soon recovered the characters' voices and settled into their rhythm once more, leaving Álvaro as a faint presence at the edge of her senses.

When, thirty minutes later, she had finished the play, she threw the book onto the floor by the mattress and balanced the torch so that it stood on its end and shone at the ceiling. The room brightened. Downward shadows were cast. The discs of mould on the walls and ceiling formed a kind of constellation. Che and Marx and Mao kept watch, their gaze kind and gentle, like loving fathers, but in this half-light, their contours broadened and their skin yellowed, adding a touch of menace around their mouths.

—I wonder why Mama keeps coming back to this role. She must like it. Or get a kick out of it. I don't understand it. It's weird, to be honest, thinking about it. What d'you make of it?

She could tell by his breathing that he was not asleep.

—Álvy?

—I told you I haven't read it.

—But you know the play. We saw it together once.

—I don't remember.

—When we first started going out. Mama was performing in it, and you wanted to see her. Which is also kind of weird, now that I think of it.

—That's not weird. I wanted to get to know your family. In Spain that would be totally normal. Only in England would that be considered weird.

—So you remember?

—I don't. We've been to so many plays together.

She lay on her back and crossed her arms over her front.

—God. You're useless.

In the ensuing silence he must have perceived her need of him, because he turned his head so that she could see his profile: his straight nose, his jutting chin, his left eye straining to look back over his shoulder.

—What's wrong with you? he said. It shouldn't bother you that I don't remember. It doesn't mean I don't have other memories of the things we did together.

He sighed then and turned onto his back. They were not touching, but the gap between them was narrow enough for the hair of their arms to stand on end and make contact across it. They had not had sex in Paris, or since, and the longer the hiatus went on the more they hardened against each other. Rather than facilitating intimacy, the things they did now functioned as shields against each other, making them feel safe and justified in their separate corners, but also threatening to crush them.

—You're thinking too much about the happening, he said. Put it out of your mind. Go to sleep.

—What d'you think of it, though, really?

—Right now, nothing.

—Come on, Álvy. Talk to me.

He kneaded his eyeballs with his knuckles. Ran his fingertips along the darkened troughs under his eyes. Blinked deliberately as if to remove a fog from his vision.

—The group is taking the right course, he said. That's all you should care about. The fact that your idea was rejected shouldn't matter.

—It doesn't.

—What is it then? You should lead by example and embrace the group's decision.

—D'you think it's the right one, though?

—It doesn't matter what I think.

—It does to me. You voted against me.

—Don't think of it like that. I voted for what I thought was the best course of action for the group.

—So you do think Iris's idea is a good one?

—I'm not going to do this with you, Eva. It always ends the same way.

He rolled onto his side again, and let out a loud, concluding sigh. She tugged his shoulder so that he should lie on his back again. He yanked himself free of her grip and sighed even louder.

—I'm worried, she said.

—About your mother?

—She is still my mother. We're planning to interrupt her play and put her on trial in front of the TV cameras. That's a big deal.

—You're being sentimental. That woman is asking for it.

—Like MISS JULIE? In the play?

—What?

—I mean, are you saying my mother is a masochist?

—Are fascists masochists?

—I think they might be.

—Well then she is.

She poked him in the spine:

—Your parents actually are fascists, and you'd never do anything like this to them.

—Don't bring my parents into this. Theirs is an entirely different context.

A pause, and then:

—And, actually, for your information, I can imagine taking action against my parents. I've often thought about it.

—All I'm saying, Álvy, is that I don't think we should wholeheartedly embrace the first idea Iris comes up with.

—Is that all you're saying?

—Yes.

—Well, d'you want to know how it looks from the outside? It looks like you don't like that your sister is asserting herself.

—That's only how it looks in your drug-addled brain.

—You've been begging her to contribute more to the commune's work, and now she does and you bite her head off. The truth is, you prefer how things were before, when your sister was just bankrolling this place, and you were left to call the shots.

—You're being unfair.

—You're the one being unfair. To your sister. You think she's wishy-washy.

—All that talk about following her instincts and searching out her own experiences. It's too much for me.

—In Paris, you acted exactly like her.

—What? No.

—You did what the fuck you wanted, when you wanted.

—There was a rebellion going on. Not a moment passed when I wasn't contributing to the large—

—Contributing to your own little cabaret, maybe.

—You bastard.

—When we hooked up with these Maoists, from day one, you didn't stop telling them off for being inflexible and dogmatic. How many lectures did you give them about how the new politics has to take account of the individual? Then we get home and what d'you do? You start giving it to your sister for being too flexible, too much of an individual.

—You're saying I'm a hypocrite?

—I don't know. I just look at you when you behave like this and I scratch my head and I think, no one can win. Whether we move this way or that, you're always going to find fault with us. There's nothing we can do to get your approval. Unless we're Doris, of course. Then we can do what we like and still you'd think we're great.

—What do you mean? I'm not like that with Doris.

—You put her on a pedestal.

—Shut up.

—You put her on a pedestal because, unlike your mother, she's found a way to be an egomaniac that doesn't depend on selling her soul to the tabloids and the fashion magazines. And you want that for yourself too. But you know you can't just copy her. You have to figure out your own way, and you haven't yet, so you go around rejecting, rejecting, rejecting, because nothing you see is *it*.

—I live for the group. What more do I have to do to make you believe that?

—You'll only need the group till you've figured out a way to do all of this on your own.

—Wow. The truth comes out.

—Which makes you just like your sister. You don't like to see it, but you're similar. Iris uses us as well. In her case, for company. She doesn't really care about us, as people. She just cares that we're here when she comes back from her parties. She likes having us around because we look after things when she's out and we look out for her when she's in.

—You arsehole.

—It's just a pity you don't dress more like a hippy girl, and be sexy sometimes, then at least I'd get something out of it.

She rolled onto her side, so that now they were lying back to back. The promise of expression was that it would alleviate pain and make it bearable. The danger was that it would unearth older and deeper strata of torment.

—To top it off, you're now saying Iris is sexy.

—Not Iris. The cool ones you see around.

The Guineveres. The watery-eyed ladies of the lowlands. The belles dames of legend to whom Bob Dylan and Jimi Hendrix crooned.

—You men would ball anything. You've always said you couldn't stand Iris. So this must mean you can't stand me either.

—When you're like her, you're right, I can't stand you.

She rubbed her palms up and down her cheeks, as if scrubbing them with soap.

—I'm always myself. When am I ever not myself?

—You're always yourself, yeah. And what you are, is a chameleon. You say one thing to the Maoists, and another thing to Doris, and another thing to me, because you think you're the only one who sees the whole picture, and we just see these little parts, we're blind to the rest, and it's your job to manage us all, to lead us to the light. But you're careful not to go too fast either, you don't want to reveal it all to us too quickly, because somewhere you like that we're limited, that we don't quite reach the standard. It means that when it comes time to do your bidding, we'll do it. We'll go along with whatever you say—

She whirled round and began to slap his back.

—You fucking-fucking-fucking-fucking bastard.

He reared up into a seat, knocked her hands away, put his face into hers:

—Stop it. Now. I mean it.

She cowered, half-expecting him to slap her back, on the cheek, as he had done on one occasion during a quarrel. It had not been hard, his hand had been open, and he had been sorry, racked with remorse, and had kept his promise never to do it again. But the memory was there all the same. It could not be erased, and it often returned to make her flinch.

Satisfied with having produced this fear, which was the closest he would ever come to being right in an argument with her, he collapsed back down onto his side.

She stared at the back of his head.

He burrowed his cheek deeper into the pillow.

—I sacrificed a lot, she said, by setting up Wherehouse. I could have been—

—I know, I know, a proper actress like your mother.

—I could have been a lot of things. But, yes, an actress, as well, if I'd wanted to be. Don't think I don't think about the money I could be earning elsewhere, the name I could be making for myself. The reviews. The flowers. The nice dressing room. The comforts. I think about these things every day. I mean, look at where we live, the state of it, how could I not? But instead of fuelling regrets, I think of what I've missed and I tell myself, Eva, it can't be for nothing that you've given all of that up. What you do, what Wherehouse does, has to be extraordinary. It has to be worth it.

Eva knew Álvaro was not comfortable, either, with the power that Iris and Doris had so quickly assumed in the collective. He too had been happy with the previous regime. Under Eva's leadership, the group's ethos of equality had not required him to relinquish his natural privileges. When he had spoken, he had been listened to. He had not had to do women's tasks like cooking or keeping house. He had not had to get out of his seat to answer the door or change the record; his cup of tea was brought to him, it was never his turn to make it. According to the biological laws, he had occupied a position of slightly elevated equality, from which no one threatened to topple him. The old regime had been nice like that. But Iris and Doris were not nice. They were unpredictable. Tricky. They could not be trusted to respect the unspoken rules. Which was why Eva could not understand why Álvaro was supporting them. Was he not afraid, as Eva was, of where they were leading them?

—Iris's plan isn't going to save this place from demolition, she said.

—I don't think anyone really believes it will.

—Then what are we doing it for?

He must have felt her gaze on his skin because he now turned round and met it square on.

—When you're thinking about all of this stuff, Eva, do you ever think about what we'll do? When this place comes down? Is there a plan B?

Eva shook her head. Artists, real ones, did not make backup plans. Those with a cushion to fall back on invariably fell back on it. When things got tough, they lay down, which was what they had intended to do all along. It was why they bought the cushion in the first place.

—Until Wherehouse disappears, she said, there's only Wherehouse. Thinking about what comes next would only make it a reality.

—That's mystical thinking. Deluded.

—What's deluded is people planning for the end of what they love. That's what really destroys things.

Suddenly worked up, visibly hot, Álvaro thrashed about until he had rid himself of his jeans. One sock came off in the melée; the other stayed stubbornly in place.

—What is it, Álvy?

—I'm hot.

He subsided, panting.

—And also I'm thinking, after this place gets torn down—

—What?

—we could go to Spain.

Eva examined his face in an effort to determine whether or not he was serious, and when she saw that he was, said:

—No, we couldn't, you fool. You've overstayed your student visa. It was a miracle you got through immigration after Paris. If you leave again, they won't let you back in. Not a chance.

—You overestimate Her Majesty's Government.

—You underestimate them. You've just been deported from France. Your name is known to the English authorities.

—Maybe I don't want to come back.

She was stunned:

—You don't mean that.

—Maybe I do. Going back to Spain has always been an option.

—You're a known Leftist, Álvy. An expatriate agitator. I'd bet my life you're on some list.

—Franco can't live forever. Change will come. We could be part of that change.

—Not interested. I'm staying here. England is my home. I thought you'd made it yours.

—We could live more cheaply in Spain. Even under the regime, a person lives better. We could get a flat of our own.

—With what money? We'd have to get jobs.

—My parents would help. You know they know people.

—Not this again. You want to manage a factory? Or work in a bank?

—Those aren't the only choices. We could work in bars in the evening and make art during the day.

—You mean exhaust ourselves at night and sleep all morning, dabble for an hour at something worthless before we start work again, like all the other pretend artists in the world? We don't have to go to Spain to do that. We could do that here. We'd have plenty of company.

—So, as ever with you, it's all or nothing.

—Yes.

—I'd like to see you cope with nothing.

—A half-measure *is* nothing.

And with half-measures, they, Eva and Álvaro, would be nothing. For love, like art, could not flourish in circumstances dominated by money and meaningless work. Love required complete economic and personal freedom. Leisure time. The opportunity to engage in absorbing activities, which, when shared, led to deep union. This was what made love so rare. It required special people who were prepared to free up their lives for it.

—So tell me this, he said. If I stay—

—Sounds like you're about to make an ultimatum.

—Listen. If I stay, are we going to be together? You promise we'll stay together as a couple?

—I'm not following.

He gathered up the bedsheet until there was a mass of folds resting on his chest, around which he put his arms, a surrogate embrace.

—Do you fancy Sunny?

—Álvy. He's a Sikh.

—So?

—So, no. I don't fancy him.

—So there's only me in your heart?

—Yes.

—Then we should get married.

She was not expecting a proposal, but neither was she surprised that one came now. It was a kind of vengeance that most couples unleashed upon one another, was it not? *If we are unhappy, if we dislike each other, if we must suffer for the fact of no longer being single, then it is probably about time we got hitched.*

—Well?

—I'll think about it.

—That's the same as maybe. You hate maybes.

—You can't spring this on me and expect an answer straight away.

—That's too much to ask? Jesus. Most men would—

—I don't give a fuck what most men would do.

—I was going to say they'd take your response for a no.

—Most men are fucking idiots.

—I feel like a fucking idiot right now.

She had a horror of weddings, the congratulations and the cheers, the forced sentiments, the standing around, glass in hand, with a permanent grin on your face.

—It couldn't be a church thing. Nothing Catholic.

—Course not.

—You say that now, but when the time comes you'll start wanting to please your family.

—No, I won't. We'd do it our own way.

—Okay, I just need some time.

—You shouldn't need time.

—

—All right. How long?

She hesitated, her desire to give in locked with a ferocious resolve to hang on to herself. Could she be taken over and remain intact? Had there ever been a marriage that was not about possession or being possessed? Her parents' perhaps, and that had ended as any ordinary marriage did, with the same accusations, the same recriminations. Who got to be the exception?

—I'll tell you in a few days. But don't bother me with it in the meantime. Don't come at me, asking. That's guaranteed to make me say no. Leave me be, forget we ever talked about it, and I'll let you know when my mind's made up.

The Sing-Song Tribunal had been a marriage story. At its centre was the character of LIXIN, a peasant girl born in rural Sichuan who runs away to Shanghai to escape an abusive father. In Shanghai LIXIN becomes a dancer, in other words a sort of high-class prostitute, at a nightclub called Sassoon's Sing-Song House. At Sassoon's, LIXIN meets GEORGE, a wealthy English businessman, already married, who becomes one of her regular customers. Max, when writing the play, had wanted it to contain many grand themes, so at this point, at the meeting of LIXIN and GEORGE, the play explodes: there is cabaret, there is glitz, there is poverty, there is squalor, there is capitalism, there is imperialism, there is violence, there is rape, there is Western arrogance, there is Chinese pride, there is worker uprising, there is World War II, there is civil war, there is revolutionary war, there is Mao's countryside commune, there is a communist victory parade, and ultimately, in a final courtroom scene, there is retribution. But in essence, stripped down to its bones, with all the singing and dancing and fighting taken away, the question the play poses is: will GEORGE divorce his English wife and ask LIXIN to marry him? After three hours of *will they, won't they?*, in the end he does. GEORGE marries LIXIN, then together they marry the Cause.

Eva's role was that of the young LIXIN, covering the period from LIXIN's childhood in the countryside to her arrival in Shanghai. The role required her to be on stage for most of the first half. Her final appearance was at the beginning of the second, when LIXIN's entry into womanhood was represented by a solemn ceremony in which she hands her mask over to the adult LIXIN (who, since her mother's rejection of the role, was being played by a man called William).

As late as the final run-throughs, Eva had not yet succeeded in getting to the end of her bit without slipping up and causing an embarrassing interruption. Every day, after her last scene, she rushed into the wings and immediately burst into tears because she knew that, despite months of rehearsals, still she had not learned to walk by herself; rather she was being carried like an infant by the rest of the ensemble through every step of her performance. When she did not know the lines, or when she overplayed, or acted statically, or was in the wrong position, they covered for her, pulled her up and along, prevented her from falling down completely. Everyone did their bit to help. Her mother more than anyone else. Her mother — the true actress amongst the mere enthusiasts — always seemed to be nearby, hovering there, ready to step in. Eva saw flashes of her mother's costume, THE JUDGE's wig and scarlet robe, whenever she turned her head. She heard the quiet directions that her mother gave her when she passed behind. By moving into the spaces that Eva left unfilled on stage, her mother assumed responsibility for Eva's shortcomings. With nothing more than a look, her mother seduced bigger and better gestures out of her. At the end of each rehearsal her mother gave her little written notes saying, *Loosen up!* or *Tighten up!* (depending), or with recommendations to listen to a particular piece of jazz or to read a certain poem. Sometimes she simply wrapped her arms around her and kissed her and whispered into her ear, *You're doing the best you can, darling, and that's all you can do.*

And still, every time, Eva cried. It was blatant: she was not up to the part. There was no chance she would be ready for opening night, or for any night after that. She did not have her mother's talent. She did not have any talent, full stop. That was the truth of the situation, which she knew because her father did not spare her from it.

—You're not up to the part. There's no way you'll be ready for opening night.

These, his exact words, spoken at the top of his voice, in front of everybody. And even that was her fault. She was requiring her father to be hard. She needed to be drilled by him, made to behave in the way he thought was right, because she was so often wrong. As a director, her father was guided more by what he did not want than by what he wanted. He did not tell her: do this. Instead he said: do not do that. And he punished her when she persisted. The method was not hard to understand. Eva was the reliable stone on which he broke open his mouth, and she could not complain about being badly treated because she only had herself to blame; she was not heeding the basic laws.

From the wings, through the tears in her eyes, she watched the rest of the rehearsal and did not fail to notice how much lighter the play was, how much faster and smoother it ran, now that William was in the role of LIXIN and she was banished. How happy everyone looked, how relieved. And how dark it was where she stood.

After rehearsals, her mother normally went straight to her room without saying goodnight to anyone, and it was understood that she was not to be disturbed. But once, a few days before opening night, Eva went to her, with the intention of telling her that she was dropping out. *Mama*, she was going to say, *it's all been a mistake. I'm the wrong choice. I'm not an actress and don't ever want to be one.* Her mind was made up, she would not be appearing in *The Sing-Song Tribunal*. William would have to play the entire part, adult and child, all by himself.

—Mama? she said, knocking on the door. Mama, are you still awake?

Inside, her mother was on her back on the bed, still in costume. Iris was lying beside her.

—Oh. You're already in bed? Sorry.

The springs of the mattress creaked as her mother turned onto her side and beckoned Eva in:

—It's all right, darling. This is the life of the actress. The world gets to see us in all our states.

Approaching the bed, Eva picked up THE JUDGE's wig from

where her mother had dropped it on the floor, and put it onto the dressing table. She turned the chair round so that it was facing the bed and sat down. Leaned onto her thighs so as to avoid speaking down to her mother and to ensure, instead, that they were on a level.

—You're still in your costume, Mama, she said. It'll get creased like that.

—Sorry. I can see you're tired. I'll come back in the morning.

Alissa reached out a hand and touched Eva's knee.

—Stop apologising for yourself, child. You're fine where you are.

Her mother's hand slipped off Eva's knee and onto the floor, and she kept it there, so that she now lay with one arm hanging off the side of the bed.

—Mama, said Eva, I want to tell you something.

—Hmm? her mother said. The rehearsal went well, didn't it? Everybody did good work today, I thought.

—Mama, said Eva, if you'll permit me to say—

Her mother drew her fallen arm up and put it lying on her side:

—What is it, Eva?

Behind her mother, Iris sat up and rubbed her eyes. Peered out over the undulation of their mother's hip.

—Mama, said Eva, I think, well, I think I'm in a phase where I don't think I'm an actress at all.

—Not an actress?

—I feel I'm only giving the impression of being one. Like, it's all been blown out of proportion and I'm an *ab-so-lute* fake.

—Nonsense.

Her mother pressed her elbow into the mattress and propped her head up on a hand.

—For your age, she said, you're doing remarkably well.

—For my age, maybe. But I think that's the point. My role is the young LIXIN but I don't think it's for a young person. It's too hard.

—Eva, precious—

Her mother threw her legs off the bed and came to sit up.

—This is just the jitters. It happens to all of us. Go to bed. Get some rest. You'll feel all right in the morning.

—No, Mama. I mean it. I can't do it. Don't make me, please.

Her mother brought her palms to her face and breathed loudly into them. Now, revealing herself again, she said:

—Let me share something with you, Eva. A professional secret. Are you listening?

Eva nodded, though she did not like the sound of what was coming.

—All actors get cold feet. It happens to me all the time. The key to getting past it is to look at what's causing it. What thoughts are causing the fear? For me, it's always the same. I can't bear the thought of myself as successful in a society like ours. As a result, I get these feelings of wanting to sabotage my own work. I won't be happy until I destroy everything. But you've got to remember that society doesn't need perfect art. It just needs people who try to make art. Of any kind. Good or bad. People who are willing to fail, that's what helps societies grow and what, in the end, brings about change in the ww—

Her father, seeing the door ajar and the light on inside, had entered without knocking.

—Oh good, you're still up. Doris, come in!

Doris slinked in. Came to stand beside him.

Eva turned away a little, so that the newcomers could not see the distress on her face. She heard her mother say:

—What do you two want?

Eva pinched the bridge of her nose and fought against her tears. She could not accept the fact of all of these people around her in this moment, this total experience, because it meant a loss of control. She was, at once, desperately angry and desperately trying to avoid it. If this double feeling was like anything, it was like standing before the highest mountain, on the cusp of ascent, while being forced down, down into the ravine, the blackest stream.

—Eva, Iris, said her father. Go and wait outside please.

—Leave them where they are, said her mother. I want them to hear whatever you have you say to me.

—You want to turn them against me.

—Only you have that power, Paul.

Eva heard her mother call her name. She turned to see her mother on her feet, taking off THE JUDGE's robe.

—Can you give me a hand please, darling?

Eva wiped her face quickly before helping her mother undress. She folded the robe over the back of the chair. Then crept over to the bed and sat down beside Iris.

Her mother, standing just a couple of paces way from her father and Doris, unzipped the black jumpsuit that functioned as the base layer of her costume and undressed as far as her underwear, the combination of high-waisted pants and sensible bra (minus a girdle) that her father used to say he liked because it showed her social conscience. Without covering herself, she rummaged in her bag for her pills, downers at this time, and took two together without water.

—It's past midnight, Paul, and I didn't sleep last night. So if you've got something to say, for God sake say it, so I can go to bed and be done with you.

—Stop being so defensive. We just need to talk.

Her father took her mother's dressing gown from the hook on the door. Threw it to her. She plunged her arms into the gown's sleeves. Tied a knot at the waist. Plonked down at the dressing table and began to cream her face. All the while keeping her eyes on Paul and Doris through the mirror in front.

Doris looked around for somewhere to go, but there was nowhere.

Her father leaned sideways against the wall. Rubbed the stubble on his face.

—In the interests of saving everyone from hurt feelings, he said, we should talk, the three of us, and come to some kind of understanding, wouldn't you agree?

—No, said her mother, rubbing circles into her forehead. I don't need to talk. I just need to rest.

—You owe Doris an apology.

—Oh? For?

—You know what for. The way you spoke to her today. The way you've been speaking to her.

Planting her palms on the dressing table, her mother used it to lever herself to her feet. She replaced the dressing gown with a night-dress from the clothes pile on top of the chest.

—I simply told Doris not to touch my children. She was being inappropriate.

—Inappropriate? said her father. Quite the contrary. Seeing Doris with the children has made me think about how we've been as parents. The way she takes time with them, the way she listens to them, plays with them. It's a lesson for us.

Her mother took off her bra under the night-dress. Dropped it on the floor. Signalled to Eva and Iris that they should move further down the mattress to let her in. Then she got under the sheets and patted the space beside her as an invitation to her daughters to join her. Iris did. Eva stayed where she was: engulfed by shame for her parents' behaviour but at the same time desperately wishing for an argument so nasty that the play would have to be cancelled.

—Should I have to say it, Paul? her mother said then. It was out of line for Doris to take Iris in her car to meet her family. None of your other girls was ever given such leeway. From now on, Doris isn't to be left alone with either of our daughters at any time. She is not to touch them or talk to them, ever.

—Don't be ridiculous. I've never heard—

—You have more freedom than most men, and I'm content for you to use it. But please don't abuse it, Paul. Respect the lines we've drawn. Now, I'm about to turn off the lamp. Can you turn the main light off on your way out?

—Not until you give Doris the apology she deserves.

The anger that had obviously been simmering now flew up

and broke in her mother's throat as a maniacal laugh. The laughter seemed to travel to every part of her; to every limb; to every tip; to every nerve ending; consume her.

Eva clasped her hands over her face as a mask, and the outside world disappeared. There existed only a tiny point in space, where the index fingers parted, which contained within it the absurdity of life in all its possible forms. A moment, then, and this point turned inside out, and the world returned.

Her mother switched off the lamp. Alone, the main light caused different shadows to fall: dark discs beneath everyone's eyes; long gullies down their cheeks.

—We're not leaving until we sort this out, said her father. How about you, Doris? Maybe you should begin? I know you've something you'd like to say to Alissa.

—Okay, said Doris, well, ah—

—You've been giving Doris a hard time at rehearsals, her father cut in. And it's very unfair.

—The first thing you learn working in the theatre, said her mother, is that you can't take things personally.

—Cut it out, said her father. You can see how hard it is for Doris to do this. Just apologise, for fuck's sake.

How it had always worked was that an understanding would arise between her mother and father — unspoken — that his present affair was nearing an end, and then, barely even willed, it would end. It was not a system without rules; rather it was a system in which the rules did not need to be stated. But maybe that had been the wrong way about it. Maybe by stating the rules they would have avoided the mistake of deeming themselves wiser than the rules.

—I'm going to be honest with you, Doris, said her mother. Really, what you do or don't do, or whether I like you or not, is irrelevant. Because this situation is only temporary. You'll be gone from us soon, and you won't have to worry about me or this place any longer. You clearly have feelings for each other—

She clasped her hands together to suggest the coming together of two bodies.

—and I try hard to see things through your eyes. But I can't bear dissension between myself and Paul. And I won't tolerate anyone manipulating my daughters. So, yes, it'll be coming to a close soon.

Eva was clutching her own throat as though to prevent the anxiety from rising into her head.

Iris — *wouldn't you know* — had zoned out and was staring blankly at the ceiling.

Her father brought a hand to his forehead and closed his eyes.

—Doris is doing good work, he said weakly. She has become indispensable to me.

—I understand it might seem that way, said her mother. But a deal's a deal. Perhaps my husband didn't tell you this, Doris, but the director becomes obsolete after opening night. When the play is up and running, it has no more use for him. So, evidently, we won't be needing a director's assistant either, and I'm against you staying on as a permanent member. It wouldn't be, well, it wouldn't be right. You understand, don't you? I've nothing against you, personally. Truth be told, I'm trying to protect you.

—From? said her father.

—From us.

Her father had gone white, and a twitch had come to his right leg, making it jig arrhythmically.

Doris, on the other hand, appeared fine. She had a hand on her hip and was sort of pouting nonchalantly.

—Maybe you're right, Alissa, she said. You've been open with me from the beginning. I've known all along how things were going to go, I can't say I didn't.

—But things have turned out a little differently than expected, said her father, visibly panicked. You're different from what I expected.

—Your wife is right, Paul, said Doris. I don't want to come between you.

—My wife? said her father. What if I told you—

—Paul? said her mother, a warning.

—what if I told you she wasn't my wife? That we weren't even married?

Which was how Eva found out. That was how she was told.

The voices of children flew wildly around the auditorium. Clichés were given new punch. Insults became sparkling and light. Phrases which in an adult's mouth would have been dead weights rose up and circled round, escaped through the doors and the cracks, penetrated the ceilings and walls, reaching every part of Wherehouse. Eva was decidedly not in the mood. Had it been up to her, she would not have allowed this. But the course of things was no longer under her command. The reins had slipped from her hands. It was Iris who held them now; it was she who had called the children in.

That morning she, Iris, had knocked on the terrace doors and scoured the bomb sites; at lunchtime she had waited outside the local school gate, hoping to run into the specific types she had in mind to recruit. Of the twenty or so she approached, eleven agreed to come, which ought to have been plenty. But Doris, then, unable to tolerate the idea of a team composed entirely of boys, had insisted on doing a runaround of her own, which had yielded five more: all girls from the same extended clan, prised with great difficulty from the high-walled edifice of familial and neighbourhood control.

Eva sat alone on the stage, her legs dangling off the sides, her eyes closed, her fingertips pressed into her temples: adapting to the new reality. The children had every right to be here, and to make whatever noise they wanted. The theatre was as much theirs as hers to fill. She just needed a minute to find the heart to hand it over to them.

They — these sixteen sons and daughters of King's Cross, for whom talk other than shouting was impossible — were going to take part in the happening. According to Iris's plan, the Wherehouse members were going to lead them in a procession through the streets as far as the London Carlton, where the interruption and then the televised trial would take place. During the procession, the children were going to hold lighted Chinese lanterns, as though delivering fire from the dark parts of London to the bright.

Taking a long breath through her nostrils, Eva opened her eyes and looked around the auditorium floor. The children were dispersed in groups of two and three around the six workbenches. At two of the benches the children were making red armbands, which were going to be worn to distinguish the happening participants from the general public. At the four other benches they were making the lanterns. Laid out on the stage floor, there were already about thirty completed lanterns from previous workdays; Iris's idea was to make at least twenty more today.

The children's work at each table was being overseen by a Wherehouse member, a Maoist or both; the interaction between the children and the overseers was what was producing most of the racket. The children were excited, having been admitted both to the mighty league of grown-ups and to the magic circle of entertainers (to their minds, the collective was simply a kind of human circus). The adults here appeared to them as figures of all that was alien: they dressed in a fashion for which the children had no reference, they spoke in an English which the children did not always comprehend, they displayed attitudes and airs which the children had seldom encountered before. Everything the children saw, they wanted to touch; everything the adults touched, they fought to be the first to handle. Once they had learned how to do something, such as how to bend the bamboo strips around the lantern frame and glue them into place, they immediately assumed the role of experts in that thing, and ran around to the other tables showing the others how to do it, regardless of whether the others were involved in that activity or not. They helped each other with heartbreaking generosity and criticised each other without shame. They were tender one minute, violent the next; they fought and forgave with matching vehemence. Not knowing how long this experience would last, they plunged into it, squeezed from it all that they could, without ever forgetting that they were not the kind of people who normally did this sort of thing, and therefore were constantly anxious to know if they were still welcome to be here, and how long it would be before they were not.

The only light in the room came from candles and torches and oil lamps. In the dimness, Eva watched with only a weak sense of her own involvement; a feeling of detachment which saddened her because it reminded her of her mother and father, who, when setting up The East Wind, had not been interested in connecting with the local community. They had decried bourgeois intellectuals who thought it was necessary to submerge oneself in the proletariat. Instead they had seen themselves as a beacon, attracting outsiders similar to themselves into King's Cross. Royal Court theatre buffs and counter-cultural oddities and society movers and shakers: her parents had been obsessed with taking these exotic creatures out of their natural habitat and placing them here, in this swamp, and leaving them to sink or swim.

Unlike them, Eva really desired submersion. She wanted to be more than just a member of a commune, she also wanted to be a citizen of the locality. But she found it hard to make contact with the natives. The closest she had come was in the neighbourhood pubs, where on a few occasions she had succeeded in striking up a conversation or gaining entrance to a game of darts. But she only went to the pubs if Iris was going, and she followed Iris's lead about who to associate with and who to avoid; she did not dare to do any of that alone.

It came easily to Iris. Iris had a common touch. Which must have been self-acquired, for she had not been taught it at home. Watching her sister now, Eva was once again struck by this fact, and felt envy on account of it. Iris approached the children without trepidation. She spoke to them seriously, without condescension, and did not have to change the way she spoke in order to gain their acceptance. She answered their queries with forthrightness, and expected the same in return, in this way making it known that she would be more than merely tolerated; she would be treated as an equal and an ally. Patiently, she taught them how to look at things, to take notice, to handle with care, to worry about process as much as outcome. For one of their jokes, she gave them back two, and, taking her lead, they only laughed if they actually thought she was being funny. Of course they had no intention of inviting her into their lives afterwards, they would have been warned against getting too intimate with people like her, but within these confines they trusted her. If they encountered a problem which their own overseers were unable to fix, they rushed to Iris with it. They would not accept anyone else's word, they would only deal with her.

Doris, too, was able to coalesce with the children, though her approach to them differed from Iris's. Coming from a similar background as the children, she presumed to know them, perhaps more than she actually did, and was impatient with them for their not having seen beyond their limited horizons already. She spoke their idiom fluently, but she tended to use it to cane them with, to drive them like stubborn donkeys towards the know-how that she believed they ought to have acquired by now, if one day they wanted to get out of their situation. It was clear that, for herself, Doris did not care for children. She did not feel their absence in her own life. *Why always children?* Eva had heard her say during a discussion on the boat home from France. *Ain't it more beautiful that desire should end where it begins, and not produce all of this messy extra material? Nothing into nothing, that's the way of the universe, and the way I intend to live.* Eva was sure that her father would have liked to have more children, and she was thankful that Doris was denying him this. Eva did not know how she would have responded to seeing her father showering attention on a second brood in order to make up for his neglect of the first.

Álvaro was helping to make the red armbands. Initially he had been assigned to the lanterns, at a table occupied by three girls, but he had demanded to be changed, believing that he would get on better with the boys. He enjoyed the boys' company, though Eva was not certain if they enjoyed his company as much in return. In him, there was concealed a child that wanted to play. He seemed to believe that if he could reveal that child, be that child, he would forget how illusions were made and everything would seem real again. But the boys were suspicious of the eagerness that attended this belief. Perhaps they saw what Eva saw: that, more than feeling respect for the children as they actually were, Álvaro envied them their potential: who and what they could one day be. He hoped much from them, believed them composed of a finer clay than the rest of disappointing humanity, when the fact was that most of them would grow up into commonplace people. They merely had not yet had the opportunity to be corrupt or shallow or decadent. But they would get their chance. In capitalism, everyone did.

Eva was aware that Álvaro's primary motivation for getting married was to have children, and that he wanted to get married so soon because he wanted children young. He did not want to be an old father, as his own father had been. Eva alone was not enough to justify Álvaro's existence. A wedding in itself would not satisfy him. A woman's oath of fidelity was meaningful only as a means to the greater prize. Only children — sons — would dignify his life. Eva had often spoken to him, abstractly, about the idea of family, and what it meant to him, and she had got the sense that, for him, having children was a way of taking revenge against a future which he could not control. A child of two or three was already a moral being: he moved the right way, made the right noises, and knew what he should and what he should not feel. Álvaro seemed to believe that when Leftists got cynical about family and refused to have them, all they were doing was leaving the field open for Rightists to populate the world with their moral copies. Radicals had a duty to reproduce.

Eva looked at the question through the opposite side of the glass. She believed responsible revolutionaries should not have children. When children were born, they had to be the first consideration. Until they were grown, one did not have the right to live for oneself. To bear children was necessarily to enter a state of ceaseless torment as one wondered how one could bring them up well and in what way one could leave them a means of support. Unless Eva begged from her grandparents, which she was not prepared to do, she would not be well off enough to afford a housekeeper, nor would she want to contract out her maternal responsibilities to a stranger like that. She would be forever torn between domestic chores and her artistic fulfilment, which ultimately was her deepest health. Were she ever to become a mother, so as not to become like her own mother, she would in all probability sacrifice her art for the children's sake. She would trade politics and performance for a dull peace. But the result, the final tariff would be her own illness and death.

As for the future, a part of Eva had already given up on that. She was haunted by the threat that even if a nuclear war did not destroy the planet outright, her children would be born deformed or mad. In her waking nightmares, misshapen children, cretins, crawled on the floor around her feet, pleading for succour that she could not provide. Having physically healthy babies would be no consolation either; it would not put an end to the terrors. For how would she know, even with normal children, whether or not she was toiling for worthless ones? What would she do if they ended up being conservatives? Rightists? Fascists? And — the question had to be asked — would it be any better if, against the odds, they turned out to be Leftists? Destined to spend their lives seeking solidarity and communion in an even more hostile world? Talking about equality and freedom as higher principles when the majority had long learned to see them as meaningless words? What contribution would Eva have made then, except to help engender another generation of failures?

When adults suffered something they could not bear, when they were defeated, they transferred their feelings to their children. There was nothing to suggest that Eva would not do the same. She, like everyone else, would begin by wanting to make amends to her children for being the child of her own parents, but before long she would be taking revenge on them with the same motive in mind. It made a difference to Eva whether she was in agreement with what Doris thought, and whether Doris regarded her as being like herself; on this subject, however, her agreement was unforced. The childless, by their ignorance about whether children proved in the end a happiness or a sadness, won greater happiness than those who were parents.

—I thought it'd be worthwhile to bring the female minority together and have a quick encounter. To see where we is, and what we might come up with, apart from the pack.

On the quiet, Doris had called Iris, Eva and Barbara out to the yard. It was a muggy day, the sun's heat trapped under a thick blanket of cloud. Coming from the dark and musty building, it felt like a different climate. The light was white and diffused, scorching Eva's eyes on first contact; she had to squint and shield her face until her vision adjusted.

Doris was standing near the warehouse wall, her boot lifted onto a pallet in order to raise up her thigh, which she was using as a ledge to rest both forearms on as she leaned forward. She had taken her shirt off and draped it around her neck, as a boxer does a wet towel. Positioned as she was, her breasts drooped into the cups of her bra, offering a privileged view of her cleavage and the upper curves of her large olive-coloured nipples.

Eva made a visor for her eyes by interlinking her fingers and holding them across her forehead:

—What is this, Doris? she said. A tit-in?

Doris scratched an itch on her belly, just above the line of her belt:

—Is I offending you?

—Pff, said Eva. Can we just get right to it? We shouldn't leave the children unsupervised for too long.

Following Doris's lead, Iris had tied a knot in the front of her tunic in order to reveal her own stomach, which had the added excitement of a piercing in the navel.

—I'm sure the men can hold the fort for five fucking minutes, she said.

—I just wanted to have a quick convo about our progress, said Doris. I's worried that the people in the group are working at different speeds and have different strengths.

—With respect, said Eva, that's always how it goes in groups.

—I get it, said Doris. But I do think there's an unevenness in this group that could turn into a problem. Most of the men—

—Oh, I see.

—ain't even read *Miss Julie* yet. I suspect some of them ain't ever going to bother.

—I bought thirteen copies, said Iris, out of the collective budget, so that everyone would have one. They have no excuse.

—Everyone here's read the play, I take it? said Doris.

The other three kicked pebbles and scraped the ground with the soles of their shoes. Then looked at each other and nodded: *yes, they were good girls, they had done the homework.*

—Listen, Doris, Eva said, you won't know this because most of your performances are solitary, but the group dynamics here are pretty normal. There's nothing to worry about. When it comes to the crunch, everyone will do their bit. The men included.

—You's right, said Doris, I do normally work alone, but I's been around.

She took her foot off the pallet and straightened her torso. Took her shirt from around her neck, spun it into a tube and replaced it. She then put her hands on her hips. As she breathed, the bones of her ribcage emerged from and sank back into her flesh.

—I's seen me fair share of group happenings. And as far as I can make out, they have one thing in common. They reflect the inner resources of the group. A chaotic group produces chaos. A bored group produces boredom.

—And this group? said Eva.

—It's plain to me, said Doris, that the resources of this group—

—Emanate from the yoni, Iris finished for her.

—From the what? said Eva.

—You heard me, said Iris. Stop playing dumb to be difficult.

—The vision for the happening is Iris's, said Doris. Its origin is female. And its engine—

—Is also female, said Iris. Us four here. This has happened organically. We didn't impose it. And it works, it's beautiful. Now we need to make sure that, as we give the happening its final shape, it retains its female quality. Its cunt-identity.

—Meaning? said Eva.

—Meaning, said Iris, that it should keep its feminine power and not be taken over by the dicks, and claimed as theirs, after we've done all the groundwork. The birthing.

Eva was surprised by how angry Iris sounded. She looked at her sister, tried to find her eyes. But Iris had turned her head the other way.

Doris took a folded page from her pocket and passed it to Barbara.

—Take a look at this. It's from Iris's scrapbook. An interview with Alissa.

Barbara unfolded the page.

While Barbara read, Doris walked from one end of the pallet to another, stepping up on it, then stepping down, knocking it with the cap of her boot.

—Reading that article, she said, I was reminded why I don't read fashion magazines.

Once Barbara had got the gist of the article, she passed it to Eva. It was an interview promoting *Miss Julie.* Already in the second paragraph, in response to a question about feminist criticisms of Strindberg and his play, Alissa was delivering a rant about the women's lib movement.

—I'd take what my mother says with a pinch of salt, said Eva, handing the page back to Doris. She'd say anything to annoy the Left and get herself some attention.

Doris folded the page and put it back into her pocket.

—I ain't never taken your mother's bait before, she said. But this article flicked a switch in me. By attacking other women, she's made herself my business. I can't ignore her any more. I's satisfied she's a legitimate target.

—I'd go further than that, said Iris. She's the right target for this moment.

—I disagree with the woman in the article, said Barbara as she tucked her fringe, which had come loose, back into her military-style beret. But it has to be said, a lot of people don't like the lib women. I'm not sure that alone makes her the right target.

—I's surprised to hear you say that, said Doris. The lib women is basically Maoists. They want to drive buses and play football and use beer mugs and not glasses. They want men to take the pill.

—Come on, said Eva, how many men you know are ever going to take the pill?

—It's not that I oppose the lib women, said Barbara. They just come across as immodest to me. Women should resist pressure to enter into movement activities that are focussed solely on themselves. They shouldn't close themselves off like that. Only a general revolution, a proletarian one, will bring equality for all.

—Women ain't going to be liberated, said Doris, if they spend all of their time fighting other people's battles.

—Women who are angry should read Mao and join the Revolution.

—You say revolution, but there ain't just one any more, right? There's many parts that make up this larger thing called revolution. When the history books is written, they'll say that the biggest part was the struggle of women against men.

Barbara shrugged, agreeing to disagree.

Doris stepped one foot forward to rest it on the pallet edge.

—Speaking of women against men, I went to your mother's play last night.

This made Eva unexpectedly furious:

—You should have told us. We'd have come with you.

—I wanted to go alone, to see for myself. And I has to give it to her, your mother I mean, she's still good at what she does. She'll be the making of our happening.

—Sounds like you have something to tell us.

Doris swayed slightly, as she transferred her weight between the front foot and the back.

—Here's what I's thinking. The only way our interruption is going to work is if it don't actually interrupt the play. We do our procession, one. We gain access to the theatre, two. We storm the stage, three. But, at that point, the play itself shouldn't stop. It should continue, as if nothing has changed, even though everything has changed because we's in it.

—That would mean convincing the actors to continue acting, said Eva. How would we do that? Surely once the actors see us come on, they'll run off or refuse to keep going.

—That's the risk we run, innit? said Doris. When we take over the performance, it'll be up to the original cast to decide if they want to join us or not. The radical ones will, the reactionaries won't.

—Are you saying we should mount our own performance of *Miss Julie*? said Iris.

—Something like that, said Doris. We'll learn the parts of the play in advance so we can continue where the original cast has left off.

—And Mama? said Eva.

—She's the crux, i'nt she? The rest of the cast will be more or less disposable, but we'll have to try to keep Alissa on stage. The telly cameras will be expecting to see something involving her. They won't be interested if she ain't there. Our aim has to be to make her perform with us.

—How though? said Eva.

—Dunno yet. Whatever we come up with, we need to remember that Alissa will always have the power to stop the performance. Short of killing her, we can't prevent her from stopping it. At some stage she'll decide she's had enough, and she'll stop. Then that'll be it.

—So the point, said Eva, is to see how far we can push Mama, before she tips over?

Doris shrugged:

—She can tip over all she likes, as long as she stays on stage and in front of the cameras.

*

Later, when the children had been sent home, Eva went to see Doris in her room.

—I wanted to ask you something, she said. Not about the happening. About Papa.

Doris had been washing her face at a bowl. Now she dried her face and hands. Threw the towel into the corner.

—You don't have to worry about him. He's alone at home but has everything he needs. He always makes sure of that.

Eva stayed by the door because she had not been invited further in. She rubbed away a hot feeling on her neck.

—That's not what I meant. I was going to say, did he ever—?

Doris leaned back against the wall. Bent her left knee and brought the sole of her foot to rest against the bare brick.

—What?

—Did he ever hold you back?

Doris changed foot: brought the left to the ground and the right to rest against the wall.

—What do you want from me?

—Sorry, it's just—

—What is it?

—Álvaro asked me to marry him. And I don't know what to tell him.

Doris sighed and put her hands in her trouser pockets.

—You could start by telling him whatever it is you's thinking.

Eva put a hand over her right cheek and shook her head: no.

—You don't want to marry him? If that's the case, he has a right to know, as soon as possible.

—I don't know if I want to marry him or not.

—Then why don't you tell him that? Express your doubts.

—How could I?

—It's the truth, so just tell him.

Eva shook her head again:

—I should probably just do it. I feel he's a lonely person and would be lost without me. His family in Spain are Rightists. He thinks he can go back, but I don't think he ever can.

—You's wrong, Eva. People always go back. People return to what they was born into, eventually. The question is, would you go with him?

—No.

—Well, tell him that. Truth is always the best option, because it's the radical option, because it's true.

Eva felt like she wanted to cry.

Doris saw Eva's distress, though she did not appear softened by it.

—Eva, look at me.

Eva lifted her face.

—You should know something, said Doris. They all try to hold us back.

—You can't say *all*.

—All. In our society—

—But he's Spanish.

—I's talking about the West, everywhere.

—All men in the West are the same?

—In one aspect. Their education about us. Men of all different classes, everywhere, has that in common. They's taught to respect us, yeah, but they believe that by respecting us they win the right to set the limits of what we can and can't do, and to punish us if we cross those limits.

—Was China different?

—You'd have to ball some Chinese blokes to find that out. But I doubt it. When I look around the world, at all the different cultures, the only difference I can see between them is the openness of the violence that's used in our punishments.

—Isn't it a bit better here, though? In England? Papa helped you, didn't he?

—Until he thought he'd helped enough. Then he started wanting to control me. I had to fight him to get where I is today. Still do.

—Sometimes I think his head is still in the thirties.

—Well, things *was* different then. If your father was asked what was wrong, he knew. If he was asked what should be done about it, he also knew. When I joined the Party after meeting your dad, that's what I were looking for. That certainty from before. Because I didn't really have it for meself. I felt lucky to've met your father because he had the conviction I thought I needed. And he still has it.

—All the bloody Christian stuff?

—I don't need that kind of conviction any more. But it's part of his mindset.

—Well, Álvaro isn't Papa. He's an atheist. And I do think he wants the best for me.

—Chances are he also wants to choose what's best for you. Or he will, when the time comes.

Eva fought not to show her upset at hearing this.

—But what do I know? said Doris. Álvaro could be the one golden exception.

—So you regret marrying Papa?

—I don't regret nothing I's done. I don't believe in regret. Everything that happens is necessary.

—Bit drastic?

—I don't think anyone really regrets what they's done. What do you regret?

Eva looked out the window where the white light of the day was fading.

—This is really about your work, innit? said Doris then. You's ashamed to admit it's your first priority.

—Maybe.

—I's a hard time being relaxed about my work, too. Performance is a matter of life and death for me. It's serious. I don't have a sense of humour about it.

—I don't think I do either.

—So then the question is, is you going to let Álvaro hold you back? Whether you marry him or not, is you going to let him? Because in the end it's up to you.

—I never knew you were such a—. Sorry.

—You ain't thought about these things before?

—A bit. Not much.

Outside a pair of crows was perched on the gutter, their heads jerking this way and that, never settling. Eva watched them in silence for a while. Then:

—D'you have something against my mother?

—I'd have plenty of reason to, but no, I don't.

—She'd have plenty of reason, as well, to have something against you.

—Back then it was messy, but I don't think she hates me.

Eva went red and looked down:

—Isn't it weird, though? That she's made a career out of *Miss Julie*. Because it's a triangle, isn't it? Christ. We probably shouldn't be talking about this.

—You're right, we shouldn't be.

Doris crossed the room and took hold of the door by its edge:

—But you should know, Eva, that I don't hate your mother. I don't want to see her harmed. I don't do extreme things any more. That phase of my career is over. And anyway, in those crazy early performances, I never harmed anyone else. It were only ever meself.

Do you, comrade Bradburn, want to unite yourself to comrade Thurlow so as to constitute a communist family, to serve the people of Britain in its march towards a popular insurrection and the installation of a revolutionary government?

The oath itself was a lie, given that the Party no longer really believed that Britain was about to have a revolution, and that the leadership were at that moment redefining the whole idea of revolution itself so that it no longer meant violent overthrow of the state and instead only meant a change in the way current society was run. Had it been her parent's plan to make their lie official? Had they intended, at some stage, to get the legal certificate and the stamp? Possibly. But they never had. Much to the delight of her mother's family. Overnight, her grandparents became enamoured of the idea of communism. Communism — *the good fight!* — was keeping opportunists like her father clear of the Thurlow money. Communism meant that her mother would keep her name, and that Eva and Iris would benefit from the family connections. *Long live the Revolution!*

For her father, the lie had been based on principle. He wanted the Thurlow money, but he did not want to want it. For her mother, principles were not the first concern. She wanted to know what marriage was like before properly committing to it. To have joined the ranks of the legally married women, just like that, would have felt like a renunciation; too fast. Caution prevented her choosing a future that might be poisoned by remorse. She wanted to see if there could be a marriage which was a beginning and not, as she feared, the end of life.

So a swearing ceremony in a community hall, covered with pictures of Lenin and hammer-and-sickle flags, and with a big banner saying THE UNITY OF THE COMMUNIST FAMILY FOR THE PEOPLE'S UNITY ON THEIR WAY TO SOCIALIST REVOLUTION was the flimsy thread that tied her parents together. Yet it had never snapped. Obsessively they pulled their own way, and obsessively they returned to each other. They intimated in each other things they could not understand in themselves alone, but nothing was ever explicitly said, so they never unravelled the power of the connection between them, until it had actually unravelled and was gone.

Max, who had been a special witness at the ceremony, also ended up being party to the eventual break. When, years later, Eva asked him about it, he said to her: *There were important things you didn't see, Eva, because you were just a child. I don't see why you shouldn't know about them now. Only you must promise not to hate the messenger.*

—You must help me, her mother had said to Max one morning before rehearsals. You must talk to Paul. He has gone mad. You must make him see sense. I thought he'd soon tire of this girl. His affairs have always had a time limit. But Doris isn't like the previous ones. He has lost his mind over her. I've told her she has to go, but she won't. Paul won't let her. There's no reasoning with him, and I fear if I push too hard, well, you know what could happen then: the bastard will leave with her. Please, Max, speak to him on my behalf. Convince him to get rid of her. Tell him she can stay until opening night, but then she has to go. Do you hear me? She simply has to.

Max, though he did not want to, arranged to meet Paul at a restaurant on Wardour Street. Max knew his friend would be late so he took a book to read while he waited. The restaurant was long and narrow and French, packed with little square tables. The late-dinner crowd had installed itself in the brighter, smokier space at the front. Max put himself at the very back, alone and in near darkness, ordered some wine and read by the candlelight.

Paul arrived a mere twenty minutes after the agreed hour. He had brought Doris, even though Max had expressly asked him to come alone. Paul snatched the book out of Max's hands and looked at the cover.

—Not you as well, he said.

—It's not that bad actually, for a debut. I'm pleasantly surprised.

Paul hissed and threw it down on the table.

—Sorry we're late, said Doris.

Max kissed Doris's hand, knowing she was not accustomed to it.

—Don't worry, *Doris*—

He spoke her name as if pronouncing for the first time a commodity only recently imported from abroad.

—by now I'm used to it.

She retrieved her hand and wiped it discreetly on the back of her skirt. Max smiled at this gesture: for her type, nakedness began at the hands; to have attention drawn to them in this way would have left her feeling exposed.

Paul paced around in search of a better table:

—It's a crime to be buried back here like moles. Ah, there's one.

He marched them to a table that had just been vacated by the window. Impatiently, he drew a circle in the air over the dirty plates as a signal to the waiter to clear them. The three of them sat uncomfortably — well, Doris appeared uncomfortable, Max and Paul were content simply to observe — while the waiter wiped the plastic covering and set four fresh places. Max thought about instructing him to take the extra seating away but decided against it. It seemed Alissa was to be present even when she was not.

Max put his glasses back on to read the menu. Having eaten here before and therefore knowing what to avoid, he ordered for everyone: mussels to share followed by sole and another bottle of white wine.

—All right for you, Doris?

—Lovely, she said, though it turned out she was ignorant as to what mussels entailed.

—Oh, so you're Jewish, Max said. Are you observant?

—No. But me dad has always been against them.

When the mussels arrived Paul attacked them with his fork, a method that often left the little bits of flesh torn, and the area around his plate spattered with sauce. Max used an empty shell as pincers to prise them out more delicately, and he was happy to see Doris followed his approach even if it might have appeared disloyal. Paul did not seem to notice or to care. He was immersed in a monologue about a production of *Timon of Athens* that he had recently seen. Max winked at Doris before beginning an argument with Paul about a small point he had made. Because she knew nothing about the subject, Doris would not have been able to judge the rightness or wrongness of their views, but she was smart enough to recognise a false debate. Here, parading as genuine argument, was a series of puns, anecdotes and boasts, punctuated occasionally by weighty pronouncements, all met by rapid agreement. Each was not saying precisely what he thought, but rather what he believed would impress the other and make him respond. Each anticipated and directed the other's replies. Each fell into and out of the other's tone. Paul's speeches were a kind of citation of Max's. Max uttered words which followed directly from those that

Paul had just spoken. No part of their exchange was not infiltrated by the need to compete.

Their talk passed from interpretations of individual productions to the question of a national theatre, and from there to the Lord Chamberlain, the squalor of the West End, and the indecency of requiring good plays to show profit. Neither of them mentioned *The Sing-Song Tribunal*. Max had objections to the amount of cuts Paul was making to his script, while Paul was unhappy that Max's interventions during rehearsals were undermining his authority as the director; they both expected that, by the end of the night, without their being mentioned, these things would be resolved of and by themselves.

Max observed Doris as she tuned in and out. He imagined she was switching allegiance according to the flux of her feelings, one minute wanting to see Paul dominate, the next enjoying his having to bow low. At no point did the men make an effort to talk about anything that might interest her or require her participation. They understood that she did not have their culture, and so, out of a perverted sense of consideration, kept her separate. Her part was to be the perfect audience: quiet as a mouse, stirring at tense moments, drawing in breath at startling revelations, never restless or indifferent, glad to be being improved. Needless to say, Alissa, had she been here, would not have been similarly tame. In that seat she would have sat, as tough as ash, surrounded by an air of assurance and ease, and matched the men, one for one, two for two. More, she would have brought out the richest parts of herself and made the men tremble by means of them, for she was of a different kind, stronger and more thoroughly alive than ever a woman should be.

After a while, Doris began to express herself in the only way the situation allowed: by sulking. As she picked the bones from her sole, she put on an interest in anything other than what Max and Paul were saying. The other diners. The passers-by outside. The wax on the bottle in which the candle was stuck. Max did not reveal his awareness of this change in her. On he talked, and Paul too, their voices now hoarse as they strained to make themselves heard over an increasingly rowdy table nearby. They seemed to relish the challenge that these more difficult conditions posed, adding volume and range without abandoning the exclusiveness, the intimacy of their dialogue.

—Is anyone else coming?

Max broke off mid-sentence:

—What's that, Doris?

She cleared her throat. Put more force into her voice.

—Is we waiting for someone? There's an extra place set.

Perplexed, Paul turned to peer at the plate, the glass, and the knife and fork wrapped in a paper napkin, as if searching for something hidden amongst them. Doris watched him until her patience ran out, then raised her arm to get the waiter's attention. For a long minute she sat like this, believing that by being good she would get noticed in the end. When this failed:

—Shit this.

She put two fingers into the corners of her mouth and whistled. The room fell quiet. Heads turned. Paul's brows shot up. Max coughed wine out of his throat.

The waiter approached, scowling.

—Hi, look, I'm sorry, Doris said to him, I don't mean to be, you know, it's just there's only three of us eating, i'nt there, so can you take that place away, d'you mind?

The waiter looked down at what remained of their meal: dried streaks of sauce and little piles of bones.

—Well, everyone is finish, no? I can take away all?

—Yes, please, said Max with feigned solemnness. Take it all. Then the bill when you're ready, thank you.

Once the table had been cleared, Max leaned into the empty space, then Paul, each trying to hide behind the other, and started sniggering behind their fists like schoolboys.

—What the hell was that, Doris? Paul whispered.

—Give over, Paul, Max said. You know damn well what that was.

Max took out a wallet containing a number of notes of large

denominations. Without waiting for the bill to arrive, and as if to show his lack of concern for money — though this was not his conscious intention — he dropped three tenners on the table, far too much, and then threw some change over them as an extra tip.

—Let's get out of here.

They went first to a milk bar on Old Compton Street, then a pub two doors down, and when that closed to a basement club where there was jazz music and dancing.

—We should go home soon, Doris said at each stage. We have the final dress rehearsal in the morning.

But the men did not listen. And Max could see that, in truth, she did not really want to go. Because for the first time that evening, perhaps for the first time in her life, she was having fun.

—Having a good time? said Max.

—Yeah, actually, she said. I like it here.

She was the sort of girl for whom going out would have never been amusing. Gossiping would have felt trivial. Being pulled onto the floor by boys would have felt bullying, and she would have resisted it. Dancing, on the rare occasions she acquiesced, would have felt like the performance of a duty; the most she might have mustered was a listless dragging of her feet. Max enjoyed seeing her surprise as she found things came more easily with Paul and him. They took turns: while one danced with her, the other guarded their little table under the cellar arch, which meant she was rarely off the floor. She was by no means a natural, having had little practice up to now, and was therefore extremely self-conscious at the beginning; watching the other girls — so chic, such verve — she looked like she wanted to weep. But after a lot of encouragement and with the help of the rum, she began to move more loosely, and the more loosely she moved, the deeper the music penetrated, until eventually she was stamping and twisting and twirling and reaching through the blue smoke to make contact through the fingertips. There were moments, perhaps, alone in the toilet or resting against a wall, when her heart might have sunk if it occurred to her that, at a time when the world was haunted by the image of a hand pulling down a big black lever, or of a finger pressing a button, here everyone was, spending their money just to drink and dance. But these moral torments, if they happened, would have been brief. Overridden quickly by admonitions from the men to smile and be happy.

For they were competing for her attention now. Perhaps as compensation for having ignored her in the restaurant, or perhaps because in this environment it was good to be seen to be guardians to a girl, they performed for her a kind of duel of concern. They could not enjoy themselves if she did not; entertaining her was to be their only entertainment, and they tussled to prove it. They lit her cigarettes. Replaced her drinks. Went to and from the bar to fetch her glasses of water. Made her aware, discreetly, by touching the corresponding spot on their own faces, when her make-up required fixing. Cleared space for her on the floor by pushing backwards against the crowd. Removed from her orbit any men who looked like they might bother her. And, by all of this, made her feel, in a small way, a woman, while making the public believe that she possessed more, much more, than her drab appearance promised.

As a further kindness, they kept their conversation away from intellectual subjects and instead talked each about the other. Shouting into her ear, or across the table, Max told her what he thought she ought to know about Paul, and Paul about Max, each trying to astonish her with their candidness. There was humour in their stories, and not a little teasing, though they always expressed themselves in the proper way; they were careful not to be coarse or unreasonable, and to respect the limits which, over the years, they had set for each other. The broad outlines of their accounts matched; it was only in the details that they contradicted each other. Doris would have tried to balance their respective versions, one against another, with a just impartiality, though at the end she surely would have found it easier to trust Max, because he had nothing to gain from embellishment or fabrication. He was not chasing her affections. Admiring yet heedful, even a little formal, he demonstrated no desire to win her away — even though his job, he did not forget, was to do just that.

—At Cambridge, Max was a fucking spectacle, Paul told her. While the rest of us clung on to our uniforms, a brown Norfolk jacket was the usual thing, or maybe, if you were in the gay set, a bright yellow jumper and the blazer of a good suit, Max went round in these outrageous loose-fitting blouses that he found in a jumble sale but claimed were actually worn by peasants in Russia. Can you imagine it?

—Well, *he* was a pompous son of a bitch, Max said. He always took care to let you know that he regarded Southerners as inferior. Christ, such a merciless bore. Only in the North was life real. The work done up there was the only kind of any value. Northerners were generous and warm-hearted and democratic, Southerners merely snobs and parasites.

—It was Max who recruited me, Paul said. I spent much of the rest of my first year missing tutorials in favour of selling the works of Marx and Lenin around the colleges with him. Anything Max did, I also wanted to do. What he was, I became. The thing about Max was, it wasn't only the radicals who liked him. He was new money, an arriviste, but the uppers, too, went out of their way to include him. They loved him as much as the rest of us did. After all, he had what has always counted.

—And what's that? said Doris.

—Money, power, said Paul. And of course he was handsome then. People found him irresistible.

—He's still handsome, said Doris, winking at Max.

—Oi you, said Paul and poked her gently. You should have seen him then, though. If you'd been around, you'd never have gone for me over him.

—That's enough of that, Paul, said Max.

—Well, it's true, isn't it? Everyone went for you first, over me. Alissa included.

—Do shut up and go top us up. I'll take Doris upstairs for some air. She looks like she's going to melt.

Paul obeyed, and Max accompanied Doris outside onto the street.

They stood, fags in hand, exposing their sweating arms to the breeze, observing the cut of the passing revellers. Doris was drunk, probably a little ill, but clearly happy. She would have been enjoying listening to the men; she would have liked that they were so eager for her to understand them. Their lives sounded important, which would have made listening to them feel important. When asked, she gave little pieces of her own life, too, but not much. That did not matter now. Nothing she could say about herself would keep their focus on her so firmly as speaking about themselves.

—Is it true what Paul said? she said.

—Paul says lots of things. Eventually you'll learn which nuggets to cash in and which to discard.

—About Alissa, though. Her liking you first?

Max had gone to great lengths not to mention Alissa. Now that she had finally come up, he felt the sense of relief that follows a period of restraint. Alissa was there, like a scab on the leg; it was unnatural not to want to scratch it.

—I don't know about that, said Max. I was friends with Alissa before Paul was. There's nothing more saucy to recount than that.

—So you weren't an item, you and Alissa?

Max looked pensively upwards, to the cut of clear night sky running between the buildings.

—Not really.

Doris sucked on her fag.

Max glanced at her sideways:

—Did Paul say differently?

Exhaling a thin line of smoke through her pursed lips, Doris shrugged:

—You want to know what Paul says about you?

—I don't know. Do I?

—He says he's obliged to work much harder than you for the same results.

—What a bull merchant.

—That things just happen for you without having to spend any effort, while he has to struggle and strain to get anywhere. Is he talking about Alissa?

—Maybe. Okay, listen, quickly, before he comes back.

Alissa had been a year behind them at Cambridge. At the time of their first meeting, Paul and Max were in their second year, while she was a recent arrival, one of about twenty Newnham girls auditioning for the Amateur Dramatic Society. Paul and Max, who had joined the Society as a means to spread the communist message, were in the rehearsal audience. At Cambridge the ratio was ten men to each woman, so they had come only in part to judge the talent of the girls; their other motive, which they did not conceal, was to single out prospective sweethearts. Max, too, played that game then.

The audition process was gruelling: a monologue, a song, a mime and several improvisations, all watched by about a hundred people, including the other contenders. Alissa, Max remembered, was then a strange-looking creature of doubtful sex: skinny and flat-chested, hair cropped short, lines of experience already engraved onto her young skin. Unlike the other girls, who acted as if obeying distant ideas, she moved like she was thinking with her body; even the simplest of gestures appeared an interplay of all her muscles. At the same time, there was no ostentation in her performances, nor cheap efforts to seduce. There was instead the letting out of forces that might otherwise have turned to nervousness; a craving to live like mad for the pleasure of others. Initially, Paul did not see any of this. Another girl had caught his eye. A blonde whose prettiness was a close approximation to the forms shown on telly and in the magazines. It took Max to shake him out of his trance and make him see that Alissa was the only one deserving of their attention. The only mature girl there. And, if they looked properly, with an open and modern mind, the only really beautiful one. Compared to her, the rest were just fluttery adolescents.

Alissa was one of only six girls to become a member of the Society that term. According to the inside voices, she had been ranked first and already tipped for an upcoming lead. Max wasted no time in inviting her to tea. After that, they started going everywhere together. Boating up to Grantchester. Walking over Coe Fen. Having late dinner at the Taj Mahal. Max, heir to an arms empire, and Alissa, from a well-known family of hotel owners: wherever they were, people took notice. Rich, striking, rebellious: just by walking into a room, they made a difference. The Cambridge couple that everyone wanted to know, and that everyone already presumed would end in marriage.

—While neither Alissa nor I created this illusion, Max told Doris now, we were guilty of failing to stop it magnifying and spreading. We liked the attention, I suppose. But the fact was, ours was a platonic relationship. A meeting of minds only.

They met to talk about politics and to read plays and to help each other with their essays, and that was all. Paul, however, wracked by jealousy, refused to believe it. Such simple devotion of man to woman, without any sexual attachment, was unfathomable to him. Max had to have been courting Alissa, there was no other explanation. And that being the case, Paul would court her too.

—Don't misunderstand me, Max said. Paul didn't force himself to love Alissa just because he thought I did. As soon as he got to know her, he did fall for her. I just brought them together. I was the mediator.

Paul made a direct appeal to Max. He was terrified of exclusion, he said, and begged Max to invite him to his meetings with Alissa. The subsequent meetings of the three, which took place in Max's room and sometimes lasted for twelve, fourteen, sixteen hours, sent more than a whiff of scandal through the Cambridge corridors. Much to the threesome's delight, stories of sexual games and political plots and esoteric rituals began to circulate. When Alissa announced that she was going to audition for the female lead in the forthcoming Society production of Strindberg's *Miss Julie*, Paul managed to convince Max not to go for the male part. *You're a VANYA, Max*, Paul told him, *You're a MACBETH. Maybe one day a HAMLET. But, for goodness sake, you're not and never will be a JEAN.*

When the cast list was posted on the board, with Paul's name under Alissa's, Max called them to his room and opened a bottle of champagne in their honour. When they had polished that off, they went out to crawl the bars. So elated were they, and so involved in each other, they missed Alissa's curfew. They walked her back to Newnham with the intention of helping her to sneak in. Paul helped Alissa to scale a wall, from which she could climb over the spiked railings. The spikes cut her hand and pierced her skirt, but numbed by giddiness and drink, she managed to get over without seriously harming herself. From the other side, she beckoned them to follow her. Paul did not hesitate. Once over, and only slightly grazed, he turned to goad Max on — but Max, in the light of a single match, was shaking his head. *No, you two go ahead*, he said. *MISS JULIE and JEAN.*

—Here I am, Paul said now, coming out of the club with their jackets and cardigans across his arm. Miss me?

—Where are our drinks? said Max.

—Still in their bottles. I gave up waiting to be served. I've decided we're bored of this place.

Paul handed Doris her cardigan:

—So has Max told you yet?

—Told me what? she said.

—That he hates jazz.

Max laughed:

—It's true.

Doris put her cardigan over her shoulders:

—What are we doing here then?

—Paul likes it. I come for him.

—Aye, a real martyr.

Paul leaned into Doris's ear, as if to tell her a secret, but spoke loudly enough for Max to hear.

—Really it's the jazz people he hates.

—All pretension, said Max. No substance.

—What did I tell you? said Paul with a sly wink.

—They didn't seem so bad to me, Doris said. No one laughed at my dancing.

Max touched her arm sympathetically:

—Aw, bless you.

Paul invited Max to join them at The East Wind for a nightcap.

—Kind of you, Max said, but I think I'll stay out and see what other trouble I can find.

He slapped Paul on the back. Kissed Doris on both cheeks.

—Go and be happy.

—Don't stay out too late, said Paul, if you're coming to rehearsals tomorrow.

—We'll see.

Emboldened by drink, or perhaps by sudden feeling, Doris stepped in to hug Max. His thin frame accepted her embrace and allowed it to linger.

—Doris Lever, he said. It's perfectly brilliant of Paul to have found you.

Once back at the flat in Marylebone — he was the only member of The East Wind not to live in the lodging house — Max went straight to the desk and wrote Alissa a letter. He would not be returning to rehearsals, he told her. He had decided to leave England again, for the scene here depressed him, and, despite the best efforts of The East Wind, he saw little hope of it changing. As far as he was concerned, *The Sing-Song Tribunal* no longer belonged to him. It was Alissa's property now. She could do with it whatsoever she wished. His only request was that she should arrange to have his name blacked out of the brochures and the promotional posters for the production. He no longer wanted to be associated with it. As for Doris, his advice to Alissa was this:

The time has come to put an end to this pantomime you are too good ever to have appeared in. Paul, I have never shied away from telling you, is not a worthy counterpart for you. He is a pygmy and you are a giant of the age; he does not gain from having you tower over him any more than you do from having him cower beneath you. You need him only in order to glory in your feat of loyalty and to reproach him for his disloyalty, and in this manner you torture him and you mortify yourself.

The moment has come to disentangle yourself from this mad dance of dependence. Stop devastating yourself by Paul's failures. Set him free. Leave him to his girl, who represents the most he can hope to win in this lifetime. You, on the other hand, are made for more. Go. Be the woman who gets there. In your heart of hearts, is that not what you desire?

Max put the letter in the envelope, wrote *Alison* on the front (it had been his idea that she adopt the stage name *Alissa*) and left the letter on the table by the front door so as to remember to post it in the morning.

Max had not come to rehearsals for a couple of days, no one had seen him or heard from him, so as soon as Eva saw his handwriting on the envelope, she understood the importance of its contents. She picked the rest of the letters off the hall floor, put them under her arm, and slipped through the lodging house door to the steps outside. Glanced up and down the empty road. It was her job to hand out the post. A responsibility she took seriously. Helping out in this way functioned in her mind as a kind of apology to the other actors for her deficiencies, and made her feel a little less useless, a little less hated. She scanned the envelope again and thought about the morality of what she was about to do. It was wrong; it would make her even less popular if she was found out; and she was going to do it anyway. Something — the sense of a larger duty — was urging her on.

At speed, with her thumbnail, paying little attention to how it was tearing or to the problem of how she would restore it, she opened the seal. Read the letter quickly once. Then read it more slowly a second time. Stuffed it back in.

Her heart pounding, she glanced up the road again.

Then down at the tattered envelope.

And, in the next instant, felt an immense wave of relief.

The lifting off of a terrible weight.

For, while it was true that she could destroy this letter and by that means prevent her mother ever setting eyes on it, it was also true that she could give it to her, open and read as it was, and in doing so say to her: *End this game, Mama. Stop this play. If you can't do it for Max, if you can't do it for Papa, then do it for me. Put me out of my misery.*

I

JIANG QING

1974

<u>xvi.</u>

Late September was when things ripened in the garden. Peaches, apples, apricots, jujube, pears, and on the branches, everywhere, heaving breasts and bright flashing eyes. Around the South Lake, the reeds had grown thick and the bulrush seeds were scattering in the breeze. The surface of the water was covered by lotus leaves. The sky was clear, the air crisp. The sun, infused a dark red, was sinking, and the shadows were long and slanted. The world was serene, though there were many sounds: Jiang Qing could hear them reverberating in her chest as she looked up to see whether the heavens were obeying her meteorologist.

—He told me that dusk would overtake us at a quarter past six exactly, she said to her assistants, who were standing around her, following her gaze. If he's right, we have an hour of daylight left. But let's get the lanterns going now anyway, before it darkens. The effect of the transition will be more powerful that way.

They were in the moon-viewing pavilion on the centre of the lake. Earlier, Jiang Qing had had the imperial-era lanterns taken out of storage and hung around. Lanterns of crystal and glass tied along the beams and balustrades. Lanterns of silk gauze on bamboo poles dug into the surrounding earth. Hundreds of rice-paper and bast lanterns fastened to the branches of the bare willow trees nearby. And many more, made of shells and feathers, in the form of water lilies and ducks, floating on the water. On her command now, her assistants spread out and began to light them all.

—Be extra careful with your tinder sticks, she called after them. These lanterns are irreplaceable. I won't tolerate damage caused by clumsiness or ineptitude.

Her original plan had been to hang her birdcages alongside the lanterns, so that Mrs Marcos could admire her parrots and cockatoos and white-eyes also, but it was pointed out that the chirping would interfere with the listening bugs hidden inside the lanterns, so that idea was dropped. Instead Jiang Qing put up some modest examples of her calligraphy.

SERVE THE PEOPLE WITH HEART AND SOUL
FIGHT SELFISHNESS
REPUDIATE REVISIONISM
TRUST THE PARTY
TRUST THE MASSES

—A bit vain, don't you think, Ma, said Li Na, whom Jiang Qing had asked to come and help. Putting your own work up there.

—I don't think so. It's my handwriting all right, do you like it? But the slogans themselves are from and for the people. I'm trying to counterbalance this rather traditional setting with voices from the New China.

—I don't know. It seems a bit—

—They use calligraphy practice in the prisons now. It's a great way to straighten a person out. I'd assign you a tutor, if I thought you'd stick to it longer than a minute. I worry about your ideological progress, Li Na, really I do.

Li Na shrugged and turned away. Busied herself with the presentation of the food on the central table, rearranging the platters so that the tastes and colours were more harmoniously spread and the better dishes easier to reach. Jiang Qing watched her out of the corner of her eye. Li Na had complied with Jiang Qing's order to come dressed like a proper Chinese. Lenin suit. No make-up or sunglasses. Flat shoes. Her one slip was to forget to remove a plastic grip from her hair — the kind that members of artistic families used to make statements about themselves — but this was easily swapped for a plain pin. Jiang Qing herself had gone for an off-white blouse and brown skirt, and, to keep off the chill, a lambswool cardigan and a silk scarf tied at the neck. Having been informed of Mrs Marcos's unusual height, she had permitted herself a small heel.

—What time is she coming? Li Na called back over her shoulder.

Jiang Qing was shaken out of her paralysis:

—She'll be here any minute.

—You're going to get in trouble, Ma. You're going way off programme with this.

—I'm told our guest was delighted to receive my invitation. That's all that should count.

—When word gets out, it's going to piss a lot of people off.

—Just focus on doing a good job, my child, okay?

—You're in hot water, Ma. Don't say I didn't warn you.

With the help of her loyal Red Guards, Jiang Qing had managed to get a message to Mrs Marcos inviting her to a private meeting before the ballet performance. *I hope you don't find me presumptuous,* the note had said, *I'm simply impatient to know you. It's said that a single meeting is too short to make a friend, yet I feel this won't apply to us as we already have so much in common.*

—Are you nervous? said Li Na, coming to help Jiang Qing straighten the alignment of the chairs.

—No, said Jiang Qing. Have you been practising like I said?

—A little. But I'm not nearly good enough. Honestly, you should get Nancy Wang to translate for you.

—I can't bring in anyone official. This has to be off the record.

—I was being sarcastic.

—I don't even know what that means. You'll do a better job than her anyway because you'll tell me precisely what Mrs Marcos is saying. Nancy is good, but in my experience she tends towards approximation. Today I want word for word. No flights of poetry, got it? This isn't your moment for freedom of expression.

—Are you really going to make me do this?

—I was up late last night going over my *Thousand English Sentences*. I used to know them off by heart, but it has been such a long time since I've practiced, I fear I've forgotten everything. Objectively, it shouldn't be that hard, should it? These foreigners only have twenty-six letters to deal with, we have two thousand. But I've lost confidence. I don't quite trust myself. I need you by my side.

—Well, I'm here. You've won.

At the entrance to the pavilion, one of Jiang Qing's assistants was on a stepladder, lighting one of the harder-to-reach lanterns. Aware of the unevenness of the ground there, and judging the ladder's position precarious, Jiang Qing went to stabilise it. Li Na accompanied her.

—It's of great importance to hold yourself with dignity in front of Mrs Marcos, Jiang Qing said to her daughter. You mustn't do anything that will cause China to lose face abroad.

The assistant came down, bowed his thanks to Jiang Qing and transported the ladder to the pillar on the other side. Jiang Qing went there with him and held the ladder as before.

—Don't look too interested or smile too often. Don't open your mouth too wide, you sometimes do that. And don't use gestures. Keep your hands under the table. Restrict your face. Don't expose your teeth.

The assistant came down and took the ladder away, and Jiang Qing and Li Na went back into the pavilion. Seeing nothing else that needed her immediate attention, Jiang Qing went to the balustrade and looked out onto the lake. Li Na came to stand beside her, and together they watched a second assistant in high wellingtons wade into the water and create miniature waves with his fingers in order to send the floating lanterns further out. The sun was projecting brilliant gold reflections onto the water, overwhelming the little points of light from the lanterns. *When it gets dark, though, yes then the effect will be—*

—I want you to pay attention to yourself, daughter. Be vigilant. Don't allow yourself to be hoodwinked. How Mrs Marcos behaves with us is not necessarily how she behaves in her own home. People, remember, discover a sense of decency when they get to another country. You shouldn't assume that her demeanour is typical of a Rightist. If you find yourself getting drawn in by her, if you feel in any way overawed, you must rub your eyes and call to mind all the dirt and the darkness that we know to be lurking behind every reactionary's façade.

Li Na turned round and leaned back onto the balustrade so that she was facing Jiang Qing. She wore an expression which announced she had something to say but required an invitation to say it.

—What is it? said Jiang Qing.

—Are you warning me? said Li Na. Or yourself? Sounds to me like you're worried *you* might get drawn in.

Jiang Qing laughed:

—Is this your famous sarcasm? I've been exposed to many Western influences in my time, but they've simply bounced off me. Why? Because I've undertaken a close study of our own history and traditions, our own folklore, and have tapped into the pulse of popular creative art. I've realised that the Revolution has its own beauty, and that the struggle against Western decadence and the cult of the ugly is a social task of supreme importance. This has served as an antidote.

Li Na raised her eyebrows in a manner that acknowledged what had been said without accepting any of it:

—So you're immune.

—Not naturally. One isn't born with a special resistance. One has to work to develop one.

Li Na hooked a hand onto her hip, a gesture denoting what? Pique? Incredulousness?

—You've given me some good advice there, Ma. Now can I give you some in return?

Jiang Qing smiled. *How wonderful the young are. How they seem to have something we do not. A spirit. An openness. A fat cheek for slapping.*

—I don't mean to be disrespectful, truly, said Li Na, but when you speak to people it sometimes sounds as if you're arguing with them. Tone it down a bit with our guest. I doubt she'll be used to it. Foreigners generally aren't.

—You speak like an expert on the subject, my child. Get many foreigners, do you? in your neck of the woods? A rural Chinese with the mouth of an Overseas. That's what you are.

—I've given you my advice, for what it's worth. You can take it or leave it.

Jiang Qing walked to the centre of the pavilion, fixed something on the table that did not need fixing, then walked back to her daughter.

—Do you remember what the Chairman wrote about looking at problems all-sidedly?

—

—Well?

—Give me a second, I'm thinking.

—When was the last time you studied his great essay *On Contradiction*? Shall I refresh your memory? In that profound and prophetic work, the Chairman tells us that to look at problems all-sidedly one must understand the characteristics of both aspects of a contradiction. Not only China, but also America. Not only the proletariat, but also the bourgeoisie. The peasants and also the landlords. The past and also—

—The future, yes, said Li Na. *No contradictory aspect can exist in isolation. Without life, there would be no death. Without above, there would be no below. Without misfortune, there would be no good fortune. If one sees the part but not the whole, the trees but not the forest, it's impossible to resolve a contradiction, and therefore impossible to accomplish the tasks of the Revolution.*

—It's coming back to you.

—Know the enemy and know yourself?

—Good. I haven't entirely failed as a mother.

One of Jiang Qing's Red Guards entered the pavilion and saluted. Jiang Qing broke away from Li Na and went to him.

—What can you tell me?

The guard glanced over at Li Na.

—It's all right, said Jiang Qing. My daughter is safe. You can speak freely.

—She's left the guest villa, Commander. She'll be here in a matter of minutes.

—Be precise, soldier. How many minutes?

—Three, maybe four.

—Have we managed to get a picture of what's going on inside the villa?

—The central secretariat are having trouble picking up voices on the recording devices inside. It seems the guest and her people are running showers to cover up discussions. They're also switching between Filipino and English with deliberate rapidity and using all sorts of unknown slang.

—Hmm. Well, we have the recordings. We can decipher it all later. Has anyone managed to see in?

—One of our agents in the villa did manage to get a quick look. He reports that the revolutionary pillowcases that you sent have been changed.

—NEVER FORGET CLASS STRUGGLE?

—Those ones. It appears Mrs Marcos brought her own.

—And what are they like?

—They have their own slogans, Commander. In English. According to our man, one says, GOOD GIRLS GO TO HEAVEN.

—And the other?

—BAD GIRLS GO EVERYWHERE.

Mrs Marcos entered the Compound by the lesser-used East Gate. As instructed, her limousines parked by the Bureau of Guards; on stepping out, she was met by Li Na and a contingent of Jiang Qing's Red Guards. Together they came across the bridge on foot: she and Li Na forming a nucleus, her personal bodyguards an inner ring, and the Chinese soldiers an outer. At the centre of the bridge, at the viewing point between the two lion statues, she paused to admire the lake, and everyone stopped. Then she continued on, and everyone went with her. Once on the island, Jiang Qing's Guards melted back, and Li Na led her up the path — through the artificial hills of rock and the sisal hemps and the lotuses and the oleanders and the magnolias and the camellias and the hibiscus and the rare pair of aspens which had grown towards each other and intertwined their arms like lovers — while her bodyguards shadowed them a few paces behind.

When Mrs Marcos passed under the aspens, Jiang Qing put away the binoculars and sat into one of the two armchairs at the centre of the pavilion. Waving her assistants out, she took up her *qin* and began strumming, for that was how she wanted to be lighted upon: alone and at peace in the creation of a simple piece of music.

Mrs Marcos did not come straight in but paused, once more, at the entrance; less waiting to see than waiting to be seen. Jiang Qing had already noted her black attire at a distance and had hoped that it would appear less sombre up close. She was disappointed in this respect. A neat Western-style suit in black wool. Black stockings. Black patent shoes with a single gold buckle. A large black alligator bag. A single string of pearls, as a contrast. The kind of outfit Jaqueline Onassis might wear in an aeroplane or at a funeral. Foreigners came to China and laughed at us for wearing the same type of clothes. They thought we did not have the freedom to wear what we liked. Perhaps this was the reason for Mrs Marcos's choice today. Perhaps her intention was to be sensitive and to blend in. Jiang Qing wished she had not bothered.

Li Na conducted Mrs Marcos towards Jiang Qing. Halfway across the boards, Li Na stepped away and Mrs Marcos proceeded on her own.

The small departs, the great approaches.

Jiang Qing — her heart pounding — put down her *qin* and stood up.

Mrs Marcos was indeed a towering figure, made more so by the mound of hair frozen like ice on the top of her head. Jiang Qing found herself wanting to reach up and touch it. Take its temperature. Tap it. Crack it.

They shook hands.

Mrs Marcos's cheekbones bulged when she smiled. Her complexion was flawless. There was not a trace of make-up visible on her face, though of course this did not mean there was none there. A Chinese garden looked completely natural, as if man had never been there, but in fact this effect was achieved by careful manipulation and conscious placement of each rock as well as the daily grooming of each leaf. Even divine women were human creations.

—Mrs Marcos, said Jiang Qing, what an honour. I've heard of your reputation for a long time.

—Madame Mao, said Mrs Marcos, you extraordinary woman. I'm your devoted admirer.

Jiang Qing blushed:

—Did she really say that?

—Don't talk to me, Ma, said Li Na. Address yourself directly to the guest. Pretend I'm not here.

—Shut up.

That was a bad beginning.

—I know how it works.

Mrs Marcos's bodyguards had formed a line a couple of paces behind her. Mrs Marcos now gestured to one of them, the most handsome, who stepped forward and gave her a bouquet of orchids, which she then presented to Jiang Qing.

—From the Philippines, Mrs Marcos said.

—All that way? Jiang Qing said, accepting them. They look so fresh.

—Orchids are our strongest flower. They live on air.

Jiang Qing handed the flowers to Li Na, who made space for them on the table.

Jiang Qing indicated to one of the two armchairs, and Mrs Marcos sat. Jiang Qing sat on the other chair, Li Na on a stool behind them.

As Mrs Marcos settled herself in — her alligator bag went onto her lap and not onto the ground — she glanced around, as if expecting further additions to the party.

—What's wrong with her? said Jiang Qing to Li Na.

—From our conversation on the way here, said Li Na, I got the impression she was expecting Baba to be here.

—Has she been told the Chairman is indisposed?

—I imagine so. But, having come all this way, she probably expects to be given a slot with him.

—Tell her it'll only be us today, unfortunately.

—

—Did you say, *unfortunately*?

—Yes.

Jiang Qing picked her own handbag up off the ground and put it in the space between her left thigh and the armrest. Unconsciously, without looking, she opened its white plastic flap, and fished around inside, feeling for her handkerchiefs and breath fresheners; she did not need them but the fact that she could feel them there comforted her.

—This is my daughter, Li Na, she said, leaning towards Mrs Marcos and smiling. I've asked her to interpret for us.

—How helpful of her, said Mrs Marcos. A delightful girl. You must be proud.

—How is her English? Is it good?

—Yes, it's, umh, very good.

Yes, it's very good.

Jiang Qing understood this phrase, and the tone too, which told her it was a lie. She gave a disapproving look to Li Na, who stared defiantly back: *You're the one who wanted me here.*

—You have daughters of your own, said Jiang Qing, do you not?

—Two. After this trip, I'm going straight to America to see my eldest, Imee. She's at Princeton.

—Do you know what Princeton is, Ma? said Li Na.

—Of course I know what fucking Princeton is, said Jiang Qing. What's she studying?

—Religion and what is it? said Mrs Marcos, tapping her chin. Religion and something else, I can't remember.

—Religion? said Jiang Qing. That's a subject?

—I'm going to meet her in New York, said Mrs Marcos, so we can do a spot of shopping. Have you ever been? I do love that city. It's my *R and R.*

—Her what?

—*R and R* is what she said. I don't know what that means.

—I've never been to America, said Jiang Qing. Is your daughter happy there?

—Very.

—You aren't worried she might end up staying on and marrying a barbarian?

Mrs Marcos laughed:

—Not a chance. I'm determined to hitch her to a prince.

—

—Just a little joke. I've every confidence that after her graduation Imee will come back to the Philippines and make her own special contribution to our nation's renewal.

—I'm glad to hear it. In America everyone carries guns, didn't you know? If they don't like you, they shoot you. They kill coloured people, just like that.

—I'd like to go to America, said Li Na.

Don't get any ideas, you. You're the property of China.

Li Na and Mrs Marcos chatted together for a moment, which then became a long minute. Jiang Qing grew uneasy and started coughing.

—What topic so absorbs you? America? Are you conspiring against me?

—

—The garden is beautiful, said Mrs Marcos.

—This is the best time of year for it, said Jiang Qing.

—The sunset is glorious. I have the sensation when I look up that it's a solid thing, like a mottled shell, protecting us from what's behind.

—Is she being poetic or is she expecting a response? said Jiang Qing.

—I don't know, said Li Na. It might have something to do with her religion.

—Should I mention her religion?

Jiang Qing clicked her fingers and an assistant came and poured the tea. While they waited, Jiang Qing and Mrs Marcos locked eyes, and it was like a dream, a dream dreamed by someone else.

—We have stronger, if you want stronger, said Jiang Qing.

—Goodness, no, said Mrs Marcos. Tea is as strong as I get, at this time. At any time, if I'm honest.

Jiang Qing touched the rim of a plate of raw vegetables.

—Have you eaten? Might I offer you—?

Mrs Marcos shook her head:

—I'm going to save myself for the banquet tonight. I like to be nice and hungry.

—Are you looking forward to the performance?

—Why, of course. The theatre, and ballet in particular, is the most important thing in life.

—Did she say the most important?

—Are you going to trust me or not, Ma?

—It's only through drama and dance, Mrs Marcos went on, that people can derive enjoyment and become cultivated and humane. Have you heard of Margot Fonteyn?

Mrs Marcos appeared to tremble under the impact of this name, and without waiting for an answer, began to speak at high speed, leaving Li Na struggling to keep up.

—What's she saying?

—Shh, Ma, let her get to the end and I'll give you the gist.

—I hate to drop names but Margot is a dear friend of mine, I was in London with her last year, it was fabulous, we went dancing at

Annabel's, can you imagine? me on the floor with the great Margot Fonteyn, doing the *Paso Doble*? well, my third-rate version of the *Paso Doble* if that counts. So I simply had to invite her to Manila to perform at my Cultural Centre, and you know what? she came, the absolute darling, and oh, I'll never forget it, a highlight of my life—

—Margot Fonteyn's style is what we in China would call decadent, Jiang Qing said. Tell her that.

—Decadent? said Mrs Marcos. Yes. We'd probably call it that too.

—Tell our guest that tonight she's not going to see dancers prancing in pink tutus and pretending to be dying swans.

—Talk to her directly, Ma.

—Tonight you're not going to—

—Is there a love story? said Mrs Marcos.

—Our approach is different, said Jiang Qing. In China you go to the ballet and find yourself in a battlefield.

—I look forward to discovering how you do things here.

Mrs Marcos took a sip of tea as she listened. Placing the cup back on the saucer, she grinned broadly and nodded.

—We aren't just peddling new pieces of theatre, Mrs Marcos. With our model ballets, we're waging war against feudalism, capitalism and revisionism. We intend to create a new kind of art worthy of the great people that we have now become.

—

—What does she think about that? said Jiang Qing.

—She's not saying anything, said Li Na.

—Before, said Jiang Qing, whenever the Chinese heard a piece of Western music, or saw a piece of Western dance, they assumed unthinkingly that it was superior to our own. It never seriously occurred to them that new Chinese works, true revolutionary art, could be composed.

Jiang Qing signalled to her assistant to refill their guest's cup.

—While I share your view, Mrs Marcos said then, that our native Asian arts ought to be supported, and that new cultural seeds need to be planted at home, and the results nourished and protected, I feel we must acknowledge that, in respect of modern culture, the standards of the West are higher than ours. We have, alas, fallen behind.

—It's for this reason, said Jiang Qing, that we mustn't blindly reject all foreign things. Blindly rejecting foreign things is like blindly worshipping them. Both are incorrect and harmful. The point is to absorb the good things from foreign countries in order to make good our own shortcomings. Weed through the old to bring forth the new and make things foreign serve things Chinese.

Mrs Marcos took up her fresh cup of tea:

—Quite so.

—I don't think any other nation's ballet combines alien traditions as boldly as ours, said Jiang Qing. I can't claim our ballet is perfect, there are areas which need further adjustment, but at least we've caused a sensation and shocked the world. Now China is more influential in the West than the West in China.

Mrs Marcos, mid-sip, raised her eyebrows; mid-swallow, she tilted her head, as if thinking on what she had just heard.

—Have you been following events in Europe? said Jiang Qing.

—Events? said Mrs Marcos.

—The rebellions.

—Ah.

—The workers in the West feel a greater affinity to Mao than to their own leaders. In London and Paris, the students don't want to learn the traditional curricula, they want to be taught Mao Zedong Thought instead. This is proof that our cultural work is penetrating. Thanks in no small part to our revolutionary art, such as our ballet, Mao doesn't just belong to China any more. Like the sun, he's now the property of all mankind.

Peeking back over her shoulder, Mrs Marcos said something quickly in Filipino, and her bodyguard, who himself could have passed for a television celebrity and whose particular mark of luminosity appeared chosen to intensify that of Mrs Marcos, came forward and murmured something in her ear. Mrs Marcos nodded that she had understood, and the man receded. Jiang Qing did not comprehend what she had witnessed, and therefore thought it rude. Despite that, she had to admit she liked Mrs Marcos. What she found unbearable was the way Li Na was leering at her.

—I believe your husband likes to dance, Mrs Marcos said then, putting her cup down once more.

—Mao?

Jiang Qing ordered Mrs Marcos's cup to be filled a third time.

—Mao can't dance. Even as a young man, he was hopeless.

—I've been misinformed.

—He does appreciate dance, that much is true. He likes to watch it, if it's good.

—That's more than one can say for most men.

Mrs Marcos crossed one leg over the other. Half-hiding underneath the table, she used the toes of her left foot to slip off the heel of her right shoe, and to scratch a mosquito bite on her ankle. The bite, positioned on the skin right where the bone and the leather rubbed against each other, had become red and inflamed, clearly visible through her stockings. The gesture of scratching it was very simple, very unaffected; watching it was to see the low and the high change places.

—I wanted to ask about your husband, Mrs Marcos said, scratching away, but perhaps it's out of order to speak of the situation so frankly.

Jiang Qing rummaged inside her handbag for her handkerchiefs and squeezed them. To her mind came the image of Mao's face at the private dance party: one side of his mouth drooping open and a thick green-tinged globule of phlegm creeping over the edge of his lower lip and stretching down, down in a straight line, threatening not to break until it reached his lap.

—There is no *situation*, she said.

—Do forgive me, said Mrs Marcos. We won't talk about it. Because we're both women, I wanted to hear how it was for you. Such burdens can be lightened in their sharing. But I can see that now isn't the time.

Mrs Marcos pushed the heel of her shoe back onto her foot. There was a quiet sucking sound as it slid into place.

—I understand how hard it is. I have friends in the same position. Margot, for instance, whom I mentioned before? Her husband, Roberto, a gorgeous man, steel-grey hair, dark eyes, Latin, gorgeous, but also completely paralysed and wheelchair bound. Since the cursed assassination attempt.

She shook her head sadly.

—He understands everything that's said to him, and mouths his responses, which Margot then speaks. An interpreter. Like your daughter here. Can you imagine? A sublime dancer brought to the level of a—? Were my Ferdie in the same condition, would I be so devoted? You can't ever really say, can you? until you're actually put in that position.

The sun had sunk down into the vegetation; the jagged treetops nibbled at its lower edges. Power was passing to the lanterns, whose glow was beginning to settle on Mrs Marcos's skin.

Jiang Qing gave her assistant the signal, and Wenge was summoned from where she was waiting out of sight amongst the trees and ushered into the pavilion.

—Come on, Wenge, don't be shy, Jiang Qing said.

The girl, head bowed, stood in front of the two women. She was wearing her everyday clothes, but, having just finished the final run-through of that evening's performance, her face was heavily made up and still damp with sweat.

—This, said Jiang Qing to Mrs Marcos, is my rising star. She plays the ARMY CAPTAIN tonight.

—Did you say *she*? Forgive me, she just looks so, well, I thought she was—

—I personally chose her and prepared her for the role.

Wenge stood absolutely still, her eyes cast down. Mrs Marcos asked her a few polite questions about her work — *when did she start dancing? who is her favourite dancer? is it harder to perform a male part*? — which she answered by shaking and nodding her head.

—I've always found it amazing, Mrs Marcos said then, turning to Jiang Qing, that some people in this world are born to perform, and that it's only in order to perform that they live. Whenever I have the honour of being in the company of such people, I like to turn the tables and do a little performance for them. It's my way of giving back to those—

She turned back to the girl.

—such as yourself, young Wenge, who work so hard to make the world more beautiful.

—Did you hear that, Wenge? said Jiang Qing. What do you say, child?

—Thank you, Wenge said.

—In making the world more beautiful, you improve it, said Mrs Marcos. Art and culture and a taste for beauty leads people to goodness, that's a fact. Or maybe I'm just prejudiced. We Filipinos are for beauty. It's in our wiring. So what do you say, Wenge? Shall I sing a song for you? The only question is, what'll I sing?

She called out something in Filipino, and her guard responded.

—That's a good idea, she said now in English. I'll do 'Ako'y Isang Ibong Sawi', which is a traditional Filipino love song depicting the tragedy of a felled bird. Do you like the sound of that? It's sad but, I hope you'll agree, all the more gorgeous for it.

In a single fluid movement, she raised her hand and her guard stepped forward and took it, helped her out of her seat and led her to the centre of the pavilion.

Wenge surrendered the space by taking two steps back.

Jiang Qing waved at her, irritably, and the girl retreated as far as the balustrade.

Mrs Marcos stood with her legs apart like a man and sang like a trained soprano.

Look at her well. This is a goddess of beauty and love.

When Mrs Marcos was finished, Jiang Qing leapt to her feet and began to clap. By twisting round and raising her clapping hands, she indicated to her assistants that they ought to join in. The assistants moved into the lantern light in order to be seen doing so. Mrs Marcos bowed, not in the learned and exaggerated manner of a theatre actor but with total naturalness, exactly as a rural woman of her age would be expected to, having sung a song for her family after dinner. Seen from this close, with the naked eye, Mrs Marcos was really nothing like her image on television. Her gestures — the cameras did not pick this up — were unmistakably those of a provincial peasant.

Jiang Qing kept the applause going until Mrs Marcos had sat back down again. She then dismissed Wenge, telling an assistant to get the girl back to the Great Hall as quickly as possible.

—You're right, Mrs Marcos, she said once Wenge had gone. Even without understanding the words, the song broke my heart. Is it a popular song?

—I suppose you could say that.

—Does that mean the people in the Philippines are sad?

Mrs Marcos laughed:

—Madame Mao, in my country there are many poor people. It's common knowledge that the Filipinos live in slums and hovels. But what counts is the human spirit, and the Filipinos are smiling. They smile because they're a little healthy, a little educated, a little loved. That's the formula. The real index is not the economic index but the smiles on people's faces.

—In China, said Jiang Qing, the poor also smile, but in their case it's because they have Mao. Thanks to him, they don't need sad songs. They sing about their desire for change, for action and for revolution. They give thanks to Mao because he has shown them the way out of poverty.

—Yours is another world, said Mrs Marcos. In the Philippines, you go and talk to poor people, and what do they want? They want only to be successful. Is there a philosophy of success? If so, the Filipinos know all about it.

—Success is what a Filipino believes in, growing up?

—Why, yes, though personally I didn't have to. I had the fortune and misfortune of being born into a powerful family, where success was taken for granted.

Jiang Qing kept a stone face: the dossier had clearly stated that Mrs Marcos had grown up in poverty, and the dossier was rarely wrong.

—The truth is that I'm not fit to be a poor woman. I often wish I was. I sometimes think it would be easier than carrying all of this responsibility on my shoulders.

—There's no shame in being poor, Mrs Marcos. Mao himself was a peasant.

—Of course there's no shame in it. Just as there's no shame in being rich either. I happen to like rich people. I don't mind saying it. I take pride in the contemporary unpopularity of that view. They're charming, they're generous, they've learned to appreciate the same fine things that I appreciate.

Jiang Qing glared at Li Na, who was obviously relishing having these words in her mouth.

—Wouldn't you say that in order to eradicate poverty, you must eradicate private wealth?

—Logically speaking, that may be so, said Mrs Marcos. But the world isn't logical. Societies aren't logical. The rich, in fact, play an essential role in modern society. They keep the arts going, for one.

—We believe the masses should be in charge of the arts, said Jiang Qing. Culture should be produced by them and reflect their concerns.

—What the poor need are dreams.

Mrs Marcos's face had hardened.

—I supply those dreams to them. That is what I work so hard to do. I fulfil their wishes by being a star.

Her smile returned, her teeth sparkling.

—Something you surely understand, Madame Mao, having been an actress yourself?

Before Liberation, people used to talk of *dreams of youth*. These were dreams which one acquired early in life and which, it was supposed, one never lost, regardless of one's subsequent fate. Even if one ended up living a dog's existence cowering under the landlord's whip, one's dream was meant to stay in one's possession, deep within the psyche, untouched by the elements, pristine in the face of oppression, a source of hope even in hopeless places. What the Revolution showed was that, if such dreams did not die, it was only because they had never really lived. They were illusions whose power was drawn precisely from one's certainty that they could never come true. Bred in capitalist laboratories — the so-called *boardrooms* — and injected by means of the popular media into the mind, they caused dissatisfaction to grow there. When she was young, Jiang Qing, too, had been a victim of such dreams. Not the dreams of a people, but an individual's dreams. Dreams a revolution could not contain.

—Memories are depressing, she said now.

—You can't cut off memories, said Mrs Marcos.

The guest had come to the edge of her seat. Taking hold of the armrests, she now tried to slide the chair forwards. Jiang Qing gestured to her assistants to help her. Mrs Marcos stood up in order to allow them to lift the chair and carry it closer to Jiang Qing's. Seated again, Mrs Marcos was now close enough that Jiang Qing could see the lantern light shimmer in her lacquered hair, and to differentiate first between the sectioned waves, then every single strand.

—I don't remember much about my acting, said Jiang Qing. I'm similar to a Western person in that sense. I look forward, seldom back.

—You must remember something.

—It's not that I don't remember, but, like a photograph of a dead friend, that time is painful to think about, and far away. Looking back, I find it hard to understand.

—We all did things when we were young.

—I prefer to think about positive things.

I wasn't like some of the other girls. I didn't seek fame. It's true I went to fine restaurants, but all I ordered was a portion of steamed bread, which I nibbled at slowly, one quarter at a time. And I never took anything from men.

—Your past is nothing to be coy about, Madame Mao. You're the most powerful actress in history.

—No—

Jiang Qing spoke dead seriously.

—that is Greta Garbo.

Mrs Marcos laughed, which shocked Jiang Qing.

The shock must have shown, for Mrs Marcos immediately stopped laughing.

—The Americans have been unfair to Garbo, said Jiang Qing, by failing to give her an Academy Award. I believe this is the fault of those in power in the United States and not of the American masses. Capitalists are afraid of the likes of Garbo. Rebels. People with true dignity.

—Garbo? said Mrs Marcos. Let me see. When I think of Garbo, I think of how lonely she appeared. She projected this air of solitude. Maybe it's inevitable. Everyone who strives to be unique has to come to terms with being alone. Look at us. First Ladies are the loneliest people of all.

The women had dropped their voices to a whisper, and were leaning into each other, scrutinising each other's faces. By now it felt like there was a mental channel connecting them. Li Na, although she had dragged her stool right into the intermediate space, had disappeared from their view.

—Of the parts you played, said Mrs Marcos, which was your favourite?

—I don't know. I was NORA once. In *The Doll's House*.

—No, no, no, no—

Mrs Marcos shook her head and waved a finger in the air.

—you're no NORA. No, that's not right. You don't leave the house. You don't run away. If anyone, you're a MISS JULIE. You see the fight through to the end.

—How can you be sure?

—I'm a MISS JULIE. It takes one to know one.

Mrs Marcos reached out an open hand.

Jiang Qing looked at it:

—What does she want?

—I think she wants you to give her your hand, said Li Na.

—I want to read your palm, said Mrs Marcos.

Jiang Qing glanced around the pavilion and out into the garden. In the radiance of the lanterns, her assistants stood in their designated places like marble statues in a museum. But they were alive, she had to remember that. They had eyes. And they had ears.

—I've always felt I had a gift, said Mrs Marcos. I can't claim to be clairvoyant or anything like that, but I'm able to attain a certain perspective on the future. Little that I've foretold in the past hasn't come true.

—My mother was superstitious, said Jiang Qing. She believed that when a person is sick, their soul is capable of slipping out of the body and wandering about. I'm not my mother.

—I'm not your mother either, said Mrs Marcos. Think of this as a game between friends. You don't have to take anything I say seriously, if you don't want to.

Jiang Qing glanced at Li Na, then back at Mrs Marcos, then back at Li Na, who urged her on by enlarging her eyes and twitching her lip.

—We must let history tell the future.

—Go on, Ma, it's just a bit of fun.

Jiang Qing opened her palm and placed it in Mrs Marcos's hands.

—What's your date of birth? Mrs Marcos said.

Jiang Qing told her her birthday according to the solar calendar, the lunar calendar and the Gregorian calendar.

—Now close your eyes, said Mrs Marcos. Empty your mind. Breathe in through your mouth and let the energy rise to your hands.

Jiang Qing felt Mrs Marcos's fingernail trace the lines in her skin.

—Here's the sky line, said Mrs Marcos. Here's the man line. Here's the—. No, don't look. Keep your eyes closed. Follow my finger with your mind. Yes, that's it. This is the earth line. The sun line. The health line. The horizontal bracelet lines on your wrist are complicated.

Jiang Qing felt Mrs Marcos massaging the bones in her hand and fingers.

—Are your palms starting to sweat?

—Yes.

—Good. Now shall I tell you what I see?

Because they could not be seen arriving together, Jiang Qing and Mrs Marcos travelled to the Great Hall in separate cars. Jiang Qing told her driver to take the surface roads rather than the tunnel, and to tail Mrs Marcos. Dark had fallen on the city. Jiang Qing looked out through the windscreen at the rear lights of the limousine ahead. A mesmerising dance of red and orange lights, over which her own thoughts were layered; thoughts which appeared not as language but as a series of rapidly changing images: *Did she enjoying looking at me? Did she like being near me? Did she think I was attractive? Did she think I was stupid? Did I bore her? Did she think I was talented? When she laughed, was it at me?*

At the Great Hall, the two cars parted ways, Mrs Marcos's to the main entrance where a welcoming committee was waiting for her, Jiang Qing's to the officials' entrance at the side. A hundred metres from the door, Jiang Qing banged on the car ceiling and told the driver to pull over.

—What's wrong? said Li Na.

Jiang Qing turned to her daughter, who had her elbow on the window ledge, and her cheek resting in her hand. The darkness, suspended in the air like a powder, created lines on the skin of Li Na's face — across her forehead and around her cheeks and under her eyes — which made it look as though the girl was being haunted by old age already.

—What do you think she meant?

Li Na flashed a look at the driver.

Jiang Qing pressed a button, and a pane of glass rose up, sealing them off from the driver's seat.

—Don't obsess, Ma. It was just a game. Forget it now.

Do you miss acting? Do you ever think you'd like to do it again?

Because, you know, there will be life after Mao. Your fate line tells me so. This was what Mrs Marcos had said. How could Jiang Qing just forget that?

—Daughter of mine, I want you to know, she said now, that I don't believe Mao could ever be replaced. Just as there aren't two suns, there aren't two Maos.

—So why even mention it? said Li Na.

—I just wanted to reassure you.

But had not Mrs Marcos also said that the people should honour the wife when the man had left his chair empty?

The proximity of your marriage line and your life line denote a person who would make an able prime minister. Which is not as outrageous as it sounds. The reason England is not as backward as the Eastern countries is because it has often been ruled by queens.

—Mao can't be equalled, said Jiang Qing now to Li Na, just as the sky cannot be scaled. But do you know something, child?

What a husband does rubs off on his wife. She becomes like him. Colder. Harder. Less hesitating. Without fear of opinion. It's enough that a wife simply be herself to the utmost, and she will win.

—I'm not afraid of anything. I'm not afraid of what comes next.

—What're you talking about, Ma?

—I'll do everything in my power to ensure Mao's legacy isn't betrayed. I won't baulk at doing what's necessary to keep the leadership of the Party in the hands of a true proletarian revolutionary.

—Ma, don't talk like that out loud.

A wife had a choice: age obscurely or vie for a place in the community of leaders. By choosing the latter, she gave her nation a second chance to realise its ancient dream of being ruled by a being pure of heart. But a wife ought not deceive herself either. She had to struggle in order not to be trampled on. Outlasting her enemies required terribleness, which was part of greatness. Criticism of her would flare up while men who deserved such criticism would keep their good names. That was the way of things. But to her it would not matter. She wanted, above all, to be of use to her people. If that meant being a victim, she was glad to be a victim of this sort. *I have always been criticised for being excessive*, Mrs Marcos had said, *but that's what mothering is. You need a mother in government to make it whole.*

Jiang Qing pressed the intercom button:

—Drive on.

A moment then and they had arrived. Jiang Qing did not wait for the car door to be opened but got straight out and bolted inside.

—Where are you going, Ma? Li Na shouted after her.

—Make your own way to the auditorium, Jiang Qing said. I'll see you there in a minute.

She entered the backstage through the offices, bursting through double door after double door. The corridors outside the dressing rooms were filled with dancers milling about. On seeing Jiang Qing, they went silent and pressed their backs against the walls; once Jiang Qing had passed through, they dashed off in different directions. Jiang Qing opened the dressing room doors, one by one. Inside, the dancers putting on their make-up looked at her questioningly through their mirrors; those in the course of dressing themselves covered their nakedness with their hands.

—Where's Wenge? she said them, to which they responded by blushing and looking at the floor.

Coming to the final dressing room, Jiang Qing paused with her hand on the knob. She could hear crying coming from inside.

She flung the door open.

Wenge was sitting on the ground in the corner. Still in her ordinary clothes, her knees drawn into her chest and her face was in her hands.

Jiang Qing scanned the room: the girl was alone.

—What happened? Why aren't you dressed? The performance starts in five—

Then she saw it. A slogan painted in white on the wardrobe door. WHITE WITCH'S WHORE

As she approached the wardrobe and opened it, Jiang Qing felt no anger, for her entire will in those seconds was focussed on getting

Wenge into her costume and onto the stage. Nor was there anger when she saw what had been done — all five of Wenge's costumes slashed and spattered with paint — because she had not yet fathomed her inability to change the circumstances in which she found himself.

Anyone could have done this. A list of suspects a hundred names long could have been drawn up in a matter of minutes. In all likelihood, there were several people involved, from various levels of power. Yet the first and only person whom Jiang Qing thought to blame was her daughter. Li Na — it was obvious — had ratted her out.

There was a moment, then, when Jiang Qing saw memories of Li Na as a young baby and felt once again the obligation to be a mother to her. To stay at her side and protect her. Now, overwhelming this, came the feelings of failure and disappointment. Jiang Qing believed she had given birth to a being which would forever long for her affection, when in fact she had produced an unfeeling demon, a creature who stiffened if she caressed her.

Li Na, my child, you have been my great hope and my ultimate despair. When I batter you, crush you, flatten you, then will you think of me?

Jiang Qing turned to Wenge, who was now on her feet and holding up an arm, its elbow bent, the forearm covering her face, as if parrying invisible blows.

Going to her, Jiang Qing put an index finger on Wenge's raised arm and applied only a tiny amount of pressure to it; all that was ever needed. Once Jiang Qing had full access to the girl's face, she struck it: on one cheek with the open palm, on the other cheek with the back of the hand, a full swing behind it.

In the precise moment of Wenge's falling down, there came a burst of applause from the auditorium.

Then more applause.

Then more, unceasing.

Jiang Qing delayed only to give Wenge a final kick, managing despite her haste to land it skilfully between the girl's legs, before leaving the dressing room and running to the green room. There, amongst the crowd, she caught a glimpse of Zhu Xi in his ARMY CAPTAIN costume, chatting nonchalantly to another male dancer. When Zhu Xi noticed her, he turned towards her to reveal himself — and to flash the bandage on his broken finger — as if daring her to confront him. She ignored him. Pushed through the bodies into the wings and onto the darkened stage.

On the other side of the curtain, the applause was still going on and had not lost any of its force.

Holding her breath, she drew the edge of the curtain back and peeked out.

The entire audience was on its feet and facing towards the central door, where Mrs Marcos, expertly spotlighted from above, had entered and was now moving slowly down through the stalls towards her seat in the second row. In her limousine she had changed into a red gown, trimmed in gold thread, with a train of the same material. The audience, as they watched Mrs Marcos, knew that they were being looked at, greedily, by their colleagues in the neighbouring seats, and the public in the top galleries, and by Mrs Marcos herself, and even perhaps by Mao even though he was not there in the room. Knowing themselves to be under this scrutiny, they acted in order to be seen, with the result that their applause was rapturous but not pure. Mrs Marcos smiled and waved and soaked this poison up, as was the duty of someone who was awaited, expected, and had now come.

Do you see yourself in me?

I do, Mrs Marcos replied. *Perhaps it's because we've lived through the same times.*

But in different places. On different sides.

From where you are, you see more than I can see. I understand myself from what I see you understand about me.

Can you see that I'm proud of you?

Yes. One must be proud of one's enemy.

Then my success shall be your success also.

Mrs Marcos took her seat, and still the applause went on. Every actress dreamed of irrepressible ovations, of hearing her name shouted out, of being covered with rose petals raining down. But from this false and shallow crowd, the applause was divorced from its true feeling; Jiang Qing felt it to be mocking and malicious.

Finally three strikes of the gong reverberated and the applause gradually died. Behind Jiang Qing, the dancers from the first scene took their places on stage. The auditorium lights began to dim. Jiang Qing felt a hand grip her arm and pull her back from the curtain.

—Come away from there! Chao Ying rasped.

He dragged her into the wings.

Facing her now was a whole gallery of expressions in the opposite wing. A multitude of eyes. Some of them blinking, some unmoving. Which gave her the feeling of being spied upon and made her uneasy, though in fact this was only her fear of herself, for she knew it was her own soul in the wings that was spying on her, and that her role was to be its audience.

What did it feel like to be on stage? Mrs Marcos had asked her.

Nothing out of the ordinary, she had replied. *I knew what to do. I had a purpose. I had faith in myself and in my right to be there.*

So what has changed?

The orchestra started to play.

Jiang Qing closed her eyes and began to follow with a finger the lines on her palms. She wanted to avenge herself on all men and make them suffer. But it occurred to her that maybe that performance had already happened. Maybe what had been was not the rehearsal but the event, playing itself out. All things reverse and return: the curtain was rising, revealing a theatre after a performance had concluded and everything had been put away. So what was this? Present time. Herself, in the dark, still acting.

IRS

1968

<u>xvii.</u>

The door opened and Keith peeped in:

—They're ready for you.

Sitting at her dressing table, she looked at him through the mirror in front.

—I'll be right there.

—You okay?

—Just getting my head together.

—Anything I can help with?

She smiled:

—Take your face out of here. I won't be a minute.

He left, and she returned to the tarot cards laid out on the table. The question she had asked them was a simple one, *Should I go through with this?* but their answer was not clear. Crossed at the centre of the reading, the Tower and the Page of Cups seemed a warning (*her past would return to destroy her plans and would in turn be destroyed by them*), yet surrounding those cards were a number of minor figures from the sword suit which appeared a call to proceed (*the discord with her mother was blocking her creative and emotional energy, the only solution was open and aggressive confrontation*).

Unable to decide between these equal truths, and knowing it was disrespectful to repeat the experiment — the master spoke but once — she swiped the cards off the table. After she had done this, she examined herself in the mirror and saw, to her alarm, that she looked as alarmed as she felt. She turned off the sitar music on the stereo and, staring into her own eyes, took a few breaths in silence. Divination was meditation. It required a clear and tranquil mind. The cosmic influences did not penetrate every wall; one had to be receptive to them. Her mistake had been to approach the cards in a preoccupied state.

Escaping her reflection, she unlocked her chest of drawers and retrieved a box that she kept there. A gift from Max, bought on his trip to China with Doris, it was finished with black lacquer and decorated with a painted scene of a boy pulling a rickshaw. Returning to the table, walking over the tarot cards on the floor without noticing, she unlocked the box and emptied its contents: an old leather-bound edition of the *I Ching* and a felt pouch containing the special coins used to consult it. Slowly and deliberately she untied the pouch cord and poured the three bronze coins into her left palm. Closing her right palm over the left to form a sealed vessel, she shook the coins, once to her left, once to her right, then back to the centre, trying to empty her consciousness of everything that interfered with her inquiry.

She threw down the coins together and noted their values on a scrap of paper. She repeated this six times. Summing up the values of each throw, she looked up the corresponding diagram in the book. She read the accompanying prophecy once to herself, then recited it a few times aloud:

Work on what has been spoiled,
This will bring you success.
It furthers you to cross the great water.
Before the starting point, three days.
After the starting point, three days.
Which settled it. She would go by what she had understood.

Leaving the book open on the table, with the coins resting on the verso side in order to keep the pages from turning over, she fetched the bottle of LSD from its hiding place behind the broken radiator. She shook it and raised it to the lamp to check the liquid level. Satisfied that this had not moved — she would not use product that had been tampered with — she measured thirty doses into a bottle of Babycham (for the adults) and half that amount into a bottle of fizzy lemonade (for the children). She then crushed some Thorazine and some vitamin B12 tablets and funnelled the resulting powder into the bottles using a folded bit of paper (this would help protect their minds against bad trips). She used one of her ornamental chopsticks as a spoon to stir the solutions. Then she screwed the lids back on and went to the wardrobe to change her clothes.

Off came her jeans and her kaftan and her beads and her bangles, and in their place her Wherehouse boiler suit, which had been dyed black but come out grey-brown. She swapped her sandals for black boots. Pulled back her hair and clipped it up. Took out her earrings and her nose stud. Creamed off the caste mark on her forehead and the varnish on her nails. The only concession she made to her own style was to put on her diamond-shaped glasses (one lens red, the other black). At the door, bottles in hand, she turned back into the room, as if to say goodbye to it, but in fact not really seeing it. Her mind was busy with the ethics of spiking other people's drinks. A question on which she stood squarely on the side of: *acid-in-the-reservoir*. She wished someone had done this to her a long time ago.

The collective had gathered in the auditorium. The Maoists were dressed in their usual army fatigues, Mao's *Sayings* in their chest pockets and Mao badges on their lapels. The rest of the adults were in the newly dyed boiler suits. The children were in navy scout uniforms stripped of their distinguishing patches and epaulettes. Everyone's face had been painted black. Tied around their heads were white headbands like those the Vietnamese wore when in mourning for their dead. Several members carried toy pistols in their belts. Others had rifles slung over their shoulders. Chosen for their realism, the weight and finish of the metal, these weapons glinted in the light provided by the lanterns which were spread across the worktables and the stage floor. Cubes, pyramids, lozenges, globes, cylinders, stars, fish, animals, fruit, flowers, the smallest about a palm width in size, the largest reaching up to the men's waists: together the lanterns emitted an ancient sort of brightness which cheated Iris's mind like a dream. Gazing about, it seemed as though she had never really seen what these walls were like, or these ceilings, or this floor. Now that she was going to lose it all, she surveyed it avidly, and felt love for it.

—A toast, she said, holding the bottles up for everyone to see. To mark the end of our preparations and the beginning of our performance.

She handed the lemonade to one of the older girls. The other children, fearful of being passed over, crowded round the girl and demanded to know how the lemonade was to be divided out. A rationing system was quickly established by measuring how many fingers of liquid the bottle contained. As each child took their swig, they were closely monitored by the others — their hands hovering around the bottle, their eyes keenly gauging the motion of the liquid inside — to ensure they were taking no more than their share.

Álvaro accepted the Babycham from Iris with a bemused smirk: *fucking hippies and their rituals.* He knocked a mouthful back and passed the bottle on. The bottle made its way around and everyone took a gulp, except for two: Doris refused by saying she had given up alcohol years ago, while Keith had been warned by Iris in advance about ingesting anything that day; before drinking, he caught her eye, and she gave him a subtle signal — a narrowing of her lids, a shivering — which told him not to go on.

—What's this about, Eva said when her turn came.

Iris offered to take the bottle back.

—It's just a gesture. If you don't want to participp—

Eva, distracted by an argument that had flared up amongst the children, took a healthy draught and returned the bottle to Iris, before going off to intervene.

For show, now, Iris took her own serving. She put the bottle to her mouth as if to drink from it, but kept her lips shut against the liquid that washed against them. Taking the bottle away, she wiped her lips roughly with her sleeve and looked around. No one was paying any attention to her.

That morning, a rare occurrence, Simon had come alone to her room. He had walked straight in without knocking, and put the LSD down on her table, and said:

—This is for you. If you dose it out properly and don't squander it, it'll earn you enough to live for at least a couple of months.

The dressing gown that he lived in was gone. He had a clean shirt on, and a suit jacket, and a functioning pair of leather shoes, and a cap to cover his scabby head: outside clothes, none of which she had seen him in before.

—So I was right, she said.

—Does that make you happy? You'll be fine without me. Better off.

His prosthesis was stuffed into the pocket of his trousers, his look for the exterior world, designed to attract fewer stares on the streets.

—You'll have to take care of yourself from now on, he said.

—Like, find a job? Get a trade?

—Is there something wrong with that?

—Is that what you're going to do, Si? No, wait, don't answer that. I don't want to know.

With his good hand, he pulled up his belt on one side so that it sat higher on his belly:

—Did you see the Indians in the basement have scarpered? I saw them with their suitcases this morning.

—Scumsuckers. They owe us two weeks.

—You can say goodbye to that.

—I wonder where they'll go.

—That's a question you should be asking yourself, Iris. It

wouldn't be sensible to move in with your father. You can't look to him for support.

—Don't worry about me.

—I don't. I know you'll be okay.

By shrugging, and sniffling, and throwing her eyes around, she tried to avoid the pain that came with hearing these words.

—You know, Si, she said then, the world has changed since you were last in it. The sixties are ravenous. You're going to get eaten up.

—I survived a war.

—Child's play, compared.

He went out to the corridor and put his rucksack on his back. Turned to look back through the open door.

—Tell me one thing before I go, he said. Are you going to go through with it?

—The happening? Don't see why not. What have I got to lose?

—Just remember your mother isn't the enemy. Go easy on her. You won't have to use force, she'll submit to you, if you approach her properly.

—We'll see about that.

—War is the father of all things. Have you heard that said? Your mother can't help what she is. Any more than you can. Everyone has the same fate. You hit her, someone else hits you.

—Spare me the soldier's wisdom, Simon. Right now you're nothing but a deserter. If you're going, go.

And he did.

She went to check his room and found it empty. The cupboards bare. His money tins gone. Absences that she had imagined would one day be. Which just went to show. Nobody knew the beginning of anything, but the end was never so hard to see.

Now she poured the last of the Babycham onto the floor and threw the bottle away. Went over to Doris to have her make-up done.

—How you feeling? Doris said, rubbing the shoe polish onto her forehead and cheeks.

—Determined, said Iris.

Doris tied the white band around Iris's head:

—Too tight?

—That's fine.

Doris offered her a red armband:

—You going to wear one of these as well?

Over Doris's shoulder, Iris checked who else in the group was wearing one. Almost everyone.

—Are you? said Iris.

—Why not? Doris said.

—Fuck it. Put it on.

Now that Iris was in costume, they were ready to go. Eva lined up the children at the auditorium door and assigned a lantern to each of them. To the younger children she gave the smaller lanterns to hold directly in their hands; to the older ones she gave the larger, heavier lanterns, some of which hung from poles. The children, though wound up, bursting with excess energy, had assumed a bearing of absolute seriousness. None of them boasted if they received their favourite lantern, nor complained if they did not; rather they took immediate ownership of the one assigned them, inspecting it, turning it round, testing for the best way to display it.

Once the remaining lanterns had been distributed amongst the adults, Eva — whose red-painted helmet set her apart and accorded her an air of command — led the whole group out onto the street. The drizzle that had been falling all day had now stopped, but the skies had not cleared, and the breeze carried large drops of water blown off the roof tiles and out of the gutters. In the gloom of this terrace, at this hour of rapidly vanishing colours, the glow from the forty-four lanterns reached as high as the roofs and as far as the road's end. It was beautiful. Yet, as an image, it was also delicate. If the rain came again the lanterns would be extinguished, and they would have to march in the wet, unlit. They would be miserable. The people would laugh at them.

Eva put the children into formation first, then integrated the
adults. Eva herself was to supervise the front, while Sunny, who was
taller, was put in charge of the tail. The other adults were to act as
marshals, forming a human chain on either side of the column, in
order to protect the children and prevent outsiders from joining in.
Iris was to go in the middle, flanked on either side by Glen and Eggie,
who carried poles joined by a length of wire across which a line of
lanterns hung. Keith was assigned a particularly visible place in the
front corner. Eva did not dare to allocate Doris a fixed position, so the
latter decided to float around near the back. Álvaro stayed outside of
the procession, capturing it on his expensive new camera, a gift from
Doris.

Having established the column's composition, Eva walked up and
down its length, checking that everyone was happy and prepared, and
that they remembered the rules of the march. Then she took her place
at the front and rang her bell three times. The bell, taken from the old
East Wind prop room, was of the kind that schoolmasters once used
to call children in from the yard. Now its effect was to call the local
people to their windows. Lights in the surrounding houses went on.
Curtains twitched. Faces peered out.

We believe in nothing and everything.

We are human and we are divine.

West and east, and neither, we are Wherehouse.

The procession set off in the direction of St Pancras station. These
streets, smelling of coal; this grimed brick and this new concrete;
these blocks of buildings: Iris knew them like the back of her hand.
During the summer she had spent at The East Wind as a child,
she had explored every inch of Somers Town. A fugitive from her
parents' prison, she had wandered down every terrace and alley,
making friends with anyone who would have her: the boys. Street
football and fighting and marbles and conkers and piseball and tig
and running and running, forever running, it seemed, from one gang
or another. She had been happy here, amongst these low people,
and refused to admit she was different from them, despite her own

difference being impossible to hide. They understood her better than she understood herself. Anyone who had been to the museums and the theatres, anyone who knew about Latin irregular verbs and poetry and Shakespeare and soliloquies and scenes and improvisation and mimes, anyone who did not fidget or pick their nose or whisper or slouch, anyone who sat upright and alert and said her lines perfectly, anyone like that was not one of them.

Now, passing by her old haunts, as if acknowledging a holiness in them, the marchers maintained a religious kind of silence; a quiet conveyed by the noise of their footfalls and the bell that Eva rang to set their rhythm. From the children there came none of their usual chatter. Instead, solemnity. Graveness. Actions that appeared to be important because the children had learned to think they were important. Somers Town was their territory. How they appeared here mattered to them. The people in these parts — their families, their neighbours — were among the hardest in Europe. Everybody was tough. Shut off and bravely carrying a burden. And yet, at the sight of the passing children with the lanterns, they, many of them, stopped what they were doing and felt a softness grow inside them which, if it had been acknowledged, might have reduced them to tears.

The procession carried this quietness into the welter of Euston Road. Eva waited for a break in the traffic before leading the parade out. Once evenly spread across all four lanes, they halted to form a human barricade. The adults on either side of the column shook their lanterns and waved as a signal to the oncoming cars to stop. Drivers honked their horns and cursed out their windows, but the marchers did not move. They were waiting for Doris to return.

At the corner of Chalton Street, Doris had broken away from the march and run to the phone kiosk outside St Pancras. She had several calls to make. To her contacts in the television stations and the radio studios and the newspapers, as well as some gallery owners and artists she knew, all of whom had already received cards in the post inviting them to come to the London Carlton to witness the happening. *Did you receive our invitation?* she was going to say when she rang them now. *No, it wasn't a joke. It's real, it's serious, and it's about to start. We'd like you to be there because we want to tell you about the possibility of peace, of stopping rape and abuse, of not having a tyrannical government, of not being slaves in the money system, of finding other ways to organise our lives. We want to bring that message to you.*

Minutes passed. The traffic on Euston Road had come to a standstill. Drivers were getting out of their cars and approaching the blockade, shaking their fists and pointing their fingers and threatening to call the police if they did not move. Pedestrians were stopping where they were going and turning to gawp; some of them had come off the paths and onto the road in the hope of getting involved. The adult marchers held hands to make an external cordon, through which the children calmly peered, as if aware of their own special value, of the necessity of their being kept safe, and of the madness of the world on the other side. Álvaro snapped photos of the confrontations, the public foaming and fuming, the marchers soundless, impervious. At one point, a respectable-looking man, who had left his car running several places back while he took it upon himself to face up personally to the obstructors, looked to be on the verge of violence. The American Maoist Tray stepped in, for he was the largest and had menace; no room for fear in all of that flesh.

—Stand back, sir, Tray said to the man. I won't engage with you till you've taken two steps back. What's that you're saying? If you call me that again, I'll smash you.

When at last Doris came back, she gave Eva a signal — *It's done* — and the procession moved off, clearing Euston Road to the sound of cheers and jeers, and entering Mabledon Place, keeping to the paths now. They went round the crescent at Cartwright Gardens, passing in front of one of the Thurlow hotels, then onto Marchmont Street, before turning left onto Tavistock Place, and proceeding into the wastes of London's student-land, where the difference of but one street divided the slums from the palaces, and where nobody was a neighbour to anybody. Despite the twists and turns, the column remained unified. Most pedestrians gave way to it; those that refused it flowed around like water, flooding the roads and stopping the traffic once more. People noticed the parade, they could not fail to, but none of them cared enough to wonder what it represented.

Gower Street, Bedford Square, across New Oxford Street and High Holborn, into Covent Garden. At Seven Dials the procession paused, making a circle around the central column, while Iris and Keith relit the lanterns which had blown out.

—The kids are getting tired, Keith whispered.

—I see that, said Iris. They'll pick up again when we get to the theatre and they see the film cameras.

—Will the media come?

—I hope so.

—So it's happening, huh? This.

—We won't get into trouble.

—You mightn't. People like me pay a higher price.

—I won't let anything bad happen to you, I promise.

—You can't promise that.

Although the children rarely saw this part of London and were initially alert to the noises and the faces and the lights, the novelty was wearing off. The streets had become for them nothing but measured distances to be crossed. The final stretch down Monmouth Street seemed interminable. The children stooped their shoulders and dragged their feet. Because their arms were tired, they no longer held the lanterns high but let them dangle by their sides. On St Martin's Lane, outside a café of the sort the children's parents could not afford to enter, a table of queers drinking colourful drinks mocked the parade as it went by. This was the only moment during the hour's journey when Iris thought she might lose her temper.

Outside the London Carlton two film crews were waiting, along with a photographer and a couple of arts journalists carrying tape recorders. As soon as the procession appeared, the lenses swivelled round and began to record, which, as predicted, gave new life to the children. Their backs straightened. Their strides lengthened. Again their lanterns shot into the air.

The procession funnelled onto the path and occupied the entire front of the theatre, stretching the length of the façade, leaving barely enough space on the pavement for pedestrians to pass in single file; most felt the need to step out onto the road to get round. The cine-cameras prowled around the gathered children. Bulbs flashed in their faces. A saxophone player sitting on the opposite side stopped playing.

The adults in the group unfurled a banner. Sunny held one of the poles and Barbara the other. The message reached across all of their heads.

IT IS RIGHT TO REBEL

The Maoists had originally wanted them to hold up portraits of Mao, but the others shot this idea down. The banner bearing Mao's saying was the compromise the group came to, and not everyone was happy even with that. Iris was vehement in her opposition to any text being displayed at all, arguing that what had already been said no longer needed saying, that an expression twice used was of no value.

Eva rang the bell and the children made a line under the banner. She rang the bell again, and they turned one towards the other. Again, and they formed groups of threes. Then parallel lines. Then crosses. Then figure eights. Then squares. Then circles. Each child an atom in a process of union and dissolution, pattern and chaos; particles of light exploding and coming back together. The photographers mingled with them. The journalists stuck their tape recorders under their noses and tried to get them to talk. But, beyond their expressions of concentration and the visible pleasure they were taking in this vaguely military display, the children had nothing to say.

One of the film cameras had attached itself to Doris, who was standing a couple of paces in front of the group, using it as a backdrop for an interview, it seemed. Iris was too far away to hear what she was saying.

The other camera was foraging round, looking for anyone who was willing to talk. It found Álvaro.

—What are you? the man behind the camera asked him. What're you doing here?

—We're here because Europe is at death's door, said Álvaro. Europe is dying, and it doesn't even know it.

—Dying?

—We adore our culture. We're proud of its opulence. But this opulence is scandalous, *me entiendes*? Founded on massacre and oppression. We invented slavery only to make ourselves look as great as we do.

—Aren't you just drop-outs looking for attention?

—No, sir. Listen and you'll learn what we are. We're the children of Europe. Sons and daughters of a violent civilisation. No one should be surprised if we choose to be violent. Violence was the bath into which we were born.

The cameraman turned to Iris:

—Is that true? Have you *chosen to be violent*? Who are you going to hurt?

Iris was checking her watch.

—That's a good question, she said, looking up. If you'll follow me, I'll answer it.

She gave a signal to Tray, who then signalled to Sunny and Rolo. These three joined Iris and Keith at the edge of the group, and together they — the breakaway cell — hotfooted it towards Cecil Court, where the theatre's stage door was located. The film camera tailed them.

—Where you off to now?

—Just keep the camera rolling, said Iris, and your mouth shut.

After they had turned onto the lane, Iris heard Doris calling her name behind her. She stopped and turned round, then had to take a step backwards because both cameras were rearing into her face, their spotlights blinding her.

Doris positioned herself in front of Iris, leaving enough space between them that her gestures should be visible to the cameras.

—I want to give you something, she said.

—Everything has been timed, Iris said. We shouldn't delay.

Doris unzipped her boiler suit, and from somewhere on her body, produced an object wrapped in a square of canvas.

—Hold out your hands.

Iris looked at the others, who had formed a loose semi-circle to one side, their faces moving in and out of shadow as the lanterns hanging from poles rocked in the breeze. The men were glancing around nervously, from the cameras to the stage door and back the way they came, expecting the Bill to arrive any moment, and to be pounced on, even though they had not broken any laws yet.

Seeing their impatience, Iris obeyed Doris by raising her open palms. Doris placed the object into them. As soon as she felt its shape, its heaviness, Iris knew what it was. She did not need Doris to use her index finger and thumb to carefully unfold the canvas wrapping to reveal it.

In the early sixties, Doris's name had begun appearing in the cultural press as part of a loose band of emerging artists whose work explored the body and extreme behaviour as a means for art. By the middle of the decade, DORIS LEVER was shorthand for the genre of live performance that encompassed activities such as pissing, spitting, cutting, bleeding, hitting, whipping, hanging, screaming. Eventually she would come to reject *the art of defecating in public and nailing oneself to things*, as one critic called it, in favour of a more ascetic aesthetic, but, for as long as she had been a part of that movement, she was recognised as residing on its far edge. She was known for being able to endure acute physical exertion and unusually high levels of pain.

Her breakthrough came with *Sugar Keeps Your Energy Up and Your Appetite Down*. Presented in the summer of sixty-five in a gallery close to the wall in West Berlin, it involved her sitting at a table in the centre of a room with her legs encased in plastic Perspex boxes filled with flies. Onto the skin of her legs honey had been rubbed, which the flies obediently gorged on. As her skin was being eaten away, bite by tiny bite, she invited spectators to sit in the empty chairs around the table, have tea and converse with her. The recordings of these conversations — subsequently released on vinyl and cassette as

Sugar Can Be the Willpower You Need to Undereat — revealed that a wide variety of subjects were discussed, from the philosophical to the mundane. Copies of the recording now sold in auctions for hundreds of pounds.

But the work that would make her famous would be *Johanna's Got a Gun*. First shown in London in late sixty-eight, *Johanna* would be Doris's first piece in which she did not appear in person, signalling her move away from the medium of live performance towards video and multimedia. It would consist of a series of cine-recordings and photographs documenting a violent happening carried out by the Wherehouse radical performance collective, in which Doris herself participated. The work would occupy several rooms of the Institute of Contemporary Arts, but its centrepiece would cause most of the controversy: a looped film of Doris handing a gun to one of the collective's leaders. This gun, which Doris had procured illegally (a crime for which she was charged and fined) was the one used by the collective to gain access to the London Carlton theatre during a performance, and to attack the cast and terrorise the audience. Another contentious feature of the exhibition would be a video of Doris loading the gun with bullets. There would also be real bullet holes in the gallery ceiling, replica guns scattered around the floor, and a wall covered with Chairman Mao's sayings about guns:

POLITICAL POWER GROWS FROM THE BARREL OF A GUN

ONLY WITH GUNS CAN THE WHOLE WORLD BE TRANSFORMED

IN ORDER TO GET RID OF THE GUN, IT IS NECESSARY TO TAKE UP THE GUN

I was the gun, Doris would say in an essay published in the accompanying catalogue. *I wasn't present in the theatre except as the gun. I gave them that gun, and in doing so, I made them responsible for me, and me for them. Their morality became my morality, and vice versa. If they killed someone, it would've been on my conscience as much as theirs. With a gun in the house, death is always a possibility. In the*

*end, no one died, but everything else they did with the gun were actions
I partook in. I was the bullets that struck the ceiling. I was the noise. I
was the screams. I was there, creating and destroying, even though my
body was quite a distance away.*

Iris did not dare to touch the gun with her bare skin. But neither did
she drop it or throw it away. She kept it resting in her open palms,
positive that if she did not move someone would take it from her.

—This is real, she said. Where did you get it?

—Where don't matter, said Doris. What matters is you have it.
The happening weren't going to work without it.

—Simon? Did you get it from him? One of his contacts?

—I said, it don't matter where it came from.

—That fucking dipshit. Is it loaded?

—I hope you won't have to find out.

—Is it or not?

—You's free to take out the magazine and check.

—I wouldn't know how.

—D'you plan to use it?

—Are you loose up top or what?

—So why d'you need to know if it's loaded or not? Carrying a
weapon is not the same as using one.

—How d'you make that out?

—If it's kept in the hand, and not fired, it functions as a tool of
persuasion only. You won't get far with those toy guns. I's got some
experience in this game. Only the real thing will produce results.

—Why didn't you bring this up before. Why spring this on us at
the last minute?

—Too much for you? Would you prefer I give it to someone else?
Sunny, how about you? You know what Mao says about guns. D'you
want it?

Sunny shook his head:

—This is Iris's call to make.

Iris, by turns electrified and perturbed, continued to hesitate. The cameras' spotlights were switching between the gun, Iris's face and Doris's face, at times moving in sequence, other times deviating one from the other. Iris watched how the gun's aspect changed in the different configurations of light, the barrel appearing slightly longer or slightly shorter, the handle slightly slimmer or slightly thicker. It was not an ugly object. Some people even thought guns were beautiful.

Doris gently pushed on Iris's wrists so that her hands, and with them the gun, moved closer to her body.

—I want you to be in charge of it because I know you'll do the right thing.

—Whether I use it to not, we won't get away with having it. You're asking us to consent to our own arrest.

—If you go down, I'll be going down with you.

—I wouldn't know how to use it anyway, even if I wanted to.

—Can you use a Hoovermatic?

—What? Yeah.

—Then you can use this.

Tray began to speak, and the cameras shone their lights on his face:

—Hurry up and decide, Iris. We have to go.

Iris looked at Tray, then at Keith who was standing beside him. The politicos, the freaks: no one was doing it right. No one was learning anything. Revolution was a permanent way of life. Not a history lesson. Not a drugs party. Not a programme for the next century. It was here. She had to show everyone, now.

—All right, she said.

The cameras swung back to her, in time to see her wrap her fingers around the gun. Having no pocket or belt to put it in, she was forced to keep it in her hand. She was surprised by how cold it was and how quickly it warmed to her.

—How about you guys? she said. I don't blame you if you want to bow out now.

No one moved, except for Doris, who was already retreating back to St Martin's Lane, escorted by her loyal cameraman, to whom she was giving some sort of speech.

—You not coming with us, Doris? Iris called after her.

At the corner of the lane, Doris turned back:

—I'll be there in spirit.

The breakaway cell, now really armed, skulked to the stage door. Iris, Keith, Sunny, Rolo and the second cameraman lined up in that order against the wall. Tray knocked.

A man's voice arrived muffled though the metal door:

—Who is it?

—Delivery, said Tray.

—We don't open this door during performances, said the voice. Deliveries have to be made before the play starts.

—This is a special delivery, sir, Tray said, his accent making the scene feel like the telly. Flowers for Alissa Thurlow.

—Go to the front. One of the staff will sign for them.

—But, sir, these are from the Prime Minster. Official note paper.

After a long moment, there came the sound of the emergency lever being pushed down. The door opened just a crack, but enough for Tray to get his fingers in. Grimacing with effort, Tray wrenched the door wide. The doorkeeper, still gripping the lever, was pulled out with it; as he stumbled into the lane, Tray elbowed him in the neck, and he fell onto his face with a crack. Tray tied his hands behind his back with wire, while Sunny stuffed his mouth with a pair of underpants and sealed it with duct tape. The two Maoists then dragged the man — a frail-looking gent in a black suit, no younger than sixty — in through the stage door, and the others followed after them.

Tray led, pushing the man in front, as a kind of guide and shield, both. They went up a flight of stairs, on which the man fell numerous times and needed to be hauled to his feet, then took a sharp left onto a narrow passage leading to the dressing rooms. The first door had her mother's name on. Knowing that she would be on stage at this time, Iris kicked the door open, and Tray pushed the man onto the ground inside. The only light in the room came from a small reading lamp on the dressing table; the main light was off, and no one thought to turn it on. The obliging cameraman pointed his spot at the man's feet so that Sunny had light enough to tie them to the radiator. Watching this — the rigour both in Sunny's gestures and in the doorkeeper's expressions of fear and pain — Iris felt something she had never consciously felt before. It was not pleasure exactly. But rather a kind of cleansing. Seeing the man suffer did her good. There was a ridding quality to it. Her own scruples had momentarily vanished, and it was not all that horrifying. The not-done things were done every day. The only difference on this occasion was that they were being done through her. The balance of good and evil in the universe, the final sum, had not shifted one bit.

Back out in the passage, the group opened the dressing-room doors one by one. As anticipated, the rooms belonging to the other principal actors — Virginia de Courcy playing CHRISTINE and Eric Humphries playing JEAN — were empty. The final two rooms were larger and shared by the bit-parts, THE PEASANTS: one for the women, the other for the men. Sunny stood in front of the women's door, his fake rifle cocked; Iris in front of the men's door, the gun pressed against her right thigh. *Three, two—*, they flung the two doors open at the same time. Iris heard the protestations of the seven women next door (*ever heard of knocking? who the hell are you? robbed a toy shop, have you? piss off out of here, we'll have somebody to you if you don't*) before she registered the faces of the seven men in this room: the black pencilled around their eyes, the cracks in their foundation at the bridge of their noses and the creases of their foreheads, the bemused fluttering of their eyelashes, and then, from behind their yellow teeth, their roars of laughter.

Iris stepped into this laughter — into the fag smoke and the bad smells on which it was conveyed — and in a single fluid motion raised the gun past her ear and over her head and pressed the trigger.

She felt a shock to her hand and a current run down her arm that culminated in a pleasurable vibration in her chest. This sensation, when it had passed, left behind itself an obscure longing for itself, and she was tempted to shoot again, just to retrieve it. The sounds of the bullet leaving the barrel, and the ceiling splitting, and the plaster falling, she barely noticed, though they must have been impressive, for the women in the next room fell silent, and the men here ducked down or went to cower in the corner.

—Any more sneering out of any of you, she said, and you'll be leaving here on a stretcher. Understood? Now make a line against the wall. Come on, on your feet. Hands behind your heads. Facing me, that's it.

While the men were arranging themselves, one of them lunged forward as if to grab Iris's right arm, which she had kept lifted, the gun pointing up. Tray, who was shadowing her, thrust his boot into the space in front of her and caught the man's knee, making him stumble, then slump onto his side. He rolled on the floor in agony, his leg pulled to his chest. Tray smote him in the face, then pulled him up by the skin of the neck, like a dog.

—Fucking hero, huh? Get into the goddamn line.

The gunshot brought the stage manager down into the passage.

—What the bloody heck is going on back here? Iris heard her rasp.

Then came the sound of Sunny and Rolo grappling with her, and taping her mouth, and tying her up in one of the empty dressing rooms. One of the things that, afterwards, Iris would remember most vividly were the dull, echoing thuds of this woman's limbs banging against the walls as she struggled to free herself from the men's hold.

Iris supervised while Tray transferred the male actors, two by two, into the next room. Sunny and Keith had already put the women sitting on the floor, with their legs crossed and their hands behind their heads. The men were ordered to do the same. Rolo kept watch in the passage. Keith guarded the door. Tray and Sunny loomed over the captives threateningly. The cameraman panned across their faces. Iris, brandishing the gun with the casualness of the novice yet to comprehend its ultimate power, explained to the actors what they should do next.

—Wait for your call. Go to the stage. Act your parts as normal. Did you all hear that? Act your parts as if nothing has changed.

These actors were THE PEASANTS. About halfway through the play, in a section Strindberg calls a *ballet*, THE PEASANTS leave the barn where they are celebrating Midsummer's Night and enter MISS JULIE's house. They occupy the empty stage, drinking and dancing and singing, then exit just before MISS JULIE comes back in.

—Tonight you're going to be joined on stage by some special guests, Iris told THE PEASANTS. Some of them will be children. Don't be alarmed or make any sudden moves. Don't fall out of character. Feel free to interact with them, they're harmless, but if you mistreat any of them, or use them to interfere in our performance, you'll get a bullet in your kneecap. I won't hesitate, you hearing me?

The setting of this particular production of *Miss Julie* was contemporary, so instead of nineteenth-century dress, the actors were wearing hippy and bohemian clothes, like revellers at a music festival. A lot of attention had been paid to the details of the costumes, which had been designed not to look like costumes at all but rather authentic examples. But the result, at least to Iris's eyes, was to turn authenticity into a lie. There was nothing glaringly out of place in the actors' attire; it was simply that the authenticity had turned fake because it had started to reflect on itself and postulate itself as genuine.

—All of this is being filmed, said Iris. There'll be more cameras in the auditorium. These are for our purposes, to make our art. You can just ignore them. Don't play to them. Be yourselves, in your roles. And don't delay your exit. Leave on cue as you always do. Got that? Play by the rules, and no one will get hurt.

THE PEASANTS gave no sign that they had understood, but nor did they show any appetite for rebellion. Everyone just stayed in their places, their eyes cast down, waiting for the call to come through the tannoy. It was quiet in the dressing room to the point that Iris could hear the air entering and leaving people's nostrils. She herself was experiencing an unruffled calm, a sort of unenforced stifling of her emotions, a prerequisite state for high-powered people in important posts probably, but hitherto alien to her. Seeing all of THE PEASANTS crammed into this tight space brought home to her just how numerous fourteen bodies were. Doris had been right: without the gun, it would have been impossible to get so many people's cooperation. The gun already felt quite normal in her grip. It had bonded to her, and she to it. In the same places in her body where sex happened — on the insides of her thighs, and around her vagina and arse, and in her chest, and at the back of her neck, and on her scalp — she felt the desire for another opportunity to fire it.

After a while, her attention was drawn away from THE PEASANTS by a scratching noise outside the door. She turned to see Rolo grinding the soles of his boots into the floor, as if to crush an insect; beside him, Sunny was licking his lips and swallowing, seemingly overcome by a sudden parch. Moving her gaze back inside, she noticed that one of Tray's eyes was winking, his fingers twitching. The LSD was beginning to take effect.

Iris made eye contact with Keith. The black make-up had changed his aspect most dramatically of the group. It had completely altered the natural expression of his face. Only his eyes had escaped the metamorphosis: bloodshot, bugging, they expressed a profound anxiety as to what would happen next.

The Tannoy crackled and a scratchy voice came through:

—Eleanor, this is Jerry. Are you in the dressing rooms? If so, can you come back to the stage please?

Then a minute later:

—Ballet, places. Ballet, places. Three minutes. That's three minutes. Sorry for short notice. Eleanor seems to have disappeared.

Immediately the dreaminess that had settled on the room cleared, and everything was action. Tray, Sunny, and Rolo formed an advance guard, leading THE PEASANTS into the passage and out towards the stage. Iris and Keith took up the rear. From this position, Iris watched THE PEASANTS flow out onto the stairs, take a left through an anteroom and file into wings stage right. By the time Iris got there, Tray, Sunny and Rolo had neutralised two more crew members (the assistant director Jerry and an odd job man) and left them tied together underneath the props table. Virginia de Courcy, the actress playing CHRISTINE, witnessed the skirmish from the opposite wing. She let out a shriek, loud enough to be heard in the auditorium and to cause the actors on stage to drop their lines, before dashing into the backstage rooms on the other side of the theatre. Iris gestured to Tray that he should go after her; by holding a hand to her mouth, she gave him to understand that he should not return until Virginia de Courcy — three-times *Evening Standard* award winner and daughter of Francis de Courcy CBE — had been properly dealt with.

Iris directed THE PEASANTS into the corridor behind the backdrop, from where they were to make their entrance through the rear door. Leaving them there to wait, she went across to the other wing, stage left, and took up a position between the central scenery flats. The cameraman came with her, filming the view from over her shoulder.

A kitchen scene filled the entire stage: modern fitted cabinets with a washing machine and a spin dryer and an electric cooker and a Kenwood Chef in pride of place on the white countertop. Her mother was standing in the strongest point, between the sink and the table, dressed almost as she did offstage, in the uniform of the traitor generation: a blouse and pearls and a figure-hugging skirt to the knee. Eric Humphries was in black-and-white livery of the sort still used by waiters in upmarket hotels.

—*Am I to obey you?* her mother was saying to him.

—*For once*, Eric was replying, *for your own sake, I beg you!*

Behind the backdrop, THE PEASANTS began to sing a lewd song, softly to begin with, then increasing the volume, as if they were approaching from a distance.

—*The other servants are coming here to look for me*, Eric said then, *and if they find us together we are lost.*

To which her mother said:

—I know these people, and I love them, as I know they love me. Let them come here, and I'll prove it to you.

By now her mother had noticed her. Iris could see her mother's eyes moving across her body, quickly, not resting, but rather accumulating flashes with which she could gradually build a more solid picture. Only when the play allowed it, did her mother permit herself a proper look: Eric dropped to his knees in front of her, and she rested her hands on top of his head and pulled it into her pelvis, and, while Eric rubbed his face into her skirt and cried *Please! Come!* she stared out into the wings, as if into nothing, but in fact right into Iris's eyes.

Defying the urgent pace demanded by this moment in the play, her mother stayed like this, transfixed, for several beats. Iris maintained her stare. It was said that motherhood bestowed a strange power on a woman, that she never hated her child, however terrible the child's wrongs. Iris thought now that maybe this was true, for in her mother's eyes, while she did see disgust and disappointment and whole oceans of rage, she did not see any hatred. An observation which did not provide any solace. *What does a child have to do, can she do anything, to be more than merely not hated?*

On the opening night of *The Sing-Song Tribunal* — back then — she spent the first half in the spot box with her father, helping to operate the Kodak cine-camera which had been set up there to record the performance. The final rehearsals had not gone well. News that the Soviet Union had invaded Hungary had caused another split in the ensemble between those, headed by her mother and including Doris, who wanted The East Wind to renounce once and for all its association with the Party, and those, like her father and Max, who wanted to remain in the Party and give it one last push in a Maoist direction. There had been terrible quarrels, discipline had completely broken down, and now her father was prepared for a flop. Having buttons to press, and spools of film to change, and having Iris there to distract him, helped stave off the oncoming horror.

During scene three, when Eva as the young LIXIN enters Shanghai for the first time, he whispered to Iris that the performance was going better than he expected. But he warned his daughter not to allow this to become her fixed opinion, for he could not tell how the people were receiving it. Being such a motley collection, a general assembly of coteries and cliques, the audience was impossible to read as a single mind. After the intermission lights came up, there was a silence, one quickly broken by a couple of whistles and boos — though muted, these were enough to wring out Iris's heart — but in response someone said:

—Shh!

And some else called out:

—Bravo!

And then an applause welled up, rising to a hurricane of acclaim.

Her father gripped her arm hard enough to hurt her.

The transition from pre-emptive disappointment to joy was instant, the height of the climb extreme. Far beneath them, suddenly, lay the valley of grief carved out in their fabric by past failure. *A halftime applause. Unheard of.* He hugged Iris and kissed her, and said:

—I knew it. I fucking knew it.

Before the crowd had left their seats, while the route was still clear, he dashed up the aisle into the foyer, across the bar, and through the backstage door. Iris went with him, clinging on to the back of his shirt in order to keep up.

—Where's Doris? her father said to everyone they passed.

Doris was meant to be in the wings, acting as stage manager, but when they got there, she was nowhere to be seen. In the semi-darkness backstage, the actors were walking around in circles, bewildered, embracing and re-embracing each other. Mouths open, eyes wet, hands reaching out, they grabbed Iris and wanted to grab her father too, to hug him, but he pushed them away:

—Where's Doris? Have you seen her? Where did she go?

Someone said he had seen her heading towards front of house, so they doubled back the way they came.

Though the half-open backstage door, father and daughter had a view across the bar into the foyer. By now the crowd had left the auditorium and the place was packed. Everyone was here. *The Times. The Guardian. The Telegraph. The Daily Worker.* The West End people. The Royal Court people. The university people. The Party people. The art people. Even the local King's Cross people who, on Doris's insistence, had been given free tickets. And there, now, was Doris herself, in homemade clothes which were not the fashion, her black hair sprayed into a stern bun that belied the unrestricted manner with which she moved through the gathering. Iris was too far away to hear what Doris was saying to those she spoke to; she knew only that Doris had become very smart very fast, a proficient user of the vocabulary, a meeter and greeter, an ardent believer in herself.

As they watched Doris weave through the bodies, Iris could sense her father was fighting against the urge to go out there after her.

Never go front of house during the intermission, was his line. *Do not be the man who makes an appearance. Do not be the man who greets his audience, and talks to them informally, and asks them how they are. Do not do it. Be anyone but him.*

But then he swung open the door fully and stepped out into the torrent, and took Iris with him. Immediately they made a difference. Like a siren going off, they became the object of everyone's eyes. Heads turned, looks widened, cheeks collided. In strained accents, the people — these sharp and cross examples of the English, so used to being encased in brick rooms and freezing — overcame themselves in order to give her father the inevitable praise. Iris, her ears already attuned to the unspoken layers, could detect an air of surprise in their voices that her father, this Northerner, a Party man no less, should have produced something worthy of their consideration, in need of no excuses or special allowances. *They didn't spot it coming, did they?*

—Magnificent, Paul, darling.

—I simply can't believe what you've managed to achieve all by yourselves. Is it true it was all done without a grant?

—Look at this place. When I heard what you were planning, I just knew it would turn out fabulous.

—You've brought us all together, when we're all so busy. And that's what one wants. An event. When can we expect the next?

He took hold of Iris again, and, as they moved together through the crowd, he used his free hand to scratch a patch of eczema on his forearm, brought on by the stress of the last few days. Being in the presence of these people affected him violently; Iris could feel it in his grip, how it tightened when someone approached and loosened when they went away again.

Although Doris was still in their sights, she was tough to keep up with, for she was everywhere. Slipping this way and that, into the empty spaces. Welcoming people, introducing them to others. Approaching the orbit of those whom no one else dared approach. Snubbing the significant people in her own good-humoured manner. Apparently unmarked by any social stigma, unburdened by her accent and her origins, deftly transforming the crowd into a party.

They, father and daughter, made good progress through the throng, faster than Doris because they were ruder, but then, suddenly, they lost her.

Thinking that perhaps she had gone outside, they pushed through the main doors. Under the entrance canopy clad with translucent red corrugated plastic, a smattering of people glowed in its reflected light. Not seeing Doris amongst them, Iris peered up and down the terrace, which was illuminated by a line of paper lanterns, also red, hung from the lampposts to mark the theatre's opening. A line of cabs stretched along the pavement; the neon lights in the shape of the words THE EAST WIND were reflected in their windows. A gang of local boys loitered on the opposite side of the road, immersed in the soft rays of red, *What's going on over there?* written on their faces: the audience's audience.

—Excuse me, said a young man to Paul's left. Are you Paul Bradburn?

Her father, identified, became uncomfortable in his body and started to fix himself.

—Can I just say, said the man, I really admire—

Paul interrupted him by pointing at the cigarette he was smoking:

—Can I have a drag of that?

—Sure, said the man. Let me get you a fresh one.

—That one's fine. I just want a puff.

The man handed her father the half-smoked fag. Iris watched him suck on it, wetly. Then drop it on the ground and pulverise it with the sole of his shoe.

Back inside, Iris glimpsed Doris's black hair near the bar and pointed at it. They made their way there, both smiling at the thought that, outside right now, the people would be explaining them.

Her father tapped Doris on the shoulder, and she turned round: *Not her.*

—Sorry, I thought you were—

—Paul, darling, lovely to—

But they were already moving off:

—Thank you, sorry, yes, thank you for coming, we'll catch up ss—

Paul waved at Simon behind the bar: *Have you seen Doris?*

Simon touched his ear to say he could not hear him over the noise.

Have you seen Doris? Paul said silently, exaggerating the movements of his jaw.

Simon raised a bottle of wine: *Want some of this?*

I don't want anything. Have you seen—?

Simon, seeing Iris now, waved at her, and Iris waved back. He poured wine into one glass and lemonade into another and put them on the counter. They muscled through the bodies. Her father intimidated someone off a stool and put Iris on it. Iris gulped the lemonade: an extremely rare treat.

Simon ruffled her hair:

—Nice?

She burped.

Simon laughed.

Her father pointed at the wine.

—I don't want that.

—It's not for you.

Simon slid the glass towards a man sitting on the next stool.

—Hello again young Iris, said Mr Lever. Having fun?

Iris could not answer because she had filled her cheeks with lemonade and was trying to get the gas to come out her nose.

—Do you know who this gentleman is? Simon said to her father.

Her father looked at Mr Lever: *No*.

—This is Doris's father, said Simon.

—Ah, Paul shook Mr Lever's hand. You came.

—Paul invited me. Would've been rude not to accept.

—Ha, yes, well, I'm glad you received the invitation. It's a coincidence, actually, that I bumped into you because I was just looking for—

—You must be the brother, Mr Lever said. Paul's told me about you.

—What's that? said her father, furrowing his brow in confusion.

Simon caught her father's eye and gave him a quick signal, a circling of a finger around the temple, to say that the man was a bit senile or something.

Iris spat the lemonade into her glass and released a guffaw.

Simon wiped the spilled lemonade with a cloth and gave her a stern look.

—Yes, Mr Lever, said her father, raising his voice and stressing his diction, it's nice to meet you at last.

—You don't look nothing like each other, said the father, wagging a finger in the space between Simon and her father.

—So people like to say, her father said.

—Weren't you at the war as well? said Mr Lever. You're of the age.

—Second thoughts, her father said to Simon, nodding at the wine bottle, give me a glass of that.

Simon went to get him a glass.

—Sorry, said Mr Lever. Did I offend you?

—Course not.

—I has a mouth sometimes. I don't get out much, is what that is.

—I'm glad you came. Doris is very special to me. To all of us. None of this could've happened without her. She was an enormous help. You should be proud of her.

—Next she'll be wanting to get on the stage herself.

—Oh, no danger of that. Her talents definitely lie elsewhere.

Mr Lever shook his head as if to say he did not understand what talents he was referring to, and why a place like this would need them.

—D'you mind me asking, why ain't you behind the bar as well? Look at your poor brother there.

He gestured to Simon who was pouring her father's wine.

—Doing everything. In his condition.

Her father took up his glass.

—You're absolutely right. I do feel quite useless now that the play is up and running.

—What's wrong with you? said Mr Lever.

And then to Simon:

—What's wrong with him? Why don't he do anything?

—Don't worry about my brother, Mr Lever, said Simon, wiping the counter and giving her father a wink. We give him plenty to do. Behind the scenes.

—Hope so, said Mr Lever. The devil is God being idle on the seventh day.

Her father downed his wine in four successive gulps. As he drank, he glowered at Simon.

—D'you want to know what I think of the play? said Mr Lever now. I were telling Paul here—

—You're mixing the names up, Mr Lever. He's Simon. I'm Paul.

—What's that?

—I said—. Never mind.

—I were just saying to Paul, it doesn't have much of a plot, the play, does it? I couldn't understand a word of it, but I enjoyed watching.

—Thank you.

—I's a few things I could say about China, if I was pushed.

—Well, what you must understand is, behind the Chinese façade, the play is really about England. Europe. The struggles here.

—Well I never. That quite passed me by.

Her father gulped from a fresh serving of wine:

—The thing is, Mr Lever, when you're like us, when you've had your fill in life and you don't care any more, you tend to be philosophical. You put things obliquely. Turn things into symbols. That's our failing.

Mr Lever slapped her father on the arm:

—Look, don't get down about it. You's all did your best, di'nt ya? Ain't that what counts?

Mr Lever turned to Simon:

—And you's happy with it, i'nt ya?

Simon shrugged:

—Yeah, it's not bad.

Mr Lever turned back to Paul:

—Listen to your brother. He's the expert. He knows what's good and what's not.

While her father was talking to Mr Lever, Iris clocked Doris going up the mezzanine steps to the office. She tugged on Paul's sleeve, and again, and again, until he took notice of her, and followed her gaze. He slammed down his glass and said:

—Mind Iris for a minute, can you, Simon?

And:

—Fine to meet you, Mr Lever, we'll catch up later.

Then made straight for the stairs. Climbed them two at a time. Ducked under the STAFF ONLY sign that hung on a chain across the top. Entered the office.

Iris kept an eye on the office door while she finished her drink. Simon poured her another one, which she drank the same way. She waited for a moment when Simon and Mr Lever were not looking before jumping down from the stool and running after her father upstairs.

She pushed open the office door and peeked in: she had seen them at it before, many times, and did not get tired of it.

After a good innings, they both noticed Iris in the doorway.

Iris ducked out and ran down the stairs. Her head pounded. Her hands tingled. There was blood in her mouth from where she had bitten the inside of her own cheek. She tried to pass through the bar without being seen, but Simon called out to her.

—Iris, where you off to? Come back here!

She threaded her way through the bodies to the backstage door. Ran down the corridors to the dressing rooms. Her mother was the only member of the ensemble to have a room of her own. Iris found it crammed with people: friends and well-wishers picking at the food laid out on a special little table and sipping on champagne in real flutes. Her mother was sitting at her dressing table, Eva on an overturned basket beside her. The people crowded around them. Pressed their hands. Kissed them. As Iris tried to push through, the heat and the scratch of ruffles and sequins against her skin made her face flush a deep red.

—Oh God, said Eva when she saw her sister.

—Shh, said their mother.

—Hi, said Iris when she finally made it over.

Eva fixed her shirt collar and touched her hair and bared her teeth:

—Pchs! What're you doing here? This is no place for a child, am I right, Mama?

Their mother did not answer because Edward Woddis, the theatre's main shareholder, was bending over and whispering into her ear.

—Can't you just piss off and stay off, for once? said Eva.

Iris bit the inside of her cheeks and tried to catch her mother's eye. But her mother was staring up towards the ceiling as she listened to Woddis.

Iris took hold of her mother's sleeve and pulled on it.

—Mama?

For she had just understood why she had come here.

—Mama? Mama? Mama?

She had come to warn her. She had come to say: *Mama, they're at it again. Papa and Doris are fighting.* And to ask: *Why don't you fight with Papa like that any more?*

—Mama, listen to me, please.

Doris wants Papa to leave with her. And Papa said he's going to go. You're losing, Mama, don't you see? Iris saw it in her mind; it was a kind of premonition. A rupture was going to happen, and her mother was doing nothing about it. *Don't just sit there, Mama, do something.*

Her mother swatted away her hand and held up a finger: an order for her daughter to stop being annoying and to wait her turn.

The truth was in Iris's mouth, and for once she was ready to spill it. Speak, speak, was this not what her mother was forever telling her to do? *So why aren't you listening?* The frustration that she felt in her groin crept up into her stomach and her throat and was now close to consuming her. She felt her eyes go fuzzy and saw spectrums in the room where the sounds were and tasted burnt meat on her tongue.

—Eva, darling, her mother said then, detaching her ear from Woddis's lips and leaning forwards so that she could speak quietly and still be heard. Take your sister out of here. Take her to Simon at the bar. Or better yet, find your father. He's the one who's supposed to be looking after her tonight.

—Mama, come on, said Eva. I'm one of the actors, I can't be seen front of house. Get someone else to take her.

—For heaven's sake, Eva, said Alissa, do as I say, and don't make a scene.

Iris watched her mother's face turn towards her. The coloured clouds parted and reality returned to stare at her.

—Iris, I can't talk right now, all right? Have you forgotten what night this is? Can't you see what's happening around you? Go with your sister and I'll see you after the show.

Eva, enraged, seized Iris's wrist and dragged her through the crowd out of the room. In the corridor, Eva swung Iris forward and pushed her in the back, hard enough to make her stumble. The floor vibrated, and in the places where Iris's feet fell, luminous circles like ripples in a pond appeared.

—You always have to get in on things, don't you? said Eva. You can't stand that this is happening to me and not to you. You won't just let me have it.

Eva led Iris to the dressing room she shared with the other actresses. Two of the actresses were inside, sharing a single cigarette. As soon as the sisters came in, they shared a look of exasperation and left without saying a word.

—You see what you do to people? Eva said to Iris when they were alone. No one wants to be around you. I don't care what Mama says, I'm not going front of house, that's not what real actors do. So you're going to have to wait in here on your tod until the show is over. Christ, you really know how to get in the way.

Iris looked around the room: two mirrors, four chairs, one wardrobe, a standing lamp, and, blowing through these objects, wetting her face like a mist, the colours purple and turquoise and yellow — and that was where her memory stopped.

What she did next, what she did to her sister in that room, she had no recollection of. Later, when accused, she would not deny doing it. Nor would she even deny planning it (the rope and the duct tape *were* in her pockets). It was simply that she could not remember performing the actions. Any images of the incident that she could summon came, not from her own memory of it, but from what others told her about it. And, in fact, most people refused to tell her anything because they did not believe that she could not remember. *How is it possible, even for you, to forget doing such a thing? Of course you remember. You're just using your illness as an excuse.* Really the only one who seemed to believe her was Doris. Doris did not mind telling Iris what she saw that night. Which meant Doris's memories were what filled the void in Iris's mind. Doris's memories became hers.

After her fight with Paul in the office, Doris came downstairs alone. Paul had left before her, returning to the spot box in the auditorium. The bar had emptied out, just a few stragglers left. Simon called out to her as she went through, but she ignored him and went straight for the backstage door.

Alissa was waiting for her at the props table in the wings.

—You're cutting it fine, Alissa whispered.

Alissa was first on stage in the second half. Rather than entering from the wings, however, she was to come into the auditorium through the central door, and walk alone in the dark through the stalls, holding a lighted lantern and chanting. Doris's task was to accompany her as far as the auditorium door: carry the lantern, open the doors, and make sure Alissa's costume, THE JUDGE's red robes, did not get caught in anything.

Alissa walked two paces behind Doris along the corridors. Because her hands were busy holding the lantern, Doris had to push through the doors with her back and hold them open with her foot. Alissa did not think to assist her once. Doris checked that the bar was empty before allowing Alissa to come through.

Still behind the counter, Simon gave Doris a searching look, which she pretended not to see.

In the foyer, Doris lit the lantern and hooked it onto its pole before giving it to Alissa. Once she had found the right grip and had steadied the lantern, which was dangling in the air above her head, Alissa positioned herself in front of the auditorium door like a queen poised to enter her court. Doris lifted the back of her robes, walked back a bit, then let them drop, in order to straighten them out and give them extra volume. Then she went to the door. Held the handle. Waited for the signal.

Suffusing the passing seconds, there was silence, there was solitude, there was shame.

Keeping her ear close to the door, Doris watched Alissa only halfway, out of the sides of her eyes.

Alissa kicked out the bottom hem of the robes and looked down left and right to see if they were falling evenly.

Through the door, the audience quietened, which told Doris that the auditorium lights had been brought down. She waved to Simon, and he turned off the foyer lights.

Alissa's aspect in the glow of the lantern was serious, set in purpose.

—Whenever you're ready, Doris whispered.

Alissa made some last adjustments to her stance, her posture, her grip. Finding stillness now, she exhaled loudly once, as a sign, and Doris opened the door.

The inside atmosphere wafted out. The dark beckoned, and Alissa — the bearer of a fiery red sun — crossed in. Doris watched her progress through the slightly open door. In the stalls, black danced as it was swallowed up by the encroaching light. The swish of robes dominated the silence, until, halfway down the aisle, Alissa's voice rose up into an incantation whose involuted modulations caused the crowd to murmur and sigh.

Doris closed the door and made her way backstage in the dark. Most of the actors were in the wings watching Alissa perform. Doris weaved through them in search of Eva, whose entrance came next. Unable to find her, she went to the dressing room that Eva shared with some of the other women. The door was locked.

—Eva? she said. Are you in there?

A muffled voice replied, yes.

—You're not supposed to lock this door. Where did you get the key?

Doris put her ear to the door. She could hear movement inside.

—Eva? Can you hear me? This is your call. Five minutes.

Doris went back to the wings but stayed close to the dressing-room corridor, into which she found herself glancing continuously. In rehearsals Eva had always been prompt to the stage, for she liked to have her costume thoroughly checked and to be on her mark well in advance of her entrance. This delay, the locked door, they were atypical. Doris could not help thinking that something was wrong.

By now, Alissa had climbed onstage and fixed the lantern into its place in the set. The stage floor was divided into three distinct locations. To the right was an interior space with a faintly Chinese feel; to the left an exterior; in the middle an intermediate site like a corridor or a terrace, neither fully inside nor fully out. Built over the stage was a large scaffold onto which were attached signs and advertisements in Chinese, English and French, giving the impression of a neon Shanghai streetscape. On top of that was a second structure with panels depicting clouds in an oriental style, from which emerged THE JUDGE's bench, as if suspended in the air. In this way, the stage was also divided vertically into three: ground, elevation, heavens.

Alissa began to climb the scaffolding ladder to the heavens. She had switched from chanting to speech and was delivering one of her long monologues. The Shanghai lights were illuminating in horizontal rows, from bottom to top, at the same rate as her ascent. It was one of Eva's favourite moments; it was the build-up to her own entrance; she had never missed it before.

Again Doris went to bang on the dressing-room door:

—Eva! You're going to miss your cue!

Doris stood there for a few beats, tapping her foot, then ran back to the wings, checked the stage, then came back to the door, rapped on it with both fists, then went back to the wings once more, willed the action onstage to slow down, *please not so fast*, then turned to look into the corridor and saw, now, coming this way, Eva, at last, in full costume.

—You want to give me a heart attack? Doris said, grabbing the girl's wrist.

Doris rushed Eva to her mark. There, she had just a few seconds to check that Eva's mask was properly tied and her costume sitting right before sending her on with a customary little push.

Simultaneously, from the opposite wing, William, the actor playing the adult LIXIN, came on. He and Eva walked towards each other downstage, met in the middle and embraced.

Doris went cold.

Eva moved differently than in rehearsals. And she looked shorter and slighter than usual in William's arms. Her hair, visible between the mask straps at the back, was lighter and cut higher on the neck.

The colour of blood, the sound of bells, the feeling of incontinence, the memory of failure, the thought of death all suddenly converged in Doris's mind: it was not Eva at all, it was Iris.

Iris and William began to dance together, and to sing. Iris knew the movements, she knew the words. Her voice was strong, her acting good and light. She did not mumble into the mask. Did not snivel on account of the heat. Did not pause, as Eva tended to do, but rather moved, moved, always forward, the thread unbroken. Her transitions from singing to speech were smooth, and her responses, now to William, now to Alissa, were clean and measured. William and Alissa had not failed to recognise her: Iris sensed their shock about this and was taking advantage of it.

It was a nightmare.

Doris rushed to the dressing room and tried the handle, but Iris must have locked it again on her way out.

—Eva, are you in there?

Doris cupped her hands on the door and put her ear into the space between them, in an effort to amplify any sounds on the other side. She heard nothing and at the same time definitely heard something: a silence in which menace was gathering.

—Eva? It's me, Doris. Answer me if you's in there. Whatever you've done, I won't be mad, I swear.

Nothing. Something.

The actors had gathered around the corridor entrance.

—What's going on? Where's Eva? Why's Iris playing her part?

Doris pushed through them on the way back to front of house:

—Calm down, nothing's going on. Iris is covering for her sister, is all. Just play your bits as normal.

In the bar, Simon was sitting on a stool at a counter, drinking a beer and smoking.

—The master key, she said. Where is it?

—Why?

—Just tell me.

Simon went behind the bar and checked the hook.

—It's not here, he said. Come to think of it, Iris was asking for it earlier. She said she'd put it back when she was finished.

—Jesus Christ.

Doris spun round in search of an object that might be of use.

—D'you have a crowbar or something?

—Has Iris locked herself in somewhere?

—Iris is fine. I think Eva might be—. Simon, you've got to help me.

—There might be something in the storage room in the back.

—Get it, please. It's serious.

Simon padded off to the storage room and came back, two long minutes later, with a hammer and a large screwdriver under his bad arm.

—Will this do?

—I hope so.

Doris ran back through the corridors with Simon trundling behind her. She banged on the dressing-room door:

—Eva?

Simon leaned against the wall to catch his breath:

—Eva's in there?

Doris kicked the door a couple of times, uselessly. Then crouched down and put her hands to her face and felt her heart pound against the corridor's narrow walls.

The actors hovered around.

—We need to open this door, Simon.

—What's going on?

—Simon, just trust me.

—All right. I'll hold the screwdriver, and you do the hammering, yeah?

Together they started to attack the wood around the lock and the hinges. The noise was easily loud enough to be heard in the auditorium, but Doris did not care; she went harder and harder. There was a loud splitting sound as the screwdriver went right through the door. Simon had to pull on it hard to get it back out.

—Put the screwdriver on the bottom hinge there.

The final hinge sprang off, and the door shifted on its axis and came loose on one side.

Doris pushed Simon out of the way and kicked it. And then again.

—Let me, said Simon, pulling on her arm.

She shook him off:

—I've got it.

One more kick and the wood chip split in the bottom right corner. Simon tore away the broken piece, creating a space large enough for her to crawl through.

Inside, the room was bathed in the clear light emitted from the bare bulbs that framed the mirrors on the left-hand side. The first thing Doris noticed was a shadow that stretched along the floor and up the righthand wall. Then she made out Eva at the shadow's base. She was lying on her side on the floor, naked apart from her bra and knickers. Her limbs were tied with rope and belts to a chair. Her skin was red and raw from fighting against the bind, though she was absolutely still now. The impression she gave was of a chess piece that had been flicked over on a board. Her head was resting on the ground. Her mouth, stuffed with underpants and sealed with masking tape, gave no sound; she had given up trying to scream. Her nostrils were pinching in and flaring out with her breath, which was slow and even. Her eyes blinked deliberately once: no more struggle, just relief and exhaustion.

Doris — on her front, halfway through the door, her torso in, her legs out — was at the same level as Eva, close enough to remove her gag, to release her, to caress her. But she did not do so immediately. Rather, for another moment, she stayed where she was, wedged between here and there, and looked. And looked. And, unconscious that she was doing so, kept on looking. For this was horror, which, if withstood, was the only beauty left, and she had intruded upon it.

Pristine. Irrepressible. A discovery more necessary than that of love. Now fading in front of her eyes, irrecoverable. Always almost gone. A vision that looked forward to the past. In search of neither audience nor reward. Without a script. Resistant to direction. No goal. Movement within the impossibility of movement; the fleeting shapes that avoided terror's grip. An antidote to the perishing of the truth. Dangerous, vital, exquisite feminine beauty: history had created this. And history, in its mystical way, had also created the violence that went into its creation. Would it be possible to emulate? To replay with equal cruelty but without causing the same harm? An artist capable of such a feat, how would she be? And who?

The next line in *Miss Julie* was her mother's: *You promise.* Everyone in the London Carlton was waiting for her to say these two words. The action could not continue without them. They were the cue for her mother and Eric to run offstage, and for THE PEASANTS to enter by the back door, and for the Wherehouse procession to storm the auditorium. The words could not be skipped. They were essential. Pivotal. But she was refusing to say them.

The audience — that mysterious black space to Iris's left side and to her mother's right — had become restless. Seats were creaking. Old men were coughing. The atmosphere was bad. Already those in the front rows would have heard the gunshot coming from backstage; those in the lateral seats would have noticed the commotion in the wings; now the whole house was tense, everyone had sensed that something was wrong; the only reason they were not reacting was because they were waiting to see how everyone else was going to react.

The magic words — *You promise* — still unforthcoming, and unable to hold back any longer, Eric broke free of her mother's hold, and stood up. He turned, loosely, out of character, to see what had seized her mother's attention. Catching sight of Iris in the wings, he flinched, then dashed off stage right, where he was tripped up and bound, and — only because he fought back so fiercely — was slapped and kicked until blood poured from his face. His cries, released in the seconds before his mouth was taped, reached as far as the cheap seats, where they were transformed into whistles and catcalls. These in turn were drowned out by the shouting and singing of THE PEASANTS, who now burst onstage through the rear door.

Almost simultaneously, the auditorium doors opened, and there was a letting in of light, and the Wherehouse procession came down the aisles. Iris's view was limited, but she could hear the children moaning. Some of them were crying. Their lanterns were knocking off the corners of the seats. Eva, barely bothering to whisper, was ringing the bell and giving panicked orders. In the audience there were gasps. A sharp laugh broke out. Some loud talking. Boos. Waves of tension.

Her mother, finally falling out of her paralysis and switching back into herself, whirled round and ran off. Once out of the audience's sight, however, she was brought to a halt by Keith and Sunny, who were blocking her exit from the space between the flats. She threw her arms up: she was not going to resist, she did not want any violence. Keith made a circle in the air with his finger, as a signal for her to turn back round.

—You're not going anywhere, MISS JULIE. You have a part to play. You're going back on.

Iris watched her mother turn back round to face her. Their eyes locked again. On stage, THE PEASANTS were doing a drunken set dance whose steps mimicked the strenuous lovemaking which MISS JULIE and JEAN were supposed to be engaging in offstage. The line connecting Iris and her mother was hard and taut; it did not break even when THE PEASANTS charged through it. When Iris blinked, her gaze went straight back to the source; her mother did not seem to blink at all.

When the procession reached the stage, Eva and the other collective members lifted the younger children onto the boards. The older ones climbed up themselves. Entering this pristine Formica world, some began to scream; some to giggle; some wandered around in a daze; some — those that had had to be carried through the stalls — lay on the floor in a catatonic state. The adults were not in much better shape. Only a minority, the freaks Glen, Eggie, and Per, had come to understand that they had been drugged, and had decided to enjoy the ride, dancing with the actors and chasing after the objects flying around their heads. The rest, judging from their noises, were confused, and afraid, and suffering. Unable to stand being in the bright lights, they retreated into the wings to sit with their heads in their hands, or, in the case of Álvaro, to turn around and around in circles like a dog chasing its own tail. The cameraman stayed in the stalls, at the base of the stage, moving this way and that in search of faces to zoom in on: no one looked like they were acting, yet no one was acting as normal either, he had never seen anything like it, it was delirious but not happy, it would make for disturbing viewing. Doris was nowhere to be seen.

Eva had intended to stay on the stage with the actors and the children, but, clearly overwhelmed by an experience she did not understand, she dropped the bell onto the boards — *clang!* — and went off, joining their mother in her little prison between the central flats. Eva did not look well. She pushed off her red helmet, which was making her feel hot, and that too fell onto the floor with a loud crack. She adopted a wide-legged stance and stretched her arms out sideways, as if steadying herself on a moving train. Perhaps thinking she was going to fall, she took hold of their mother's arm, and with the other hand began to wipe her forehead, over and over, as if to take some invisible hair out of her eyes. Their mother, although frightened by this strange behaviour, allowed herself to be held on to. Her eyes darted between her two daughters: the agitated one beside her and the motionless one in the other wing. Iris could almost see the calculations taking place in her mother's mind as to which was worse: humiliating herself in front of her public by appealing to her daughters or humiliating her daughters by appealing to her public.

A minute more, and THE PEASANTS finished their dance and went back out through the rear door. Without them, Glen, Eggie, and Per lost some of their verve, which they tried to regain by feeding off the children. Of the eight children remaining on stage, four were running around, laughing and playing; Glen, Eggie and Per found it difficult to join in their games, however, for they were games born of bewilderment and disorientation, and had no order; they curled and twisted along axes visible only to the children. Of the other four children, one was rolling around perilously close to the stage edge. A couple were lying dead still on the boards; judging from the twitching of their eyelids they were experiencing inner movement. Another looked plain psychotic, grimacing and pulling at himself and biting his tongue and wailing. One kept approaching Iris in the wings and trying to embrace her and talk to her, but Iris thought it was too dangerous to have a tripping child near a gun, so she shook him off and pushed him back onstage every time. All but two of the children had discarded their lanterns, which lay around, broken and extinguished.

Before leaving Wherehouse, Iris had prepared the children for the unexpected.

We're going to a magic theatre, she had told them. *Once inside, you might see things, colours and sounds you've never seen before, like fairies in the air, or sprites. You might also feel special senses. Experience new emotions. If this happens, you mustn't be frightened. They won't teach you this at school, but the truth is there exist worlds which we don't touch in our ordinary lives. What enters our consciousness on a normal day is not all that can possibly enter it. The universe is kind. The visions are your friends. There are, in fact, no enemies in this life. We have too much aggression inside us. We must learn to be as meek as newborn children, and welcome everything in as a gift. The belligerent, the defensive are always the first to fall.*

She had already picked out those children who were likely to have good trips and those likely to have bad. It gave her little pleasure to see her predictions borne out, though she felt no remorse either.

Everybody had to die sometime; the children might as well get it over with early so they could come back as somebody else; if they were not ready now, they would probably never be.

Her mother's cue for coming back on stage had long passed. In the play, she was meant to re-enter as soon as THE PEASANTS danced out the door. Alone on stage, she was meant to survey the mess made by the revellers, and, aware that she herself might look a mess having just come from a tryst with her father's valet, fix her own appearance in the mirror. It was then, while her mother was powdering her face, that Iris was meant to come on, taking over Eric's role as JEAN. Iris had learned the part. Every line. If her mother did not do what she was meant to, Iris would not get to do what she was meant to, which was to act. It was awful to have to depend on her mother like this; awful to want to act, and awful to rely on her mother's actions for it.

While on stage the children, like inmates in a miniature asylum, continued their deranged ballet, Iris glowered across at her mother in the wings. Her mother remained trapped on three sides: by the flats, by Keith and Sunny, and by Eva. Her only way out was to come back onto the stage. But — her arms folded, her chin raised proudly — she was spurning it.

In different parts of the auditorium, seats were banging up. People were leaving.

—Enough of these horrors! a woman cried as she went.

The majority, though, were sticking it out. Like most audiences, they were more interested in watching the actors than the play, so they were not overly concerned that *Miss Julie* was being ruined; more interesting to them was the chance to witness actors in trouble, failing, being mortified. Somewhere in the distant heavens, someone began to clap. Others then joined in, and it spread down into the balcony and stalls, and took over the entire theatre: not an ovation but a taunting *clap*-pause-*clap*-pause-*clap*-pause-*clap*.

Eva put her hands over her ears and shook her head frantically.

Iris could see her lips move: *Shut up, shut up, shut up, shut up—*. Their mother saw her chance and tried to slip round the outer edge of the flat, so as to escape into the wings stage front without being seen by the audience. Eva immediately sensed their mother's absence, and reawakened. Newly furious, she caught the back of her mother's blouse and launched her sideways into the lights.

Acid usually allowed only limited space for memory. Almost never did the visions Iris saw while tripping remind her of her own past. Reality was altered but remained unshakably itself, untainted by what once had been. Sober now, she was looking from the other perspective: things were as they were, and that was full of memories. An extraordinary image of her mother had materialised in the world — pitched headlong onto the stage, and now falling down onto her hands and knees — yet playing alongside this image, over it, in it, were memories, ordinary memories, of the kind as might occur in the course of an average day. Her mother teaching her to sing at the piano. Her mother checking her homework. Her mother accompanying her on the train to boarding school. Her mother accompanying her on the train back. These recollections caused Iris to feel the horrendous burden of her mother's criticisms. *Stop drifting away. Don't fall down. Clean yourself up. Have sympathy. Be good. Make friends. Read more. Analyse it. Speak up. Sing higher. Choose better. Which one do you want? No, not that one. Are you crazy? Do you want to be like everyone else?* And, in the same instant, they caused her to act: to step out of the wings and onto the boards.

Her mother was crawling on her hands and knees towards the stage edge, intent, it seemed, on climbing down into the stalls.

—Help! she was saying, Help! Call the police. Someone, please. I don't know who these people are. I don't know what they want. I have nothing to do with this.

Nothing?

Iris shot the gun for the second time. Aimed it upwards like before; without looking for a target, just pressed the trigger. The bullet struck a theatre lantern. Glass and bits of metal and plastic rained down onto the back of a child who was lying on the boards facedown. A section of the stage lost brightness. The cameraman ran out of the wings and pointed his camera up, to record the damage. The audience's clapping ceased. To be replaced by yells of panic, and whimpers, and loud cracks, and groans as people dived down behind the seats, or climbed over them, or crawled under them to try to get out.

Her mother, legs dangling off the edge of the boards, about to jump off, turned back to face the stage. What she saw — Iris was happy to mount this scene for her — was her daughter bringing the gun to her own temple. Pressing the muzzle into her skin hard enough to leave an imprint.

Seeing this, her mother froze.

Seeing her mother freeze, Iris smiled and took the gun from her head and pointed it at the green exit sign above the central doors.

The crowd began to protest, then choked on its own breath.

Iris drew a line in the air with the gun — dead slow, the slow that is the spending of all force to hold back all force — until its sight found the centre of her mother's forehead, her third eye.

A crack formed in her mother's hard, white resistance; she blinked.

Iris rubbed her finger along the trigger.

Act, woman.

Her mother's jaw unfastened, her lips parted.

Am I to obey you?

Iris cocked the hammer.

For once. For your sake, I beg you.

EVA

1968

<u>xviii.</u>

At last the group arrived at the London Carlton. Eva saw Doris following the breakaway cell onto Cecil Court. Doris was supposed to be staying here with the main group, and it infuriated Eva that she was not sticking to the plan. Eva could endure anything — right now, for instance, on the verge of committing acts of vandalism and violence, she was on the extreme edge of herself, but controlling it, holding it, hysteria flickering in and out of her gestures without taking them over — but she could not endure Doris's refusal to submit to her control. *Listen to me for once, I beg you.*

A few minutes later, Doris re-emerged from Cecil Court, accompanied by the cameraman who had gone with her. Relieved, Eva conducted the children into their final dance formation, then gave the other collective members the signal that they should prepare themselves for entering the theatre. Joshua arranged the children into two lines, one on either side of the door.

Turning back towards Doris with the intention of urging her to hurry up, Eva saw that the cameraman was now coming back this way, but that Doris herself, separated from him, was going the other way, down St Martin's Lane towards Trafalgar Square.

Eva grabbed Álvaro.

—Here, take this, she said, giving him the bell. Keep the children in order. Don't make a move until I get back.

She ran after Doris:

—Doris, wait! Doris! Doris!

Doris pretended not to hear until she could no longer pretend; then she twisted her neck round.

—Where are you going? said Eva.

—Look, I'm sorry.

—For what?

—This is your happening. You don't need me around any more.

—You're leaving? Now?

—Go back to the group. See it through without me.

—Don't do this, Doris. Don't run away like you do from Papa.

—Go back, Eva, or you'll be too late.

A little further down the road, a cab was parked with the engine running. A male figure inside opened the door.

—What's going on, Doris? said Eva.

Doris offered her a hug which she did not accept but was powerless to reject.

—I won't be coming back, said Doris. Sorry. You're amazing. I won't forget you.

—Where are you going? Back to Papa? I don't get it. You've been blanking him since you got back from Paris, and now all of a sudden you have to see him? Can't he wait a bit longer? Stay and help us finish this.

—I'm sorry, Eva. I've gone as far as I can go with you.

—We've just got started. Please, stay. We do great work together.

She waved dismissively back towards the theatre:

—Much better than this, I promise. This is only a test. In the future there'll be better things.

—Keep making good work. Don't give up.

Tears flooded Eva's eyes.

—What am I supposed to do?

—Go back to the group. Do what you planned.

—No, about the other thing I told you. What am I to do about *that*?

Eva let out a terrible sob. That she had ever talked to Doris about Álvaro cut her with shame; that she had brought Álvaro up again now, as an act of desperation, would haunt the entire rest of her relationship with him. This need she had for the people she admired to convince her that it was right to marry him, it would never go away.

She had to press a closed fist against her mouth to force her feelings back.

The cab's horn honked, and Simon's head emerged through the open door:

—What the bleeding hell is keeping you?

Seeing him, hearing him, Eva's hand fell from her face. The tears ran down her cheeks, unfelt, for their provenance was in emotions that had passed into shock.

—I don't believe it, Eva shouted after her. Tell me this is a joke!

So she was with *him* now? *Simon* was the reason Doris was not going back to her father? Impossible. Doris was using Simon merely. For what, only Doris could know, though it was unlikely to be for anything other than her art, the advancement of her career. Did Simon love *Doris*? If he was capable of love at all, which Eva doubted, then maybe. Maybe purloining his brother's love was precisely how he understood love, and the closest he would ever get to it.

Doris trotted away towards the cab.

—It's not what it looks like, she called back as she climbed in.

As she settled into the rear-facing seat, her hand remained on the door handle, keeping the door open as an invitation for Eva to join them. Eva took a couple of steps, then rushed forward, getting as far as the rear bumper before — *slam!* — the door closed, and Doris shouted through the open window:

—Don't pity your father. He ain't an innocent party in any of this.

Eva watched the cab splutter to the end of St Martin's Lane, then tear left onto William IV Street.

Before returning to the group, Eva fixed her red helmet, which had tipped back on her head while running, and wiped her face because it felt dirty after crying. The black shoe polish came off on her fingers. Wiping it on her boiler suit, she felt consumed by a sense of loss.

Back outside the London Carlton, the children had come out of line and were shifting about. Scratching their limbs and talking to themselves. A couple were sitting on the ground. One was convulsed in laughter. Another was gazing fixedly at a point on the pavement directly between his feet. An older girl called Mary appeared to be in a trance and stared at Eva without seeing her. Several lanterns were on the ground; one was tipped onto its side, being knocked about by the shuffling of the children's feet. Suddenly furious, Eva swiped the bell from Álvaro.

—What bullshit is this? she said.

—What's your problem? Álvaro said.

—My problem is you. I leave you with one measly job—

She shook the bell hard, and it pealed out its terrible sound. But it did not have the desired effect. The child who was laughing began to cry. Another started screaming. A third ran away and had to be chased after and dragged back. The rest had to be physically pushed back into position.

—Where did Doris go? Álvaro said.

—Who fucking knows, Eva said. She's been doing this to Papa for years. It's her habit. She leaves. No warning. Then she—

—Comes back?

—Yeah. And all is forgiven.

After the failure of The East Wind, Doris's career had progressed in parallel with her mother's, if on a different scale. As Doris, the body artist, moved up from warehouses to galleries, her mother, the actress, went from rooms above pubs to large West End theatres. At the same time that Doris began to be featured in art journals, her mother began to appear in Sunday supplements and on television. Eva kept a close watch on the paths taken by the two women, and what she found was, she did not envy her mother, with the larger fame; she envied Doris, with the smaller.

Eva envied Doris for whatever it was she possessed which impelled everyone — her father, Max, Simon, the world — to pick her. To want to look at her. To work with her. To love her. Eva envied Doris for having been chosen from nothing to be something, and for having dedicated herself to becoming that something without dropping all of her principles in the process, as her mother had done.

It did not matter that Eva was not entirely taken in by the art that Doris produced. That she thought it self-absorbed in spite of its extroverted veneer. That its political power was vastly overstated by the critics. What mattered was that, between surpassing her mother or surpassing Doris, she would have chosen the latter without hesitation. She might not have been fanatical about Doris's art, she might have thought it inferior to anything a group could achieve, yet she would compare everything she did in the future against it. And, in this, she would be just like her mother too.

Shortly after their wedding in nineteen-seventy, Eva and Álvaro would go to Doris's big show, *The Proletarian Cultural Revolution Will Be Eternal*, at the Whitechapel Gallery. The show would consist in its entirety of photographs of Simon. Simon asleep. Simon in the bath. Simon smoking at the kitchen table. Simon opening a can of beans. Simon naked on the couch with an arm over his eyes. Simon frying an egg. Simon tying his shoelaces. Simon turning on his radio. Simon with his war medals. Simon with his memorabilia from Italy. Hundreds of them, taken over a two-year period (the same two years of Eva and Álvaro's suspended prison sentence). Most of the images would be taken in the same flat, and Simon would always appear alone, though he would sometimes be seen interacting with Doris behind the camera: talking to her, or smiling at her, or, in one, giving her the finger because she had just come in on him sitting on the toilet. With the photographs printed in varying sizes, the images would cover the walls from floor to ceiling, room after room: Simon — his ugliness — everywhere. For that would be the true star of the show, its real focus. His ugliness would be what the camera seemed most interested in, what its lens seemed intent upon. Even when his ugliness would not be at the centre of a picture, still it would be at its centre; when it would be hidden, still it would be there.

Standing in front of an image of Simon's stump poised above a chess piece as if about to move it or topple it over, Eva would say to Álvaro:

—What do you think?

Álvaro would shrug and say:

—Not my thing.

Eva would feel her hand in Álvaro's hand, and the cheap wedding band pinching the skin of her finger, and say:

—Mine neither. Who'd want it on their wall?

But the truth was, given the choice, she would have given up Álvaro there and then, if it meant being able to go back to that night outside the London Carlton and to climb into that cab with Doris and Simon, if it meant her name being stencilled on these gallery walls beside Doris's, if it meant her own image filling these rooms until they became something more than her.

Why had Doris not chosen her? Was it because she believed Eva had not suffered as Simon had? Was Eva too intact? If so, what injustice. What wilful blindness. If one took the whole of someone's life, no one was clean. Marks were left by whatever one saw and did; it did not have to be war. Even a privileged life like Eva's took its toll.

A thousand wounds and a hundred holes.

Giving up Wherehouse and entering into the marriage system had done nothing except bandage these wounds over. How hard it was to have so many injuries and not have the opportunity to let air to them. Wifehood would have been easier if Eva had always wanted to be covered up, or if her love for Álvaro was such that this covering up did not feel like a sacrifice. But, as it was, waiting for a chance to undress was a torture. With Álvaro, she was but a mummy. Wrapped up in her defeat.

When will a call to nakedness come?

In the theatre foyer, the ushers had been watching the children's street performance through the glass of the door. The three of them, two male and a female, all over fifty, were nudging each other and laughing up their sleeves. On Eva's nod, Joshua, Jay, Stewie, and four of the older children pushed the door open, slipped in and formed a tight circle around the ushers. By linking arms, the Wherehouse members locked them inside the circle, then together they sidled to the right; caught like flies under a glass, the ushers were forced to move with them.

Once the way was clear, Barbara opened out the doors, and the rest of the children poured in. Inside, Eva, Glen, Eggie, and Per divided the two lines of children into three and put one line to stand in front of each of the auditorium doors. Barbara locked the main door with a bicycle chain, then ran to the booth, where the ticket seller, encased in glass, was speaking into a telephone. Barbara put the muzzle of her fake gun against the glass and said:

—Put down the phone, now.

The ticket seller's mouth began to gape and grind.

—Speak into the device, said Barbara.

Without taking the telephone receiver from her ear, the ticket seller leaned into the microphone:

—The money's in a safe.

—We don't want your money, said Barbara. What we want is for you to put down that fucking phone.

On the other side of the foyer, Joshua was negotiating with the ushers.

—Look, if you cooperate, no one will get hurt. These kids are the future, man. It's your duty to give them the space to protest. Do you really want to prevent them from doing that? It'd be easier for everyone if you just let them.

—Out of the bloody question, the head usher was saying. You need to leave right away. The London Carlton is private property. People have paid good money to see the show that's in the programme. Who are you to barge in and ruin their evening?

Eva peeked through the central doors of the auditorium. The stalls were full enough. On stage, Eric Humphries had just taken her mother round the waist and was trying to kiss her. Her mother slapped him:

—*Stop it!*

—*Are you joking or serious?*

—*Serious.*

—*You play games too seriously, and that's dangerous.*

The open door was letting light into the stalls and attracting stares and whispered remarks from the people seated there, so Eva withdrew. By her calculation, there were about five minutes to go before the group's cue to enter.

In the foyer, the children were becoming increasingly agitated. Pushing and pinching each other. Pointing into space and yelping. Crawling on their hands and knees. Eva put this down to the strangeness of the environment. The pomegranate-patterned wallpaper. The Moorish-style vases and urns. The plush armchairs and decorative plants. The panelling and carved moulding of walnut and sycamore. Midway between a posh sitting room and a brothel: *who knew how to behave here?*

Glen and Eggie were working hard to keep the children in their respective lines and to stop them dropping their lanterns on the floor. Most of the lanterns had gone out. Eva signalled to Per that he should get them going again using his lighter, but Per, basically a child himself, had taken to mimicking the children in their nervous jerkings.

—It's like I'm tripping, he was saying as he rotated his open hands in front of his face.

Son of a bitch. Is he on drugs?

Eva felt she should be angry about this. She had told Iris that no one was to be given drugs of any sort until the happening was over. Yet Eva found she could not summon any ire. All of a sudden it was like she was watching a fire from a distance. She felt great and did not give a shit any more.

The ticket seller had locked herself into the booth and was hiding under the desk. Barbara was failing to coax her out.

—All right, fuck you, said Barbara. Stay where you are.

Eva went into the adjoining bar, took a high stool from the counter and brought it out to Barbara. Together they wedged it under the handle of the booth door so that it could not be opened from the inside.

The barman had followed Eva out into the foyer:

—Hey, where are you going with that?

Barbara pointed her toy gun at him.

—Blooming heck, he said.

—Get the fuck back inside, Barbara said.

—I don't want any trouble, he said, retreating, I'm only new here.

Eva closed the bar doors behind him, inserted one of the lantern poles into the handle cavities, and slid it across to create a lock.

As she was doing this, a deep sound, a boom, like a timber plank being dropped onto the ground, resonated through the building. This caused time to stop, as the Wherehouse members glanced at each other questioningly.

One of the ushers used this moment of suspension to try to free himself from the circle. A scuffle broke out, and within seconds the two male ushers were face down in the carpet, several pairs of knees pressing down on their necks. Joshua taped their mouths, while Jay and Stewie tied their hands.

—We didn't want to do this, but you left us no choice.

In the affray, the female usher managed to crawl out under Joshua's legs. Once free, she staggered to her feet and, with the skirt of her uniform bunched up around her thighs, lumbered towards the stairwell. Eva — light-headed, happy — relieved Eggie of his lantern pole, and detached the lantern from it, leaving her with a mean-looking weapon with a metal hook at its tip. Wielding this, she went after the usher.

Violence or non-violence? Now that the east wind was blowing, the drums of war were beating: which side was Eva on? Mere thoughts could not tell her what she was going to be. She was not daunted. She would proceed. Let good or evil come as a surprise. Foretold, she would not believe it anyway.

When she reached the stairs, the fleeing usher paused to check if she was being pursued. Seeing Eva advance towards her, she hesitated.

Who in this world is afraid of whom?

Eva tightened her grip on the pole — her arms taut in preparation for a hard swing — and quickened her pace.

The woman, defiant, waited until Eva was only a couple of feet away before turning again to go up. It was almost like she wanted Eva to hit her. Obliging, Eva swung the pole; it caught the woman's ankle, tripping her up. The woman fell forward onto the stairs. Eva knelt on the second step in order to reach up and grab her foot. The woman pulled on her leg to free it. Her bones stretched in Eva's grip like an elastic. A jerk, then, and the woman, like water, came falling down.

Liquid light cascading.

Colours washing over Eva's skin.

Running off her clothes.

Pooling at her feet.

How beautiful.

When she touched the puddle with her boot, its surface rippled in all directions. By stamping in it, she created bubbles that floated up and burst on her face.

She felt elated, free of the things that had been bothering her before. *What things?* Nothing mattered in the world. Everything was wonderful, and everything remained wonderful until some people started pulling her back by the arms.

—Leave her be, thing, they were saying, That's enough, ay.

She turned to see who these people were and recognised them as

Glen and Eggie, yet all the same she felt the need to ask herself, *Who are they?*

Automatically she said to them:

—Do you see the toilet? Tie her up and put her in there.

Then to Joshua and the others, she said:

—Did you hear that? Tie them all together and put them in that toilet.

And they obeyed her, just like that. As if she had a special power. Which would certainly explain the numb feeling in her joints. She looked at her hands and they were shaking. But that was all right because they were not hers. Then the illusion failed, and they became hers, and that felt like death.

As the men were dragging the ushers across the foyer towards the toilet, the central auditorium doors opened a crack and an audience member peeped out and said:

—For goodness sake, shh!

And then, taking in the scene:

—What the ff—

At this point the door opened wider and a second man appeared:

—Good grief.

Again, for Eva, the world went watery. As she ran towards these men, she saw the air part before her.

—We're part of the show, she said. Don't interfere. Go back inside.

But her special power seemed not to work on these particular specimens, they were resistant to it, which required her to hit them with the pole: one then the other, in the soft parts of their bellies. They keeled over but came back up, so she poled them again, and they came back up again, like buoys bobbing in the sea. This left her no choice but to keep going, caning, staving, which they seemed to enjoy, for they were laughing like the plaster cherubs that decorated the foyer ceiling. When finally they fell and did not come back up, in the places where their bodies struck the carpet, bursts of colour were thrown up, and everything turned cloudy.

When the dust cleared, she saw Stewie gagging them with

underpants; then she saw Joshua pulling them away towards the toilet; then she saw the pole lying broken on the floor.

What matter?

The cameraman followed Stewie and Joshua to the toilet. When Joshua opened the toilet door with his back and dragged the audience members after him, the cameraman stuck his camera inside to capture the interior view. That done, he came running back to Eva. Jammed the camera into her face.

—You're hurting people, he said. Why? Why are you doing this? What can you possibly hope to achieve?

Eva could see her own image mirrored in the lens, but upside down. She thought about what would happen if she and the cameraman were to change places. Then he would be her image, and she instead would be real.

Done with this, Eva pushed the camera away. She felt her eyes go fuzzy and saw rainbows in the room, light breaking apart into hundreds of glittering particles. Then her vision returned with double clarity, and she could see the beauty that lived on the surface of ordinary things. The pomegranates on the wallpaper, for instance: they were dropping from their branches and breaking on the ground, their juices oozing out. Red, blood red. Lakes and lakes of it, a red so pure, so genuine, it seemed extracted from the centre of the earth, and so deep, besides, that the other Wherehouse members were wading around in it, the children splashing and swimming, everyone in a daze of pleasure. The cameraman had wandered off, which was a pity because Eva had just thought of something really interesting to say: *about red, the colour red, redness.*

She opened the central auditorium door for a second time. Bad smells came rushing out. Feet and mould and gin. Then, overlaying that, lavender. Spiced wine. Cloves. The smells had significance, as did the sounds, which were like echoes. On the stage, her mother was saying:

—*I know these people, and I love them, as I know they love me. Let them come here, and I'll prove it to you.*

To which Eric Humphries was saying:

—*No, Miss Julie, they don't love you. They take your food, but once you've turned your back they spit at you. Believe me!*

It was almost time to go in.

Eva closed the door and called the Wherehouse members to her by whistling through her teeth and beckoning with her arms.

—It's our moment, she said. Organise the children.

The collective got to work picking the children off the ground, and pulling their trousers up, and getting the lanterns back into their hands. Barbara tried to assuage the crying ones with kind words; Álvaro's approach was to take them by the shoulders and shake them:

—Shut up! Shut the fuck up!

Eva empathised with him. In a way she hated these children too. Their useless little lives, which she thought ought to be swept away. There could never be a movement that belonged to them. But right now they had their purpose. She needed the monkeys to disrupt the palace.

The procession, divided into three, made its way down the aisles towards the stage. The children, though they were walking on dry carpet and breathing in smoky air, appeared to believe themselves to be underwater, drowning, for they were staggering about making swimming motions. The surviving lanterns hovered around them, a mad dance of golden lights, like comets spinning around each other. The light picked out faces in the audience and made them brighter by making everything else darker. Amid the sadness and spiritual blackness and depression, a pair of eyes would catch fire, and that person — Eva saw — would have the sensation of being alive for a brief moment. He would hear noises in his ears and feel tremors in his hands and feet. His insides would turn right over. He would become conscious of a desire to stand up and call out. To stamp his feet. To say, *No! This cannot be! I object!* But then the light would pass on, the sensation would end, and he would be in the dark again, where he would oblige himself to scorn what he had just felt, in order to reduce its terrifying power, its strange mystery, wherein he would be lost.

The procession reached the stage having been subject to little else than silence from the crowd; the few hisses and groans that did reach them merely worked to emphasise the volume and density of what was unexpressed. Eva helped the younger children onto the stage, then climbed up herself, feeling an irresistible urge to assault the audience, to fight every one of those people: her words and her body against theirs, until they had learned to put aside practicality and reasonableness and any notion of measure; until at last they learned to scream.

THE PEASANTS were chasing each other around the stage, incorporating parodies of classical ballet moves into their movements, stopping every so often to assume semi-pornographic poses in groups of twos and threes. Glen, Eggie, and Per did not hold back; they plunged straight into the melee, dancing about with THE PEASANTS, being vulgar and making a mess of the set. The children dropped their lanterns and sat down, or lay down, or rolled about; about half of them walked straight off into the wings. Rolo, Stewie, and Jay were overcome with a sense of absurdity, unable both to forget where they were and to remember why; they, too, disappeared offstage. Álvaro wandered around, taking his photos, apparently randomly, not always bringing the viewfinder to his eye but shooting from the level of his chest. As Barbara tried to unfurl the banner, she was shaking in an effort to keep control. She only managed to reveal half of the text — IT IS RIGHT — before becoming overly aware of the artificiality infused in her actions, rendering her incapable of bringing them to a conclusion. Joshua, who arrived at the stage last, having made a detour to the spot box to disable the lighting technician, was clapping his hands and shouting a slogan:

—*The East is red, the sun is rising, long live Mao Zedong; the East is red, the sun is—*

All of this: captured in closeup by the cameraman in the aisle directly below, and by the press photographers flashing pictures from the wings.

Eva was leaning on one of the kitchen counters that made up the scenery. Her limbs had gone cold and numb from below upwards. She had the vertiginous sensation of objects on stage — the cooker, the kettle, the Kenwood Chef, the pattern on the fake wall tiles — moving closer and further from her. There were spheres like little planets in her vision, and she was sure she was about to faint. She dropped the bell, creating a black chasm in the floor that spread outwards before collapsing back in on itself.

It was the lights, she thought. The lights were too hot. She had to get out from under them.

She looked into the wings stage left, and saw Iris: *No.*

Stage right, between the central flats, amongst the spinning and slumping Wherehouse members, was her mother: *Yes.*

It was cooler there, with her.

—Mama? Eva said, seeing now that the woman she had recognised as her mother really was her mother. *Mama, thank God. I don't feel well.*

Her mother looked pale herself.

—Don't worry, Mama, Eva said. It's nothing serious. I just feel queasy, like I'm coming down with a bug. Maybe you caught it too? Anyway I'm glad you're here. I hate to be alone when I'm ill.

In that instant, a shocking applause reached them from the house, rhythmic and taunting. Out of the noise sprang colours; colours louder than the noise from which they sprang. Explosions of sparks. Extreme blue. Yellow sizzling. Luminous bursts of black.

Eva threw off her helmet and closed her eyes and blocked her ears. She felt her mother's hand on her shoulder. *Oh Mama.* She rubbed her cheek against her mother's fingers as a request for her mother to rub her head like she used to when Eva was sick as a child.

—Maa—

Without warning the floor had begun to tilt, as if they were aboard a ship in rough waters. She grasped her mother's arm in order to steady herself.

—Mama! Mama!

She opened her eyes: her mother was the only unmovable thing in the world; everything else was losing its balance. To her right, Keith and Sunny were clinging to the flats to stay upright. Behind them, the other Wherehouse members were leaning forwards against the rising boards so as not to keel over. There were too many people here, Eva reasoned. That was the problem. Stupidly, like sheep, the entire collective had come off the stage into this wing, none of them had gone the other way, which had put too much weight onto one side, causing the imbalance.

To create some counterweight, she would have to take her mother across to the other wing, where only Iris and the second cameraman were. The stage had emptied out. THE PEASANTS had come off. Of the collective, only Glen, Eggie, Per, and a few children had stayed on, and they were now exhausted after their gambolling, and were sprawled about.

So the coast was clear.

Escape was by a straight line across the boards.

But wait. The lights. The lights were hot, burning. And her mother, who was famous for never wearing make-up on stage, would be unprotected. Eva wiped some black off her face and made to rub it on her mother's cheek. Her mother struck her hand away. Eva tried again: surely her mother understood that this was for her own good? This time, her mother caught her wrist and flung it back at her. Which, in itself, was perplexing, but then her mother made a solo lunge for the stage, a sort of kamikaze dive to the left, which was completely incomprehensible, and forced Eva to grab the back of her blouse to save her. *No.* What on earth was she thinking? *It's dangerous out there. You'll get scorched.*

Her mother struggled against her hold. Eva held on in spite of her mother's wild thrashings until the seam of the blouse tore, all the way from the underarm to the waist, creating a large aperture that revealed a white bodice underneath. The sound of the material ripping went to Eva's gums, right to the roots of her teeth. Wincing, she released her grip, and her mother stumbled forwards, tripped over her own left shoe as it came off, and landed on all fours centre stage.

At once, the world flattened out. The applause ceased. Eva sucked a breath in, as did the audience, and everyone held it; pulses pounded in a thousand necks.

—Help me! her mother said then and started crawling towards the stage edge. Someone please!

It was the lights, Eva thought. She needed to get out of the lights. Someone should help her. But who? Why was no one stepping in?

From the other wing, Iris — *oh praise little Iris* — came onstage. Raised a gun to the lighting rig. Shot out a lamp. The explosion produced a great quiet in Eva's mind; the raining metal and glass, a deep tranquillity. She did not think to think about why or how Iris came to possess a real gun. It was natural that she should have one, and that she should use it to help their mother, who was in such need. *You're a wonder, sis. An exception to everything. A true renegade. Work your magic. Get rid of this daylight in the night, so we can just be here without having to see so much.*

But, instead, Iris moved her aim away from the lighting rig, and — no stopping her now — put it on their mother.

Eva went cold.

Wait, she said mentally at her sister. *I see you. I can see what you're doing. Stop. Stop, I said. I won't let you do it again. I won't let you.*

Iris took a couple of steps in their mother's direction. The arm holding the gun was rigid, the hand steady. The other hand, however, was rubbing up and down her thigh, an old habit from childhood when her palms would sweat when she was excited. Eva remembered her doing the same thing on the opening night of The East Wind; the exact same motion with her hand, Iris had made, just before attacking Eva in the dressing room.

Rub, rub, rub, rub—

Their mother, from a crawl, rose up to a kneeling position, and raised an open palm as a shield. For a few moments they stayed in this pose — Iris poised to fire a stigmata right into her mother's hand — until their mother's arm tired and she lowered it. As she did so, she began to speak. And when she had finished speaking, Iris responded. Eva recognised the words they used. They were lines from *Miss Julie*. And suddenly she remembered: this was a happening. There was a plan. A script to follow. She had a role to play, she just could not remember which one. Who was she? *Who the hell am I?* Until that came back to her, she would be consigned to the sidelines, where all she would be able to do was watch.

On the opening night of *The Sing-Song Tribunal*, at the end of the first half when the famous applause had erupted, Eva came off stage and saw all the other actors hugging each other and expressing as-tonishment, and she thought, *Why are they so surprised? What were they expecting?* Eva did not wonder at the acclaim. Her performance had been brilliant. All she had ever needed, to bring her talent out, was the heat of the lamps and the pressure of a real crowd. Once she had stepped onto the boards and appeared in front of those people, she had become entirely herself. Strong and unafraid and generous, she had carried the whole cast on her back. The ovation — *how long until everyone saw?* — was for her, and it was nothing more than she deserved.

The other actors did not come over to her. Did not hug her or congratulate her. Did not say, *Wow, Eva, you really nailed it. We owe you this one.* The opposite, they ignored her. Looked over and past her, like she was a little child who was there only incidentally and not, as was the case, a central player, the lynchpin. The longer Eva stood there in the wings, waiting to be seen, the more invisible they made her feel, until she could take it no more and ran to the little toilet at the end of the dressing-room corridor and locked the door and sat on the bowl with the broken seat and wept.

—Mama, Mama, Mama, she said through her tears, Mama, Mama—

For her mother was the only person who would be able to make sense of these feelings.

She went down the corridor to her mother's dressing room. Her mother appeared happy to see Eva at the door, and waved her in, even though she had ordered her daughter to stay in the shared dressing room during the intermission. *It'll be an adult thing*, she had said to her. *Not suitable for you. I'll be busy talking to people and won't have time to look after you.*

—I thought I told you—

Her mother saw that her eyes were red and puffy.

—Have you been crying?

—No.

—It could be the mask, irritating you.

—I'm fine.

Eva's presence changed the configuration of the room. The pull which her mother had exerted on the gathering shifted to Eva. It was to her — the next generation, her mother's hope and despair in the flesh — that everyone now seemed to direct their personalities.

—Is that who I think it is?

—If it isn't the young Thurlow, the real star of the show.

—The last time I saw you, you were—

Standing beside her mother, Eva peered around quietly, evaluating the status and power relationships in the crowd; once she knew where in the hierarchy everyone fit, she would be able move into action and enter the exchanges which she believed would bring her most benefit.

—Are you going to follow in your mother's footsteps?

—A lot of pressure for someone so young.

—Was learning the lines hard? If only my kids had your discipline.

—And what did you think? Eva asked a man who had just congratulated her.

The man patted her shoulder, pretending not to have heard the question, and moved on.

Her mother put an arm around her waist and pulled her in.

—You don't ask people that, she whispered.

—Why not? Eva said.

—People will tell you what they think, if they feel like it. It's not polite to put them on the spot.

Eva flushed red.

Her mother kissed her on the side of the head:

—It's all right. These are things you'll learn.

Eva squirmed in her embrace. Her mother's hold tightened. This striving to create and share an emotional state was an imposition, and though it may have been in the service of an ideal — mother and daughter as intimates — it was no less violent for that; mother and daughter as inmates.

Framed by the doorway, watching them, was Iris.

—Oh God, said Eva.

—Shh, said her mother. Be nice to your sister.

Iris made her way through the bodies:

—Hi.

Eva fixed her shirt collar and touched her hair and bared her teeth:

—Pchs! What're you doing here? This is no place for a child, am I right, Mama?

Their mother could not answer because Edward Woddis had got her ear.

—Can't you just piss off and stay off, for once? said Eva.

—I just came to give you these, Iris said.

To Eva, Iris gave a card that she had made herself. On the front she had drawn a picture of a leg in a cast and underneath had written, *Break a leg!* Iris would later claim not to remember making this card, but Eva kept the evidence and there was no arguing with that. Eva opened it suspiciously and read the message inside.

—Why do you bother? she said, dropping it onto the dressing table.

—This is for you, Iris said to their mother, handing her the doll she had been making during rehearsals.

Now finished, the doll was dressed in bright red robes, similar to THE JUDGE's robes their mother wore in the play, and had a yellow star stitched onto the front, its five points touchingly uneven in length. Iris would later claim that she remembered making the doll but not giving it to their mother.

—Really? You're giving me this? You've spent so much time making it, are you sure you don't want to keep it for yourself? For your room?

—No. I want you to have it. It's you, don't you see?

—It's me? It doesn't look like me. Does the star on the front mean that I'm a star?

Iris shrugged:

—If you like.

Their mother turned the doll over. On the back, the letters M and A and O had been sown.

—That's her name, said Iris.

—I thought you said it was me.

—It is you. In costume.

Eva, feeling like she had been brought into the open against her will, scanned the nearby faces to ascertain if they were watching.

After that, their mother sent Eva away with Iris. Eva took her sister to the communal dressing room, which was where Iris did what she did. Eva would never believe that Iris did not remember it. Eva remembered everything about the incident, she could recall each of Iris's actions — *rub, rub, rub, rub* — for which Iris herself appeared totally conscious. There was nothing in Iris's behaviour to suggest she was absent or in an altered state. Iris tricked her into playing a game, then brutalised her, abused her, and everything Eva now felt about this was justified. There was no grey area. The lines dividing right and wrong were clear-cut and visible; they could never be rubbed out. Eva was the victim, she had a right to feel aggrieved, she had grounds for it, she would never let anyone take that away from her.

Less clear were the events that took place on stage while she was tied up in the dressing room. At different times over the coming years, it would be described to her by many people — there were so many witnesses, looking from so many angles — but she would never quite succeed in wrapping her head around it. Not through any naivety on her part, but rather because the incident in itself was inexplicable. What her mother did, what Iris did, both: beyond understanding.

—What exactly happened?

Eventually she would pluck up the courage to ask her mother. And her mother, then, as if she had been waiting a long time to be asked, would tell her, from her point of view. And Eva would listen and accept the truth of what she heard and would never ask to hear it again. For Eva had already decided that her own version of events would be that which her mother chose to give her.

When the dressing room emptied out, Alissa locked the door and vomited into the bucket in the corner. Then she dressed and went to wait for Doris at the props table, as rehearsed.

Doris was late. Probably off in a room somewhere, washing Paul's prick with her cunt. Doris came in a state — her hair falling loose of its knot, her skin blotchy, her eyes wet — which suggested she had, in fact, been off washing Paul's prick with her cunt. Then it was not funny any more.

—Shall we?

She followed Doris through the corridors towards front of house. Doris was charged with carrying the lantern to the foyer, but she proved incapable of opening the doors at the same time. She kept knocking the lantern against the walls or dropping the pole or letting the doors slam. It was like something from *Laurel and Hardy*. Alissa ended up having to assist *her*.

In the bar, seeing Simon wink and leer at Doris was too sickening. When, at the auditorium door, Doris began to tug and drag at the back of Alissa's robes, in a way that left Alissa feeling molested, she snapped:

—Can you just stop that?

—Sorry, Doris said too late.

—Don't be sorry, just be a little delicate. You're not saddling a racehorse.

Doris let the robes fall loose. Came to stand in front. Took hold of the doorknob, preparing to pull it open.

—That's right, said Alissa. Do the door.

Alissa felt unexpectedly tense. She recognised these nerves: they were those of the marksman who had hit the target with her first shot but was afraid she would not get the bull's eye again, now that her audience were assuming triumph.

She examined Doris's face, trying, one final time, to see the girl through Paul's eyes. Max had been wrong in his letter: Alissa would not let Paul go so willingly. She would not leave Paul to this girl. Doris would not be staying. She would be gone tonight. Alissa would make sure of it.

Hearing the audience quieten, Alissa made some final adjustments for her entrance.

Then, before opening the door, Doris looked Alissa straight in the eye and said:

—I ain't afraid, you know, Alissa. With Paul or without Paul, I'm ready. Whatever comes next is welcome, even if I don't trust it. Even if I hate it.

Making not to have heard, Alissa stepped past the girl and into the auditorium.

The lights were down. The stage was dark. Alissa heard the door close behind her, and there was a long moment, before the audience realised she was there, when nothing was happening in the world. No spectators, no spectating. No performer, no performance. Empty, abandoned time. During which Alissa made the mistake of reflecting on the appalling difficulty of being an actress. If truly practised, the hardest art of all. With Doris's parting words swirling in her mind, she asked herself the terrible question:

Am I ready for what comes next?

The people in the back rows had begun to notice her. Their murmuring caught the attention of those seated in the middle, who turned round to look. The shiftings of these, in turn, caused the heads in the front to crane round. The connection had been made.

As an opening-night gimmick, Doris had handed out cheap paper fans to people as they arrived. Many in the audience were now using these fans to beat the air in front of their faces. In the lantern's red-orange glow, the fans were as flames in a blaze, animated by an alternating breeze, now from the east, now from the west, gust after gust, wave upon wave, tension and relief, producing in Alissa's ear a rhythmic pulse — *wha-wha, wha-wha* — to which she now began to sing in time.

In Max's original script, THE JUDGE's song had had lyrics, but in rehearsals, inspired by the Eastern setting, Alissa had stripped the words out and replaced them with repetitive, meaningless sounds like mantras. Chanting now in an arrangement of her own invention, she climbed onstage using the temporary steps stage right. She crossed the boards from the exterior space on that side to the central terrace. There, she fixed the lantern on a hook outside the house façade. A red overhead lamp came on, which gave the impression of a pool of light coming from the onstage lantern, illuminating only centre stage and the objects immediately adjacent to it. Crossed spots, dimly lit, bathed Alissa in what resembled moonlight. Without a mask to cover it — hers was the only character in the play not to wear one — her face shone white. Bare of any make-up, just a thin layer of baby lotion to make it gleam, her skin showed all of its creases and contours. She knew the disadvantage of this, how it made her appear uglier than she was, perhaps even a little ill, but she also knew that a clear visage was necessary to make the expressions she wanted to make, the countenances that were disappearing from the West and in search of which they had gone all the way to China: the knitted face of sadness, the lifted mouth of happiness, the tightened eyelids of anger, the wide-open mouth of surprise, the downward lips of disgust, the frozen stare of rebellion.

She came downstage, stopping close to the edge. In the haze of the stalls, she picked out the little red point of Paul's cine-camera, and orientated herself towards this, her hips facing the wings, her torso twisted so that her chest and shoulders looked out, with the result that everyone was lured into her song.

Behold THE JUDGE. The god-figure, the all-knowing narrator, the representative of authority and tradition, the spokesman for capitalism and empire; ever-present on stage, plunging in and out of scenes, sometimes interacting directly with the other characters, other times passing judgement on them from the periphery; endowed with the finest soliloquies and the most elegant poetry; blessed with a few good gags besides: unquestionably the most important role in the play. And, lest there be any doubt about it, she was playing him.

She brought the chant to a close by pulling it down into her diaphragm until it wheezed away. A pause. A long intake of breath. Then, thrown into the deep silence:

—*Be upstanding!*

The audience stayed pinned to their seats, the revolution postponed for another night.

—*Court rise. All persons having any business with the court, draw near and give your attendance.*

So began THE JUDGE's monologue. The lengthiest and most involved speech in the play. Without any breaks of voice, she started her ascent to the upper platform. As she went up the ladder, the lights of the Shanghai streetscape turned on, and the signs and advertisements began to flash. From the wings there was an explosion of drums: the heavenly court was in session, and the gods were angry. Reaching the top — she did not pause her speech even to catch her breath — she crossed the boards and went behind THE JUDGE's bench. She did not sit in the throne, but stayed on her feet, her arms at forty-five degrees to her torso, her fingertips leaning on the bench surface. This stance gave her robes volume. The tresses of her full-bottom wig hung down over her breasts, concealing them. In her bearing, the dignity that came from being part of something remote and grand.

Auditorium: one.

Stage: two.

Platform: three.

This was the third phase of her entrance. Yet she felt like she was just now emerging from a sealed room and rubbing the dark from her eyes. Looking out, looking around, looking down, a boundless view, the auditorium seemed her estate. From here, she had an unobstructed panorama of all she had accomplished. Like a man she could survey, with one inclusive glance, the house she had built using the planned designs of a woman's mind. The emotion of this made her voice crack, giving her a terrible fright. Frantically, she sought to untie the muscles in her throat. A second later, her speech returned, high-struck and powerful, bringing with it a feeling of great relief.

The audience were in the palm of her hands.

—*A civilised society*, she said, *is one that punishes, not to harm a person, but to prevent further harm.*

This was Eva's cue to enter.

But Eva was not entering.

Until this moment, Alissa's awareness had had no focus, but was dispersed around the house; now it zoomed in on the spot where Eva was supposed to emerge from the wings. Alissa recited a couple more lines, in case that might goad her daughter out, but, no, she was not coming. In the opposite wing, William was waiting, Eva's entrance being his own cue to go on. He glanced up at Alissa and gave a little shake of his head, and Alissa understood then — this was the foreboding she had — that the problem was not that Eva was late; the problem was she would not be appearing at all.

And there was more. Prior to this foresight, in an even obscurer part of her mind, she foresaw that Iris was going to appear in Eva's place. So when Iris did in fact appear — *of course, here she is now, wearing Eva's mask, of course, of course* — Alissa experienced it as a déjà vu. She had seen this scene before. She had always known it was going to happen this way.

Thus forewarned, Alissa did not flinch. Did not drop a word or skip a line. Did not allow herself to speculate about what had happened backstage, nor to give in to anger or the desire to reprimand. Rather, she maintained a fierce calm, and put her absolute trust in Iris that she would succeed in playing the part of the young LIXIN as her own.

William, maskless but dressed in a traditional Chinese woman's *cheongsam*, now entered from the other wing, and Iris met him downstage, and they began to sing and then to dance. This was the meeting of the young LIXIN with the adult LIXIN. The lyrics of the song mimicked those of a love ballad, as the adult seduced the youth into maturity. The dance was a sort of foxtrot, an alteration of slow and quick steps, at the core of which were the adult LIXIN's attempts to entice the young LIXIN to part with her mask.

William adjusted quickly to Iris's presence. He integrated her seamlessly into his actions. With Eva, he had had to play forcefully in order to overcome her hamming: her tosses and jerks, her unnecessary poses and bizarre attitudes, the fire she tried to breathe into even minor sentences. But with Iris, now, there was no fighting. Even masked, she had a translucently thin skin; he could see her feelings and could sense in advance the direction they were taking her, which made reacting to them require less effort. Through the eyeholes of her mask, there radiated an energy that even Alissa, high up on her platform, could feel as a physical heat.

Alissa put an end to the dance by summoning William and Iris up to her court. As they climbed up the ladders, Alissa reprised their song, changing the words to a warning:

—*The young cede to the old, but be warned, the young get their own back in the end.*

From the wings, the rest of the cast came on and filled the stage below, humming softly and dancing in loose formation.

Once on the top of the platform, William and Iris came to kneel in front of Alissa, as before a statue on an altar. Alissa came out from behind the bench and placed herself between the two. She rested a hand on the crown of Iris's head:

—*Do you, Lixin, in the fear of the Lord, and before this assembly, agree to become an adult member of our free-earning society, and to make every human effort to preserve its ways?*

—*I do*, said Iris.

—*Do you promise, through divine assistance, to be unto capitalism a loving and faithful servant, productive and full time, until it shall please the Lord by death to separate you?*

—*I do.*

—*Do you accept capitalism as the natural state of affairs in the world, to have and to have not, for better for worse, for richer for poorer, in sickness and in health, to love and to cherish, according to God's holy ordinance?*

—

Alissa tightened the grip on Iris's scalp as a signal to the girl that she should answer. William, without turning his bowed head, peered at Iris out of the corner of his eyes. The third *I do* was the cue for Iris to take the mask off and give it to William: the symbolic passing of responsibility for LIXIN's life. But Iris was stuck. Dumb. Inert. Rigid.

Iris used to say that, when a fit was coming on, she would sense bad smells like rotting meat. Well, now filling Alissa's nostrils was the stench of smoke and gas and melting rubber, as if somewhere unseen, in the blank place where Iris's mind had gone, the fires of revolution had been lit.

From nothing, the little finger on Iris's left hand began to quiver, almost imperceptibly. Then her head swung sharply to the right, and both her arms flew up. Then she keeled over onto her back, where her body began to writhe, her limbs to throw punches and kicks at an invisible enemy. A wet patch formed in the crotch of her costume. Her bones slapped and slammed on the boards. Her neck twisted one way and then the other, causing her head to thrash violently from left to right, as if being repeatedly struck. From behind the mask, a guttural sound came, very old and very deep, like a primeval hymn.

In future years, when Iris would come to review the cine-film of this scene, she would conclude that Alissa had had a choice in that moment. Alissa could have stopped the performance. She could have cushioned Iris's head. Or held her legs in case she fell over the platform edge. Or put something between her teeth to stop her from biting her tongue. Or called out, *Is there a doctor in the house?* It had been in Alissa's power to help. What could possibly have been more important?

But, to Alissa, it did not feel like she had a choice. Or rather, the choice she appeared to have, had in fact been made long before. Duty's pendulum swung away once more, and Alissa accepted that her daughter was separate from her, an autonomous being. Iris had made her own decision to be here, on this stage. Regardless of the wisdom of that decision, Alissa was not going to try to save her from it. Instead she was going to ensure that it was a decision not made in vain.

Without hesitating, she came to stand over Iris, stepped across the girl's flailing body so as to plant her feet on either side. Her robes shrouded Iris's hips and legs; when Iris kicked up, the red material swished and wafted and flapped.

Now Alissa bent over and caught hold of Iris's rocking skull. Gripping the front of the mask, she pulled Iris's head towards her so that she could reach the ties at the back. Keeping the head lifted with one hand, she untied the mask with the other. When the mask came free, Iris's head fell back onto the boards with a load bang. Uncovered, Iris's face had the look of someone involved in a desperate struggle against something. Her eyes were rolled upwards, the whites exposed. Her jaw was clenched. She was gritting and grinding her teeth. From the corners of her mouth, white foam spewed. To all appearances, she was trying to speak. On her contorted lips: the words she had never spoken, but one day would.

Alissa stepped away from Iris and lifted the mask into the air, its painted front facing out.

The audience — Alissa imagined — were stunned. Nothing like it had ever been seen on the London stage. From this moment on, everything that occurred in the play they would accept as part of a great work, a masterpiece. *There'll be three hundred performances.* How could it be otherwise?

Alissa made three circles in the air with the mask, as if purifying the space with it. Then turning to William, she said:

—*Because you have made vows before God and these witnesses; because you have pledged your commitment to the capitalist way and have declared the same by accepting this mask, I now pronounce you money-earner and whore. What God has joined men must not divide.*

She fixed the mask to his face, and, with Iris still convulsing on the floor, played out the remainder of the scene.

—*There, you see!*

On the London Carlton stage, Iris was speaking to their mother using lines from *Miss Julie*. JEAN's words.

—*Do you think you can possibly stay here now?*

—*No—*

Their mother was responding as MISS JULIE.

—*I don't. But what can we do?*

Iris moved downstage, took a chair from under the table, turned it round to face their mother, and sat in it. She leaned forward and rested an elbow on her thigh and cupped her left hand over her right so that both were holding the gun; this way, her entire body was orientated towards the weapon; she appeared intended for it, answerable to its needs.

—*We could go away*, she said. *Travel. Far away from here.*

—*Travel?*

Their mother got to her feet. Threw off her right shoe so that she was barefoot. Wiped the wet from her eyes. Sucked in the mucus from her nose. In order to hold closed the rip in her blouse, she was forced to cross an arm awkwardly across her body.

—*All right, but where?*

—*To Switzerland. To the Italian lakes. Have you ever been there?*

—*No.*

Eva was finding it hard to watch. When she focused on a point, on Iris's face, say, or on the gun, everything swirled around it. When she shifted her gaze to another point, her mother's torn blouse or her laddered stockings, everything then swirled around that.

—*Is it beautiful there?* their mother said, daring to take a step towards Iris.

—*An eternal summer*, said Iris. *Oranges, laurel trees.*

From their mother, another step:

—*But what shall we do there?*

—*I'll start a hotel. De luxe. For de luxe people.*

—*Hotel?*

—*That's a life, believe me. New faces all the time, new languages. Never a minute for worry or nerves, or wondering what to do. Yes, that's the life.*

—*Sounds exciting, but*—

Their mother took another step so that she was now touching distance from Iris. Iris leapt up with a force that sent the chair falling back and waved the gun in the air as an order for their mother to get back. Their mother recoiled; dashed back as far as the wing. Iris, keeping the gun aimed at their mother, set the chair upright. Then she sat on the table and put her feet on the chair as a stool. Visibly happier at this new altitude, she rested the gun on her knee, held it loosely in one hand, a more casual attitude than before: *I would prefer not to have to use one of these*, it seemed to say, *but circumstances have called me to it.*

—*You shall be the mistress of our hotel*, she said, *the pearl of the establishment. With your looks, your style, we'll be made.*

—*Sounds wonderful*, their mother said. *But, Jean, you must give me courage. Tell me you love me. Come and kiss me.*

—*I'd like to kiss you*, said Iris. *But I daren't. Not in this house. I do love you, though. Can you doubt that Miss Julie?*

—*Miss?* said their mother. *Call me Julie. There are no barriers between us now.*

—*I can't call you that. There are still barriers between us. There will always be. As long as we're in this house.*

The words, now, began to turn around in Eva's ears, the pattern of sounds dissolving and reassembling, speeding up then slowing down, as if someone had their finger on the vinyl.

—*Above all*, Iris said, *no emotional scenes, or it'll be all up with us. We must think this over coolly, like sensible people.*

Their mother had given up holding closed the tear in her blouse, so it hung down, revealing a roll of flesh above where the wire of the bodice dug in.

—*My God. Have you no feelings?*

—*Me? No one has more feelings than me. But I can control them.*

—*Don't speak harshly to me.*

—*I'm not speaking harshly. I'm talking sense.*

Iris got down from the table and cupped their mother's cheek with her hand with apparent fondness. Abruptly Iris swiped her arm to the right, using their mother's head as a lever to push her down to a kneel. Then she used the tip of her boot to knock her onto her side.

During this short sequence of actions, it was impossible to tell if Iris was in character or not. She did not try to make her gestures distinct. She moved quietly, in a way that was at odds with the idea of performance as a discrete event. It hurt Eva to witness it. This was an actress, a natural talent, functioning at the highest level. And it was also her sister. Iris. Who had received not a single day of training. Who had never been re-educated, as Eva had, to walk and sit and look and talk before a public. Who, through some secret method of auto-correction, in communion with her own reflection only, had learned to play herself with accuracy and ease. Watching her now, Eva experienced a despair that would have been inconceivable in any other situation. Hell was up on earth and had engulfed her. To escape these few seconds of anguish, she would have given away years of her life. All the work she had put into her craft, all the struggle, had been a waste. She was a fake. A fraud. Her being in this theatre at this moment, her very existence, was unwarranted. By rights, she should just wither away.

—*Is there anyone on this earth as miserable as me?* their mother said from her position on the ground.

Iris scoffed:

—*Why should you be miserable? Think of Christine in there.*

She pointed into the wings at Eva. This made Eva jump. *Christine? Yes, that's it. JEAN's fiancée, CHRISTINE is who I am.* A vague memory flashed in her mind of learning the lines, the process of it, but she could not recall the words themselves. She knew who she was supposed to be, but did not know what to say, as herself. Which was awful.

—*Don't you suppose Christine has feelings too?*

—*Oh God in Heaven*, said their mother, *end my miserable life. Save me from this mire into which I'm sinking. Save me.*

—*I can't deny I feel sorry for you*, said Iris.

Iris made a sudden dash across the stage. Reached down and grabbed their mother's string of pearls.

—*Servant, lackey, stand up when I speak!*

Iris tugged on the pearls, as if to pull their mother to her feet.

Their mother resisted by going limp and allowing her neck to be yanked up and her head to fall backwards.

At this point, a man from the audience invaded the stage from the front:

—This has got to stop! If no one else is going to put an end to this, I will!

Eliciting screams from the audience, Iris raised the gun and aimed it at the man. She did this without releasing her grip on their mother's pearls, so she now had both arms outstretched, her mother on one end, her weapon and its target on the other. In the wings, the photographer's camera flashed wildly.

—You can put that down, the audience member said. You don't scare me.

With her neck wrenched, their mother's veins had popped out and her skin had turned puce; she could barely turn her head.

—It's all right, sir, she said, coming off script for the first time. Go back to your seat, I'm fine.

A second audience member, who had attempted to leave the theatre, shouted from the aisle:

—They've locked the doors, but everyone stay calm, the police will be on their way.

A third spectator:

—Come down from there, mister, no need to play hero. Let the authorities handle it.

The man on stage hesitated, until their mother said to him:

—You're a gentleman, and I thank you. But I lied when I said I don't know who these people are. This is my daughter. I don't know why she is doing this, but I do know that if I do everything as she says, she will not hurt anyone. Please sit down.

Once the man had left the stage, Iris jerked her arm to snap the necklace. Released, their mother reeled back. Her hand flew to her throat to massage it. The pearls, their mother's own, hailed onto the countertop, then the floor.

Glen, who was crouching nearby, said:

—Aw, man, gorgeous things!

And chased after them as they bounced and rolled in various directions.

—*Servant's whore*, Iris said then, returning to *Miss Julie*. *Lackey's bitch. You dare to order people around? Not one of my class ever behaved the way you've done in your life.*

—*You're right*, said their mother. *Hit me. Trample on me. I deserve nothing better.*

—*It hurts to see you sunk so low. To find that deep down you are a kitchen slut. It hurts me, like seeing autumn flowers whipped into tatters by the rain and trodden into the mud.*

—*You speak as though you were already above me.*

—*I am.*

Iris indicated to the comatose children, and to giggling Glen, and to wide-eyed Eggie.

—We are.

Iris was now deviating from the script, but their mother was not put off by this. She took up where Iris left off. Responded to Iris's additions with the same spontaneity that she summoned for the rehearsed text. She herself did not diverge.

—*You're a thief*, Alissa said. *That's something I'm not.*

—I'm not a thief, said Iris. We're not thieves. We don't want anyone's money. We just want justice. We want you to admit your faults and be punished for them. It's a matter of fairness.

—*Are you sure about that?*

—Yes. You are old, we are young. Your time is up. You might as well give in.

—*You won't win me over like that.*

—How, then?

—*How? I don't know. There is no way.*

—Because you hate us.

—*I detest you as I detest rats, but I can't run away from you.*

—Join us, then.

—*Join you? Oh God. I'm tired. So tired.*

Their mother came to sit with her legs bent to one side. She pulled a chair towards her to use as a ledge on which to lean her torso. Crossed her arms over the seat of the chair and rested her forehead on top of her arms.

Iris loomed over her, peered down at her with beady-eyed intentness, as though surveying an injured hare whose beauty meant nothing, only her pain, for that would bring the rewards.

—And me? said Iris. Do you hate me?

—*I'd like to shoot you like an animal*, said their mother, lifting her face to the auditorium.

—*But you've got nothing to shoot with*, said Iris, shaking the gun in her face. *What are you going to do?*

With that, their mother broke. Pushed the chair away, causing it to fall loudly onto its back. The brutal treatment of props and furniture was, for her, the behaviour of an amateur, it showed a lack of delicacy and restraint. She was moving off script.

—This a fascist scene. Do you realise you've become fascists?

Iris laughed a cruel laugh:

—Listen to you. You had your time, now you think no one else should have theirs. You failed.

—Is this your revolution? If so, it's barely worth the name. It'll last a day and be dead tomorrow.

—Maybe so. But today is our day. It's only right that we live up to it. If we can bring about equality for one day, at least we'll have proved it's possible.

—You'll soon tire of your so-called equals, child, and of this madness. Talented people always rebel against equality. The winner is the person who comes first and establishes order.

—You failed to be great, so now all you want is order, order, order. You think there's no room in this world for greatness. For astounding deeds. For dreams to be achieved.

—Dreams? Are we in your dream now? What astounding deed do you want achieved here? That we torment each other to death, is that it?

—Does the violence frighten you?

—Not even remotely.

Iris jabbed a finger into their mother's upper arm with enough force to rock her. Their mother stopped herself from falling sideways again by planting her right hand on the floor. With her left, she swatted away Iris's finger. Action and reaction, prod and parry, they had been rehearsing this ritual for years but were only performing it now for the first time.

—Why are you doing this? their mother said. What do you want?

—I want you to say sorry.

—Me?

—You.

—

—Just the one word: sorry. We'd take that.

—And then?

—Then you die.

—If you want me to die here, I'm game. Look what you've done to me. In front of these people whom I love. What else do I have to lose?

—No, not yet.

—When then? How long must this go on?

Their mother came onto all fours, then got to her feet, slowly, one leg, now the other. She fixed her skirt so that it sat below the knee once more.

Iris watched her through narrowed eyes:

—Don't forget the role you're playing.

Their mother brushed down the front of her blouse.

—You could start by speaking kindly to me, she said. Treating me like a human being.

—Act like one yourself then, said Iris. You demean us. You called us rats. I shit on you. Your whole soul is warped and soiled and ugly.

Their mother refolded her collar:

—All right. Help me then. Tell me what to do.

—*There's only one answer*, said Iris, *you must go away. At once. Far away.*

—With you?

—No. You're not one of us. You must go alone.

—*I'll only go if you come with me.* We're one. We're family.

—Family? Stop pretending we're the same.

—We are, at the end of the day.

—*Are you mad, woman?*

—Maybe I am.

Iris used the gun to gesture into the wings:

—This is our house now, not yours. You must leave.

—*I can't go. I can't stay. Help me. Order me. Make me do something. I can't think, I can't act.*

—*So now you see what a monster you are.*

—All right, yes.

Iris turned the gun round so that its handle was facing out, then offered it to their mother:

—*You people, you think you've seen and done it all. You prink yourselves up and stick your noses in the air as though you were the lords of creation, but really you're nothing. You want an order? I'll give you an order.* Take the gun and go to your dressing room. Get dressed. Make yourself nice. Then shoot yourself.

—Fine. If you come with me.

—With you? You crazy bitch.

—*Speak kindly to me.*

—*An order always sounds unkind. Now you know how it feels.*

Their mother took the gun.

—*Do it!* said Iris. *Go!*

Their mother walked firmly offstage.

A detached observer, Eva had nevertheless felt entangled in the performance. She had played the punisher, too, and taken pleasure in the pain of it. Having her mother back in the wings was like a reconciliation. There were tears in her mother's eyes.

—You're crying, Mama, Eva said.

—It's just crying, her mother said.

There was nothing stopping her mother from leaving the wings and going backstage. No one was blocking her way any more. Sunny had gone to sit on the ground and pet the skin and hair of anyone who came near him. Keith was looking after the children, making sure they did not harm themselves with props or on sharp corners. Her mother's path was free. She could simply walk away. Instead she stayed and presented the gun to Eva: its handle in her right hand, its barrel and its shaft lying across the open palm of her left, half an offering, half an exhibition.

What now?

Eva thought this behaviour curious. Had they rehearsed this? Was she supposed to do something in particular? Eva did not know what to think. She had that state of mind where the absurdity of things and their plainness, their horror and their insignificance, were visible at the same time.

Then it came back to her: the plan. The public trial. The tribunal. Her mother, she who had given up the struggle, was to be struggled against. Made to plead in front of the people and forced to bow in an acknowledgment of guilt.

Eva looked onto the stage. The set was a mess. Props were scattered about. Furniture was overturned. Four children remained lying on the floor. Glen and Eggie were sitting against the backdrop, flapping their arms and flipping their fingers in the air.

Iris was standing centre stage, where she had a direct view of Eva and their mother in the wings; her head was tilted, her hip cocked, in anticipation of the next round.

The cameramen were filming Iris from two different angles: one at thirty degrees to the left, the other at forty-five degrees to the right.

In the darkness of the auditorium, figures moved about. The sound was that of a busy pub; no booing or heckling, just people talking loudly amongst themselves. On top of this, coming through the open auditorium doors, was the bang-bang-bang of the main door being barged in. And beyond that again, the faint nee-naw of police sirens.

It was all wrong. Eva's inside was all wrong, just as the outside was all wrong; there had to be a correlation. This illness she was feeling, had she caused it herself? Something chemical in her, an old poison released? A madness of the eye which had travelled to the mind and made it extravagant? She looked back into the wings, where the other Wherehouse members were lying about like hospital patients, as ill as she was. All of this was her fault. She had infected them, and together they had created this mayhem. She turned back to the stage. Haloing the scene now was a luminous circle of diverse colour. Weaving through space were rays of crystal white, crossing and recrossing, making exquisite patterns. *I must not see this. I must not think of this.*

But then the thought hit her: she had been drugged. Iris had laced their food or spiked their drink. What was happening was, she was tripping. Everyone was.

Incensed — an instantaneous jump from stupefaction to rage — she grabbed the gun out of her mother's hand.

—Give me that.

She walked forward to the frontier between onstage and off, the meeting of light and shadow. There, she froze. Overcome by the simple difficulty of coming on. It was all about fear — *I don't know if I can pull this off* — and the only way past it was to remind herself that events were not in her hands. She was dealing with someone else's words, someone else's actions more than her own. The not-owning of her actions was there from the start.

She stepped onto the stage with the gun held in both hands.

Let this be the play.

Iris welcomed her on with a warm smile.

—*What a mess*, Eva said, suddenly remembering CHRISTINE's lines. *What on earth have you been up to?*

—*It was Miss Julie*, said Iris, falling back into JEAN. *She brought the servants in. You must have been fast asleep. Didn't you hear anything?*

—*I slept like a log.*

Eva walked an arc — centre stage right, downstage, centre stage left — and Iris did the same in the opposite direction, round the counter, and thus they began to circle each other like gladiators in a ring. Iris appeared entirely focussed, completely calm, whereas Eva, furious and at the same time morbidly aware of the presence of the audience, kept darting her eyes this way and that anticipating apparitions on the stage, suspecting enemies in the shadows, expecting mockery and contempt.

—*Dressed for church already?* said Iris.

—*You promised to come with me to Communion this morning,* said Eva.

—*Did I? What's the sermon today.*

—*Execution of John the Baptist, I expect.*

—*Oh God, that's a long one.*

Eva felt the heat of the lights on her face, and the corresponding drain from her veins. Her hands were wet where they held the gun.

To be on stage was to say to many people, *Look at me*, and there were indeed many of them, a wall of faces. She had the horrifying sense that if she paused at all they would start to clap again, or to laugh, so she gave herself little internal shoves, in an effort to keep herself going.

—*What have you been doing, up all night?* she said. *You're quite green in the face.*

—*Nothing*, said Iris. *Just sitting here. Talking to Miss Julie.*

—*She doesn't know what's right and proper, that one.*

—*It's strange, you know, when you think of it.*

—*It?*

—*Of her.*

—*What's strange?*

—*Everything. You aren't jealous of her, are you?*

Iris gave Eva a staring look as she said this. The brightness in it was shattering. This was God in the light of the eye, and at the same time it had a malevolent glint, which appeared to criticise Eva's performance. It seemed to say that Iris could do Eva's part, any part, better than her. It made clear that, as she played JEAN, Iris was imagining herself as CHRISTINE as well, identifying the things that she would do differently from Eva. Iris was probably not seeing Eva at all, but only her own reflection. Adjusting her performance not to Eva's decisions but to those taken by an image of herself.

Feeling abandoned, Eva started to falter. She found herself hanging in space without the slightest idea of what she was going to say next.

—Stop, she said.

The theatre stopped, the action ceased, and what was left were two women: just them all alone on the earth.

—What are you doing with your eyes? You're putting me off. Let's try it again, and don't do it this time.

Iris did not object to this interruption. Without shifting her pose even minimally, she waited for her new cue.

—*What a mess*, Eva said, restarting the scene.

This time they got only a few lines in, as far as *Execution of John the Baptist*, before Eva halted the action again.

—I don't know why you can't just look at me, she said. Is there something that's keeping you from looking at me, just that?

They began again. This time Eva merely fed her lines to Iris in a monotone, while Iris played her part to the full. Eva prowled around Iris, at a distance, taking her in, making sense of her. Dissecting her in front of her.

—Stop pulling faces, she said.

And Iris altered herself according to her instruction.

—You're telling us too much.

And Iris agreed.

—Don't sell the words. Don't colour them.

And Iris obeyed.

—God, Iris, can't you invent anything? Haven't you got even the tiniest drop of imagination? You're being ponderous. Take a look at yourself. Where are you? Make an effort to make less effort. Wait, who told you to do that? Did I tell you to do that? Do as you're told.

Eva could not remember her mother ever praising her. Or even spending that much time with her. Iris had got most of their mother's attention. Criticising Iris was their mother's passion, to which Iris responded by suggesting impossible things to do — *I want to be a lorry driver, I want to go to Botswana* — which she knew her mother would shoot down. This made it seem like Iris had been forced to give up many dreams, but what was really happening was, Iris was seducing their mother, monopolising her, consuming all of her attention with increasingly outlandish fantasies, all the while preventing Eva from getting any of what she wanted; forcing Eva to beg.

—What do you think you are doing to yourself, Iris? Actually, all right, go ahead and pose if you want to. In fact, put your hand here like this. Bend your knees. Lift your leg. Pull your own hair. Drop down on your knees. Crawl on the floor. What are you doing with your face? Smack that look away. Harder. I said, harder.

When someone from the audience called out their own direction, Eva shouted back:

—Fuck off. Don't tell my little actress what to do.

From the foyer came the sound of glass smashing as the main door was broken in. A group of hecklers, no doubt waiting for this moment, shouted in unison:

—Saved at last!

And there was a hullaballoo.

Feeling a new sense of urgency, Eva approached Iris, who was crawling around on the floor, and fastened her hand round the back of her neck. She led her around like a dog for a few steps, then took her by the hair and led her around again, this time with Iris's face lifted up. From there, Eva pulled her up to a stand, and began to manipulate her body into a variety of awkward gestures. Iris submitted to this without dropping a single line. As Eva lifted her arms up, or bent her back over, or twisted her head and her torso in different directions, her voice climbed and plunged, widened and narrowed, burst out and collapsed in, but did not stop its flow.

—Have you no more to give? Eva shouted at her. Cut out ninety per cent. Now double it. Be more exacting. You needn't pretend you don't know what's coming next.

—Ohh! the crowd roared as Eva pitched a knee into Iris's stomach.

—Ohh! as she kicked Iris in the side, causing her to fall down onto her back.

Rearing over Iris's prone body, Eva drove her boot into Iris's ribs, then her thigh. Buried a fist into her stomach. Thumped her in the chest. Landed a blow with dreadful force on her chin, then repeated it, as though purposely falling on a bruise, simply for the cruelty of it. But in fact no real cruelty was taking place. Iris was collaborating with her according to the principle of victim control, whereby she who was on the receiving end was actually in command. When Eva smacked Iris, Eva herself was not initiating the action; the appearance of being struck was being created by Iris, while Eva was simply following her movements. When Eva used her free hand to take Iris by the throat, instead of squeezing, she was pulling her fingers outwards. Iris grabbed her wrist, in order to give the impression that she was trying to break her grip, but really she was pulling her hand towards her. It was Iris who was yanking the strings and Eva who was obeying.

—This is our Hall of Justice, Eva said. You're in the People's Court. Are you ready to confess?

—I've nothing to confess, Iris said.

—Don't give us that. Confess now and we'll be lenient.

Iris tried to speak again but Eva's grip on her neck prevented her. At least, that was the impression that Iris wanted to give.

—Speak up! said Eva. Make an honest confession! Say, *I'm to blame.*

—I'm to blame.

—You're only saying it.

—I *am* to blame.

—You want to play games, you little fuck? You've been accused, and now you must pay.

—What's my crime? Tell me. If I'm guilty, I'll admit to it.

Eva released Iris's neck by throwing it down. The back of Iris's skull struck the boards with a bang. Eva took a few paces stage right. In the foyer blue lights were flashing. People were pouring out of the auditorium and onto the street through the now open main door. Police officers with torches and guns were coming in this direction, shouting orders at the fleeing audience and at Eva onstage.

Eva turned back to Iris, who was sitting on the boards with her legs spread out in front of her and supported by both hands behind her. In that moment Eva felt a connection to Iris. Despite everything, she believed in their rapport. Iris was her sister. They were related as one breath was to another. *Same mind, same belief.*

—If you've done nothing wrong, said Eva, why would you be here?

—Just tell me, what have I done?

—You asked us here, to this theatre, so that we would eventually abuse you. You planned it this way, didn't you? We're following your directions. We're part of your stupid game. I can't believe we fell for it. The only reason we're on this stage is to help you make amends for your mistake.

—History will repeat itself if it's not properly judged.

—All right, so let's deal with the main charge first.

—What's that?

—Something you've got away with all your life. Something you've never been punished for. Now do you take the blame?

—For that night?

—For what night? Say it.

—I don't know what you want me to say. I was a child.

—All these years we've been making excuses for you. Blaming ourselves. But do you see that, in fact, it was all you?

—Some of it was me, but—

—Some? You destroyed everything. Single-handedly.

—All right, yes. I destroyed it all. But I also made everything you have today possible. Without me, none of you would be who you are, where you are. But if you really think I'm to blame for your failures, and all the problems you see, then go ahead. I won't stop you.

—So you consent?

Eva wiped her sweating brow with the back of her hand, the same one which held the gun. Metal flashed.

—Do whatever you want, said Iris.

—I want to fucking kill you.

—It's a terrible thing to kill. But all right. If you feel you have to, do it.

—You really want me to, don't you.

—What you want, I want too. I'm not going to fight you.

—That's not Zen, you know. That's just passivity. You make me sick.

—Imagine if somehow you could live life differently. If you could wake up and feel that you'd begun afresh. The past all forgotten. That's what you'd be giving me. The gift of reincarnation.

—You don't really belief that shit.

—It would be a relief. You'd be doing me, all of us, a favour. Maybe I don't exist at all anyway. Maybe I just think I do.

Now, with deliberate slowness, Iris unzipped the front of her boiler suit to reveal her chest.

That was first.

Then Eva raised the gun and aimed it there: at the triangle of stretched skin and protruding bone that met the beginnings of her sister's breasts.

That was second.

When observing one power meeting another power greater still, the order, as well as the direction, was important to know.

The next day, a photograph of Eva aiming the gun at Iris would appear in the *Guardian*. The photograph would show Eva standing to the right, black make-up smudged, her arm outstretched, the gun handle held in three fingers, her thumb on the hammer, her index finger on the trigger. Sitting on the floor to the left, about four paces away, would be Iris, her blackface mostly intact, her neck and chest bare, her eyes wide and staring straight into the barrel. In the background, out of focus, would be the auditorium, populated by blurry figures, including a cine-cameramen and a photographer and some police officers. At the edge of the image, behind Iris, Keith would be seen emerging from the wings, running, his knee drawn up to his waist, as if coming off a racing block. The headline above the accompanying article would read:

MAO CULT ASSAULTS WEST END THEATRE
THREE SHOTS FIRED, NINE INJURED

The following year, the same photograph would make it into the *World Press Photo Album*. It would be printed on page thirty-six, after the images of the Paris protests and the civil war in Nigeria and the Soviet invasion of Czechoslovakia, and alongside four other pictures from London: one of a children's march on Downing Street demanding more nursery schools, and three of violent clashes between police and anti-Vietnam protestors on Grosvenor Square. The caption underneath the photograph of Iris and Eva would read:

Mao means murder! A radical theatre collective causes a scene.

It would be Álvaro's photograph. Because Eva's thumb would

be seen on the hammer of the gun, and because the bodies in the background would have the appearance of being in motion, the image itself would look like one that had been quickly snapped in a moment of high confusion and tension. In fact, the photograph would be one of a series Álvaro would take of the same subject, in the same position, from slightly different angles. This would be possible because Eva would be frozen in that position for a long time, as much as a minute according to some reports. Álvaro had been in the wings, by his own admission high on LSD and unable to do anything productive, but when, in pursuit of a hallucination, he would happen to glance onto the stage, he would see Eva striking and holding that pose, and this would bring him to his senses. He would run on and begin to shoot, taking twelve pictures in all before Eva fired the gun. He would choose to send this particular photograph to the press because it would be the only one containing Keith. The other pictures would feel empty without the Negro. The story of Wherehouse would not be complete without his presence, rushing in. For, by a stroke of bad luck, he would be the one holding the gun when the police arrived, with the result that he would be treated more harshly on arrest than the others and charged with a greater offence.

Álvaro would believe the publication of his photograph signalled the beginning of his career as a press photographer. This would be his launch. His lucky break. A belief which would gain further power when Doris Lever would include the same photograph in her controversial show *Johanna's Got a Gun* at the Institute of Contemporary Arts in late sixty-eight. Álvaro would go to the opening, have his picture taken beside his own photo on the wall, and think, *This is it. The start of something.* Except it would turn out to be the end. Although his name would appear beside the photograph on the gallery wall, as well as in the coinciding brochure, the photograph itself would become associated with Doris, as did everything to do with Wherehouse and the assault on the London Carlton. Thanks to *Johanna*, those places, those events would become hers. Any memory that people had of them would originate in Doris's presentation of them and become bound up with Doris as an artist. It would be presumed she had orchestrated the entire happening, though she would never actually claim to have done so.

Álvaro would try to capitalise on this bit of exposure by trying to build a name for himself as a photographer of protest. For more than a year afterwards he would attend every demonstration in London, of every size, and every happening, of every kind, and shoot like a madman. None of these pictures would end up being published. He would mount a couple of shows, but these would be minor, attended mostly by relatives and friends, who would be his only clients. Far from the making of an artist, that year would be the destruction of an idealist by his contact with his own limitations, producing little more than frustration and disillusionment, and leading him to question the value of life and in the end to condemn it.

Eva's marriage to Álvaro the following year, though itself a success in the sense that it would last in time, would be in reality the joining of two failures: two disappointed people in ordinary nine-to-fives, who hated each other for not having succeeded, but who could not have lived with any success enjoyed by the other. More comfortable for them would be to share the conviction that their respective talents had never been recognised. The problem had never been that they lacked ability but would only ever be that the world was shallow and unread and terminally inclined to reward the wrong people for the wrong things. Their mother's continued celebrity as an actress, and Iris's lucrative new career as a shop owner — five branches of KYOTO FUTON open throughout the country by the time Thatcher was elected in seventy-nine — would merely be proof to them that success in the modern capitalist system had nothing to do with genius and was built on blind luck alone.

But it was a mistake for Eva — still in the London Carlton, pointing the gun at her sister — to go so far into the future. An actress must always live in the present. She must not foresee what she will do next, or what is going to happen to her. She must not anticipate. Anticipation caused stage fright.

Returning to the here and now, her thoughts came to a sudden halt. The images that had been racing though her head disappeared. Her mind temporarily disconnected from time, and she could see the smallest detail of everything around her.

On one side, the police, in exquisite costuming, mounting the stage.

On the other side, one beat ahead, Keith bursting from the wings.

In the shadows, their mother screaming.

The audience, those remaining, stamping their feet.

A camera flashing.

Her own finger on the trigger.

Iris, with her eyes, urging her on.

Everything was in place. Tinglings rushed up her vagina to her belly to her mouth. She knew where and what she was. There was but one tiny, impossible step she had to take. To take it, she was sure, was the most important thing on earth at that moment. So that she might respect herself, she had to be capable of this. Was there another route out? No, was the answer. She would do it even if she had to repent of it all her life afterwards. To right the wrong, it was necessary to exceed the proper limits. Her future greatness would be characterised by the extreme position she took now, and by the holding of that extremity for the duration of the act. It was immoral, yes, but then all great deeds, those which have remained and not been washed away, were. If the need arose, she would not only kill her sister, but herself as well. This was the conflict of right against right, in which both parties had to be ready to die.

Are you ready? Eva silently asked her sister.

Are you? Iris replied.

Eva felt the hand holding the gun inflate and deflate, as if breathing by and for itself. She saw Iris's eyes puff out and collapse also, as if they had lives of their own. It was wrong to say an actress found her character within herself, in isolation from others; the truth was, in order to find herself she had to go out of herself, into others. Eva, seeing her own likeness in the depths of Iris's consciousness, experienced a moment of panic. To be an actress was to be on trial all the time, and Iris was demanding the verdict. Eva had to act and make an end. Yet the stage fright would only subside once she had forgotten this responsibility.

You've brought this on yourself, Eva told her sister.

I'm of no consequence, Iris replied. *I'm nothing, except insomuch as I'm a part of you. Do it, so, for yourself.*

Film footage exists — it never made it onto the television, but it is there in the BBC archive, available for anyone curious enough to go looking for it — of the moment just before Eva fired the gun. In it, Keith is seen grabbing Eva's arm and lifting it up so that the gun is pointed above Iris's head. When the shot is fired, the image cuts away as the cameraman ducks down behind a seat. When it returns, Eva is bent backwards, as if she had just been thrown by an invisible force — the image quality is bad, but the front of her boiler suit looks to be drenched in piss — while Keith wrestles the gun from her hand. Then there is some more confusion, the image swinging left and right. When it settles again, Keith is being pinned to the ground by two police officers, the gun on the floor by his head.

No footage exists that answers the question of Eva's intentions in the moment she fired. Did she mean to shoot her sister? Or did she deliberately wait until Keith had moved her arm before pulling the trigger?

Ask Eva and she would say it did not matter. Sometimes she lived in a way she did not know why. She just did things and did not give meanings to them.

The play had played her, the happening had happened to her. They had all seen her. They had all watched. *What difference does it make?* What was important was, life had not been repeated.

THE
CLOSING

My dear Mao,

The month in which I am writing is May. The calendar of my daily conduct that hangs by my cell door, with my name and my so-called crimes printed on it, tells me that this is so. Summer has begun. In the garden the peonies are blooming, soon the lotus will come out and the air will be filled with its rich perfume, and by season's end I will have lain in prison for fifteen years.

That this time has passed slowly, and that its passing has impinged upon my health, is undeniable, but I have endured it, for I have been sensible with myself and have striven to be occupied. When I wake, often at an uncertain hour, I reach for one of your poems or a passage from your *Sayings* and read it over until the fearful ghosts which assail me have been driven away. I follow this with some Marx or some Lenin, which forces my thoughts to strenuous exercise, although I must say your writings are more powerful in this regard, a single sentence of yours surpasses a hundred of theirs.

In a place like this it is easy to be on bad terms with one's body and to allow it to degrade; I am determined to keep a close alliance with it. So as soon as I am out of bed, I spend at least twenty minutes at the sink, bathing my intimate parts and laving my face and gargling my throat. I will not wear dirty clothes, they must be aired and brushed and rubbed of any stains before they are put near me. And excuse what seems vain, but I do not need a special occasion in order to fix my hair and put a dab of perfume on my pulses; the ordinary day is occasion enough.

It is my responsibility, also, to keep the room in order, and I, the seventy-seven-year-old wife of China's Great Saviour, am not too proud to get down on my knees and wash the floor, as once I did as a girl in the country. When I am satisfied that I have reached all of the corners and that the dust has vanished (there is a daily check), I do an hour of *tai chi* with the hope that afterwards my bowels will move, though it is common that they defy me. Due to a lack of roughage in my diet, I am often crowded and have to strain; not infrequently I am required to unblock myself using my fingers and some soap.

As a kind of experiment with my suffering, they like to change the times of my meals, shifting them one hour this way or one hour that, or sometimes reversing the order entirely that I should dine at sunrise and breakfast at midnight, thereby preventing me from settling into a healthy human rhythm. It often happens therefore that I am deprived of lunch after my exercise, which is a terrible agony and leaves me no alternative except to lie down and replenish my energies with sleep instead. These forced, unnatural slumbers take away from my rest at night, and, filled as they are with wearisome iterations of my daytime visions, release me into the afternoon feeling heavy and out of humour. A successful evacuation can unburden me some, but I try again only if I am sure because repeated failure is likely to darken my mood further and lead to piles.

In the evenings I make my dolls. My normal output is one doll every three days, or about two per week. I calculate that I have produced over a thousand dolls since my arrest. I would like to think that all of these dolls have been distributed among the working families of Beijing, and that the children have been stirred by finding my initials embroidered on the inside of the little uniforms. But it is also possible that my dolls have been thrown into a warehouse to rot, or burned in pyres, or picked apart and their material given back to me for reassembling.

One never knows with these motherfuckers.

Last year, I took a hiatus from the dolls to write my memoirs. I had become sick of the public infamy, on which they take cruel pleasure in keeping me up to date, and wanted to correct the record once and for all. But when I sat down and looked back on my life, what I saw, it appals me to say, was only a shapeless mass. I found that, whilst I could foretell the future with some accuracy — a feat quite possible when one is informed on enough elements of the capitalist crap-heap which composes the present — the past was maddening to think upon; like a vast shroud, it seemed vague and distant, there was no saying how it really was.

Nevertheless, I was resolute. I decided I would not rest until I had recaptured the truth which I knew was there. My work was intense and orderly. I applied myself and became engrossed. I exerted every nerve in my act of remembering. And in the space of just a couple of weeks I managed to turn out fifty or sixty pages. But then, when I paused to revise, I found I was unhappy with my efforts. I have a passion for things which are done well, and I had to admit that I had failed in my account. To my dismay, I had given myself a life so special as to be unworthy of a Communist. I had depicted my experience as unique and for that reason valueless because it could not be reduced to the common experience of men.

So I destroyed everything. I tore the pages into tiny pieces and flushed them in handfuls down the toilet. They were furious when they discovered I had done this. They, even more than I, had wanted a finished manuscript. A finished manuscript was the solution to a problem that otherwise they did not know how to master. A finished manuscript was bound to contain something that could be twisted into an acknowledgement of guilt. And once they had that — my guilt — they would be able at last to get rid of me.

That I denied to them a licence for my own execution made them seethe with vengeful rage. They stamped and cursed and spat and ordered that I be thrashed with ox-tailed sticks. They came to my cell at all hours and hit me about the head with rolls of fresh paper.

—Come, you witch, they said. Sit and write. You must rid yourself of what is wrong. You must purge yourself of your filth.

And I always did as they said: I purged myself onto their paper and returned it fragrant with my vomit and my shit. Never will they get what they want from me.

This explains, dearest man, why I do not make my calligraphy visible here; why I do not allow the pen to touch the paper but instead draw on the air just above it; why, hovering and dancing, I lay my characters out in secret lines, beginning again at the top of the page once I have reached its end, as the old style dictates. I do not do this for show. I am neither mad nor pretending to be so. My actions are without pretence, conceived to ensure that my self-criticisms are not seen by anyone who might misunderstand them or use them against me. Anyone, that is, who is not you.

Please do not be alarmed that as I write I also weep. Keep my tears from concerning you. They are simply what comes when a woman has retreated from the people and the parades and the struggles of high politics, and has come to abide in her inner place, and has realised there that, though it might not appear that way now, she is not destined to be always alone. Soon I will, when I feel able, arrange to be with you in Heaven, where I hope our meeting will be what a meeting between you and me should be, after everything that has taken place. In the latter years there grew between us a wide chasm, and there is a chasm still wider now: that which separates the living from the dead.

There is, of course, no width that cannot be crossed if the will is strong, but first my duty is to ensure that I have been thorough in my analyses and have purified myself in every aspect. I must appear before you clean. For only on a blank sheet free from any mark, the freshest and most beautiful characters can you write, the freshest and most beautiful pictures can you paint.

AUTHOR'S NOTE

The Sisters Mao is a work of fiction. As they appear in the novel, Jiang Qing, Li Na, Imelda Marcos, Xiao Dangui, Nancy Wang, and Mao Zedong are in every aspect figments. Unlike the Western style of *Forename Surname*, Chinese names are styled *Surname Forename*; I have followed this throughout the novel. In most cases I have used the full names of Chinese characters in accordance with how they would be addressed in China; on a handful of occasions I have diverged from this rule in order to create a specific aesthetic effect. Throughout, I took the liberty of calling Mao Zedong simply Mao, because that is how he is known around the world, but also because I felt the shorter version lent the prose more power.

The East Wind is a composite of ideas associated with several twentieth-century European theatres: Moscow Art Theatre, Berliner Ensemble, Unity Theatre and Theatre Workshop in London, Théâtre du Soleil in Paris, and Theatre Laboratory in Opole, Poland. The Wherehouse collective and Doris's body art are inspired by various international theatre groups and performance artists working from the sixties onwards, primarily the Living Theatre, Welfare State International, the Theatre of the Oppressed, Guillermo Gómez-Peña, Hannah Wilke, Adrian Piper, Marina Abramović, Zhuang Huan, and Oleg Kulik. The London Carlton is an imagined blend of West End theatre buildings. The Odéon refers to the theatre of the same name in Paris, though it bears only fictive relation to it. The Compound is a representation of the Zhongnanhai government complex in Beijing; not least because Zhongnanhai is closed to public viewing, its manifestation here is a fabrication.

The Sing-Song Tribunal is invented; all the other plays mentioned in the novel are pre-existing works. Chapters xvii and xviii contain quotations from August Strindberg's *Miss Julie*; all are from Michael Meyer's translation, though I have made some changes to Meyer's language to bring it closer in tone to the novel. The lines of poetry quoted in chapter xiii are my version of a translation by Maoist Documentation Project of Mao Zedong's poem 'The Immortals' (1957). The quotation from *I Ching* is a slight adaptation of a section from the Penguin edition (1989).

ACKNOWLEDGEMENTS

I am grateful to Iñaki Moraza, Breda McCrea, Niamh McCrea, Eugene Langan, Barbara Ebert, Priscilla Morris, Seonaid Mackay, and Andrea Pontiroli for their love and support; to my agent Rebecca Carter for her continued tending and rearing; to my editors Philip Gwyn Jones and Molly Slight for their insights and advice; and to the entire Scribe team, especially Sarah Braybrooke and Adam Howard in the UK, Henry Rosenbloom and Kevin O'Brien in Australia, and Emily Saer Cook in the United States, for their work in producing and promoting this book.

A bursary from An Chomhairle Ealaíon (Irish Arts Council) funded ten months of uninterrupted writing. My thanks to Sarah Bannan and the literature team at the Council for this help.

STUDENTS OF THE WORLD

IGNITE
YOURSSE

WE ARE AL

Foreig

Scum

STRIKE

GHT FACTORY
CLOSURES—

T YOUR COLOURED
ORKMATES

AGAINST THE BOSSES'
"AGREEMENT"

TO AL
TRAD
UNIO

YOU HAV
↑ DUTY
TO SUPPORT Y
MEMBERS FIG
RENT RI
& EVICT
UNITED TENANTS ACT

... THE
TIME IS
RIGHT FOR
FIGHTING
IN THE
STREETS'

HEY'VE CLOSED
ORBONNE MADR
ERLIN LAW FAC
ORNSEY COLUM
EXICO TOKYO
UILDFORD AND N

WORI